Albert

the final weekend: a stoned tale

the final weekend: a stoned tale

A Novel by Neal Cassidy

Neal Cassidy
nnaight@yahoo.com

Ordering Information:
Quantity sales. Special discounts are available on quantity purchases by corporations, associations, and others. For details,
contact the author at the email address above.

Library of Congress Control Number: 2019909855

ISBN: 978-0-578-54425-0 (paperback)
ISBN: 978-0-578-54904-0 (ebook)
M & S Publishing
Published in the United States of America

for my mom, carey, k-, & scrapdog...

"i am who i am not, but who i wanted to be…"
-Neal Cassidy

Contents

Schroeder

I wrap my arm around my girlfriend, pulling her closer. Our bedroom is dark, except for the light from the TV on the wall that's showing the local Sunday news. The silver-haired reporter adjusts his red tie and starts the story.

"This just in. We have breaking news that twenty minutes ago, around noon, at a municipal train station, two heroes-"

2 ½ days ago…Friday morning

Goodkat

Letting out a slight groan, I casually open my eyes, revealing nothing, darkness. Entirely covered by my comforter, sheets, and three or four of the seven pillows on my bed, I reach over and push "stop" on my phone, turning off the alarm. I can hear the air conditioner blasting away and my ceiling fan buzzing on high, and I chuckle a little, thinking of the three speeds my fan seems to have - 'Very, Very Light Breeze', 'Very Light Breeze', and 'Hurricane'. Closing my eyes again, I burrow myself deeper into my bed, hugging my body pillow tighter, enjoying the warmth and comfort of my perfect cocoon.

After a few minutes, I find the controller to the air conditioner that's under the same pillow as my phone, the green display on the remote shining brightly in the darkness of my shell. 59. I turn it off, reluctantly unhug my body pillow, grab my phone, and pull the comforter off my head, squinting at my first sign of sunlight that's shining brightly through the blinds above my dresser. Sitting up on the edge of my bed, I rub my eyes, glance around at nothing in particular for a second while blinking several times quickly, then stand up and pull the chain on my ceiling fan. One, two clicks and the fan switches from a hurricane to a very, very light breeze. I pick up the bottle of water next to my bed, drink all of it - not quickly, but steadily - finishing it like I do every morning, then look at my phone, checking the clock. 8:29.

"Plenty of time to get to my 9 a.m. class," I tell myself. Along with the time, I notice several texts from the girl I hooked up with last night, and I quickly run through yesterday evening's events in my head:

Went to the gym, did an easy workout - 60 minutes of various cardio machines and sprints, with ab exercises every 12 minutes. Steam bath and cold pool after that. Came home, smoked a blunt, then had some whiskey while grading term finals and watching an episode of Eastbound and Down, a show my friend, Sorin, had turned me on to when I last visited him in Canada.

Finished grading papers, smoked another blunt, drank another whiskey.

Looked at porn. Decided I wanted to go out instead of jerk off. Took a shower. Sipped on a shot of whiskey while smoking another blunt on my deck, then went to one of the local bars.

It was late, but it didn't take long, and pretty soon I was talking to a student that recognized me from campus. She was hot, tall, light hair. After a few drinks, we went back to her place, fucked for an hour, she fell asleep and I snuck out, hearing, "Goodnight, Professor Goodkat," from her roommates and friends, who were still up and drinking on the porch when I came out the front door.

Still buzzed, I politely waved, said, "Goodnight," and it wasn't until I got home, that I remembered and realized I'd fucked one of them several months ago.

Passed out after downing a glass of water and taking two Ibuprofen.

I glance at a couple of the texts: "Hope you got home safe." "I have an exam tomorrow and practice until 7, but I'm free after." There are a couple more, but I don't bother to read them. I can't remember her name, Stacy, Sara. Another Sara I had sex with years ago at a hooker and pimp party pops into my head. Something with an "s," a "c" maybe. I push "save contact" and for a name, I type, "hot girl pink top/gap in tooth."

When I open my bedroom door, the warmer air hits my face. It's early May and the past few days have been oddly hot. Wanting to get going, I put on "It Takes Two" by Rob Base & DJ EZ Rock, and dance my way to the refrigerator, pull on the handle, grab an apple and two mini-candy bars. As I make my way to the sink, I stuff both of the mini-bars in my mouth, turn on the faucet and peel off the small label on the apple I'm holding under the water. After wiping it dry with the towel that's hanging on the oven handle, I toss it back in the fridge and ask myself if I left something from last night to smoke this morning; but I can't remember, so I leave the drawer to the trash can open in case I have to roll something. Getting more into the music, I glide across the room, gyrating and rapping, making my way over to where if I'd left something for myself, it would be. I glance behind a framed picture of me competing in a big-air ski competition, that's sitting at the back, right-hand corner of my desk.

"I can't believe that was almost twenty years ago," I say to myself. Nothing but my light blue lighter behind it. For the first time, I recall smoking a blunt after taking the Ibuprofen last night, so I open up the middle drawer, grab the small twenty-bag I see, one of the three Dutch Master Palmas sitting next to it, and an old pair of bonsai clippers that came with a bonsai set, a girl I used to date, HH, gave me years ago. I never even attempted to grow the bonsai, but the clippers were excellent for bud. Halfway back to the kitchen, one of my favorite parts of the song hits, and I stop, break out a couple of simple, sly moves while rapping, then go on.

After licking the Dutch on one side and cutting it, I split it, empty the insides into the trash can and tear a bit off the top, evening it out. Grabbing the little twenty-bag, I pull out a nice nug and snip at it, the clippings falling onto one of my monthly University magazines that I never read, swipe the bud into the longer section of the Dutch, roll it, then gather up the small twenty-bag, magazine, and clippers, and dance back to my desk.

I glance at the microwave. 8:34. With the music still playing, but without dancing or sliding, I head to my bedroom. A bit of coldness still lingers, and I open my closet, grabbing a nice pair of blue pants that I bought on a trip to Cyprus last year, a Lacoste black, slim-fit polo shirt, some boxer briefs and a thin pair of black socks that have small skulls and crossbones on them.

Throwing it all on my unmade bed, I head to the bathroom. When I turn on the light and see myself for the first time this morning, I'm cool with what's looking back at me. I'm 40, turning 41 at the end of next month and I feel like I'm as fit as I've ever been. Dancing around a little, mocking myself, I point into the mirror and start shooting finger pistols while checking out my six-pack and "v" on my 175 lb., athletic frame.

I close in on my face, look at the lines under my eyes. "Those bitches weren't there a few years ago," I think to myself - like I do every morning. I scan the rest of my face. "Healthy and unwrinkled, better than most people my age," I remind myself - like I do every morning. Putting more emphasis on the latter and shrugging off the former, I continue grooving and dig my right heel into the tiled floor, spin myself around, then close the shower curtain, pulling at the right end that always folds over, so water doesn't leak out when it's warming up. Going back out into the living room, I turn off the music on my phone and set it on my desk, next to my keys, cash, and headphones.

I grab the blunt and lighter, open my sliding glass door, and walk onto my deck, wearing the same thing that I woke up in - a pair of boxer briefs. The sun and heat hit me harder when I step outside, and I figure it must be at least 85 already. Watching the students and adults walking around, six stories below, I take a drink of water and spark the blunt, taking a few puffs. I take in more of the surroundings between pulls and swigs of water, noticing the small boxwoods lining the sidewalk every ten feet or so; the flags for the University that are on the lights posts this week; the small, unincorporated, businesses, some of which aren't open yet. About halfway through the blunt, I notice that most of the students are in groups of two or more, the majority of the adults are alone, and all of the students seem to be dressed alike in one way or another - same colored shorts and t-shirts. Little copies of each other. Their clothes and hairstyles, practically identical, especially the girls. I take two last, long puffs and throw the blunt over the railing before going back inside.

8:42. "Right on," I think to myself. After turning the shower on, I pull at the right end of the curtain again even though it doesn't need it, grab some mouthwash, gargling while I slather some toothpaste on my brush, and test the water after spitting into the sink. Still too cold. Staring into the mirror, brushing my teeth, going back and forth between looking at my torso and face, I zero in on the same features as before, and notice a grey hair on the right side of my head, so I carefully pluck it, making sure not to pull any other hairs with it, then test the water again. Perfect.

As I'm spreading the shampoo around my hair and the rest of my body, I remember for the first time this morning that this is my last class of the semester. "Well, not even a real class," I think to myself. I only have to hand out one small final exam as well as evaluations of my performance during the semester. "Which are always stellar," I remind myself, smiling while the water washes me off. After putting on moisturizer and deodorant, I squirt three pumps of lotion into my hand, spreading it over my arms, chest, neck, torso and lastly, my butt - an area I hadn't paid much attention to, until a few weeks ago when I saw a wrinkly, saggy eighty-year-old ass in the gym locker room.

Because I didn't shut the door, my bedroom has lost most of its cold air, and I dress in under a minute, grabbing my keys, phone, and cash on the way back to the bathroom. I spread two fingers worth of matte cream through my dark hair, close the cabinet and look at myself, hair as slick as a '70s disco dancer. Reaching back, I snatch the towel, dry my hair with it quickly, profusely, then pat it down and brush it to the side without much attention. After picking up my bottle of water, I open the fridge, find the apple, and it seems more colorful to me than before. It seems to have a little more yellow. I snatch two more mini-candy bars, head to the door and slip on my green oxford shoes, then look at my phone. 8:47. Cool.

I close my door at a reasonable level, rather than slamming it shut, like my neighbors, then take the stairs in lieu of the elevator, as usual. While skipping down the steps, I yank at the cords on my earbuds, fiddling with them for a bit, untangling them easily before the bottom floor. In sync and without missing a beat, I head towards the front door, Blackmill's "Let it be" introducing me to my day.

This side of the street is shaded by the buildings across the way, so I don't feel the heat as much as before and after I slide on my glasses, I notice a mural on an exposed, brick wall facing my front door that must have been painted sometime between when I got home last night and this morning. It's a picture of a tree losing its leaves as it blows in the wind and underneath, in simple, pink, lower-case letters; it reads, "you think you have time."

"Maybe better for the fall, not so much for the spring and the start of summer," I think to myself, sauntering down the shady side of the street.

I truly enjoy this part of the morning, walking with a buzz, music playing in my ears, turning possibly unnecessary conversations into quick nods and waves. A few of the students passing by notice me, and some of them, wave, some speak, but I only see their mouths move, and I make out the simple, "Hey or Hi, Professor Goodkat," but anything more than that, I don't bother with. I recognize some of them from past classes, some from current ones, but most I don't recognize at all. The girls that wave, smile or giggle, and after a few more blocks, ahead of me I see a small, petite redhead that I fucked a couple of months ago in the middle of a row of bushes, two streets over after a bar closed. Not noticing me, she pulls at the door to a coffee shop.

It was St Patty's weekend, and she was drunk, we both were, and she was wearing a cute pair of small, green shorts with suspenders over a t-shirt that barely covered her tits, green, knee-high socks, and green Chuck Taylors when I met her near the pool tables. She had great hair, short and naturally curly. She was loud in bed. I don't know why, but I couldn't decide if she was hot or just decent-looking.

Today she looks hot. She glances in my direction, away, then quickly back at me, and with a surprised look on her face, she smiles, gives me a cute, little wave, and mouths, "Call me."

I mouth back, "I will," even though I know I won't, and I'm relieved when she blows me a kiss and walks inside, instead of stopping to talk.

In the salon window up ahead, a huge papier-mache hairdryer and scissors that are hanging on thin wires grab my attention and while passing by, I notice various ladies inside, some cutting hair, others getting their hair cut, a few sitting in chairs against the wall, their heads covered by those huge, plastic, alien helmets. Everyone's lips seem to be moving, except for the women wearing the helmets, all of them either reading magazines or looking at their phones, and behind the papier-mache display, hanging on the purple wall facing me is a squared mirror in a white frame, lined with light bulbs, that I couldn't see before. In white lettering, it reads, "You are beautiful."

More than half-way through my walk, up on my right, I see NeNe organizing and arranging the fruits on her stand. Once I'm about ten feet away, I start walking lightly and approach her slowly, trying to sneak up on her; but before I can get much closer, she turns around to move some bananas and looking up, she notices me. "Ahhh!" she exclaims, smiling, pointing and shaking her finger at me. "You did not get me this morning!"

Nene is very short and old enough to be my mother. Always dressed nicely, she greets me with open arms wearing a dark blue dress with matching shoes and a matching belt. Her hair is short, parted neatly to the right, and I notice that she has a small, dark blue pendant in the back right section of her brown hair. I pull my earbuds out, give her a hug and a kiss on the cheek. She feels nice, comforting, warm, pleasant. I let go and pull myself back.

"That's because you're too quick for me," I say, in my deep, southern drawl.

Smiling at my comment, Nene taps my arm. "Hold on a second, honey," she says, turning around, walking to the other side of her stand. When she moves, she resembles a cute penguin, taking small steps as her body sways right, left. She hands me two bananas and an Asian pear that are in a brown, paper bag, the same thing she gives me every morning.

"Do you want anything else, honey?" she asks.

"No, I'm cool, NeNe. Thank you for the breakfast," I say, giving her a twenty-dollar bill, purposefully allowing my hand to linger in hers before letting go.

"Let me get you your change, honey."

"Come on now, NeNe, no need." I put my hands up. "You didn't charge me the last two times. Keep it," I say, reminding myself that I spend about $400 a month on this breakfast. "By the bye, you look fantastic today," I tell her.

She smiles, puts her arms up, I lean down, and she gives me a quick kiss on the cheek, hugs me again. Before I can push play on my phone and leave, she looks me up and down and shakes her finger at me, telling me for the second time this week, "You need to eat more." I give her a sarcastic grin, nod, take a bite of my apple. She smiles, shakes her head, waves me away playfully, then turns back to her bananas.

Almost immediately, I see a guy I've seen nearly every morning for the last couple of years. With gray hair, he's maybe fifteen years older than me. When I first noticed him, he was fifty pounds heavier and had a mustache. About a year ago he lost the mustache and weight, and instead of baggy suits, I started seeing him in tennis clothes and running attire. We had a brief conversation a few weeks ago at another fruit stand I had to stop by because Nene was visiting her family and not open. The owner of the stand was arrogant and rushed, electrified. He was one of those guys who became irritated easily, cursing at the bags when they wouldn't separate, prompting me to tell him he could just give me my pear and bananas and that I didn't require one. I found out my man's name was Tom, and that he had gotten into tennis and working out because of a friend. Today he's wearing a fitted suit. Seeming to be in a rush, he smiles and says, "Hey man," as he quickly passes by. His rhetoric seemed to pick up this added "man" halfway through our conversation back at the conflicted man's fruit stand, no doubt prompted by my own speech.

Nearing the end of the road and my apple, I glance up, noticing the stop light ahead of me is red. Veering off to my left and between two parked cars, I start to cut through the stopped traffic towards the other side of the street, looking to my right before coming out from behind the delivery truck in front of me. The light's still red and no traffic is coming, so I walk diagonally, merging into the crosswalk twenty feet ahead of me, looking over at the dozen or so people waiting for the sign to change. At the front, a young couple leans over a baby stroller, the dad waving and making silly faces while the mom shakes a bottle.

After finishing the last bite of my apple and tossing it in the same black trash can in front of me that I always do, I experience a deep sonder. It lasts a bit of time and I think about the wildness of it all, how many different people there are out there in the world, with their own intricate lives and my momentary deep thought is interrupted when I look up and see a giant bear staring at me. Actually, two of them. One pink and one purple. I take a couple steps to my left, then a few to my right. Doesn't matter where I go, their eyes always seem to follow me. Yesterday it was a gorilla, the day before that, two giraffes. The toy store has a new display every morning. Rounding the corner, I see my brick building ahead, mostly hidden by the trees on campus, and I pull my phone out, check the time. 8:59. "I can either walk to class and be two minutes late or grab a quick smoothie," I say to myself. Because my students are used to my usual and casual but not too late tardiness, I go with the latter, knowing that I'll get a kick out of it when they all let out a sigh of disappointment after I appear just before the "15-minute rule" can be used.

I yank on the door, hearing a small chime from above, and halfway in I almost run into a very old man in a wheelchair. He's wearing a sweater and jacket with a striped wool blanket over his legs, and behind him is a young, black woman wearing purple nurse's scrubs.

"I apologize, ma'am, sir," I say, backing up, holding the door open.

"No problem, baby," she says, pushing the wheelchair over the bump in the doorway. "Thank you, baby." She smiles at me and then looking out towards the sidewalk leans down towards the old man, whose head is tilted down, eyes barely open. "Come on, Mr. Bixby. We have to get you home. You gonna miss the start of your show. And I don't want you getting angry, because you missed it. I don't like you when you angry." Shaking her head slightly, she pushes him down the sidewalk.

There are only two people in line, and I notice a former student, Trent, working behind the counter. Wearing a bright orange polo shirt and an orange visor, with a smoothie stitched onto it, he looks hungover. A funny but lazy guy, I had him in my class two years ago. Either regularly hung over and late or not there at all, I'd busted him twice for cheating. I had to give him credit for his ingenuity, though. One time he took the label off of a Gatorade bottle, replacing it with one containing the answers to the test in place of the ingredients. He busted himself when I caught him trying to read it like an old man trying to understand the Sunday paper without his glasses. The second time brought the same result. I found him trying to understand some small print he had put onto rollers and placed on the inside of an old calculator watch. But I never failed him. I allowed him to make up the two tests, supervised, and he pulled off a D both times.

The attractive, thin woman with red hair that's ahead of me moves out of the way, and I look down at her black heels, noticing a sun tattooed on the top of her right foot. No colors, just grey. Walking past me, she looks at me briefly as she smiles, puts her lips to her straw.

"Professor Goodkat! Remember me, Trent? I had your class?!" Trent excitedly yells.

"Was that last sentence a question or a statement, Trent?" I ask, jokingly. "Of course, I remember you, man."

Appearing to be slightly intimidated, he forces a laugh; then in the same, loud voice, he says, "You're the coolest Professor I ever had. The coolest!"

"Right on, Trent. Listen, man, I'm in a rush. My class just started. Could you please get me one of those goya smoothies?" I point at the menu above his head, then look down at my phone, trying to give the impression that I don't have much time, nor that I want to go down memory lane.

"Sure thing, Professor G!" Realizing how loud he's speaking, Trent lowers his volume. "Right on, I can do that," he says, still excited, making a fist. He looks down at the fist he's made, back at me, then puts it down quickly, turns and hurriedly walks away.

Trent

"Fuck, what goes in a goya smoothie?" I ask myself, hurriedly turning around, embarrassed by my awkwardness. "I need to make this fast, so Professor G can get to his class." I can't help but think of all the hot students he's hooked up with. "Two super hot girls in my class that I know he had a threesome with, last Halloween. Everyone knows about that. How does that dude keep his job? Is it against the rules? What rules? Are there rules for this at our school? For the professors? He's a fucking cool professor. Let me go when he caught me cheating. How the fuck did he catch me? I can understand the watch, but that bottle was a solid fucking plan. Fuck, this visor sucks," I say to myself, reaching up, adjusting it. "I wish I didn't have to wear it. I have cool hair. I bet I could pick up way more girls than I do if I didn't have to." I quickly remind myself that I haven't picked up any girls from here. "Shit," I whisper out loud, looking at Professor G. He's looking at his phone, and I grab the book in front of me that describes all the drinks and how to make them. It's my third day, and I only know two of them from memory. "This job sucks. I can't believe I had to be here at 7 a.m.," I tell myself, even though I didn't show up until 7:45 and I didn't do most of my opening duties. I find the pink "G" and flip to that page. "Six ingredients. Have I made this before? Don't know. When is my break? I hope that no one is out back so I can smoke." Measuring out the ingredients as best I can, I make the smoothie fast. Peanut butter, milk, dragon fruit, blueberries, blackberries, and raspberries. Zrrrrrrrrrrrrrrrrrrr. The blender whips everything around, causing my head to hurt even more. "All that whiskey. Man, that chick was ugly." I close my eyes until it's done. "Here you go, man, uh, Professor G," I say, handing him the cup. "Do I sound stupid? Does he think I'm a total dork?" I ask myself. "No charge, Professor G. On the house," I tell him.

"Thanks, Trent. I appreciate it, man." He nods his head. "Have a cool weekend."

"I should get him to do my voicemail," I tell myself. He waits outside to hold the door for two girls I know from school, and as it closes they stop, and all three of us watch him through the window as he glides away.

I look at my phone, the cracked screen telling me that I have six more hours of work left, and I put my visor back on after a failed attempt to get one of the girl's phone numbers. I have a major headache. Reaching for the book in front of me, I flip to a drink a coworker showed me that's good for a hangover, then trip over the mop I'd put to the side earlier this morning, after only mopping half of the floor that I was supposed to; cursing I go on, not bothering to move it from its awkward spot.

Zrrrrrrrrrrrrr. I rub my eyes, hard, and when I stop I feel like I've been transported to another dimension, taking in the white dots floating in black space for a few seconds. "My head is fucking killing me," I say to myself. "I'm seriously never drinking whiskey again. I hope this drink works. I wonder if Brent even knows what the fuck he's talking about."

I finish it quickly and decide to make another, but I can't remember what's in it, so I open the book again, flip back to the page, and start measuring out the ingredients, this time adding some extra scoops.

Zrrrrrrrrrrrrr. I hear the ding for the front door and shut off the blender, annoyed that I have to, but relieved that the noise has stopped. Turning around, I see a large lady with short, frosted, hair and two little kids wearing identical, black t-shirts. "The King Cobra" they read, below a picture of a king cobra wrapped around a roller coaster. They both have their heads bowed down, punching away at the Nintendo Switches in their hands. One of them lets out an annoyed, "grrrr," then shakes his Switch up and down. "Where the fuck is Vicki?" I ask myself, looking back at the door.

"Yes?" I say, brushing my hands on my shirt.

"You mean, 'Can I help you, ma'am?'" the lady barks, agitated. She glances at her phone, squints her face, then shoves it in her pocketbook and looks back at me. "Why don't you try again and then tell me what specials you have." Mumbling to herself, she adds, "No wonder you work at a smoothie store."

"Absolutely," I respond.

She waits a moment. "Well?"

"Yes."

"Can I help you?" she fumes, growing angry.

"No thanks, I don't need any help." I chuckle a little, look her and her kids up and down, then say, "But may I suggest one of our low calorie, low-fat smoothies?"

"I want to speak to your manager now!" she demands, putting her finger in my face.

"Sure thing, Karen," I tell her, grinning and walk away, not paying attention to whatever she's shouting.

I walk back to the manager's office, open the half-closed door and lean in. "Hey Vicki, there's some chick out here that wants to talk to you."

"Is it a customer, Trent?" she asks, glancing up from her computer, a disappointed look on her face. I can't see what's on the screen, but I assume she's playing solitaire because it's the only game she ever plays.

"Yep."

"What did you do this time, Trent? This is getting old." She slaps both of her hands on her desk. "You were late this morning, as usual, and you did half of your opening duties, as usual. This is not a difficult job."

I zone out and don't listen to the rest of her mini speech. I've heard it a hundred times. Rolling her chair back, she walks around her desk, turns me around and pushes me out the door. She's still talking, but I'm still not listening, and I hope no one is out back on my break, so I can smoke. We start to walk to the front, Vicki nudging me from behind, me purposefully walking slower. I notice "Karen's" fat face and her stupid "I want to speak to the manager" short haircut, through the circular glass window on the door. She's popped some chewing gum in her mouth, and she's chomping up and down on it like it's her last meal. The door flings open when Vicki shoves me through; as I approach the annoyed lady, I suddenly turn, put my arms out, say, "Here you go, the manager," and walk backward, arms still up, to the other side of the counter.

Before I can get back to the blender, I hear, "How do you hire people like that?" and "I am a paying custom-" Zrrrrrrrrrrrrrrr. Hoping it will annoy her even more, I run it for longer than needed, even though it makes my head hurt, and I zone out, thinking about what we're going to do tonight. "Clarence should be coming by in a little bit," I remind myself. I pour the smoothie into a plastic cup, grab a straw, tear off the end, put my lips to it and blow off the rest towards the trashcan. I miss. Switching her glare between Vicki and me while she rants, the fat lady is waving her arms up and down like a turkey, making herself look even more ridiculous than before. I rest back against the counter, cross my legs. Karen notices that I have no fucks to give and she starts to flap her arms even faster. I sip on the straw, lean back a little more. "This actually tastes really good. My head is actually feeling better," I think to myself, pulling the cup back, looking at what's inside. "Fuck, maybe Brent does know what he's talking about." The lady leaves and without saying anything, Vicki shakes her head, then pushes the door open and walks back to her office. "Back to play some more Solitaire," I say to myself.

The next couple of hours go by much slower than I think they should. I have a list of things to do, but I only bother with a few of them. Instead, I spend most of my time, either on my phone, looking up cars I can't afford, or staring out the window at the girls walking by. Only five customers come in: an old couple; some single bald, nerdy looking guy; and three dudes that are obviously stoned. My break is coming up, and I notice Clarence, wearing his new uniform, through the window. He gets to the door and holds it open for a man who looks like a woman - or a woman who looks like a man, I can't tell which - and when they both walk in, I yell, "What the fuck is going on, man!?"

The lady, I can tell it's a lady now, bears a solid resemblance to Michael Jackson and she glances up at me from her phone with shock; but then, just as quickly, she looks back down and pushes on her screen, not seeming to care at all. Not taking her eyes off her phone, she slides her finger down it, then reads the menu, but doesn't say anything. When she looks back down, I clear my throat. Nothing. I clear my throat again. She doesn't look up. Clarence puts his hands in the air, gives me a look, shakes his head and mouths, "What the fuck?"

"Excuse me," I say, loudly. "You can text Annie later and see if she's okay. Someone is waiting behind you," I tell her, pointing at Clarence, and he starts rubbing the back of his neck. Shaking his head, he lowers it.

MJ looks up, shoves her phone in her pocket, then pushes up the sleeves on her jacket and shirt. "I want to speak to your manager!" she demands. "I know what you mean by that!"

"Not the first time I've heard that today," I reply, chuckling. Clarence is trying to hold back his laughter, and I take my familiar journey to the back office. Sticking my head through her door, I reach up, tilt my visor to the side and moan, "Vickiiii." After asking what I need, she hits her desk again, harder this time, and gets up quickly, stomping towards me.

"What up, fool!" I shout while walking towards Clarence. He's holding his phone up in the air, taking a picture of himself. I don't bother to look over to see if Vicki and MJ are looking at me, because I already know they are and Clarence and I reach out and clasp hands, pulling into each other as best we can over the counter. "What the hell are you doing, man?" I ask, motioning at whatever the fuck it is, he's wearing over his shoulder. "What are you going to do next, pull out some lady items from your purse?"

"First off, fool, this here is a satchel and it's handy." He holds it out and strikes a few poses, pouts his lips, acting as if he's a model. "It's stylish, man, but you wouldn't know anything about that."

"No, no I would not," I say, mocking him.

"And second off, I'm trying to find the best angle for my new profile pic. My first one in my uniform. A brother in a uniform. What do you think?" he asks, putting his arms up.

"I think you have to accept the fact that you can't really get a good angle on a circle," I respond, laughing out loud immediately after.

"Fuck you!" he says, flicking me off.

"Dude, you look great. I'm fucking proud of you. You got a perfect score on your shooting test, the first cadet ever. You're what you always wanted to be - an officer in our hometown. You should wear that uniform with pride." I put my hands up and back away a little. "Just don't bust me." We both laugh, clasp hands again, and I ask, "Did they have to special order that triple X size?"

"Motherfucker!" Reaching over the counter, he acts like he's going to grab me.

Flinching, I take a couple steps back. "Hey, guess who was in here earlier?" I say, glancing past him towards Vicki, who quickly takes her eyes off me.

"Who?"

"Professor Goodkat."

"Damn, man, that dude is cool as hell. He pulls more wool than a sheepherder." Clarence laughs a little, adjusts his satchel over his new uniform. "My favorite professor."

After agreeing, I ask, "You want the usual, man? I'll fix it and then take my break, and we can go out back and smoke." I look over, the woman still pointing at me, complaining, and Vicki closes her eyes for a moment.

"Cool with me," Clarence responds, still messing with his satchel, not looking up.

"He does look sweet in that uniform," I think to myself. I can't believe that my best friend is a cop." I scoop the ingredients into the blender. Zrrrrrrrrr. The loud sound doesn't bother me as much as before, and while pouring his smoothie into a cup, I look over just in time to see MJ leaving. "Come on, man, meet me out back," I say, handing him his smoothie. "I'm going on my break."

Bracing myself on the doorway and hanging into her office as far as I can, I tell Vicki, "My work here is done. I'm going on my break."

She looks up from her computer. "But you didn't do anything!" she screams, throwing her hands up in the air. "All you've done is fuck up!" She flops her arms up and down while saying this, reminding me of the heavy lady from earlier.

"I wonder what game those kids were playing?" I ask myself. "What time is Harry's train supposed to get in tonight? I'll ask Clarence when I get outside." After she stops saying whatever it is she's saying, I push off the frame, edging myself out of her office, giving it a moment to see if Vicki speaks again, hoping she doesn't. She doesn't and looks back down at her computer, clicks on her mouse. "How the fuck can someone play solitaire so damn much?" I ask myself. "She literally plays for hours a day." I walk to the end of the employee lockers, open mine, get the blunt out of my bag and head to the door in back leading outside, pushing the handle below the red sign that reads, "DO NOT PUSH ALARM WILL SOUND." The alarm hasn't worked in the five days I've been here.

"Yah!" Clarence screams, lunging at me when I open the door.

"What the fuck, Law Dog?!" I yell, excitedly jumping back. "Damn, fuzz. Back up, man. You know I'm coming out of this door." I walk past him, purposely bumping my shoulder into his.

"Settle down, man," he says, squinting his eyes, looking away from the sun. He sets his satchel down on a blue milk crate next to him, and making a slurping sound, takes one last, long sip from his straw.

"I think it's done," I tell him.

"Spark that thing up. I've got shit to do," Clarence says, looking behind him, to his left.

"You being so rude, I'm not so sure I'm in a sharing mood," I joke, as I pull the lighter out of my pocket and spark the end. I take a few puffs, and Clarence hook shots his empty cup into a trashcan ten feet behind him. He makes it, gives me that same triumphant smile and nod all of us have seen on the basketball court, and I hand him the blunt.

He takes a few, long drags, then looks at me and asks, "So are you going to see Schroeder later on or do you want me to stop by?"

"Yeah, I'll stop by."

"And what the fuck was going on with you and that chick last night?" he asks, in a higher pitched voice, something he does when he questions my decision making. "She was looking rough. How fucked up were you?"

"Come on, man, you know how it is. They were playing that song, fuck, what's the name of it? You know what I'm talking about. I think it's, 'I Know Who I Want to Take Me Home.'"

"Yeah, yeah, I know, man. I was there," Clarence says, passing the blunt.

I hit it a few times, then ask, "Isn't that the name of the song?"

"Yeah, I think so." He shrugs his shoulders slightly, starts to nod his head up and down. They play that song every fucking night they close."

I go back to my story. "Anyway, man, they were playing that song, 'I Know Who I Want to Take Me Home,' and I was fucked up. We had smoked all that weed and drank all that whiskey."

Clarence interrupts. "You had drunk all that whiskey." He looks down at the smoking blunt in my hand, reaches out and says, "Since you're not going to smoke it." I take a few puffs, hold it in, take one more, hand it over and continue.

"So, of course, I'm wanting to get laid. I made my rounds through the bar and dancefloor, to see what was available and I see her, and she looked good at the time." Imitating some type of surveillance system, I bring my hands to my eyes, start making beeping noises and move my head up and down, to the right and left. "I calculated the boobs, body, face factor," I say, adding more robot-and-machine-like, noises. "And then I went in for the kill and of course with my smooth moves, I didn't go home alone."

"Yeah, you looked real smooth last night." Clarence laughs, hits the blunt. "Real smooth."

"Yeah, the risk I took was calculated," I say.

He pauses, takes a last puff, holds it in for a moment, exhales. "But man, you're bad at math." Still squinting, but not as badly as before, he gives it back to me, says, "Alright, man, I got to go." We clasp hands again and hug. "I'll see you at home. And don't fucking forget to stop by Schroeder's," he reminds me.

"Yes sir," I say, putting my hand to my head, in salute. "Tenfour, Lieutenant Fuzz." I pull my hand down quickly, take a hit, and put it back to my forehead.

"Go fuck yourself, Lieutenant Smoothie," he says, giving me the bird with both fingers. He crouches down a little, slowly starts shuffling backward, and still flicking me off, he quietly says over and over, "Go fuck yourself, Lieutenant Smoothie, go fuck yourself, Lieutenant Smoothie."

"And buy some fucking glasses, Lieutenant Fuzz!" I yell, still holding my salute. "Aren't those aviators, like, mandatory for you fuckers!"

"Go fuck yourself Lieutenant Smoothie, go fuck yourself Lieutenant Smoothie," he repeatedly whispers, again and again, each time more quietly, still backing away. Before he disappears around the corner of the building, he mouths it one last time, then blows me a kiss with his two middle fingers.

I hold my salute after he's gone. "I know that fucker's coming around again before he leaves," I tell myself. "He's such a fucking tool."

Clarence

"I'm going to give it a full minute," I say to myself, hiding behind the wall, still crouched for some reason. I check to see how many steps I've taken today: 2420. Chuckling when I see the last three numbers, I wonder if my little, backward shuffles counted in my total. I grab my smaller belly, slightly shake it. "Forty pounds down, thirty more to go." I let go, look at my watch. Twenty seconds. I quickly recall us fishing in South Florida last summer, and how I was constantly eating peanut butter, marshmallow, pickle and potato chip sandwiches on the boat. "Ugh. I can't believe I used to eat that shit." Times up.

Kneeling down and holding out both middle fingers, I pop around the corner, shouting, "Fuck you, Lieutenant Smoothie."

Trent's still standing there, saluting me, with one hand to his side, blunt smoking from his mouth. "Aaaaaaaaaaaand fuck your cheesy tots, nigga!" he shouts, pulling his hand from his forehead abruptly.

We both let out a hysterical laugh, and I picture us in my truck at a fast food drive-thru, on that same fishing trip.

Because he was the soberest of the four of us, Trent was driving. Starving, we had just come off the boat, and all of us were wearing bathing suits; I was the only one wearing a shirt, and when we pulled up to the drive-thru, we were kind of loud and obnoxious, Trent especially. None of us can really remember what he said or what the last straw was, but we can all pretty much agree that the drive-thru worker didn't care for his comments on her fake hair weave. It all ended in her throwing Justin's cheesy tots at Trent and yelling, "Fuck your cheesy tots, nigga!" She nailed him right in the face. The cheesy tots literally could not have hit their mark more accurately. Before closing the window, she calmly said, "Serves you right, muthafucka."

Indifferent, Trent looked at us and said, "Guess we're getting pizza?"

I stand up. "Fucker!"

"Later!" Trent shouts. Walking away, he sticks his hand in the air, points his finger and shakes it. "And don't forget to go to Schroeders!" he yells, not looking at me, mocking me, barely interrupting me from saying the same thing.

I know he's not coming back out, so I reach into my satchel and start walking up the alley, towards the street. My headphones are a mess, and I can feel the hotness of the sun on the top of my head, and I have to stop because I can't seem to get them untangled. It takes me a minute and somewhere in the middle, I pause, look up at the sun, and wipe my brow. I go to my music selection, then to albums, and in the mood for my favorite soundtrack, I slide my finger down my phone. Scrolling to the "J's," I select track five, put my earbuds in. "I can't wait to get those headphones with my first paycheck," I say to myself, picturing the red and black, noise-canceling, over-the-ear Beats I've been eyeing for weeks, in my mind.

"*Bawwwwwwwww.*" The beat drops in a few seconds and I begin moving my right hand, act as if I'm scratching on a turntable, in rhythm with the music, and slightly leaning to the left, I start moving my body. I dance up the street with a smooth cadence, smiling, still continuing to scratch the air below my hip, the sun still shining brightly but not really bothering my eyes anymore. Gliding down the sidewalk, I mouth the words to myself, smiling and nodding my head at anyone that's looking at me. I stop, turn to my right and check myself out in a pharmacy window. Continuing to casually dance, rapping with Big Daddy Kane, I run my eyes up and down my reflection. "My uniform looks fucking sweet," I say to myself, admiring how the dark blue matches my black skin, broadening my smile even more. I reach my non-shadow, table scratching hand up to my tightly, cropped hair, run my fingers over it and scan my body again, proud of myself for the work I've put in, but still not completely pleased with what I look like. I look at my pants a little closer, making sure that the bottoms touch my shoes nicely, evenly. They do. I glance down at my feet to make sure. They still do. Looking at myself one, last time, I think about the security guard job I left last semester for the academy, a job I'd worked for two years, and my boss, Stu Pomper, who passed away last month. A great, funny guy, Stu was an aficionado on everything. It didn't matter what subject you brought up - the Kennedy assassination, wars, inventions, trade routes along the Silk Road - he always seemed to have some knowledge and always, an expert opinion. I remember him telling me how proud he was of me and how he knew I would succeed as a police officer. "Nuff Respect, Stu," I say to myself, slightly nodding my head, my reflection gesturing back. The song ends, along with my silent rap, and I stroll up the street without mouthing the words to the the next song even though I know it by heart, too.

A fast walker, I go back and forth between looking at my phone and ahead of myself to make sure that I don't run into anything or anyone, and text, "Good Morning, I love you ☺☺☺♥♥," to my mom and grandmother. After walking around some orange cones surrounding an open manhole, I message my sister, "Good luck on your exams," and check my mail to see if the real estate agent from Florida has sent anything regarding this summer's fishing trip, since all of the other guys are too lazy to put it together. I chuckle when I open my profile page and see myself trying to look hard and serious. In a quick second, I look up to the top left of the picture and see "Mr. Cuddles," my teddy bear I've had since I was a kid. Unfortunately I didn't notice "Mr. Cuddles" when I uploaded the picture. Within a minute, my mother had commented, "Nice picture. Handsome. Is that Mr. Cuddles in the background?" One hundred percent of the next seventy-two messages referred to "Mr. Cuddles." But I kept it up. I liked the attention it got from girls.

I tap "edit" and upload what I think is the best pic I took in the smoothie shop, labeling it, "New job. Starting Sunday."

At the top of my phone, a notice comes down from my sister. I don't bother to open it, because it's short. "Thanks, bro! ☺☺."

I slide her message out of the way and notice that I already have two notifications - two guys from school who have "liked" my pic. Browsing through some of my previous profile pics, I notice I'm bigger, heavier, but smiling in all of them: me and the guys at a bar in Florida; my mother, and sister and me smiling in front of the Christmas tree, all three of us wearing Santa hats and matching red and green sweaters; Trent and I at a concert, freshman year. Ahead of me, some Asian dude in a black t-shirt and jeans is walking, quickly also, but only about eighty percent as fast as I am, and I have to pick up my pace when I get close, walking comically faster past him, so that I'm not in his personal space for too long. I wait for several feet before resuming my normal pace, and a notification slides down from the top of my phone. A text from Trent. It reads, "Idea for lodging for the trip," and it has a link.

"No fucking way this dude took the time to look up a spot to stay," I think to myself, opening the message, clicking the link he sent. A page opens up, and immediately I see the same image Trent sporadically sends all of us - a huge, naked, black dude sitting at the edge of a bed, leaning down with one elbow resting on a knee, with a fucking baseball bat for a dick. "Fucking A!" I shout out loud, throwing my head back, looking away from the screen. Going back to his messages, I erase it, doing my best not to look until the image is gone. "I can't believe I fell for that shit," I say to myself. "That fucker is always thinking of some way to send that pic. How do I continue to open shit he sends me?" I tell myself as I type, "Thanks, jackass, I'll take that under advisement. And stop sending me pics of BLACK COCK!!! Keep that for your own viewing pleasure." I push send.

He immediately replies, "Awwww come on, baby, you know I only like to look at your BLACK COCK."

"Fucking tool," I text back. "And stop doing that, too." Trent had gotten in the habit and found it very amusing to position himself in places, where I would be naked soon. Whether I was coming out of the shower or getting dressed or undressed or whatever, he would hide on the other side of my bed or in my closet, and when I saw him, he would drop his jaw and gape at me with wide, open eyes to creep me out. He even went so far as to take a pic one time. Hiding in the closet, he popped out and snapped it when I dropped my towel after a shower. Turning his phone around, he looked at the pic and then slowly stood up, lowered his head, and said, "I apologize, dude. That was too far even for me." I saw him deleting the photo as he walked out. This caused him to stop his creepy peep show antics for about a week. Then he went back to doing it again.

He replies, "☺."

I glance up and see a woman with her back to me, holding a baby in a pink outfit over her shoulder. The baby looks at me with its bright blue eyes, lets out some sort of cute, little, baby sound. I start to make faces, shake my head back and forth, stick out my tongue. She giggles, the mom turns around, and going back to a neutral expression, I nod my head.

She smiles, looks back towards the intersection, and the baby looks at me again, grinning. The mother begins to cross the street, away from me, and sticking out my tongue, I make one last, silly one, the baby giggles again, and pretty soon I'm unable to hear it and I can't tell if it's because she's stopped or she's too far away, and I notice down to my right a bright, yellow piece of paper, that's blown up and rested under my foot. I pick it up and turn it around. Some sort of environmental awareness fundraiser flyer; it lists the date, time, and location, along with a quote at the bottom: 'The best time to plant a tree was twenty years ago. The second best time is now.' "Maybe something other than a flyer would be wise," I think to myself, wondering how much paper was wasted. Without balling it up, I hang it over the recycling bin next to me and drop it in.

I go back to my profile picture, see that I've already gotten six more likes and a comment - four of the likes from guys, and two from girls. I instantly recognize one of the two girls from class and without putting too much thought into where I know the other girl from, I flip to see what the comment says. It's from my sis: "Where is Mr. Cuddles? JK! You look great, bro! I love you!" I grin, push like, then look up to see how long before my light's going to change. Eleven seconds. Before I can hit "reply", I feel a tap on my shoulder. Turning around, I look down and see Ling-Ling. Well over a foot below my height, she's staring up at me, smiling, chewing on gum, waving at me quickly with her right hand.

"Hiiii, Clarence," she says, in her high-pitched voice.

"Hi, Ling-Li-," I feel another tap on my other shoulder and turn around.

Courtney greets me in the same way. "Hiiii, Clarence."

"Hi Courtney, Hi Ling-Ling."

Both of them scoot together and stand side by side in front of me. "Congratulations!" they both scream, putting their arms out, hugging me. I tense up as they grasp me, both of them squeezing tighter. They hold on and shake me for a few more seconds, then stepping back, both of them start jumping up and down, clapping their hands. "Clarence, Clarence," they chant.

"You look great, Clarence," Courtney says.

"Yeah, Clarence, you should be so proud," Ling-Ling, chimes in, looking me up and down. "That uniform looks really good on you."

"Aw, thanks, girls. I can't wait. First day is on Sunday," I say. "What are you two doing?"

Ling-Ling

Taking small steps back and forth, and holding both straps of my backpack, I tell him, "Not much, we're going to the mall. But one of us is hungover, so we're running late." Glancing at Court, I swing my foot in her direction, accidentally striking her on the shin.

"Owwwww!" she yelps, embellishing the pain. She punches me on the shoulder, I hit her back, and she hits me back again, then says, "Even."

I look at Clarence, and he's squinting a little at the sun, and he has a small drop of sweat on his forehead. "As a result, I can only spend twenty minutes at the mall, because it will take us seven minutes to walk there from here and then twelve minutes from the mall to the lecture." I think for a second, go on: "Unless I take the bus from the mall, but then there's a risk of being three to four minutes late due to extraneous variables."

"Dork," Court says, looking down at her phone.

"Why are you so hungover?" Clarence asks, looking at Court. He takes his hands out of his pockets, wipes off the drop of sweat on his forehead. "What did you two do last night?" I start to say something, but a loud, long honk comes from the street, and all three of us look over. A heavy-set lady with short hair is leaning out of her car window, yelling at an elderly woman ahead of her, who is trying to parallel park.

She hits the horn again, then screams, "Fucking hurry up!" It doesn't make the old lady move any faster, and eventually, the large woman speeds around her, blaring her horn; and when she whizzes by, I notice two kids in the back.

Court shuts off her phone and turns to Clarence. "We were at Bull Branch last night," she tells him, chomping on her pink gum, twirling a small section of her blond hair. "Leah was hooking us up as usual, and we were having a cool time, dancing and whatever." She glances over at me. "I shouldn't have taken that final drink at last call," she says, making a displeased face, cringing.

Giving her the same scolding glare I gave her last night and this morning, I say, "Well, that's what you get for taking a drink from someone you don't know." Clarence nods his head, and I decide to remind her for the third time today, "I've told you not to do that."

"Yeah, LL. I know. Thanks, mom." She rolls her eyes and looks at Clarence.

I don't stop. "Well, when are you going to listen, especially with that stupid sweater that guy was wearing last night. It had more colors than a rainbow." Both of them chuckle, even though only one of them knows what I'm talking about. "What was the name of that drink anyway," I ask her, "a Pill Cosby?" They get a kick out of my joke and after all of us stop laughing, there's a short bit of silence, and I check the time. "Eight minutes to get to the mall. We should leave now. I know Court is going to walk slow," I tell myself. Clarence begins to say something, but I interrupt him because I don't know what he's going to say or how long of a conversation it will spark. "I don't have the time," I say to myself. "I hate to seem rude, but we have to go." Before interrupting him, I estimate that if I let him talk and I'm lucky, it could take two minutes, depending on the subject matter and what Court might add. "If that's the case, then we have to take two minutes off of the mall, but what if Court takes forever like she always does? I can't risk it, and I want to get those flip flops." I run through all of this between the time I notice he's going to say something and before he actually does. It almost seems to go in slow motion.

"Okay, Clarence, we have to go. Byeeeee," I say, cutting him off, burying my face in his chest, hugging him again. Court joins me. Clarence feels like a big teddy bear when I hug him. "He's such a nice guy," I think to myself. "I'm so happy for him!"

We say congratulations again, before letting go and while both of us are waving goodbye, Clarence asks, "Are you two coming over tonight?"

"Yep, we'll be there!" I yell, grabbing Court, pulling her towards me.

"Just you two?" Clarence asks, shuffling his feet forward, grinning.

Court turns around quickly and teasingly says, "Awwwwww. Now we know why you really want to hang out with us."

I sniffle and act as if I'm going to cry. "Yeah, wish we had known this the whole time."

"No, no, no, you girls know it's not like that. I've known you two since before you were even friends with her," he says, defensively, holding his hands out, shaking them.

"Settle down, Clarence," Court says. "We know, we know, we're just teasing."

"I don't know if she can make it tonight," I tell him, looking at my watch, pulling on her again.

"But we will see!" Court shouts, with a huge grin.

"Okay, okay," he says, somewhat embarrassed, wiping at his forehead.

"Byeeeeee!" we yell, turning around, slightly jogging a few feet. We slow down to a fast stride, and pretty soon, we're walking at Court's casual pace.

"He looks terrific," she says, chomping on her gum, harder than she did when we were talking to Clarence. Five inches taller than me and wearing blue sweatpants, with some sort of yellow stain on them and a Snoop Dogg t-shirt from a music festival we went to last summer, Court walks with a confidence I wish I had. Despite the fact that she's hungover and got ready in two minutes, she looks beautiful, like she always does. Looking forward while she talks, I glance over, then pull my shoulders back. She's always had good posture. I practice how my stance and pose look in the mirror, make sure to take breaks during my studies so that I'm not hunched over constantly, and even do some of my school tasks on the floor, lying on my stomach. I feel like it balances out any forward leaning that I do. Despite all of this, I still slouch sometimes, an old defense mechanism, though not near as much.

"Yes, he does," I agree, pushing my shoulders back even more and I ask myself, "Am I chewing my gum harder?" I stop chewing it all together and drop it in the second trash can on my left because the first one is for recycling. When I do, Court bends down and picks something up from the mulch surrounding one of the boxwoods that line the right side of the sidewalk.

"Cool, look," she says, standing up and turning around, showing me a small, multi-colored, smooth stone. She puts it in her pocket and continues to walk.

"And what are you going to do with it?" I ask. "Put it next to the others in the back of your sock drawer?"

"Yep!" she replies, happily. "That's exactly what I'm going to do." She still hasn't looked at me, and despite her acute hangover, she's perky and smiling.

Shaking my head, I tell her to pick it up the pace, while still making sure that I don't walk on any of the cracks on the sidewalk.

"Yeah, yeah," she quips, stepping on a crack, then another.

When we get to the escalator that leads to the second floor, I check my watch. "We actually have a full minute," I say to myself, smiling.

"Look!" Court shouts, nudging me on my side, pointing ahead.

I glance up and see both of our reflections in the mirror, to the right of the escalator. We always stop and look at ourselves in this mirror when we use this entrance to the mall. I don't pay much attention to it, but Court does and she always points at us and shouts, "Look!" in the same excited manner that she always screams, "Look, cows!" every, single, time we see them when we're driving. I imagine a lot of people walk a little to the right on the sidewalk before the escalator so that they can see themselves in the mirror - both guys and girls.

Courtney

LL starts to veer to the left to get on the escalator, but I pull her back in front of the mirror with me. "We look cool," I tell her, tossing my hair, putting my sunglasses on top of my head. "But, of course, I look cooler," I joke, hitting her with my hip. I stand on my toes, turn my head to the right, left, stick my arms up and tap her again with my hip. LL makes a funny face, then looks at me in the mirror. "She looks so cute today," I think to myself, so I tell her, and she sticks her tongue out and makes another face. She's wearing a floral dress, with matching light purple shoes and bracelets and rings in colors identical to the flowers. Her black hair is neatly parted to the side and pulled back, and she's wearing one of her six backpacks that best match this outfit.

Riding two steps behind her on the way up, I start moving my hands back and forth, quickly, against the bottom of her dress, causing it to fly up. She turns around and holds it down, attempting to swing at me at the same time. "Don't do that in public!" she sternly warns me, giving me a serious, evil glare. "It's one thing to joke around and do it at home, and it's another thing to do it out where everyone can see!"

"Yeah, yeah," I say, brushing her off, walking past her once we reach the top, towards one of the kiosks in the middle of the mall.

The guy working it is in his late 40s, and he rubs his beer belly as we approach him. "Hey ladies," he creepily says, running his fingers through his thinning hair. We both look at him with a small hint of disgust, don't bother to say anything and make our way to the other side of the kiosk.

"What do you think?" I ask LL, nudging her. I give her a wink. "I think you two could hit it off. Maybe a little-" and I start imitating porn music. "Bow chicka, wah, wah."

"Oh, absolutely," she agrees, nodding her head. "I'm just waiting for you to go over and make a move on him." She points behind me.

I turn around and see an elementary school boy riding a blue dinosaur with white spots on it, in the kid's indoor playground. I know instantly that she's referring to the high school senior I hooked up with that was visiting our campus last semester, on a college visit.

"I do that one time..." I say, turning back around, pointing my finger at her.

She's flipping through a magazine now, and she doesn't bother to look up. "Mhmmm."

"Yeah, whatever," I say, reaching for a pink pack of gum on the small counter beside her, recalling the other high school senior I hooked up with; different year, different college visit. "There's no way she knows about that," I think to myself.

"Yeppp, I know about that one, too," she says, her attention still on the magazine.

I play dumb. "Huh? You know about what?"

LL looks at me and rolls her eyes. "These magazines are bullshit," she says, abruptly, laying the magazine back where it came from, aligning the sides, top, and bottom so that they're even with the ones below it.

"What do you mean?"

"Well, fifty percent of the time they tell you that you're beautiful and that you should love yourself just the way you are," she tells me, with a grin. "The other fifty percent of the time they're telling you how to lose ten pounds in two weeks." She shakes her head, reaches over, picks up a pink pack of the same gum I grabbed. "And that's after they give you a cake recipe in an earlier article," she adds, handing me the pack. "Thanks."

We turn the corner and back into Creepy McCreepster's line of sight. "Ladies," he says, brushing his hand through his hair again. "Anything else I can get you?" he asks, looking both of us up and down, raising his eyebrows a little. We both give him a nauseating look. He hits the handheld calculator in front of him, but I can see that it says $3.00 and I put the money on the counter fast, hoping to avoid any further conversation.

LL snatches the gum from his hand, but he doesn't catch our hints, and he turns his glare to her, winks, says, "Anything?"

"Actually, yes," she tells him. "Firstly, I'd like to know why you require a calculator for a three-dollar purchase that doesn't involve sales tax. Second-" She pauses and points at one of the small kids on the playground, then stares him right in the eyes and asks, "Do you ever get really horrific, intrusive thoughts, like what would happen if I just kicked that toddler over there across the playground, and then you say to yourself, no?" His eyes widen, and he doesn't say anything after his head pops back and he looks at my face, not my breasts this time, seeing what my response will be.

I giggle, say, "Fucking weirdo," and he turns and walks past us, tugging at his white t-shirt that needs to be washed.

This is not the "good" mall. That one is on the other side of town. It has the more expensive stores with name-brand clothes that LL and I both like to wear, along with much better make-up stores, but this mall is perfect for cheaper clothes and dresses that might only be worn once or twice. This mall also has a year-round flip-flop store, the whole reason we're here.

We pass by a number of stores that we've never gone in – a greeting card store, a men's clothing shop called "The Famous", some game and calendar store that's just opened. The dollar store we use to save money on simple items for the apartment or whatever is up on the right, and when I ask LL if we need anything and if we should stop by, she tells me that there are currently five items on our list that could be purchased there, but then she walks a little faster and tells me we don't have the time.

The shop's not big, maybe the size of five of my closets, and a blonde, teenage girl wearing a yellow tank top, sitting on a stool against the back wall, doesn't bother to look up from her phone when she boringly, lamely says, "Let me know if you need anything." Neither one of us respond, and it doesn't take long for LL to find the pair she wants.

"Here we go," she says, pulling them down. Smiling widely, she holds them close to her chest and dances around for a second. We look at what's on the walls for a few more minutes, each one of us pointing out pairs we think are cute and ones we think are ugly. I grab some that are black with gold stripes on them, put them back, look at several others, then pull them back out again, but I don't buy anything. LL walks over to the young girl and hands her the flip-flops with cute little cartoon cows on them.

The girl puts them in a small bag, gives it back to LL, pushes some buttons on the register and looks up at us for the first time. "$22.99," she says, with a neutral expression.

"Oh no," LL tells her. "If you check they're supposed to be on sale. It says-"

The girl interrupts her. "Cool, whatever." She gives LL a big smile, says, "Let's just do $10," adding, "but there are no receipts on sale items."

"Well that's much better than I expected," LL happily replies, handing the smiling teen ten dollars. The girl takes the money without pushing any buttons on the register, tells LL that her flip flops are adorable and then shuffles some papers, acts as if she's doing something work-related.

As soon as we walk out of the store, we see two of our old roommates from freshman year walking towards us with three of their friends. "Hi Courtney, Hi Ling-Ling," Tabitha and Jenny annoyingly say, approaching us. LL and I look at each other without responding to them, and I glance back to the store and notice the teen putting the $10 in her pocket. All five of the girls look exactly the same. They're all wearing white tank tops, with light brown-colored shorts and white tennis shoes. All of them have Ray-Ban aviators resting on top of their heads, the same haircuts.

"Well don't you look cute," Tabitha, says looking LL up and down. LL doesn't respond.

"So, are you two excited about the summer?" Jenny asks LL. "Any trips or plans?"

"Not really," I shortly reply, looking around, waiting for them to leave.

"Nope," LL says, bluntly.

"Of course, you don't," Tabitha says, giggling. "I'm sure you'll be studying the whole time. When was the last time you even went out and had fun?" The other four girls laugh in unison.

"Yeah, you docta, yet?", Jenny asks, purposefully leaving off the "r". All of them cackle and Tabitha approvingly taps Jenny on the left arm.

"Phew, not yet." LL sarcastically answers, stepping forward, pulling her shoulders back, standing taller. "But can I ask you a question, Jenny?" She glances over at Tabitha. "Tabitha, can I ask you a question? What are you two and your basic bitches doing out this time of year? I thought you didn't emerge from hibernation in search of pumpkin spice, until the first sign of fall?"

"Damnnnnnnnnn," I say, shaking my head, laughing at all of them. The two of them don't know how to respond because LL's never talked to them this way before, showing this type of confidence, and they just stand there in a stupor, their mouths open.

LL ends it with, "And lastly, when you basic bitches do wake up, how long does it take to figure out whose Ugg boots are whose?"

"You laugh at her because she's different," I say, looking them all over. "She laughs at you because you're all the same. Check her out in fifteen years when she's a lead surgeon." I pause, then add, "You fucking cunts."

We walk off to silence, shock, and I whisper to LL, while we're walking away, "I love you."

"I love these flip-flops," she says, smiling, while I put my arm around her. "And I love you too."

A short, old woman wearing a matching yellow and purple plaid skirt and jacket puts her hand in between the elevator doors before they close. "Thanks!" LL and I both blurt out, turning sideways and shuffling into the elevator, even though the doors are completely open now. The old lady doesn't say anything, she just nods and smiles and looks away. After glaring at us and then the old lady, a large woman in her mid-40s, who has two kids wearing black t shirts with snakes on them with her, let's out a "Hmph," and then repeatedly pushes the "close" button. I start to raise my right hand, begin to say something, but the little, old lady stops me. She gently pats my arm twice and continues to look ahead, through her thick glasses, holding her yellow and purple plaid purse, smiling the biggest smile. Both she and the woman with the unwarranted sense of self-entitlement get off on the next floor. Before the door closes, the little, old lady turns around, looks at me and says, "It wouldn't have made any difference, dearie. They're all the same."

I mouth, "thank you," and say to myself, "I can't wait to see my grandma tomorrow."

LL is pulling at the plastic piece that joins the flip-flops together. Her hands fly apart, and she jumps back, once it snaps. "Oh!" she exclaims, laughing. Behind her is a light brown cork bulletin board encased in glass. Someone has unlocked it and taken a red marker and written in all lower caps, "you don't like gay marriage?...don't have one! you don't like abortion?...don't get one! you don't like weed?...don't smoke it! you don't like porn?...don't watch it! you don't like alcohol?...don't drink it! you don't like people of color?...then take your racist ass somewhere and don't hang out with them!" I giggle, pull out my phone, take a picture of it, look over at LL and start thinking of when we first met each other in high school. We were both freshmen, and she had just moved to town. It was her first week.

I was sitting in the front of the class. I preferred to sit in the back, like the school bus, but inevitably I was always moved to the front, like the school bus, within the first week of school starting every year since I could remember, due to talking, horsing around, or whatever. The teachers and the bus drivers thought they could keep a better eye on me this way as well as keep me under control. On this particular day, I was all wired up, because my dad brought me to school and he had let me have a candy bar and Red Bull for breakfast. After asking me numerous times to "Be quiet," during class, the teacher had finally had enough and belted out, "Do you know where you will end up if you don't pay attention in class and fail?!" I could see all of her teeth and her finger was shaking as she pointed at me.

"I don't know," I replied. "At a strip club entertaining your husband?" Her eyes doubled in size and her mouth dropped. The class erupted in laughter.

After taking a couple of seconds to collect herself and demanding the class to "Be quiet!", she pointed to an empty seat in the back and yelled, "Get back in that seat, young lady! We will be discussing this with the Principal after class!" I made my way to the back of the room, accepting quick slaps to my hand and nods of respect.

Plopping down into the blue seat, I let my body slide down the chair. "Ewww," I said, recognizing the strong smell of formalin from the collected, unwashed trays in the sink next to me. "Fucking gross."

"You get used to the smell," someone said, in a squeaky voice. I turned around and saw a little Asian girl, wearing a matching, navy-blue skirt and jacket, with a white shirt and glasses too big for her face, sitting next to me. She didn't look up. Instead, she placed a little baby carrot into her navy-blue backpack. "It's a good place to sit if you want to avoid those people," she said, still not looking at me, nodding the top of her head towards a group of popular kids I hung out with, sitting together a few rows up. She pulled her empty hand up and reached into the baggie full of baby carrots on her lap, hidden under the desk. "It's also much less likely that I'll be called on by that stupid teacher," she added, lowering another carrot into the bag. "She doesn't care about this class, and she doesn't even know any of the material. She only wants to be liked by the popular kids. I was put in this class by mistake anyway." She shrugged her shoulders. "I'm supposed to be in the college-level biology course."

Ignoring anything she'd said and briefly forgetting the smell creeping behind me, I asked, "What the hell are you doing with those carrots?"

"Oh," she said with a laugh. She took her hand out of the bag and showed me her face for the first time. "I'm feeding Cool Bandit."

"What the hell is a Cool Bandit?" I asked, raising myself up in my chair, leaning over the aisle, trying to look in the bag. Smiling, she opened it a little, leaned it over so that I could see. Inside, was a black, brown, and white guinea pig. It was making little squeaking noises and looking up at me. "Awwwwwww," I squealed. Immedi-

ately wanting to rub Cool Bandit, I reached my hand down, but pulled it back fast and looked up to make sure the teacher wasn't looking. I brought my arms to my chest. "She is so cute!" I whined, quieter this time, definitely not wanting to draw attention to us. I looked up at the little Asian girl and asked, "Is it a she?"

Smiling, she nodded her head, grabbed a baby carrot from the bag, and handed it to me. "My name is Ling-Ling," she whispered.

"My name is Courtney," I whispered back, taking the carrot. Ling-Ling smiled, and after waiting a few seconds for the teacher to make her way to a part of the board that definitely blocked her view of Cool Bandit, she leaned the bag to me. After eagerly accepting my carrot, the piggy quickly retreated to a corner of the backpack.

"She needs to get used to you," Ling-Ling, said.

"Hey, Ling Long Song." We both looked up and saw Danny, turned around, looking at us. Stretching his eyes wide with his fingers, he slowly shook his head back and forth. "What Wong Ling Long Song," he said, continuing his childish mimicry. Ling-Ling, sunk into her chair, closed the backpack, pulled it under her legs, and her smile disappeared.

"She's cool, you fucking twat," I said, snapping my fingers to get his attention. Still holding his eyes, but not moving his head, Danny looked at me. "What's not cool is you sending pics of that pathetic excuse you call a dick to me on a Friday night after drinking with your loser friends in your parent's basement, due to the fact that you have the house all to yourself, because your father's getting cucked, watching Tyler, Britney and Cody's dads run a train on your mom in a nearby motel." Danny dropped his hands and looked around to see if anyone heard what I said. A few did, and they were laughing at him. I motioned with my hand for him to turn around while giving him a look of disgust. When he did, he bowed his head down in shame, showing more of the white collar he had popped up, under an already-popped black collar. "Jesus," I said, closing my eyes, shaking my head.

"There will be a time when he'll look back at himself and laugh as hard as I do now," I said with a grin, turning back to Ling-Ling. Her smile came back, and she excitedly sat up in her desk, handed me another carrot. She opened the backpack a little. "Weeh, weeh, weeh," I heard from the bag. "What are you doing after school, LL?" I asked, looking into the bag at Cool Bandit, handing her the treat. The piggy let me pet her for a brief second, then ran to her corner. I sat back up and looked at the little Asian girl in front of me. "Do you want to hang out or do something?"

"Whaaat?" she responded suspiciously, sitting back a little in her desk. "Are you serious?"

She never switched that fucking class.

"Come here," I tell her, grabbing her by the arm, dragging her to the ladies' room on the right.

"I have to go soon, Court, be quick," she says, pulling out her phone, while I look in the mirror. I set my glasses on the black marble counter, run my hand under the faucet, triggering the water to come out and flick some at LL.

"Whoops," I say, smiling, waiting for her to react.

She runs her hands under the faucet in front of her, flings water on me, and we go back and forth, getting each other wet, until she finally stops and yells, "Stop Court, I have to go to my lecture!"

Pulling out my phone, I hold it up to take a pic of myself. Just then, a Hispanic woman bursts through the door, chasing what I hope is her small child. The lady is only wearing one sandal and swinging at the little boy with the other one, yelling something in Spanish. Laughing, with chocolate all over his mouth, the boy gets down on all fours and slides under one of the stall doors. The woman shouts something else and opens the door, but the kid slides into the next stall, and this goes on for another full minute. Disappointed, I finally give up and stop taking selfies. "Oh my god, I can't even," I complain, flipping through the pics, noticing the sandal wielding mom in the background in all of them.

"Settle down, Beavis," LL tells me. "They took five photos on the first moon landing and every time we go to the bathroom you take seventeen."

"Fuck you and your flip-flops," I say, laughing, giving her the middle finger.

"Have you tried going to your profile and posting, 'worst day ever' and then replying to every comment, 'I don't want to talk about it,'" she adds, giggling, pulling out her phone.

"Ohhhhhh, Fuuuuuuuck, You! Ling Long Song!" I snap back, jokingly shoving her. I immediately know that she's comparing my current actions to a ritual repeatedly practiced by all of our roommates freshman year. Pursing my lips, I start to dance a little. "Did you text Schroeder yet?" I ask, looking at myself in the mirror.

"Just did," she says, edging out the door. "I'm off like a prom dress." She gives me her cute, quick wave, and before the door closes, I see her turn and jog towards the exit.

Schroeder

"Every single morning it's the same thing," I think to myself, rolling over, waking up for the second time today. "The few times that I have to get up before her, I'm a ninja. When she wakes up earlier, I feel like I'm listening to someone playing the drums in a rock band." I push the "home" button on my phone, revealing a picture of my girlfriend at a diner we went to a few months ago. She's wearing a blue jean jacket and a trucker hat of mine, with a green and blue cricket team logo on the foam front. Raising the beer, she's giving a cheesy grin. She hates this picture. I love it. It's 1:29 p.m. I'd been woken up earlier this morning, by her whale horn of an alarm at 6:29 a.m. She refuses to turn it down, for fear that she'll oversleep and miss her train to work. For the next hour, I covered my head with the pillows, trying to drown out the sound of her unnecessarily loud kitchen and bathroom noises and her five trips in and out of the bedroom, finally falling back asleep about ten minutes after she'd slammed the door on her rush out. I'd gotten up at 10:31 to go to the bathroom, but was able to get back to sleep quickly, due to the fact that everything was dark, because of the still-drawn shades and because I'd traveled to and from the bathroom, in a purposefully groggy, rushed manner, with my eyes mostly closed, so I didn't "lose any tired".

I grab one of the t-shirts off of the floor, on my side of the bed, noticing that it's inside-out, but put it on anyway. Scanning the floor, looking for two socks, I find a grey one on top of a crumpled-up green shirt in the corner and a black one with red stripes, sitting on my bedside table, laying behind a glass of warm hefeweizen that has an orange in it. Not bothering to find the matching sock for either one, I put both on, look at my phone, and scroll through the same multiple texts I wake up to every day: a few peeps looking for bud and my mom and my girlfriend telling me good morning, they love me, and to "have a good day." Both of their texts have smiley faces, and I reply quickly to both of them, hoping they won't text back.

About five feet before the kitchen, I pick up speed and jump onto the fake wooden floor, sliding all the way to the refrigerator and open up the bottom door. I grab a bottled coke from Mexico, the ones that use real cane sugar, put it in the freezer and look over to my right at the covered, red frying pan on top of the stove. Pulling up the lid, I take in the smell of fried eggs, cut-up sweet sausages, straw onions, tomatoes, garlic, and blue cheese, then I notice a square of aluminum foil on a black plate next to the sink. I already know what it is.

While waiting for my Coke to freeze up a little, I answer a few of the texts, asking people what they want, telling them when they can come by, making their appointments at least a few hours from now, so I can get high and play PS4, unbothered by anyone, at all, especially my girlfriend and her lengthy text discussions. While responding to everyone, I roll two blunts, because I know I'll want two and I don't want to have to put together the second one in the middle of chilling and playing *God of War*. I go back to the bedroom and prop our pillows against the bed frame, fluffing them a little, making it so they'll be comfortable to lay in, but also convenient enough to eat in, then I turn on the TV and PS4, open up the game and push pause once it's loaded and ready to play.

I slide back into the kitchen and over to the table, where I put the leftover blunt from last night and notice a pink, post-it note next to it that my girlfriend left. It has little hearts on it and says, "Stop smoking so much!" and "Take out the trash, please." I pick it up and lay it next to the plate, with the peanut butter and honey sandwich on toasted wheat bread that's wrapped in aluminum foil, open up the main window and screen, and smoke half-blunt, enjoying the silence that comes with being home alone and not being reprimanded for puffing. When I'm done, I toss it out the window, and close only the screen so the kitchen will air out. Opening the freezer, I grab the Coke and five, frozen chocolate chip, bakery cookies out of a plastic container, that's hidden under some bags of frozen vegetables on the second shelf.

Once I get to the bedroom, I lay the cookies stacked on one another and the bottled Coke on my bedside table, instantly realizing that I forgot to open the top. I come back from the kitchen with an opener and plop down onto the bed, having to adjust the pillows some before I'm satisfied with my sitting arrangements. After taking a swig of the Coke, I stuff a cookie in my mouth and start rowing my boat. I play for the next few hours, taking breaks right around every hour to smoke. On the first break, I pull out the other one and smoke half of it, grab some more cookies and put another bottled Coke in the freezer. I heat up and eat the breakfast my girlfriend left, before my second smoke, but I have to get another Coke out of the fridge because the one in the freezer has frozen up too much. This one has a pink post-it stuck to it, that reads, "Stop drinking so much Coke!" No hearts. I ball the note up, toss it in the trashcan and smoke one of the remaining blunts. An hour later, I smoke the remainder of the last one, then go back to the bedroom and play until I defeat one of the Valkyries.

I glance at my phone, realize that Goodkat and some of the guys will be coming by soon, so I turn off the PS4 and TV. Grabbing the two, half-drunken bottles of Coke and empty plate, I slide into the kitchen, wash my plate and fork and a red bowl, which has a small amount of milk and Cocoa Puffs in it, the leftovers from my girlfriend's quick breakfast. After taking a shower, I decide to jerk off before anyone comes by, but while I'm leaning over the sink, trying to bust one out, I'm interrupted by a text from my girlfriend.

"You at home?"

I reach for my phone, with my non-lubed hand. "Yep," I quickly reply, halfway going back to my duties, hoping that will be it. It isn't.

"Jesus, Schroeder! Jerkoff, much?! Your Fitbit just went from fifty steps all morning long to 783 in three minutes! You better not be looking at porn!" she texts, halting my mission. I'd forgotten that we'd linked these fuckers up to an app on her computer when we bought them last week.

Knowing I'm busted and with the mood gone, I throw on my boxers, shorts, and t-shirt, right side out this time, and text back, "Only to you my, S- P- ☺☺." Before she can respond, I add, "You know I would never watch that, especially now that we're together ☺♥."

"Ok. That's what I thought. I love you, L-. Be home in an hour or two."

"I love you too, my S- P- princess."

A notification comes in at the top of my phone. It's a text from Professor Goodkat, and he says he'll be by shortly to grab an "O".

I type, "Right on, man," push "send," put my phone down, jerk at some of the toilet paper, to wipe my right hand clean, and instead of tearing, it unravels at a quick speed, falling to the floor, rolling behind the toilet. "Shit," I say, chuckling a little, retrieving it. I rub any excess lube off my hands, wash them, then delete my history and close the tab on my computer that's sitting on the bathroom counter, facing the sink.

I'm pickier with Goodkat's orders, always offering him my higher quality green at a better price, picking out the best buds for his ounces. I pull out a bright green and purple one, smell it and toss it in the baggie, add some more until it weighs out to twenty-eight grams, then throw in two extra nugs. For some reason, I remember that I haven't brushed my teeth today and I half-jog into the bathroom, uncap the bottle of Listerine and take a swig. After opening the door above the sink and navigating through my girlfriend's 98% ownership of the cabinet, I find my electric toothbrush, but not the battery that's usually sitting upright, next to it. I look in her brush where it sits, losing power, because she's taken it out again to replace hers that's dead, due to her not taking it out when she's done. I've told her a thousand times her battery will lose power like this, but she says it's too much of an annoyance and also difficult to take it in and out every time, especially in the morning when she's in a rush.

I hear a knock on the door before I can make the second round on the front of my teeth, so I stop. Knowing it's Goodkat, I shuffle my scruffy, red hair around, tucking parts of it behind my ears, but because my hair's not too long, most of it just falls back and I look at my reflection in the mirror, my bright, blue eyes staring back at me, my girlfriend's favorite part of my body.

While making my way through the living room, I hear knocks to the rhythm of "Shave and a Haircut," but only the first five notes, not the last two and I open the door to see Goodkat, standing six inches above me. He's wearing a blue and white plaid bathing suit, a grey, deep v-neck t-shirt, and flip-flops. I can't see his eyes because of the old-school, circular, 1930s Dillinger looking, sunglasses he has on.

"Hey, what's going on, man?" he asks, removing his glasses, folding them up.

"Not much, man," I say, accepting his hand and half-hug greeting. "Come on in."

He walks in and sits down on the yellow chair, next to the sofa. "So, what do you have going on today, man?" he asks, setting his keys on the coffee table in front of him. I look down and see a black Range Rover key, along with a silver and gold key, and a small, rubber Viking ship key chain, with a crown and "QBH" written on the sail.

"Not much at all, man," I tell him. "I finished all of my projects earlier yesterday." I plop down on the brown, leather couch. "My girl has class and her internship today, so I had the morning and most of the afternoon to myself," I say, smirking, thinking about how sweet and relaxing the day's been without having to have a conversation every twenty seconds.

"Right on, man," Goodkat says, with an agreeing nod and smile. "I know you enjoyed that. What did you play?"

"*God of War*, man. Have you checked it out?"

"No, not yet," he says, resting back in the chair. "I've been playing *Fallout 4*, but I only play every so often. I don't get into it as much as you do." I can tell that he doesn't mean anything negative by his comment. "Maybe once every two weeks, for a couple of hours, but I dig it when I play." Relaxed, he points at the paused game on my TV. "I'll check this out after I'm done with it." He gives a short laugh. "But it'll probably take a year."

Before I can say, "Right on," I change my mind and nonchalantly, say, "Cool."

"Job still sweet?" he asks, looking around the room.

"Yeah," I answer, a little too excited. Sitting up, I lean forward, put my elbows on my knees and ramble for the next few minutes, going on and on about two jobs that I've closed in the last week and how my bosses couldn't be more pleased, adding how much I love working from home and nothing beats doing your job high, wearing only your boxers.

Goodkat doesn't interrupt. He just nods his head with the occasional, "Right on," maintaining eye contact the entire time, never seeming disinterested. I catch myself babbling and stop mid-sentence, sit back and try to chill out a little. "My bad, man. I didn't mean to bore you with all that."

"Come on, Schroeder," he says, somehow managing to lay even further back, into an even more relaxed position than he was already in. "I'm glad you're doing well. That's fantastic, man. I knew you would when I had you in class." Before I can say, "I can't believe that was ten years ago," he goes on. "Trent on the other hand." We laugh, knowing that he's saying this in a joking manner; then both of us trade two Trent stories of our own, and we agree that although he makes some stupid decisions and is irresponsible and lazy, you can't help but like the guy.

"How are things with you, man?"

"Things are fine by me," he answers, stretching out one leg. "School is ending. Going down to see a friend next week and then taking a trip for a month or so."

"Where?"

"I have no idea," he says, with another short chuckle. His storytelling doesn't take as long as mine, and he sits up, clasps his hands together. "So, what do you have for me, man?

Grinning, I say, "Something you won't be disappointed in."

"Haven't been yet. By the bye, did my advice work?" Goodkat asks.

While trying to recall what his advice was, I reach into the already open, wooden drawer beside me and grab his ounce. When I do, I also pick up a small, black and white battery-powered dog that my girlfriend and I picked up at a street fair in Santorini, last summer. I toss the baggie to Goodkat, who casually catches it in one hand, right before it hits the table. He lays some folded up cash I hadn't noticed was in his other hand, on the table. A $100 bill is on the outside, and I don't bother to pick up the money. Sensing that I need some help, he says, "About getting rid of your girlfriend's annoying friend."

"Yes!" I exclaim, pointing at him with both hands, now knowing exactly what he's talking about. "Thanks, man! You were totally right! All I had to do was mention to my girlfriend that her friend was pretty, and I haven't had to put with that annoying bitch since."

"I told you," he says, confidently, nodding his head up once. "So, what are you up to tonight, man?" he asks, standing up, instead of leaning back into the chair again. He puts the baggie in his pocket without ever really looking at it, then grabs his keys.

"We're actually going out with Trent and those guys tonight," I answer, turning the dog upside-down, looking for the small power switch. When you turn the switch on, the dog sporadically jumps around, flashing its weird, red eyes on and off, while making an odd, robotic bark. Wanting to give Goodkat a laugh before he leaves, I flip the switch on the bottom of the dog without picking it up, but nothing happens. Turning it over, I open the bottom where the batteries go, except there are no batteries. They take AA, just like our toothbrushes. "Motherfucker," I say, to myself. I set it on all fours on the glass table and get up. "Harry's moving back to South Carolina on Sunday to start his business, so we'll probably be with them all weekend," I say, walking behind Goodkat, towards the door.

"I like Harry," he says, not bothering to turn around after opening the door, continuing down the hallway. "Dude reminds me of me."

"Later!" I yell. He raises his right hand in the air, doesn't say anything, and disappears down the stairs.

About thirty minutes later, Trent comes by, and I immediately make fun of the khaki cargo shorts he's wearing, when I open the door. "What the fuck could you possibly need so many pockets for?" I ask.

"Fuck you, Ginger Spice," he says, shoving me as he walks past me. "What the fuck are you doing? Working hard in your boxers all day? And where is your super-hot girlfriend?" He starts glancing around the apartment, exaggerating his search by peering quickly to his left and right, up and down. "Please explain to me how the fuck that happened," he asks, looking at me. "Did she lose a bet?" After he's finally done talking, he sits in the same yellow chair that Goodkat relaxed in, the same chair that everyone that comes over to buy weed sits in. If they sit down.

I flick the back of his head. "Ow," he moans, flinching a little.

"You want a beer or something?" I ask, with my back to him, walking to the kitchen.

"Yeah," he answers, getting up and following me. "What ya got?"

I don't answer and open the fridge to let him see for himself. We went to the store yesterday and bought two of those six-packs where you can mix any single beers that you want. Bottled or canned. He reaches in and grabs an IPA, one that I'm sure he won't like and that he picked based solely on the label, but I don't say anything and grab a bottle of breakfast stout that has a picture of a baby boy with blonde hair eating from a bowl with a spoon. I pop open the tops with a small, pink bottle opener that's shaped like a flip-flop because I don't feel like walking back to the bedroom to get the one that I left there. After setting it and the bottle tops on the counter next to the fridge, I walk over to the closet and grab a small, black fan that I should have gotten out earlier, place it on the floor, point it to the window and plug it in. Trent is already standing by the window, hunched over a little, pushing up the half-open blinds, so that he can see outside. I sit in the chair, grab the lighter, and a blunt that I rolled after Goodkat left, from the glass table. We click glasses without saying anything; both of us take a swig and Trent makes a dissatisfying face, and pulling back the bottle, he looks at it.

"Cool picture," he says, taking another swig, making the same face, and shaking my head a little, I say, "Cool shirt," then light the blunt.

He looks down at his purposefully faded, red t-shirt. It says, "Long's Rod & Tackle," and has pictures of various fishing tackle and equipment and a fishing rod at the bottom, where underneath it reads, "The longest rod for when you're getting wet." Thanking me, he pulls a piece of his shirt from his chest, let's go. "I got it at the mall." I close my eyes, shake my head again.

"So, you bummed out Harry and Justin are leaving?" I ask, passing the blunt. He takes a puff.

"Yeah, it sucks." He pauses. "Can't believe all of us graduated." Without exhaling, he takes an even longer hit and sets his beer on the window, with the label facing in. It has two, wooden coffins on it, one of which has a pawn from a chess set lying in it, the other coffin, a king piece.. Trent blows a billow of smoke into the kitchen. "I know Justin's bummed out," he says, looking at me.

"Man, blow that out the window! What the fuck do you think the fan is for!?" I yell, motioning to the fan, imagining my girlfriend getting home, complaining about the smell, going on a tirade about it. I take a couple of sips of my beer and Trent takes another long pull.

"My bad, man," he says, with the raspy voice of someone who just took too big a hit. Yanking up his shorts, he passes it back to me while bending down and blowing smoke out the window. He grabs his beer, looks at it, but doesn't take a sip. Sounding slightly glum, he says, "We'll have an epic weekend." Still inspecting the label, he starts peeling one of the corners back. He quickly looks at me and changes his tone. "Going to get fucked up and laid!" He clinks my bottle, then raises his and takes a swig.

"Right on," I agree, bringing mine to my lips.

I take a puff, and Trent makes a similar, unpleased face. He shrugs his shoulders, chugs the rest of his beer, lets out an "Ahhhhh," when finished and then proudly places the empty bottle on the counter and lets out a long burp.

"You want another?" I ask, closing the screen.

"Nah, I'm cool. You bringing MC Hottie tonight?" he asks, moving his eyebrows up and down.

"Yeeep," I proudly respond.

We play video games for the next hour, and somewhere in there, after telling him about my girlfriend's decorative towels that I'm not supposed to use and how amazed I am by her insanely excessive use of toilet paper, I learn about Trent's lunch.

Trent

"I'd just gotten fired from the smoothie place and-"

"You fucking got fired again?!" Schroeder asks, snickering. He pauses the game, falls back onto the sofa, starts laughing harder.

"Yessss, Strawberry Shortcake. I got fired."

"Again," he adds.

"Yes, again."

"Do the guys know?" he asks, sitting up, unpausing the game.

"No, but I'll tell those bitches later. Now back to the story." Schroeder kicks me in the face. "So, I was super hungry and wanted some Mexican."

"And you had just been fired." Schroeder chuckles after interrupting me again, roundhouse kicks me, then rips out my spine.

"Fucker!" I punch him in the shoulder, in real life. "Now shut the fuck up. So, I'm hungry as balls, and I want some Mexican, mainly so I can take advantage of the fact that all of them serve unlimited, free chips and salsa. I go to that new place that just opened up, you know, on Nosegay Lane." He nods his head, doesn't say anything. "So, I ordered the cheapest enchilada they had on the menu and ate that and the rice and beans that come with it and like, four bowls of chips and salsa. The salsa was hot and spicy as shit, so I asked the waiter for mild, and he says, 'This is the mildest we have, señor.' So anyway, like two minutes after eating, you know how I am after Mexican, man." I put my hands on my stomach.

He chuckles a little, says he's the same way, and I go on.

"So, I rush through the dining area, clenching my cheeks, trying to make it to the bathroom. I bust into a stall, sit down and after releasing what I will just rate as a "9.5," I realize there's no fucking toilet paper!" I dart my head around Schroeder's living room. "I look left, right, up, down, behind me, on the toilet. No fucking toilet paper! But then, and I swear to you, Schroeder." I raise my hands and look up, trying to show the seriousness of the situation. "A beam of light shone down on a small handle, I hadn't noticed before, on the wall to my left and I turned it, and a small light turned on, and I thought I heard a hymn." Excited, I look back at him. "It was a fucking mini-fridge, Schroeder! A fucking mini-fridge, with cooled, chilled toilet paper!" After throwing my hands up further in the air, I collapse back into my seat. "I spent the next fifteen minutes in there."

"Chilled toilet paper? You're kidding me?" he says, laughing. "That's fucking amazing!"

Nodding my head, still shocked, I say, "I know, I know."

Just then, I hear the click of the front door and Schroeder's banging, girlfriend walks in. With short black hair, a hot, dark-skinned body and nice, nice tits, she comes from behind me and stands in front of us. "I'm guessing she weighs one hundred pounds, tops," I think to myself, trying not to be too obvious about checking her out. The outfit she's wearing only makes her that much hotter. Small, yellow shorts and a t-shirt, with a chinchilla wearing sunglasses. At the bottom, it reads, "chinchillin."

"Hi, my love," she says, smiling at Schroeder, looking past me, as if I'm not even in the room.

"Hi, honey." He pauses the game and stands up.

She lays the backpack she was wearing when she came in on the floor, next to my chair, then gives him a hug and a kiss. "Hi Trent," she says, turning around.

"Hi," I surprisingly respond back, quickly looking up from her ass. She pays no mind to me and turns back to Schroeder.

"Were you busy all day, my love? Did you get those projects done that you said you had to finish?" she asks, hugging him again, pulling him in tight. She gives him a kiss on his chest, then on his cheek and his lips.

"Yep," Schroeder says, winking at me. "All day long, honey. I just got finished before Trent came over." He motions towards me, waits for me to back him up.

I shake my head in agreement. "Yep." She gives me a skeptical look, lets go of Schroeder and heads into the kitchen, talking about something while walking away. Schroeder unpauses the game, I take my eyes off her butt, and I can still hear her saying something ten seconds later, when she walks back in, holding the beer tops and bottle opener Schroeder had put on the counter earlier.

"Clean up after yourself, Schroeder," she says, holding them out for him to see.

He doesn't look away from the screen. "My bad, my love."

"Schroeder, were you even listening to me earlier?" she asks, putting her hands on her hips, twisting her right foot to that angle that all girls do.

Without looking away from the TV, he says, "Yes, you were talking about how the train was held up at the first station for ten minutes and after waiting you ended up having to board another train, because the one you were on was going to take too long to fix and then some guy seated next to you was coughing--" Having proven his point and impressing me, because I had no idea he was paying attention, Schroeder stops repeating her story. Looking away from the screen, he flashes her a grin. "See, I was listening. And then you came in here to reprimand me for the tops and bottle openers."

"Not reprimand, my love," she says, in a concerning tone. "Just remind you so that we have a clean apartment." She smiles, jumps a little. "I love you."

"I love you too, honey," he tells her, blowing her a kiss from the couch.

I give a puzzled look meant only for myself and mouth the words, "What the fuck?"

She heads back to their bedroom, jabbering about, "some bitch" on the subway, and before I can ask, Schroeder leans towards me. "I barely pay attention, I just pick up on keywords and infer and listen for interrogative statements."

"Inte-what?" I ask myself.

"When she asks a question," he says, correctly assuming that I don't know what inter—whatever means.

She returns not long later, still chattering, this time about a coffee she got at school today that tasted bitter. "Do you think that's odd, my love?" she asks, looking at him. "That I get a coffee there every day, but today it tasted bitter."

"Nah, could be a bunch of things, honey." He punches me in the face and then sweeps my legs. "You know how most of the employees are at places like that. Most don't care. Who knows, the beans might have been old." Schroeder stops talking and leans to his left on the sofa, when he dodges one of my kicks, then continues. "There could be a bunch of other extraneous variables that could cause this. No need to worry."

"Extrane-what?" I ask myself, missing his head again with my punch.

"You always worry too much and think something is bigger than it is. Just relax," Schroeder tells her.

"Okay," she responds, still looking concerned, but not as much. She changes her mood quickly and holds up a wine bottle opener, says, "And my love." She shakes it until Schroeder looks at her.

He pauses the game, looks up. "Yes, my love?" He sees the other opener in her hand. "My bad," he says again, showing his teeth.

"And you didn't make the bed."

"My bad. Will you fix me a sandwich?" he asks, flashing even more of his teeth.

Slightly irritated, she says, "Yes. What do you want?"

Schroeder explains in specific detail the sandwich he wants, and she goes back to the kitchen after standing and listening and mimicking a waitress taking an order. He unpauses the game and asks, "What time should we meet you guys out tonight?"

"Whenever the hell you want." I lean to my right, then my left and stand up fast, screaming, after beating him for the first time. "Aha!" I drop the controller, raise my hands in victory.

"One for twenty-two is not bad, Trent," he says, laughing at me.

"Schroeder!" His girlfriend storms out of the kitchen, holding a framed picture in her hand. "What the hell is this?!" When she gets closer and holds it steady, I can see that it's a picture of her and at the bottom, in red marker, it reads, "Employee of the Month." "You think this is funny?" she yells, throwing the picture at him, but not too hard.

"It was a joke, my love!" Laughing, he stands up. "I thought you'd like it."

"You make your own fucking sandwich!" she shouts, storming back into the kitchen.

Arms outreached, Schroeder calls out, "My loveeeee!" She pulls her hand back, gives him the finger, keeps on walking and in a low voice so that his girlfriend won't hear, he points and says, "Back to the kitchen!"

"I'm going out on that victory," I tell him, setting the controller down. "I'll let you sit here in shame and disappointment for a while."

"Oh yeah, Trent," he says, "that will be bothering me for quite some time." He beats his closed fist over his chest a few times. "I don't know if I'll be able to sleep tonight."

"Hook me up with an eighth, before I go?" I ask, knowing I have no money.

"No problem." Schroeder opens the cabinet next to him, weighs it out, then throws it to me. "Here you go."

"I'll pay you when you come over tonight," I say, stuffing the little bag into my pocket.

"Cool, figured," he says, giving me a quick glance.

A few moments later, she comes back in, holding a sandwich, almost showing it off. Sitting down next to Schroeder, she puts the plate on the table in front of him. He reaches for his food, but she pulls the dish out of the way, grabs the sandwich and takes two, huge bites. With a full mouth and lettuce and other bits hanging out, she mumbles, "My sandwich, make your fucking own."

"What the fuck?!" Schroeder says, pretending to be angry. He flaps his arms up and down, putting on a show. "I worked hard all day long, supporting us and putting you through grad school, and you do this to me!?"

"Mmmhmm," she mutters, nodding her head.

He stands up and puts his hands on his hips, moves his right foot, mocking her earlier stance. "It takes me an hour just to pick out an outfit and travel to work," he jokingly adds. I laugh, and she takes another large bite of her sandwich, holding it close like she's eating in the middle of a prison cafeteria. Halfway through his ranting, Schroeder slowly leaps towards her in a joking attempt to steal the sandwich. She hugs it closer, avoiding him easily.

"I knew you were going to do that. My sandwich," she says. "Yours is in the kitchen."

After coming back with a similar sandwich, he sits down next to her, leans over, kisses her on the cheek twice and says, "Thanks, honey."

"You're welcome, my love," she says, putting her hand on his knee. Rocking back and forth slightly, she sets her sandwich on Schroeder's plate, instead of her own and he just grins, kisses her on the cheek again and takes another bite of his.

"Alright, Lifetime channel. I'll see you two tonight," I say, standing up, giving Schroeder a look of shame.

While walking to the door, I hear at the same time, "Later, man," and "Bye, Trent."

Stopping, I turn around, and say, "That is if she lets you go out tonight, man." I snap my wrist and mimic the sound of a whip, repeating it three times.

Shaking his head, Schroeder chuckles, takes a bite of his sandwich and his girlfriend flicks me off, then kisses Schroeder for the millionth time since she got here.

On my way back to the apartment, I run into an anti-gay demonstration at one of the local churches. A lot of the churches in the area have been showing their support of gay marriage lately, so these protests have been popping up around town. They're non-violent protests, with the people from both sides mostly just screaming at each other, pointing fingers. The local police are always there in case anything gets out of hand, but it never does. On the church lawn, to the left of the sidewalk that leads up to the chapel, the anti-gay demonstrators are shouting; some of them raising their fists, others holding signs showing images of flames, fire, and the devil, with slogans reading things like, "SINNERS GO TO HELL", "SAME-SEX MARRIAGE IS A SIN", "BURN IN HELL". I shake my head, embarrassed for them, wondering why they not only care so much about what someone else does with their own life but why they have such an intense hatred for someone they simply disagree with. The cops on the sidewalk smile and laugh, most of them chatting with each other, some of them shaking their heads in agreement with the people on the right side, some trying to calm down the ones on the left. I notice JG, Lil E, and Rap, three guys I know from school, picketing at the front, and I immediately stop in my tracks, start laughing at the signs the three of them are holding and what Lil E is wearing. "Yo! JG, Lil E, Rap!" I yell, with my hands around my mouth, trying to get their attention. Seeing me, all three nod and chuckle, then throw up peace signs and a closed fist.

Dressed as Jesus, Lil E is holding a sign with a red arrow on it that's pointing to the protestors. It reads, "I'M NOT WITH THESE GUYS". JG's sign also has a red arrow pointing to the protestors, and it says, "THESE GUYS NEVER MISS A GAY EVENT". I take a couple more pics, rereading Rap's sign again, that's written in red and green and has a picture of Santa Claus on it. "STOP PREMATURE CHRISTMAS DECORATING". After flipping my phone around and taking a few selfies with them, I yell out, "You fuckers rock!" while pumping my fist. They throw their hands up again, Rap launches a few round ornaments into the crowd on the other side, and I send a couple of the photos to Clarence, Harry, and Justin, adding that same pic of that naked black dude sitting at the edge of the bed.

When I walk in the door, Clarence is on the couch by himself, playing *Read Dead 2*. He'd been playing the game for months but hadn't beaten it yet, instead choosing to roam the countryside to see what else he could find, who else he could kill. He has a plate of nachos and a two-liter bottle sitting in front of him on our coffee table, and as he lifts the Mountain Dew-filled martini glass, I see a Cool Ranch Dorito, in place of an olive, and flick him on the back of the head. He doesn't flinch. "You classy motherfucker," I say. "What time is your driver picking us up tonight?"

I notice the monster nacho that's set aside, at the top right corner of his plate, the one that's topped perfectly with cheese, meat, tomatoes, and sauce, the one I know that he's saving for the end.

Holding his glass daintily, he turns around, looks at me, nods, takes a sip, says, "I told him ten o' clock, but it'll probably be ten-thirty. You know how Bentley is. That bitch is always late." He sets the glass down, snags the Dorito from the rim, and throws it in his mouth.

"What the fuck is Justin doing?" I ask, looking around the apartment. "And what the fuck are you doing over there?" I motion towards the nachos. "If you want to keep fitting into that sweet tracksuit you're wearing and your Lieutenant Fuzz uniform, you should lay off that and that Game Boy cocktail."

"What the fuck do you think he's doing?" Clarence sarcastically answers. "And it's called moderation, fool. Look it up." Hiding behind a snow-covered tree, he kills two guys with a long-range rifle.

"Awwww yeah," I say, flicking him in the back of the head again, this time harder. "Let's make that gravity bong and get fucked up!" He doesn't flinch this time either, and after taking a deep breath, he pauses the game, stands up. I look up at him and break into a fighting stance, start dancing, punching the air. He laughs and pulls down the zipper on his jacket a little. I think to myself, "I can either take him on and get body-slammed onto the couch, or I can interrupt Justin's spank session and get this last weekend of partying started." I go with the second option. Acting like I'm going to kick him, I raise my leg, then run off to the hallway instead and hide behind the wall, returning once I hear him sit back down and start the game. I reach down towards his plate, stop, look over at him. "Do you mind?" He shakes his head, and I quickly grab the monster nacho, throwing it in my mouth.

"Motherfucker!" he yells, standing up, and I sprint to Justin's room.

"Juuuuuuustin. Oh, Juuuuuuustin," I whisper, lightly tapping the door repeatedly, turning the locked doorknob, back and forth. "Oh, Juuuuuuustin."

"Uh, hold on, I'm studying," he blurts out, and I hear some shuffling and other noises; a drawer closes, then he opens the door.

"That must be a hardcore study session," I say, standing up, folding my arms. Breathing slightly hard, Justin's cheeks are red and his short, black hair, usually parted neatly to the side, is matted in the back and sticking out.

"It was," he tells me, pushing his glasses up his nose, trying to walk past me.

I block his path, don't let him get through the door. "Studying after your classes are over, huh? No more school work, yet you claim to be studying?" I ask, interrogating him, inspecting his room. I look at his bed, desk, floor, put my hands to my eyes, start acting like some sort of high-tech scanner. "Duh, duh, duh, duh, duh, duh." Imitating a host on a crime documentary, I announce, "I see no 'hardcore' evidence, such as moisturizer, a nearby towel, tissues, not even a single sock on the floor. I see nothing compelling, nothing that would lead me to believe-"

"Get out of my way, dumbass," he says, trying to shove his way by me. I hold my ground and finish.

"Nothing that would lead me to believe self-gratification has occurred. Yet…" I pause when I spot Justin's mouse. "You have made a grave mistake!" I exclaim, and he looks over at his desk, quickly. "Notice," I say, pointing to the mouse, leaning into him, pushing the side of my face against his. "Notice that you have left your mouse on the left side of the table!"

"Ahhhhhh!" Justin screams, throwing his head back. "Fuck off!"

"Guilty, motherfucker!" I yell, grabbing his shoulders, pushing him onto his neatly made bed. "Come on, bitch! Let's get fucked up! It's our last weekend!" I pretend like I'm jerking off, then shake my hand a few times at him, palms up, pretending to spray him with my nut. "Let's gooooooo!" I turn around and run up the hallway to flick Clarence in the back of the head again, harder, regardless of the consequences.

Justin

I get up from my bed, slowly, dream-like and pull the corners of my red-and-white-striped comforter down and to the side, straightening it. After putting one of my pillows back in place, I fluff it a little, yank at its cover and for some reason, even though I couldn't care less about Trent knowing that I was jerking off, I move my mouse back to the right side of my desk. "I'm actually glad he interrupted," I think to myself. Embarrassing as it is, it's something familiar, something that after I leave for my internship won't happen again. Harry's permanent departure on Sunday has been on my mind a lot, depressing me and I look over at the mirror, above my dressers. What little I do have on top of the dressers - a bottle of body spray, a burnt figure from South of the Border, and a Jack Burton action figure - are neatly placed in the back left corner. I'm wearing a blue, ribbed tank top, something I would only wear here, not in public, and I zone out, gazing at the pictures that are stuck between the wooden frame and mirror: various photos of us partying, at the Indy 500, in weed fields in Jamaica with some Rastafarians, at the Hedonism II resort on the same trip, all of us in a boat on a fishing trip in Florida, and our first party on our first night in this apartment. I glance over all of them, remembering the road trips and plane flights to and from, the laughs and small details of each trip. It all seems like it was yesterday and it all seems like it was so long ago at the same time, and still in a dream-like state, I reach out for the picture of our first party here, slowly pull it out from between the mirror and wood. All four of us are in it, drunk, smiling, each with a drink in our hand. My gaze shifts to my best friend, Harry, his thick arm around me. "Third grade," I think to myself.

I pushed my glasses up and turned my lock on locker #315 to the right, three times, stopping at H ½, two times to the left, to G, and then one time to the right, to H and pulled. The locker wouldn't open, so I repeated the process, this time turning the worn-down, copper dial, slower, making sure the arrow lined up perfectly with the letters. It opened this time, so I set my Star Wars backpack on the floor, resting it against the lockers to my left, unzipped the two zippers that met at the top and took out my homemade locker divider that I'd made in June. It lined up correctly and slid right into the top of my locker. I started to evenly distribute my school supplies, my mother and I bought in July, uniformly and in their correct locations, when I heard, "Grrrrrrr," from my right and then a fist hitting the locker next to mine, locker #316. Looking around my orange door, I saw a boy, smaller than me with brown, spikey hair, wearing light plaid shorts and a Spider-Man t-shirt. Lightly tapping his locker, he was pulling at the lock, unsuccessfully trying to open it. With all of my excitement and precision to detail in setting up my locker, I hadn't noticed him.

"These things are tricky," I said, smiling, looking at him. I pointed to the locker and didn't say anything else, asking for permission to try. He scrunched his lips up some, didn't say anything either, and frustratingly handed me a slip of paper. I took it and read off the letters aloud while turning the copper dial. "E." I made sure to line the arrow up just right. "Like I said, these things are tricky. B ½." I glanced back at him. "It usually takes two tries no matter what to open the lock. A. And you have to make sure you line the arrow up," I said, pulling the latch, up, opening the locker, "just right!"

He was bouncing up and down and clapping when I turned around. "Thanks, my name's, Harry," he said, smiling, reaching out his hand. "I just moved here. I don't have any friends."

"I'm Justin." I said, taking his hand. "I'll be your friend."

My eyes tear up a bit, and I know I could cry if I let myself, I swear I could bawl, but I fight it and wipe what little tears have formed in my eyes with my tank top. I also know that if I had to talk to someone right now, that if one of the guys walked in at this moment and wanted to speak, I wouldn't be able to. I wouldn't be ready to fight it. I would break down right here.

Putting the picture down back in its place, I gather myself, raise my shoulders up and down some, clear my nose, push my glasses up, then look in the mirror. My eyes are a little red, but it doesn't look like I've been crying. Trying to get my mind on something else, I think about the gravity bong we're getting ready to make, along with the night we're getting ready to have, and I come out of my dream a little. A few moments pass, and I awaken from my fog completely, when I hear Trent yell, "Hey, Sir Beats-A-Lot, get the fuck in here!"

My mood brightens a bit, and I walk towards the living room, telling myself not to think that tonight, tomorrow, tomorrow night, Sunday morning, that all of this will be over and gone before I know it. Trent and Clarence are in the kitchen, cutting out the bottom of a Sunny D jug and filling up a cooler with water, respectively.

"How the hell do you drink that shit?" Clarence asks, pushing Trent before either of them notice me.

Both of them glance over towards me, then go back to their tasks. While pointing my Swiss army knife in the air and waving it, Trent answers. "It's good for you, man." He puffs his chest out. "Just look at me. Been drinking it since I was a kid. Plus, it goes perfect with Reese's Puffs cereal." He starts licking his lips, looks at Clarence, stops, then starts again, suggestively this time, while raising his eyebrows up and down. Carrying on, he begins thrusting his hips forward and backward.

Shaking his head, Clarence says, "Just hurry up and cut the fucking bottle, man." He turns off the water, lifts up the cooler.

"You don't want me to rush do you? What if I cut my hand off?" Trent says. He points my knife at Clarence, shaking it up and down. "You need to think about that."

"Then you could beat off with the left one," Clarence tells him, on his way to the coffee table. He stops, nods in my direction, says, "Take a course from the master." Both of them laugh at my expense, and Clarence sets the cooler on the glass top, spilling some of the water over the edge, onto the coffee table.

I flick Clarence off. "So, how was work today?" I nonchalantly ask Trent, walking behind him, to the other side of the counter.

"Fine," he answers, making the last cut on the container, the bottom of the Sunny D jug, falling to the floor.

"Dumbass, the trashcan is right here," I tell him, motioning to the overflowing can, picking up the bottom piece, tossing it on top of the mound in the corner. "And why don't either of you ever take out the trash? Or clean up?" I ask, looking at both of them. I pause for a moment, motion to the water on the table. "Clarence?"

"I'm sorry, what was that again, Grand Master–" Clarence starts chuckling. "Fap?" He begins laughing even harder, and Trent joins him.

"Fucking morons," I say, turning my attention back to Trent. He's piercing the bottle's orange cap with my knife, wiggling it around to make room for the bowl piece. "So, nothing exciting happened today, huh?" I ask. I turn, glance at Clarence and he's looking at Trent, trying not to laugh.

Trent looks up from finishing the hole. "No, why?" he answers, grabbing the bowl piece, noticing us smirking. "Oh, fuck you fuckers," he says, motioning at us with my knife. Clarence and I burst out, howling, and Trent drops the orange top and bowl piece on the floor.

Clarence points at me. "First drink is on you tonight and the second one is on Harry." I lose sight of him when he says the second part because I bend down to pick up the bowl that rolled towards me.

"What was the over-under range on the bet?" Trent asks, grabbing the top off the floor. He sticks his hand out, palm, up, without looking at me, expecting the bowl piece.

I drop it in his hand. "I had nine to eighteen days, Harry had nineteen to twenty-eight days, and Clarence-" I stop talking, look over at Clarence, and allow him to finish.

"Clarence had one to nine days," he says, raising his Mountain Dew martini, nodding to Trent. He takes a long gulp, finishing it, then lets out a satisfying, "Ahhhh."

"You rat bastard! Have you no soul!?" Trent yells. "Profiting off of my loss! You have no idea how this makes me feel!" He starts sniffling, pretends to get choked up.

"I know exactly how it makes you feel," Clarence says, resting his arm on the back of the couch. "I've seen you, work, man. Or should I say, I've seen you avoid work." He laughs, shakes his head. "You're like, the worst employee ever. How the fuck did you get fired today?"

"It doesn't matter, man. I just got fired. That's all you need to know." Trent looks down, puts the bowl back in, pops his head up, shouts, "Now let's get fucked up!" He raises the finished piece in his hand, then grabs three beers out of the fridge.

"Oh, no," Clarence says, shaking his head. "You're definitely going to tell us now."

Knowing that both of us will either bug the shit out of him until he does, or that Clarence will pin him down on the floor and torture him by hanging spit from his mouth, over his face, until he tells us, he yells, "I was fired because I was carrying fifty dozen eggs in from a delivery and I dropped them when I tripped on the sidewalk, because I was watching this hot chick bend over in a skirt!"

"Bahhhhhhhhh!" Clarence starts convulsing and falls back onto the couch, slapping his thigh. Not surprised by yet another termination, I chuckle, but I get nowhere near the enjoyment out of that he does.

Clarence stands up and for the next five minutes, using various facial expressions, he gives several impersonations of Trent, that include him falling to the floor, wiping away fake eggs, but continuing to catch a glimpse of "that ass," as he calls it.

We sit on our stained, dark, plaid L-shaped couch and I start to dry off the glass counter with a towel I brought from the kitchen while making Clarence pick up the cooler, cleaning off some of the different colored circular rings that were already there. "Why the fuck did I even get coasters if you dumbasses never use them?" I ask, throwing the towel at Trent when I'm done.

He catches it. "Settle down, Sir Wanks-A-Lot and give me that lighter."

I slide the lighter with our university logo from my side of the table to his. "Here you go, O' unemployed one. Don't miss that gazing at Clarence's ass."

Trent stares up towards the ceiling, acts like he's gazing into the sky or space. "Ahhh," he says, dramatically. "I remember when I first discovered jerking off. I thought it was for losers and dudes that didn't get laid." He looks at me. "I've never told you this story."

"Oh please, enlighten me," I say.

He begins. "It was the summer before my senior year of high school. I'd been dating this chick for about eight months, and she was house-sitting for her parents' friends for the summer. I was getting laid a lot, but for some reason, I can't remember why maybe she was on her period or something, I decided I was going to jerk off, I was going to test out what all the fuzz-" Trent pauses, looks at Clarence. "My bad, man." He finishes his sentence. "Fuss was about." Clarence hits him on the shoulder but doesn't interrupt. "This chick I'm dating is somewhere, work, wherever, and I go into the bedroom and start to jerk off. I don't remember what I was thinking about, most likely some other chick, probably her younger sister and it doesn't take long to nut, and I'm like, 'This is fucking sweet! Why the fuck have I not been doing this sooner!' It was like the flood gates had opened, literally. I was still getting laid, but I was jerking off all the time." He acts like he's jerking off, every now and then pretending to cum. "I was beating it in the woods, behind the shed, in the bathroom. After rolling all of this off, he catches his breath, looks up to his right. "Here's the worst part of the story. My mom caught me not long after, well, not literally. She found some DVDs in my laundry and made me go see our priest. He said, 'Son, it's not a sin to jerk off, but it is frowned upon.'" Trent ends his story by sarcastically saying, "Yeah, like the big guy is looking down on me while I work one down, disappointed, saying, 'Technically this is my fault, for not being more specific, but I am not happy about this at all.'"

We laugh, and Clarence says, "Yeah, I can't say I'm worried about that at all when I'm pummeling my meat." He pauses, shows his teeth, sucks in some air. "But I can admit to some shame and questioning some of my porn choices when I'm done." He looks at both of us, and we're already nodding our heads.

I push the jug down into the cooler, letting it fill up with water and Trent fills the bowl with some bright, green bud that has beautiful, visible crystals on it, from a small bag he says he got from Schroeder. "Big surprise," Clarence tells him. He passes the lid to me, and I barely fasten it onto the top of the jug, taking the lighter from him next. I light the bud and pull up the bottle, watching it fill with smoke while they cheer me on with different, motivational chants, including references to my jerking off, like, "Go, Grandmaster Fap!" and "Take it all, Beat Boy!" Unfastening the cap, I put my mouth over the top and push down the bottle, taking in all of the smoke.

Each of us finishes our own bowl, then go another round, and at some point, we start to talk about a music festival we went to last summer. We reminisce about the bands we saw, the ones we liked, the ones that sucked, the girls, how hot it was, and Clarence and Trent commend me, for the thousandth time, about my thinking to go to the grounds of the festival two days before and burying two bottles of vodka for us to have at the event. I'd even made a treasure map for extra comedic value.

After we make it back to the couch, Clarence looks at me and says, "Alright, motherfucker, start it up."

It was first semester, freshman year and I was trying to find a flash drive in Harry and my dorm room. It had my paper for History 221: European Imperialism on it, and I knew it wasn't on my side of the room because I had nothing out of place and everything was right where it was supposed to be. Instead of trying to find a needle in a haystack in Harry's messy, disorganized side, I decided to walk across the hall, to Clarence and Trent's room. Stepping in the middle of the white, circle patterns on the green carpet, like I'd always done since the day we'd moved in, I made my way across the hall and knocked on the door, hard and quick, immediately recognizing the smell of marijuana from their room. All of them, especially Harry, had tried to get me to smoke, but I'd always said no. "I'm going to kill him if he doesn't know where that flash drive is," I thought to myself, knocking on the door again. The paper really didn't take me long to write. I'd easily gone over the ten-page requirement, because my knowledge and genuine interest in the subject of my paper - the causes behind European expansion arising both within Europe itself and in the decline of the powerful states in the Indian subcontinent, Africa and the Far East - had prompted me to keep on writing. I hadn't saved it on my computer, only the flash drive, and I knew if Harry didn't know where it was, then I'd have to start all over again, and it would most likely be subpar to what I currently had.

Trent opened the door, and a cloud of smoke blew out of the room. "What's uppppp?" he said, smiling, greeting me with extremely red eyes. He looked left, down the hallway, then to the right and pulled me in quickly, slamming the door behind me. The room was filled with smoke and set up exactly like ours, both of their beds sat up high, propped up on sets of dressers on one end, desks on the other. Just like ours, their beds were high enough and far enough apart, so that there was enough room between the desks and dressers for chairs, allowing them to sit and study under their beds. They both also had fabric material with different designs on them, hanging from the ceiling, held up by string and circle screws, surrounding their twin beds, giving them privacy whenever they hooked up. Trent's was dark plaid, and Clarence's had different colored dinosaurs on it. Between the back of their desks and the door, they had a couch, chair and coffee table on one side and a TV, DVD player and two mini-fridges, on the other.

"Jus, take a hit of this!" Harry yelled, holding up a marijuana cigarette, motioning me towards him.

"You know I'm not going to smoke that," I told him. "Where's my flash drive? Have you seen it? I need to print out my paper!"

"If you take a hit of this, I'll tell you where it is," he said, teasing me.

"Fine!" For some reason, I grabbed it out of his hand and smoked it a few times, letting out some coughs while questioning him again.

"Dude, relax," he said. "Last night I put it behind that picture of us on your desk because I had to use your computer and I was all fucked up, and I didn't want to misplace it. It's there." He patted the seat beside him. "Now sit down."

"No, no, I have to do this right now," I told him, ending my rare visit.

I closed the door behind me, and when I heard it shut, I felt guilty about leaving quickly, so I immediately turned to knock again, but before I could, I heard Trent ask Harry, "I know we've only hung out a few times, but why do you live-" and before he could get out anything else, Harry interrupted.

"If you ever ask me that question again, we won't be hanging out."

"Dumbass," I heard Clarence say.

I went into my room and found the flash drive behind the pic-ture of Harry and me at our high school graduation. We were both wearing maroon caps and gowns and gold sashes, our school colors. I'd always hated those colors. Instead of putting the flash drive back in its usual place, I put it back behind the frame, forgot about going to the library to print my paper, and with an unusual and unex-pected feeling of euphoria, I went back to Clarence and Trent's door, strolled in without knocking and for the next thirty minutes, with a confidence I'd only shown around my mom and Harry, proceeded to say the oddest, most profound things that came to my mind, ending with me trying to convince the guys that the "Why did the chicken cross the road" joke was about suicide. Enjoying the show, they con-tinued to let me talk, without interrupting once. The golden moment came when I grabbed one of Trent's burritos from his freezer, threw it in the microwave, and ate it while complaining about how it was half-cooked and half-frozen. Breaking their silence for the first time, Harry asked, "Then why the hell are you eating that nasty, half-cooked thing?!"

Still completely blazed, and using my half-cooked burrito as an example, I talked for the next thirty minutes, going off on some tan-gent about how life is pointless and entropy is unavoidable and filled with callous and casual destruction, telling them "shit happens".

We smoked again during my last rant, and I saw Trent give Harry a nod and mouth, "My bad."

As a result of my reaction to getting high for the first time, now, sometimes when we smoke, we each take a turn saying any odd, weird, dumb, or profound thought that comes to our mind, or that we've thought of or seen since the last time we played.

"Alright, bitches," I say, confidently, leaning back, starting a game I know I can finish. "If you replace the 'w' in what, where and when, with a 't,' you answer the questions." Trying to look cool and casual, I rest my right arm up on the back of the couch, but since it's too high and uncomfortable, I put it back down.

"Deeeeeep," Trent says, rubbing his chin.

Clarence takes a sip of his beer, says, "That's pretty cool, man," then puts his hands up. "Alright, alright, I'm prepared. I knew we would do this a lot this weekend." I think about the last part of what he said longer and more than I should, and my confidence is replaced with that same drab feeling when I'm reminded this is our last weekend together.

Before I can harp on it for too long, Trent yells out, "Me too, man! I was thinking the same thing! I got a lot of 'em!"

"Wait your turn, fool," Clarence says, waving him off. "Respect my man's game." Clarence reaches out, we slap hands, and he holds mine for too long, tightening his grip slightly. He doesn't say anything; he just looks at me for a moment, without any expression, then nods. Letting go of me, he points and shouts to Trent, "Respect my man's game, nigga!" and I feel better.

"Then go!" Trent shouts back.

Clarence flicks him off. "If two vegans are arguing, is that still considered a beef?"

We all laugh but Trent quickly stops, and excited to go, he says, "Alright, like I said, I'm ready for this weekend."

"The 'this weekend,' part of his statement doesn't really bother me," I try to tell myself.

"Is the 's' or 'c' in 'scent,' silent? Huh, huh?" he asks, looking at us for our approval.

Clarence and I look over at each other, shake our heads, then bury them in our hands. I look over, mocking him. "Prepared for this weekend?" Joking about it will make me feel better.

Clarence adds, "Yeah man, that's, end of the night, we all fucked up, and everybody's high so you can say anything, type of dumb shit." He raises his voice a few levels. "You don't open up with that! Prepared? Shit." After waving off Trent, Clarence looks at me, and we slap hands again, quickly.

"That's cool, Clarence, you'll see. I wanted to open up weak and attack later!" Trent says.

"Sure, sure," I say, motioning my hand to calm him down. "You'll get your turn again." I go ahead with my next one. "We'll never know what memories we have forgotten."

"I can barely remember the memories I do remember!" Trent jokes. Clarence and I laugh, and I think we both believe what he says.

"Half a dozen is a very inefficient way of saying six," Clarence blurts out.

Hiding my mouth with my beer, I inconspicuously point at Trent and whisper to Clarence, "Wait, wait, maybe you shouldn't be mentioning that around you know who."

"What the fuck are you two talking about?" Trent asks.

"Uhhhhh, eggs, you, hot girl, skirt, bending over, dropped eggs, fired from your job?" Clarence holds his mouth open, leans his head to the side.

Trent flicks us off. "Fuck you, fuckers!" He takes a sip of his beer, leans towards us. "Okay, boys! How about this? If you cut holes into a net, there are fewer holes than before." We both chuckle and Clarence and I admit that it's not too bad and sensing our acceptance, Trent puts his hands out, acts like he's holding a net. "Seriously, it has fewer holes every time you do it!" he explains.

"We get it, we get it," I tell him, looking at my phone. "Okay, last round and then we have to go. We have to meet Harry." I throw out one that I know will really fuck with Trent. "The only time that incorrectly is not spelled incorrectly is when it's spelled incorrectly."

"Jesus, that's a lot to keep up with!" Clarence exclaims. Trent takes a moment to laugh, and I'm sure that he doesn't get it, but I don't care and I don't bother to explain it to him.

"Name something cooler than when you were in the sixth grade, and you walked into the cafeteria late with McDonald's, because you had a doctor's appointment earlier in the day." Clarence snaps his fingers, swings his arm after saying this, and Trent and I, knowing precisely what he means and loving what he said, both slap his hand, and Trent gets up from the couch.

I stand up quickly to stop him, to make him take his turn, but the effects of the gravity bong hit me hard. "Damn," I say, wobbling a little. "I feel like I'm floating through time and space itself."

"Been there before," Clarence says, and Trent agrees.

"Come on, let's go out and meet some ladies!" Trent shouts, inching away, nodding his head towards our bedrooms.

"Nope!" I say, snapping out of my haze. "You can make your statement and then we can go." I look at Clarence.

"Damn right."

Trent thinks for a second, then quickly blurts out, "Okay, why don't they make Band-Aids in black, yellow, or brown?" We don't say anything. "You know, for like, different races and stuff?"

We hold our thumbs down, collectively boo him, Trent lowers his head, and Clarence says, "Come up with something good next time, so we can feel some pride for you, instead of the usual shame and disappointment."

Trent

I rush into our bathroom before Clarence can get there because after I shower, I need time to let the gel harden my hair so that when I mess it up fifteen minutes later, it holds an unkempt, "I don't give a fuck look" on purpose. Since it's Friday night, I use some of his good-smelling body wash, instead of grabbing my mostly empty bottle of shampoo. I squirt more than is needed onto an orange sponge my mom sent me in a "care package" on Valentine's Day, scrub my chest, torso, arms, dick, ass, and thighs, letting the soapy foam run down and clean my lower legs and feet. I don't bother to wash my hair, because the greasier it is, the easier it holds, and I won't have to use as much gel. When I get out, I dry off with my already wet towel, sniffing it halfway through to see if it smells. It does, but not too bad, and I throw it back over the shower rod, wipe some steam off the mirror and squirt gel into my hands, running them through my hair in all directions. Brushing my hair back, I run over it several times, to make sure it's as even as possible, then part it to the right and cover myself with some of Clarence's body spray. When I open the top to my deodorant, it reveals a "barely there" slab of blue over the plastic piece, and I tilt it to the side, wiping my armpits, trying to get something out of it.

I yank the chain on the shark hanging above my desk, lighting my room up with blue and yellow neon colors, and search my dressers for some underwear and one of my t-shirts with Clarence's picture on it, choosing the one with a cropped photo of his face on the body of a jackass. For years I'd been taking photos of him and putting them on t-shirts. It started in high school when I used his senior picture. Since then, I've collected quite an extensive collection. One with an image of his grunting face on the body of a bulldog, one with him wearing a banana hammock for some joke we pulled, one with his family Christmas photo on it. Last time I counted, I had eleven. After glancing over and noticing a few strands of grass growing out of my keyboard, I pluck them out, dropping them on the floor. "Fucking douches," I say out loud. One of the guys, I don't know who, because no one will admit it, had thought it would be funny to put seeds in my keyboard and grow grass. I step into the shorts I was wearing earlier and run into Clarence in the hallway.

Wearing only a towel, he must have heard me get out of the shower. "Nice hair," he says, pushing me against the wall. He glances down at his image on my shirt, shakes his head.

"Psssh, you wish you had these golden locks," I tell him and he reaches his hand up quickly, towards my head, acting as if he's going to fuck with my hair. Falling for his bluff, I flinch, like I always do, and chuckling, he shoves me one more time with his ass, then heads down the hallway.

Zipping up my shorts, I walk into the kitchen, reach into the fridge, grab a can of Clarence's Red Bull, then open the freezer and pull out Harry's vodka and an ice cube tray that's half-empty. I throw all the cubes in a glass, then pour some vodka, followed by what little Red Bull is needed to fill it up and take a big chug. After adding in a bit more of each, I drink what's left in the can, enjoying the taste, something the other three guys make fun of me for. I put the vodka and empty tray back in the freezer, grab three blunts and Justin's knife. Once I empty the cigars out onto the top of the trash in the corner, I head over to the couch, take another swig and break up the buds with my hands, then spread it in the wrappers. Justin comes out while I'm rolling the last blunt.

"Looking good, grandpa from the 1930s."

I only respond with, "Blmph," because I'm busy licking the wrapper.

He grabs a glass, opens the freezer and says, "What the fuck?!" Pulling out the empty ice tray, he turns around, holds it up to me. "Can't you fill a fucking ice tray?!"

I pretend I still need to moisten the wrapper, even though I'm done and just respond with some sort of question-like noise. "Mmmpphhh?"

"Dumbass," he mutters, walking over to the sink, filling up the tray. "And stop drinking Harry's vodka, you damn mooch," he adds, after putting the tray back, before pulling Harry's vodka out and pouring some for himself.

"I'm sorry, pot, what did you call the kettle?" I ask, no longer pretending to be occupied.

"Don't worry about what I'm doing over here," he responds, chuckling, grabbing his orange juice from the fridge.

I get up from the couch, walk over to the kitchen, we clink glasses, and both of us take a drink. "Let's kill this weekend!" I yell, thrusting my hips at him. I pound the rest of mine, open the fridge, grab two more Red Bulls and make two of the same drinks as before, this time using Clarence's vodka, instead of Harry's.

When Clarence walks in, I hand him his drink, we all touch glasses and Justin shouts, "Here's to tonight!" and all three of us finish them, fast, and Clarence asks, "You fools ready to roll?"

I grab the blunts from the counter, run into the bathroom, mess my hair up, then brush it around, trying to find what I think is a "perfect" scruffy look. After a few minutes, I get what I like and head out to a waiting Clarence and Justin.

"Let's go, Primp Bizkit," Clarence jokes, opening the door, letting Justin out.

"Oh, good one, I haven't heard that before," I say, running and grabbing the door, opening it back up before he can close it on me.

While we're waiting in line for the bar, Justin turns to me and asks, "Isn't this the bar that you got kicked out of last Christmas?"

"Hell yes, it is!" Clarence shouts, standing on his toes, waving his hands, trying to get the attention of the bouncers dressed in black t-shirts and black jeans.

They don't even look in our direction, much less see him, but that doesn't stop me from yelling at him quietly. "Man, settle down over there!" I glare at him, shove him a little. "What the fuck?!"

"Relax, man. They aren't going to recognize you. You aren't wearing your Santa suit!" he says, yelling out the last part too loud.

Justin starts chanting, "Santa, Santa!" and worried, I glance at the entrance; but one of the bouncers has left, and the other one's talking to a group of fraternity guys, and Justin opens his mouth, acts like he's going to shout something again, but doesn't.

It was last year and I'd just been fired from my job as a mall Santa for using my phone to take personal photos of girls sitting on my lap. Evidently, there had been some complaints. Still dressed as

Santa, I walked into the first bar I found, immediately downed several shots and a bunch of beers. At some point, the bartender decided to switch the jukebox, from my selection of heavy metal to something more holiday-themed and absolutely hammered, I began, screaming and cursing at him, even threw a few bottles.

I told the guys I'd been escorted out, but a video that appeared online the next day showed I'd been "escorted" out a window. You could hear me yelling, "I won't be coming to your house on Christmas!" after I picked myself up off the sidewalk, dusted myself off.

"Go fuck yourself! We're Jewish!" one of the guys yelled.

I have Clarence pay my cover charge, and duck my head down and to the right, as I walk in. Neither of the bouncers recognizes me, or they don't give a fuck; we stroll through, and I immediately start looking around, checking out the girls. There are plenty here, due to it being a lot of people's last weekend and I assure myself that more girls than usual will be looking to hook up. The bar is crowded, so we make our way through the mob of people, to the back. On the way, I look to my right into the mirror behind the bar, seeing myself in the crowd. After stopping and taking a second to look at myself, I go on, trying to move some of my hair that didn't please me. A waitress is clearing one of the booths against the wall, and I notice a guy near the end of the bar who wants the open table, too. I recognize him from some class I had, sophomore year, and he's closer but I don't have a group of sorority girls blocking me, so I get to it first. Glancing over at him, I thank the waitress, and he just gives a frustrated look, pulls out his phone and accidentally runs into one of the sorority girls, while walking away.

Clarence slides into the left booth first. I follow, and Justin tells us he's going to get the first round. "Cool," I respond, nonchalantly, always welcoming any free drink and the postponement of my paying.

Justin's phone beeps and his face sinks after he looks at the screen. Disappointed, he tells us, "Harry said, he's going to be late." He glances around the bar for a moment, then looks back at us. "He said, that he probably won't be here till 2 a.m. or later. They're held up at one of the stations. Something's wrong with the engine."

"Damn, that sucks balls," I say, telling myself I'm glad I'm not the one stuck in some train.

Clarence picks some lint off his gray t-shirt, casually asks Justin, "What time is his train leaving on Sunday, anyway?"

Irritated, Justin answers, fast, "I don't know, like, 12 or something. What do I look like, his mother?"

I would jump all over that, but I can tell that Justin didn't care for Clarence's question, so I don't. "Here you go, man," I say, holding out $20, uncharacteristically offering to pay. "I'll get the first round." He waves it off, telling me I hooked them up with bud.

"What do you guys want?" he asks. I tell him I don't care and Clarence tells him to pick since he's buying. Justin puts his hand out, nods at Clarence, who slaps it, nods back, then Justin walks over to the edge of the bar, and waits behind two ugly girls that I don't pay much attention to.

After checking out some of the sorority girls, specifically a blonde with yoga pants, I notice the guy who lost the table to me. Still talking to the girl he ran into, he's slightly touching her arm, as he waves to his friend, another guy I recognize, and I ask Clarence, "Speaking of Sunday, what time are you starting?" I look over at the small pile of coasters on the table. The top one has a 1950s-looking, chick, in a one-piece bikini, holding a tray with a beer on it. I take that one and the five underneath it, shoving them in one of my pockets.

Clarence looks up from watching what I'm doing, opens his eyes a little wider, says, "One." He nods his head up and down, grins, then looks back down at the coasters. "I can't wait," he says, confidently, biting his upper lip, pumping his fist, slightly.

"You're going to kill it." I sit up, bang my hands on the table. "So, what type of advantages do I get?" I ask, slapping him on the chest, leaning back again. "Advanced knowledge of DUI checkpoints? Maybe a small cut of any confiscated weed?" I glance over at Justin, and he's still waiting behind the two girls, but it looks like he's losing his position to a group of guys. "You know." I pause for a moment. "Since you're my brother, and now you're a brother with a badge."

"You-"

I hit him on the shoulder and point to Justin.

The girls have left, and one of the guys who's cutting in front of Justin - it looks like there's three of them - forearms him, hard, shoving his way to the front of the bar. The other two, also much taller and larger than Justin, push their way in front of him, one of them giving him a look of disdain as he does. Justin looks over at us, throws his hands up, and mouths, "What the fuck?" Reaching up, he taps the shoulder of the first one, but the guy in the red polo continues to halfway lean over the bar, talking and flirting with the bartender, so Justin pushes up his glasses, taps him on the shoulder again.

This time, the guy stands up, turns around and towering over Justin, he yells, "What the fuck do you want?" Caught off-guard, Justin can't respond before the guy shoves him to the ground, and we start to slide out of the booth, when I put my hand on the table, stopping us both.

"What do we have here?" I say, pointing into the crowd.

"Aw, shit," Clarence says. We sit back down, and he adds, "This ought to be good." He puts his hand on my shoulder. "Fuck, I wish we had some drinks for this."

"No shit."

Douchebag in Red Polo Shirt

"Yeah, what the fuck do you want?!" someone yells from the crowd. Glancing over, I notice a guy in a button up shirt with a name tag, walking towards us. With grey hair and khaki pants, I'm guessing he works here. "Great the manager," I say to myself, figuring he's coming to stop me from pounding this dork into the ground, but I'm surprised when he looks down at the guy with glasses, shoves him a little, then shouts, "What's going on, is there a problem?!" He yells louder this time, almost like he's purposefully trying to get the attention of as many people as he can. He taps me on the shoulder, then nods to my friends, Mike and Matt.

Surprisingly the little tool looks me straight in the eyes and says, "That douchebag right there is my fucking problem."

The manager's eyes widen, and he turns to me, asks if I'm going to let him talk about me like that. Surprised that he's going to allow me to do this, I glance around the bar, check out who all is going to see the show. Anyone that was only briefly interested before is now fully invested; everyone in the bar looking our way, waiting to see what happens next. A group of sorority girls is fixated on us, some of them sipping from the straws in the frosted drinks in their hands, and I smirk a little, wonder which one I'm going to take home to bang tonight. Matt yells, "Fuck him up!" and after Mike hits me on the back, I cock my fist back and swing right at his nose.

Trent

Harry catches his fist square in his hand, stopping the guy's swing immediately, inches from Justin's face. A few shouts of cheers and surprise come from the crowd, and the douchebag in the red polo looks up at Harry, either with fear or shock, probably both; and Harry stops smiling, becomes very serious, and the same frightened look comes over his two friends' faces. Taller and more substantial than all three, Harry takes a step forward, starts squeezing the guy's hand; and I can tell that it doesn't feel pleasant, because of the look on his face and the fact that he's bending his knees, slowly lowering himself to the ground. "You have two choices," Harry says, loudly, staring at the guy, who's becoming shorter by the second. His friends start to back away, instead of intervening, and Harry looks at them quickly, nods without saying anything, and they stop, both of them putting their hands up slightly. He glares back down at the guy, who looks like he's about to cry and continues. "You can either run our tab on your card tonight or-" He leans down and whispers in his ear.

Nodding his head up and down, the guy waits for Harry to finish, then whimpers something I can't make out. I assume he went with the first choice, because he taps Harry's hand that's still squeezing his fist and Harry lets go, and the guy stands up, but not too quickly, relieved. "You can bring eight vodka and Red Bulls over to that table," Harry instructs him, pointing over at us.

Humiliated and adjusting his shirt, he looks over at us. We wave, Clarence points at his recording phone, and I hold up an "ok" sign with my hand, mouth to him, "You look great."

Harry points over at Justin. "Now apologize to my best friend, you fucking cunt."

"Hey, I'm really-"

"Go fuck yourself," Justin says, flicking him off, walking away.

The people watching, which is practically everyone in the bar, are laughing and clapping and some of the girls look Harry up and down while the guy shuffles away, and goes back to his friends, near the bar. They don't have anything to say, and after they act like they don't even know him, he walks up to the laughing bartender he was flirting with earlier and fills Harry's order.

Harry walks up behind Justin and puts both hands on his shoulders, shaking him in front of us. "What the fuck is up, boys?" He slaps our hands, slides in after Justin does.

"2 a.m., huh?" Clarence sarcastically says.

"Come on, man," Harry says. "You know I have to fuck with y'all."

"Nice get-up," I joke, pointing at his nametag, which has his company logo on it.

He flicks me off, brushes nothing off the table, then tells us that he got on the train right after the conference ended and that he decided to come straight here, instead of going back to the apartment. "I had to leave my bag up front," he says. "They wouldn't let me bring it inside."

"Well, at least untuck that fucker," I tell him. Noticing the guy, he almost made cry, carrying our drinks, I point and say, "Oh, here comes your bitch."

He sets the tray on the table, without looking at us and Harry stands up, starts untucking his shirt, says, "Got us all night, right?" He pats the guy on his shoulder a couple of times, then rests his hand there.

"Yeah," he says, softly, looking at us, then back down at the table. His friends are nowhere in sight.

"What a great guy!" Harry hits his back a couple of times, hard. "Now go order us the same thing with shooters and then there's no need for us to see you again," he says, motioning for the guy to leave.

"So, how was the conference?" Clarence asks, picking up the drinks, giving each of us two. We all clink glasses, take a chug.

"It was good," Harry answers, after taking down half his drink. "I actually learned more from other attendees than I did the conference." He tells a few boring details that I don't really pay attention to while finishing the rest of his glass and after he grabs his second one, he says, "Enough about my trip," and looks at Clarence. "When the fuck do you start on Sunday?"

"1 p.m., brother," Clarence answers, tapping Harry's already-extended glass. Before Clarence can say anything else, I interrupt the two of them, tell them no more work talk and that we're here to get laid. They chuckle, but Justin doesn't, and he forces a smile, just before the bartender walks over.

With dark hair and wearing a small, sleeveless, plaid shirt, she comes over with a tray of more vodka and Red Bulls and four shooters. "That was fucking awesome!" she says, throwing her hair back, exposing more of her melon-sized breasts from her unbuttoned top. "My name's Allyson." Smiling at Harry, not paying any attention to us, she takes a few of the drinks off the tray.

"Thanks," he says, reaching for the shot glasses, helping her pass them out. "I'm Harry."

After she touches him on the hand and leaves the table, still without looking at anyone but him, Justin jokes, "Well, that didn't take long."

We all chuckle, Harry brushes it off, and I pull one of the blunts out of my pocket, put it in my lips, not bothering or caring to look around to see if anyone notices. "We have weed to smoke," I tell them.

Clarence raises his glass, the three of us do the same, and he says, "And alcohol to drink."

Harry motions towards the bartender, then a few more hotties at the bar. "And we have bad decisions to make."

We all look at Justin. "Gentlemen, you had my curiosity." He pauses for a moment, raises his glass higher. "But now you have my attention!"

"Aye!" all of us shout out.

We bang glasses, some of the purple alcohol falls onto the table, and after shooting them, we grab our vodka and Red Bulls, take large swigs, and Harry points out a hot girl, who's wearing a skin-tight, pink dress and really, high, black heels. Balancing herself on the bar, she's talking to another hot girl, who's dressed in a similar tight, blue dress. Nodding our heads, we all agree while checking them out, but when the one in pink lets go of the bar and stumbles to walk, Clarence says he doesn't see the point. "It ain't sexy," he tells us.

"What?" Harry asks, pulling his glass from his lips.

"Look at her, man," he says, motioning towards her. "She looks like a newborn calf trying to walk."

"I beg to differ," Harry responds, shaking his head, and I agree with him.

Without taking my eyes off them, I tell Clarence, "She can walk like that all the way to my bed." I peer at the one in blue, over my finger and the top of my glass, while taking a sip, watching her as she turns around and leans against the bar.

"She looks like a slut anyway."

"What the fuck?" I pull my glass down, ending my spy session and look over at Justin.

"Now, you need to take those words back," Clarence says shaking his head, tapping the table gently.

Justin raises his shoulders a little, puts his hands up. "She looks like she might fuck any random dude."

Harry hits Justin on the back of the head. "That's what we're looking for, dumbass. Chicks that want to have sex with random dudes! Damn!"

"Low self-esteem and questionable morals are a plus too!" I add, taking a swig. "Now let's smoke!" I shout, the blunt flopping up and down in my mouth. "Harry's been gone since Tuesday, and we only have a couple of days."

Harry

"It's so weird that this is our last weekend together," I think to myself, on our way outside. Jus is in front of me, and I notice the small "bald spot" on the back of the left side of his head. I think about all of the times I've teased him about it, and how he's always answered, "That's where my hair parts!" I wonder when the next time I joke with him about it will be. "Will we be talking on the phone? Will it be as funny?" I ask myself.

We walk a small distance into the alley, stopping next to two mountain bikes, chained to a closed, iron gate that leads to the service entrance of the bar. It isn't much of an alley, just a short walkway between two buildings that leads to another restaurant and a parking lot in the back. Like several of the other ones throughout town, this one has a name sign of someone, maybe a donor or town honoree, hanging above the street entrance. The black, metal letters illuminated by the gold light from behind read, "Rusty York Alley." I wonder to myself who Rusty York is or was, take a chug of my drink, the bouncer let me bring outside, and Trent lights up the blunt. After a few hits, he passes it to Clarence, who pulls on it a couple of times and then asks Jus if he wants it.

"Pssh," he answers, acting like it was a dumb question. "What do I always say?"

Trent quickly responds, "Don't look at my browser history?"

Clarence, just as fast, adds, "The door's locked because I'm in here studying."

Jus, looks at me while they laugh, slapping each other's hands, and as I start to say something, he puts his finger up. "Ah!"

When I look down the half-lit alley, at the line outside of the bar, I notice a group of girls standing together and instantly recognize two of them, Lily and Ginger, from a couple months ago.

I strolled outside, glanced to my left, to my right, down the sidewalk, looking for Lily's blonde hair. When I walked towards the taco stand, where she told me to meet her, a hot, skinny, black girl, wearing a light blue tank top and jeans, appeared out of nowhere, grabbing me by my arm and stopping me. "You look good," she said, staring me up and down.

When we got to the apartment, I fucked her, and she let me cum on her face, but she ended up throwing up on the side of my bed twenty minutes after. I wiped her off with some handi-wipes from my "lady drawer," then cleaned everything up, as she continued to say she was sorry. I made up an excuse of having to get up early, which was fine, because she was embarrassed and ready to leave anyway, so I ended up driving her to her parents' house. A two and a half hour round-trip.

She texted me a couple of times to apologize the next day, and I was polite, told her not to worry about it. I ended up messaging her a few weeks later, one drunken night, but she said she was looking for a relationship, not just hooking up, and we haven't talked since.

Noticing me, Ginger gives her a nudge. Trying not to be obvious, Lily turns around a few seconds later. I take a sip of my drink, wave. Neither of them smile, but both wave back and I look at the other ones in the group I haven't talked to, making a sober decision of who's the hottest, in case I need to refer to it later in a drunken state. It's still Lily, and while checking out her long legs, I wonder if she's upset about that night, but I don't think so, because she's still peeking at me while talking to Ginger, both of them smiling this time. Jus says something, maybe calls my name, but I ignore him, bring my glass to my lips, wonder if she'll still fuck me.

"Hey, Harry!" Jus shouts, hitting me on the shoulder, waving the blunt in my face.

I wipe some condensation off the bottom and sides of my glass with my shirt, slowly, just to mess with him. Joking, he pulls it back, and after I reach out, grabbing it from his hand, I realize how small it is.

Clarence gives a short laugh. "Go ahead and finish it."

Trent, mocking me as well, says, "Yeah, all for you, man," and Justin nods down the alley, tells me to hurry up, so we can get back inside.

I look down at the blunt that's about the size of my fingernail. "What the fuck am I supposed to do with this?" I ask, looking up, trying to decide who I'm going to choose, Jus or Trent. I immediately exclude Clarence, because we all know he has a huge dick. I go with Jus since he handed me the blunt and Trent hooked us up with it. "This thing is smaller than your dick," I tell him, flicking it towards his feet. "I've been gone and haven't smoked since Tuesday, and this is how you guys welcome me back?"

They start chuckling, look at each other and Trent reaches into one of his seventeen pockets, while Jus steps on the small, smoking piece in front of him. "Here you go, fucker," Trent says, handing me a blunt, and when I put it in my mouth, he lights it for me. "All for you."

I take a few puffs, blowing a cloud of smoke at Jus, then take another long hit, and look up into the sky, closing my eyes when I exhale.

"So, what did you say to those guys, anyway?" Clarence asks, pulling out his phone.

I grin and still looking up, say, "I told them that you two were recording and that if he didn't choose option one, option two would be highly more embarrassing and painful for him and his friends than it already is."

Disappointed there wasn't more, Trent says, "That's it?"

"That's it. Well, I might have squeezed his hand a little harder." I look over at Trent, out of the corner of my eye, chuckle and lower my head, take another puff.

They all laugh, and I'm glad that Jus seems happier than he was in the bar. Clarence pulls up the video, holds his phone up for us to see. We watch it a few times, and he keeps pausing at the moment I catch the guys punch.

"Fucking hilarious," Trent says. He starts directing, telling Clarence when to pause when to rewind and Clarence tells him he already knows when to pause and when to rewind. "Dude, back the fuck off," he says, nudging Trent, who spills some of his drink on Clarence's phone. Clarence shakes it off, wipes it, puts it in his pocket and grabs him by the arms. "Dumb motherfucker."

Anxious, Trent tries to get away, telling him, "But it was your fault." Clarence quickly steps forward, puts his right leg behind Trent's legs and pushes him, catching him as he falls backward. Trent's body jolts, but he maintains his drink somehow, not spilling a drop, and Clarence slowly lowers him to the concrete. Holding up his glass, Trent glances at the puddle underneath him. "Man, not on the fucking ground," he says, looking back at Clarence. "There's water and shit there. We have to go back inside." He calms down because he knows Clarence won't drop him, but when Clarence laughs and suddenly lowers him even further, Trent looks at the dirty water quickly, back at Clarence and looking a little more concerned, demands, "Don't you do it, fucker!" After a moment, he starts laughing and can barely get out, "If you…put me…in this…fucking puddle!"

"You'll what?" Clarence drops him down another inch. "You'll have to walk back home and go through your Abercrombie and Fitch shorts?

"I think they're American Eagle," Jus suggests, pointing at Trent's cargo shorts and I comment I think they might be Old Navy.

"He won't drop you if you promise to never wear those again," Jus says, looking at Clarence.

"Respect!" Clarence yells.

"Fuck you, bitches! My cargo shorts are sweet!" Trent shouts, and I raise my glass, adding, "And functional."

Clarence eventually lifts him back up, and I look down the alley again. Lily and her friends have moved on, inside by now, I assume; and when I glance through the rest of the line, the majority are guys, and none of the girls interest me. "Alright, Jus," I say, turning back to him, "final rounds this weekend." I immediately regret saying it that way, because I know he's upset about it being our last weekend, but it's too late to take it back or say it another way, so I just puff on the blunt a few more times, finishing it.

Smiling, he starts dancing, as if he'd paid no attention to my choice of words and says, "There is no reason." He pauses, stops moving. "For the alphabet to be in order." He starts dancing again, and I instantly recall when I first heard him say this. It was lunchtime. Sixth grade.

After giving me the other half, Jus, took a bite of his sandwich and said, "Did you know there is no reason for the alphabet to be in order?"

I'd been talking about how cute I thought Beth, a girl in the same grade as us, was. We had kissed at one of the birthday parties we'd gone to that summer and Taylor Swift's, "Love Story" was her and my favorite song at the time. When I asked him how cute he thought she was, if both of us having the same favorite song meant anything, and if I should try to kiss her again during her birthday party at her home in Wildwood this weekend, this had been his response.

"Yeah, that's great," I said, looking around the table, forgetting what I was talking about.

After finishing his sandwich, Jus opened up his Reese's Peanut Butter Cup, and when he peeled back that orange label, for the millionth time, in front of me, I couldn't take it anymore. "I have to see what they taste like!" I screamed, grabbing one of the cups. I ripped off the wrapper, took a bite, then stuffed the rest in my mouth and just sat there, chewing it slowly, enjoying the taste of what I'd been missing.

"What are you doing, Harry?! You're allergic!" Jus yelled, grabbing my arm, trying to shake me out of my Reese's bliss.

I turned my head slowly towards him. "Mmmmmmm, worth it." Swallowing the last bit, I reached into my backpack, grabbed my epinephrine injector, calmly stabbed myself in the leg and asked him, "Can you get the school nurse?"

"What the fuck, Harry?!" Jus shouted again, freaking out even more. Flailing his arms above his head, he ran around our small table once, stopped, then yelled, "Stay right there!" while sprinting away to get the nurse.

I ran my fingers through my mouth, collecting whatever was left, savoring the taste of what I'd never been allowed before. Then I passed out.

"I've never even thought about that," Trent says. He starts randomly saying letters, looking down at his hands while he counts them on his fingers. "Q, U, Z, V, A." He looks up at us. "Yeah, it doesn't matter, does it?"

I look back at Jus, smirk, then glare at Clarence and Trent and blurt out, "How did whoever invented the clock know what time it was?"

"Yeah, how the fuck would someone know?" Trent asks, looking at Jus for an answer.

Jus looks like he's getting ready to say something, and I think about the hot blonde, her hot friend, the hot bartender and how I don't want him to go into one of his lengthy explanations to answer Trent's question, so I say, "What do you have, Clarence?" and Jus puts his glass down.

"I love when an ATM charges $3 for you to get your own money, and then tells you to cover your pin, so you don't get robbed."

After we're all done agreeing, Clarence glances at Trent, then says something about living like a king on payday, eating out and buying drinks, and living like a pauper at the end of the two weeks, eating noodles and sneaking airplane bottles into bars. Trent looks up from the puddle Clarence threatened to drop him in, sees all three of us staring at him and he puts his arms up. "What?!"

"Oh, my turn. Okay." Still not realizing that we're referring to his lifestyle, he goes on. "You guys are going to love this." He waits a few seconds, and none of us say anything. "Okay, okay, when a giraffe goes to work, does he wear his tie on the top or the bottom of his neck?" As weak as it is, all three of us laugh, probably because we're high and he turns to the side, starts sliding his hand up and down his neck and chest, laughing at himself, repeating, "top or the bottom, top or the bottom?"

"Zzzzzzzzz!" Just then, a light bulb with a green cover over it, next to the iron gate behind Trent, sparks and starts to flicker on and off. The three of us turn our heads back when we hear Clarence tell Trent, "Do us a favor and walk either twenty steps behind us or twenty steps in front of us when we go back in." The light bulb makes another "Zzzzzzzzz," popping sound, stops flickering, returns to normal, and I can't see anyone waiting to get in the bar from where we are anymore, and when we walk around to the front, there's no line at all.

Trent yells at us over the music that's gotten louder. "Go to the table, and I'll take care of our drinks!"

Jus and I give our empty glasses to Clarence, and he puts them on a wooden railing that lines the wall, opposite the bar, and I slide into the booth behind Jus. All three of us watch Trent unsuccessfully hit on the friend of the girl that Clarence said looked like a newborn calf trying to walk, and after talking to the bartender, he comes back and asks Clarence to get up, so he can sit against the wall. "She said she would bring them over," Trent says, sliding into the booth.

"Huh, who?" I ask, still looking at the legs of the girls he tried to talk to.

"The bartender. She said she would bring the shots and drinks." Trent waves his hand slowly in front of my face. "Hello, Harry balls."

I imagine the girl wearing the tight dress in my bedroom, bent over my desk, and when the bartender brings our shots over, she takes them off the tray, four at a time, looks over at me and says, "That was so cool," or something like that again; but I don't pay much attention, partly because I'm really high and partly because she doesn't seem as hot to me anymore, which surprises me, because I'm really high. I say "Thanks," again, politely, even though it annoys me a little that repeating the same thing was the only conversation she could come up with. "Oh, and thanks for the drinks," I tell her, smiling quickly, glancing at the guys, hoping she won't stay too long. She laughs, says, "You're welcome," looks at Jus, Clarence, and Trent for the first time, and maybe sensing that I don't want to talk long, she touches my hand again and leaves.

Trent slides our shot glasses in front of us, then raises his and yells, "To this weekend, bitches!"

"Tequila? You couldn't get something else?" Clarence asks, looking at his glass.

"Yeah, like Jaeger bombs or something?"

Jus immediately yells, "Yeah, like Jaeger!" after I say this, and when I look over, his eyes are red, and he laughs a little, then quietly says, "or something."

Chuckling, I push him, he shoves me back, and Clarence yells, "This shit is going to get us fucked up!" and when Jus and I raise our glasses again, Trent looks at us and says, "You rookies need to learn how to control your tequila."

"Ha. Fuck that," Clarence tells him. "The last time you had tequila shots, you climbed out of the sunroof in Justin's car and surfed down Main Street."

Trent laughs, shrugs his shoulders. "Hey, I took a calculated risk."

We bang our glasses, the three of us yell, "But man, you're bad at math!" and we all throw back our shots.

"Melissa!"

Over an hour late, Schroeder just texted to let us know they'll be here soon. After Jus read off the message, Trent noticed a girl he's hooked up with before, someone the three of us know, not so much by an introduction, but by his stories.

"Melissa!" He's slightly slurring her name when he screams, and she turns and excitedly waves at him, standing up a little straighter than she was. A blonde, she's short and wearing an extreme amount of makeup. The two things that we definitely know about her are that she has webbed feet and that every time her and Trent hook-up after they fall asleep, she pees in the bed. Touching each other's hips and upper butts when they hug, she buries her face in his chest, and they talk for a little bit, mostly him whispering things to her we can't hear. Giggling, she waves at us, walks away, and Trent watches her ass until she disappears into the crowd of dancing people and we start howling when he turns around.

"Nice shirt," I say, pointing at him. Melissa's lipstick, eyeshadow, blush and whatever else she was wearing had left an imprint on his shirt, literally forming a face.

"It looks like someone attempted an abstract painting of a clown," Jus tells him. Trent pulls his shirt out, looks down, says, "Fuck." We lose it, start to laugh harder, getting the attention of some of the people around us, and Trent can't help but chuckle and it takes a full minute before the three of us can calm down. After Jus takes a pic, Trent does his best to wipe it off, having to dip a napkin in his vodka and Red Bull to remove some of it. Unable to get it all, he says, "Fuck it," throws the napkin at Jus, and Clarence notices Schroeder and his girlfriend in the crowd looking for us, so he stands up in the booth as best he can, his knees wedged under the table. Seeing Clarence, Schroeder gets his girlfriend's attention, and holding hands, they walk over. His appearance surprises me because he's wearing a decent, button-down shirt and nice pants, his hair actually somewhat combed.

"Hey guys, what's going on?" he says, throwing up two fingers. He drops one of them, flicking us off.

We reciprocate, and his girlfriend hits him, something we're used to. "Schroeder!"

He puts his finger down. "My bad, guys," he says, putting his hands up. "I truly apologize for giving you fine gentleman the bird." He glances over, she rolls her eyes, hits him again, but this time she grabs his arm afterward and pulls herself closer to him, rubbing where she struck.

"Hey guys!" she says, cheerfully. His girlfriend's wearing a tight, jean dress with gold buttons lined up the middle, and she tugs at it a little after waving. We all say hi and I check her out some more, but not too much, out of respect to Schroeder.

"Hold on, boys," Schroeder says, touching his girlfriend on the shoulder, assuring her he'll be back quickly. He walks over to the table next to us and starts talking to the two guys sitting there. They nod their heads, raise their beer mugs a bit, and Schroeder grabs the two empty chairs at their table, then slides them in front of our booth.

"Why so late?" Justin asks, stoned, joking, leaning over me slightly, maybe looking at Schroeder's girlfriend a little too much.

"Oh, we just got back from having dinner with her parents," Schroeder tells him, sitting down. His girlfriend puts her hand on his knee while Schroeder adjusts his chair, gives Jus an, "I can see you checking out my girlfriend" glare, and Jus looks at his drink quickly, takes a sip, leans back in the booth.

"How was it?" I ask, looking back at Schroeder, then at Trent, who's eyes are fixed on her legs.

"Everything was cool until she said, 'Daddy, please pass the salt,' and both her father and I reached for it." Schroeder adjusts his chair again, and his girlfriend keeps her hand on his leg, starts rubbing it.

"What?! Seriously?!" Clarence says, quickly, loudly, leaning on the table towards Schroeder.

"Yeah seriously, man," Schroeder says, putting his arm around his girlfriend, who's chuckling, nodding her head up and down in embarrassment. "Awkward as shit."

"Well, did they like you?" I ask.

"Of course," he tells me, putting his hands up. "What's not to like?" He pauses a moment, leans forward, says, "It was cool, though," and after glancing back at his girlfriend, he turns back to us and shaking his head, mouths, "It wasn't."

Peering at Allyson, Trent raises his hand, starts waving it, trying to get her attention, and he asks Schroeder, "Did you sell them something?"

His girlfriend leans her head to the right, in front of Schroeder's face, gives Trent a disapproving look, and Clarence tells Schroeder, "Yeah, you could be their hookup. No way they wouldn't like you then." She can't help but giggle.

"Yeah, you could have taken some pot brownies over for dinner," Jus suggests, hitting my shoulder, leaning into me.

"Hmmmmm," Schroeder jokes, rubbing his chin, slowly turning to Clarence. I don't think I should be talking about this in front of you, should I?"

Clarence puts his finger in the air, whirls it around. "Wee-woo, wee-woo."

Because he couldn't get the bartender's attention earlier, Trent stands up in the booth, starts waving his hands and while Clarence is yanking him back down, Trent motions to the dancefloor and says, "Hey, Courtney and Ling-Ling are here."

Schroeder's girlfriend takes her hand off his leg, walks over, and I watch all three hug, after throwing their arms in the air. Wearing short red shorts and a black t-shirt that says "*Hellbilly Deluxe*" in red, Courtney looks fantastic as always. I can't help but think about us fucking at the Rob Zombie concert last summer.

We had snuck off from the others, found a motorhome at the far end of the parking lot and after glancing around quickly, to make sure no one was in sight, she wrapped her legs around me as I picked her up, moved her dress and panties out of the way, slid into her, threw her against the side. After a couple of minutes, a red-faced, old guy stuck his head out a small window a few feet from us, and slurring his words badly said, "Thanks for the show." Courtney threw the beer can she was holding that had been spilling all over my back at him, I picked up my shorts, and we ran through the parking lot, back inside, laughing and holding hands the entire way.

She starts dancing, moving with the other two, and I tell myself that if I were to be serious with anyone, it would be her.

"You guys won't fucking believe it!" Schroeder yells, hitting his hands on the table. He waits a moment for me to turn my attention back to him. "At the end of dinner, her dad was drunk as balls, and when my girlfriend and her mom went to the bathroom together at the end of dessert, he leaned over towards me, breath fucking reeking of whiskey, and asked, 'So, how does my girl's pussy taste?'"

We just gape at him in disbelief, our eyes wide open, his too, and no one says anything for a moment until I shout, "What?! Are you fucking serious?!"

"No fucking way!" Trent says, chuckling. He glances at his empty glass, then looks up at Allyson.

"That's why I told you guys it wasn't cool," Schroeder says, and he goes on to tell us that his girlfriend's father passed out at the table before they left. Clarence shakes his head slightly, finishes the rest of his drink and along with Trent, focuses his attention on Allyson for a moment, before turning to me and saying, "Is she coming back over or what?"

After a while, Clarence puts his fingers to his lips, lets out one of his loud whistles, and she quickly peeks over from behind the counter.

Shooting me a smile, she tucks a white towel into her waistband and gives the glass in her hand to the guy working next to her. Irritated, he motions at the large crowd in front of them, but she waves him off, grabs a tray, and makes her way through a group of sorority girls that are all wearing the same dark green sweatshirts and chanting some song.

"Let me get this mess out of the way," she says, laying the tray down, clearing our empty glasses. She glances over at Jus, and he tightens his lips, widens them a little, nods his head down slightly, giving her what Clarence refers to as the "white person" greeting. Motioning to Clarence, Trent lightly touches her on the arm and jokes, "Don't worry about it. We'll take him home soon." He glances over at Clarence, who's not paying attention because he's talking to Schroeder; and when he pulls his arm back and winks at her, I cringe for him when she gives him an awkward smile, then looks back at the glasses she's collecting. He falls back into the bench and hits Clarence, trying to get his attention, wanting to move on quickly from his second rejection of the night.

I look back at Courtney, and she waves at me, then leans towards Ling-Ling and says something to her. "We've always had such a cool time. No dumb awkwardness, no wanting to get away, just fun," I say to myself, thinking about it much more than I ever really have, due to the timing.

"What else do you guys want?" Allyson asks, looking at me.

Already smiling, I tell her, "If you don't mind, fourteen vodka and cranberries and fourteen shots."

"Of tequila!" Trent shouts, failing to get Clarence's attention.

"No, not of tequila," I say, turning back to her. I grab some of the glasses, put them on the tray, and Jus grabs a group of them also, swiftly, as if it were rude for him not to have offered beforehand. "Could you just come up with something, Allyson?" I ask, widening my smile, glancing at Courtney.

"This guy is going to hate it when he sees his bill." She touches my hand, giggles, and I start to say, "He deserved it" or something like that, but I decide there's no point, and when she makes her way through the group of dark green sweatshirts, they're singing a different song.

Courtney

"I really like her," I whisper to LL, before throwing my hands up in the air, giving Schroeder's girlfriend a hug. She looks really good tonight, and when I ask her where she got her outfit, she tells us she buys all of her clothes in Europe.

Not bothering to look down at what she's wearing or show it off, she pauses for a moment, then adds, "When I go visit family. It's the easiest place to find something that fits me." She says all of this without making a big deal of it or bragging about shopping in Europe, and I think to myself, "It makes sense," because she's small and tiny, like LL, and it's super easy to find cool clothes for that type of figure over there. When we walk over to everyone else, Harry, who's wearing a starchy, button-up shirt that looks like it cost two dollars, is pulling two chairs over from a table two guys are leaving, and before he can turn around, I slap him on the ass, hard and shout, "What's up?!"

He jolts up quickly, let's go of the two chairs, then turns to me and mouths, "Motherfucker."

"How was your trip?" I ask, giving him a quick kiss, hugging him tight and he smells good, like cedar or something woodsy.

Copying LL's wave and high-pitched voice, Trent says, "Hi, Ling-Ling." She sticks her tongue out at him, then looks over at Justin and gives him the same, cute and quick greeting Trent was just making fun of.

After grabbing my ass, Harry pulls back, smiles at me - he's always smiling - and I look up at his prematurely graying hair, stroke the back of his head a few times. "It was cool. Wish I could have been here," he says, his hands still resting on my hips. "How was your week?" I tell him about a job interview that went well, one that didn't, and he jokes about some things at the conference, afterwards informing me that his truck was acting up and he had to take the train back here. Harry has a way with people, this ability of making you feel like you're the only woman, the only person in the room when you're talking with him; and for some reason, I wonder if he's blinked at all since we started talking. I can't remember.

When LL sits down in the chair next to Clarence, Schroeder casually tosses a bag of bud in her lap.

Mortified, LL quietly yells, "What the hell, Schroeder?! Not in public! What if someone sees?!" She darts her eyes around the bar.

"Calm down over there," I tell her, reaching my hand past Schroeder and his girlfriend. LL looks around, then hands me the bag, fast.

"No one cares," Schroeder says, feeling bad about what he did, hoping his words will make it better.

Clarence taps LL on the leg, below her yellow skirt, says something calming to her that I can't hear and I stuff the sweet-smelling bag into my purse, then slide Schroeder two $100 bills. "So, what have you two been up to tonight?" Clarence asks, LL, who's no longer looking around the bar, but still a little anxious.

"Oh! We had a great time!" I sarcastically answer, turning to LL. "Didn't we?"

"Oh yeah! A great time!" Holding up two fingers, LL moves her hand around the table. "Two hours we sat there." She stops at me. "Two hours!" After putting her hand down, she tells them it was terrible, then looks back at me. "The only thing you've made me sit through that's been worse was the *Twilight* films!"

"How can you say that?! You've seen all five!" I shout back.

"Because you made me!"

I can still smell the bud in my purse, so I put it in an interior pocket, and zip it up, while thinking about smoking it with LL, either tonight when we get home, or tomorrow, depending on whether or not I hook up. A group of Kappa Deltas near the bar start to sing "Happy Birthday," and Justin asks her why tonight was so bad.

LL slaps her hands together. "Well, for starters, it was a speed-dating event."

"I thought it would be fun and different! Plus, it was free alcohol!" I shout, wanting to make my case first.

Trent stops looking around the bar, raises his glass and agrees with me, saying, "We should have started there. Free booze and the girls would have been desperate." The Kappa Delta wearing a tiara takes a shot after they're done singing and I wonder why Trent dresses the way he does.

"Sounds good to me." I quickly look at Harry after he says this, and he unconvincingly adds, "The part you said, about being fun and different and free alcohol, not what Trent said."

I give him a look, and Justin asks LL, "So it was bad but not as bad as *Twilight*?"

She tells them about the guy who asked her if she looked up someone's criminal record before she went out with them, the 40-year-old who lived in his mom's basement, her first "date," who was wearing an ankle monitor. "He was a nice guy," I say, adding, "it might have just been an ankle weight." LL rolls her eyes, then tells them about the guy who believed thunderstorms were the government's way of covering up space battles.

Schroeder says that can't be real, and Harry asks, "You're kidding, right?" Without saying anything, she nods her head at Schroeder, shakes it at Harry, then finishes with two more, the "flat earth" believer and the guy who paid $2 for her to get a drink with "premium liquor". "He told me I could pay him back later," she says. "I'm not joking. He was serious."

After all of the guys are done making fun of LL's dates, Schroeder, who's been massaging his girlfriend's neck for the last few minutes, says, "Yeah, I fucking hate small talk. Ten percent of it is nodding to whatever the person is saying, and ninety percent of it is thinking of an excuse to leave."

"No doubt, man," Justin says, glancing over at LL, who smiles and nods her head a few times.

Schroeder's girlfriend pulls down on her dress a little, looks at LL, and whispers, "I can't believe you actually met someone who believes the earth is flat."

"We should show them the video!" Trent shouts, sitting up in the booth, looking at Harry, then over at Clarence. Trent makes a fist and slowly swings it towards Clarence's face. Clarence catches it, and all of the guys chuckle, except for Schroeder.

"What the hell is going on? What are you talking about?" Schroeder asks, looking at Trent, who points at Clarence's phone, and I glance over at Harry, who doesn't say anything.

With Trent looking over his shoulder, Clarence plays the video. "No way!" Schroeder yells, asking him to replay it. Justin flicks Harry's ear, tells him to make it closer next time, then glances over at LL, who's giggling at his joke.

After watching it several times, Harry tells them to calm down, saying, "Alright, alright. No big deal. Just a few douchebags."

"So, we actually did make out better than you two," Clarence says, then looks at Trent. "We got free drinks and a show." Trent agrees, says the girls here will probably be just as desperate and he starts looking at the crowd behind me.

A waitress comes over to the table, and I can tell she's interested in Harry, by the look she gives him and the glance she gives me afterward. Without thinking about it, my hand had drifted to his leg sometime during LL's rant about our night, and it had remained there. After setting some drinks and shot glasses on the table, she smiles at Harry, tells him, "I know you'll like this."

She doesn't look at me, purposefully, leaves after he thanks her by name; and knowing he doesn't need to bother, he says to me, "I asked her to just come up with something for the shots," and I don't care.

I take the straw out of my cranberry and vodka, because my grandmother always told me, "Straws give you wrinkles around your lips," and it tastes good, a little bit too much vodka, which I like. The shots are colorful and taste fruity like I expected them to be, and Schroeder's girlfriend doesn't like it. She makes a face, sets her half-full shot glass on the table, and Schroeder picks it up, finishing it.

"Imagine if you went to one of those speed-dating events and you ended up kissing or making out or whatever with someone, and you found out they were your cousin," Harry says.

"Ewwww," LL says, cringing. "That's so gross."

"I don't know. Depends on how hot she is," Trent says, trying to wipe some red smudge off his shirt.

"Dude," Clarence says, shaking his head. He takes a gulp, looks at us. "Or what if you met someone who had really low self-esteem and after talking to them and building them up, they decide they're too good for you."

Schroeder throws in one, too. "Or if you met someone who asked you your zodiac sign and you just said T-Rex, because none of them are real."

This reminds me of when LL and I were in high school. We would look at horoscopes in our rooms together, trying to make connections in our lives with the words on the pages, imagining endless things. About a month ago, she came home with a paper, thinking it would be fun to look at them again, to reminisce, so we broke open a bottle of wine, got high and spent the next couple of hours, joking and laughing on her bed.

"So, you start Sunday, right?" Schroeder's girlfriend asks Clarence.

Seeing her hand on Schroeder's leg, I notice mine still on Harry's and take it off.

"Yep, 1." Clarence motions to Harry. "Right after we drop that fool off at the station." Not sure why I hadn't done it sooner, I reach over and take off Harry's nametag, hand it to him and make a mental note to look up some shirts online for him this weekend. We clink glasses, some of them touching, some of them not and everyone shouts some sort of congratulations to them, and after all of us drink, Harry reminds everyone that he leaves at noon.

"We should do breakfast or something," LL suggests, looking at me, then everyone else.

"That's kind of why I said something," Harry says, teasing her.

Schroeder's girlfriend mentions a diner she really likes, and Schroeder rolls his eyes, tells us he can't stand the place and doesn't like going there. Annoyed at first, she smiles and starts rubbing his leg harder when he says, "Besides, why would I go out to eat when I have her cooking at home."

Harry says we should just have breakfast at their apartment, and after asking him if he's sure about his departure time and eating at home, LL suggests some restaurants close to the train station, telling them, "Knowing you guys, it's more likely you'll be too relaxed and unmotivated at home to be on time."

"I'll take that into advisement, Ling-Ling," Harry says, with a short laugh. She makes a silly face, knowing he's making fun of her and the way she is about timetables and tardiness, especially when traveling.

Trent speaks up. "I'll just have the girl I hook up with tomorrow night make me breakfast." Looking out to the dancefloor, he continues, "Maybe eggs, some bacon and-"

"I hope your right hand is a good cook then," Clarence says, interrupting him.

All of us laugh, then we start talking about how lame and needlessly lengthy the graduation ceremony was, Schroeder's girlfriend tells us about her internship, and Justin informs LL and me about another Trent firing. When Clarence motions to my t-shirt and says something about the concert, I think about Harry, the motorhome, and giggle a little when I recall that old guy and throwing a beer at him. Looking down at the red lettering on my shirt, I wish I'd gotten two, for when this one wears out. I glance over at Harry, who's checking out the bar, just like he was the last time I looked at him, and Schroeder calmly asks the table, "Anyone want to smoke?"

Everyone answers yes quickly, pretty much at the same time, and LL finishes the last of her first drink. I make fun of her for taking so long, and she flicks me off, picks up her second vodka and cranberry and jokingly says to Schroeder, "As long as you don't try and give anything to me." She pulls her straw out, puts it in her empty glass, Justin smiles at her, and I wonder when the hell they're going to at least just kiss, and Harry taps me on the leg, asks me to scoot my chair out of the way so he can slide out of the booth.

Pointing towards the bar, Harry says he's going to talk to the bartender, and when I glance over, I realize he's talking about the girl who was at our table, and it bothers me a little, but I shake it off. Holding up an empty shot glass, Trent yells, "And get us tequila instead of this crap!" He tries to move out of the booth, but Clarence doesn't budge, and after Trent pushes him a couple of times and Clarence still doesn't budge, he stands up and tries to hop over him. Tripping halfway over, Clarence has to catch him by his cargo shorts, so that he doesn't fall over, onto LL, who's thrown her arms up, spilling some of her drink.

"What's the damn rush, man?" Clarence asks, standing up, shoving him a little. Trent apologizes, she laughs it off, and because she's the only one worried about it, LL holds her glass to her right side, hiding it from the bouncers as we walk by, even though Justin told her they don't care. One of the bouncers, the one with the ponytail, looks Schroeder's girlfriend up and down with an uncomfortable, creepy glare, while she walks past him, only stopping once he notices me staring at him. Quickly putting his head down, he pretends like he's checking his clipboard.

Trent sits on one of two bikes near an iron gate, and after he notices they're chained together, he gets off. Looking disappointed, he scans the area around us and says, "I was hoping I could find something to build a ramp."

"Think about how stupid that sounds." Trent starts to say something, but Clarence puts his finger to his lips, then repeats himself. "Shhhh. Just think about how stupid that sounds."

Schroeder pulls a blunt out of his pocket, and Justin tells him we should wait for Harry. "I ammmmmmm," Schroeder jokes, acting offended.

Trent nods his head towards what's in Schroeder's hand. "Dude, there's like eight of us. How's that thing supposed to last?"

"Please," Schroeder says, reaching into his pocket, pulling out three more blunts.

"Respect," Clarence tells him, pumping his fist slightly.

Schroeder starts to dance a little, and Clarence and Justin and Trent join him, all of them giving each other the same weird little handshakes while they gyrate their bodies.

"So, are you two going to fucking kiss or what?" I whisper to LL.

"Shhhhhh!" She glances at the guys, who aren't paying attention to us at all, much less hearing what I'm saying, then looks back at me. "Shut up," she mumbles, opening her eyes a little wider, staring at me. She looks back at them again, and when I start to say something else, she looks at me quickly, out of the corner of her eye. "Shhh!" I open my mouth a little more. "Shhhhhhhhhh!" Schroeder's girlfriend looks over at us and smiles.

"When-"

"Shhhhhh!"

"If you-"

"Shhhhh!" LL tries not to, but she starts giggling, and I can't help but wonder if Harry's inside, hitting on that waitress, bartender, whatever.

"So, what do you two, think?" Justin asks, looking at us.

"Huh? What do we think about what?" I say, stepping between him and LL. Regretting that I hadn't danced with them and disappointed they'd stopped, I begin shaking my body, grab Justin's hand, and he starts to move with me.

"About when to make eye contact with someone," he says, laughing, continuing to dance.

Trent walks away from us, turns around and starts strolling towards us slowly, then looks at LL and me. "Like, if you're the only two walking down a hallway or the street or whatever. When do you make eye contact? Now, now?" he asks, taking small steps. While all of us shout out different answers, LL glances at Justin and me, starts dancing too, and pretty soon everyone else joins in, all of us having our own party outside.

"I get the same type of uncomfortableness when I'm paying in a check-out line," Schroeder's girlfriend says, swinging her arms in the air.

"That's true! I feel the same way!" Clarence shouts. "And they make you feel that way without even saying anything! It always seems to take me forever to get my wallet and card out!" He touches his heart, leans his head back. "Ah, the pressure!"

Everyone is too busy gyrating and laughing, so no one notices Harry when he walks up and says, "Why the fuck are y'all dancing!?" We remain quiet, and he can tell we're trying not to laugh, that none of us are going to say a word, so he says, "Fuck it," and starts dancing with us, without knowing why.

Some of the smoke from the blunt gets in my eyes, so I step back, start waving my hand in front of my face and hand it back to LL. Harry and Justin are sharing a blunt, so are Clarence and Trent as well as Schroeder and his girlfriend.

"So, is your friend coming out tonight?" Clarence asks, looking at LL, then me.

"Awwww, Clarence," LL teases. She takes another couple of puffs, passes it back to me.

"Why, do you want to give it to her, Clarence?" I ask. Schroeder's girlfriend spits up some of her drink.

Trent puts his hands out, starts thrusting his hips back and forth. "Awwww yeah, Clarence!"

"Sorry, not tonight, but she's definitely coming out tomorrow night," LL says, adding, "I asked her, but she had previous plans."

Disappointed, Clarence kicks the pavement, says, "Ok, cool," then flicks off Trent and Harry.

"So, guess who we're having lunch with tomorrow!?" LL shouts, looking at everyone.

"Who?" Harry asks. LL hands me the blunt, tells me she doesn't want anymore, and a light behind Harry, makes a loud, popping noise, then starts flickering on and off.

"There it goes again," Justin says.

"What, the light?" Schroeder asks, throwing what little blunt he has left, into a small puddle on the ground.

"Yeah, it did the same thing the last time we were out here," Harry tells him. He looks back at LL. I'm sorry, Ling-Ling. Go ahead. With who?"

Clutching her drink, she begins jumping up and down. "You have to gueeeeess!"

Harry's eyes get fuller, and all of the boys are much more attentive, the five of them actually taking an excited step towards her because they now know who it is.

"Say it ain't so," Justin says, taking a sip of his drink. He pulls his glass back, looks at it, then pulls something out of it.

"The Grandmaaaa!" LL exclaims.

Nodding his head, Trent says, "The fucking Grandma."

"The motherfucking, Grandma!" Clarence yells. He starts shaking his hips, moving his hand in the air like he's scratching a turntable, and all of us start dancing again. Schroeder's girlfriend asks what's going on, and Schroeder tells her that my grandma is a legend and he'll explain it later.

"Tell us a Grandma story!" Trent begs, before taking his last hit. He throws it in the puddle, and it immediately goes out, starts floating towards mine and Schroeder's finished blunts, and when I don't say anything, he pleads, "Tell us a Grandma story, please. Schroeder's girlfriend needs to know!"

"Grandma story!" Harry shouts, putting his fist in the air.

"No, you boys are going to have to settle down," I tell them, turning to Schroeder's girlfriend. "She's just a nice, sweet, old, lady." I point at all of the boys. "And don't let anyone tell you any different." I look at Schroeder last, and he puts his hands up, defensively.

"I would never," he says, shaking his head, smiling mischievously.

"Yeah, sweet," Harry says, snatching their blunt out of Justin's lips, surprising him. Justin hits him on the arm, grabs it back, and Harry punches him on the shoulder, then turns back to us. "Sweet as...."

"Don't you say it!" I yell, pointing my finger at him.

Before we get inside, Justin teases LL about hiding her drink beforehand, so when Harry holds the door for all of us, and she walks through, she takes a large gulp while walking by the same, creepy bouncer from before.

"Time to check out the ladies!" Trent yells, looking back at us.

"Twenty bucks says he gets pissed on tonight," Clarence says, nudging Harry.

"Nah, I'll keep my twenty," he replies, shaking his head. I know exactly who they're talking about, so I don't bother to say anything, and we all follow Trent into the dancing crowd of young guys and girls.

They're just starting "It's All About the Benjamins" by Puff Daddy when we walk in, the dope version, where he dedicates the song to the class of '98. I drop my jaw a little, slowly turn to Clarence, who loves this song as much as I do, and he's already glaring at me, wide-eyed, his mouth open as well. "Oh shit," he says, slightly moving his arms and shoulders, followed by his hips, then legs. All of us love this song, but not as much as the two of us, and keeping pace with him, I sway a little, barely moving at all, just snapping my fingers every few seconds through the intro.

"It's your song!" LL shouts, pointing at us.

"Come on!" blasts out of the speakers and Clarence and I start rocking out, swinging and moving everywhere, singing the lyrics to each other once they start, and when I realize it's not the censored version, I get even more riled up because I know I'll enjoy Lil Kim's rap, my favorite part of the song, even more. We hug after it ends, and the DJ plays some slow, cheesy, popular song that a lot of people like, and Schroeder shakes his head, says, "This shit makes me want to sit in a bathtub surrounded by candles, and slit my wrists."

When we get back to the table, we have new drinks, more shots, and Trent nudges Harry, tells him, "Nice job on the delivery, man."

Harry and Justin grab the orange-colored shots, pass them around, and all of us down them, without any type of toast. Sweating, Clarence looks at me, touches my arm and beaming with excitement, says, "Man, I'm riled up."

"Me too!" I say, hugging him. He apologizes for being sweaty, and I tell him, "I don't care," and all of us agree these shots taste much better.

Schroeder's girlfriend actually finishes hers, and hands it to Justin, who takes LL's and my empty glasses, then puts them on the table. When this lame song came on, there were a couple of boos from the crowd, and someone must have said something or complained to the DJ because he stops playing it halfway through and puts on something else. The dancing mob shouts in approval, and Schroeder's girlfriend grabs his arm, starts pulling on him. "Come on, Schroeder. I want to dance." He doesn't give any resistance, and the DJ's song selection is solid for the next hour or so, and the only ones who go back to the table are Justin and Harry - Justin twice, to get everyone's second drinks.

LL and Justin dance, but don't touch each other in any way, nor give me any other type of sign that brings me hope of them hooking up tonight, or tomorrow, or the day after that. Trent makes a couple of trips around the bar, unsuccessfully trying to find a girl, coming back to the group within five minutes every time, saying to Clarence, "Eh, no one to talk to," or something like that. Harry's been glancing around the bar the last thirty minutes, particularly towards a blonde and brunette in the left corner, and when LL asks me if I'll go to the bathroom, he bends down, whispers in my ear, "I might walk around a little," and when he says that I know that he definitely will. He kisses me on the cheek and acting like I don't care, I turn to ask Schroeder's girlfriend if she wants to go with us, but she's moving her hands over Schroeder's, whose are on her hips, him behind her, so I don't bother. Harry starts talking to Trent, and when we get to the bathroom door, I let go of LL's hand, look back before following her in, and the two of them are walking in the direction of the two girls Harry was checking out earlier. I know our relationship and the way it works, what both of us want, but it still hurts a little, and I don't understand why he couldn't have hung out longer, given the circumstances.

When we walk in, there are two girls at the counter. Wearing similar, black dresses, one is really short and petite, has dark hair; the other one, much taller and fuller, has red and they remind me of some of the ads I've seen on Pornhub. The mini trailers that show a taller, larger woman lifting up a smaller, shorter girl against a wall, then fucking her with a strap-on.

They glance into the mirror at us, look back at each other, then continue talking, and the taller one starts applying lipstick. Above the mirrors, a yellow neon light that says, "TAKE A SELFIE" hangs from the ceiling. When I look behind it, at the reflection in the mirror, it somehow reads, "FAKE A LIFE." I pull out my camera and LL points up, says, "So cool." Annoyed, as if we'd intruded on them, one of the girls lets out some sort of grunt, and they turn off the faucets that were running for no reason. I wait for them to leave, take several pics of us, kissing LL on the cheek in one, and after we look at them, LL frowns a little, looks in the mirror, and says, "I always look the same in pictures."

"Give Justin a blowjob tonight, and maybe you'll look different," I tell her, giving her a wink.

"Court!"

"What?! At the rate you two are going, it's never going to happen!" I throw my hands up. "You need to make a move! He needs to make a move! Somebody needs to make a move, for God's sake!"

We join the others, dance for another ten or fifteen minutes, and when I look around for Harry, it doesn't take long to find him. He and Trent are talking to the two girls, both of whom are wearing light-colored, summer dresses, and I quickly realize they're paying more attention to Harry than Trent. I put it out of my mind, then hug LL, grab her half-empty drink, down all of it and keep dancing.

Clarence starts wiping his forehead with some napkins he picked up from the bar; on our way back to the table, Schroeder's girlfriend tells Schroeder not to drink so much, and Harry and Trent join us, not long after we sit down.

Holding four plastic cups, Harry sits down next to me, in the chair I was sitting in earlier. "She said they don't give out glasses after last call," he tells us, handing out the drinks. Trent passes around the cups he has, then mostly just looks around the bar, while all of us break off into smaller conversations.

Harry's as polite and fantastic as he always is, but not as flirtatious as he was when we were last sitting here, and I know we're not going home together tonight. Once he finishes his drink, he kisses me on the neck, whispers, "I'll call you tomorrow," and after he leaves, I pull out my phone, open up my contacts.

Clarence

"And you fuckers need to stop making it so obvious you're checking out my girlfriend!" Schroeder shouts, swaying a little, pointing at Justin and Trent, then slowly to me. He smokes a ton but doesn't really drink all that often and I can tell he's pretty drunk. Laughing, trying to be serious, he adds, "All the time!"

"Dude, it's your own fault for having such a hot girlfriend. You signed up for that. If you don't want that problem, go out with an ugly chick," Trent tells him. He leans on Schroeder and looks past him at his girlfriend, who's been dancing with Courtney and Ling-Ling for the last fifteen minutes. "Damn, how did I miss that?" Trent says.

Schroeder looks up at Trent, who's now laying all over him. "You mean like the one who leaves you in a small pond every morning after a night of hooking up?

"Fucker!" Trent says, getting off of him.

"I guarantee you wake up in 'The Scarlet Pumpernickel' tomorrow."

"The fucking what?" Trent asks, looking at Justin.

Justin laughs, and I have no clue what the fuck he's talking about either. Chuckling, he says, "If you don't hook up with Melissa tonight, I'll clean your room and fix you breakfast, lunch, and dinner tomorrow, but if you do, you have to clean the living room and kitchen."

"Psssssh! I'll take that bet!" Trent tells him. Justin puts his hand out, Trent slaps it, then starts glancing around the bar, and Justin looks at me, mouths, "Sucker bet," and leans back in the booth.

Copying Justin, Trent leans back in our booth and starts imitating everything he does and says, until I point out the time. "You better hurry up," I tell him.

"Tick tock," Justin says motioning his finger back and forth.

Trent plays it cool for a couple of minutes, and when he tries to leave, he realizes I'm not going to move, so he jumps over me, without tripping this time. He flicks us off, walks away, and I glance over at Justin and Schroeder. "He'll be back in under ten minutes."

Schroeder cups his hands around his mouth and yells, "Good luck without Harry!"

"What are the odds that I win that bet?" Justin asks, bringing his drink to his lips. "100%?" Schroeder's body starts to lean to the left, and he catches himself, sits up quickly, then laughs. "On a scale of 1-10, one being low, and ten being high. What are the odds he's going to get pissed on tonight?" Justin leans forward, puts his hand up to me as if he's holding a microphone.

Playing along, I answer, "A motherfucking, ten! That dude has no game! Watching him struggle to score is like watching soccer. I will admit he's a blind squirrel that can find a nut every now and then, but a ten, a motherfucking ten!" I hold up my hands, spread my fingers, then slam my hands on the table. "That dude is getting pissed on tonight!"

We watch him walk around for a while, not approaching many girls, having short conversations with the ones he does, and we start making up dialogue, each of us taking the role of Trent or the girl he talks to.

"Why yes, I do have a small penis. How could you tell?"

"No, I'm sorry, I don't dance with men who can't hold a job longer than 48 hours."

"Yes, my name is Trent. I'm looking for a night that doesn't require a bathing suit. And a mop."

After a while, we get bored, start talking about nothing in particular, and more than once some guy tries to move in on Courtney, Ling-Ling, and Schroeder's girlfriend, only to be turned away by one of the girl's outstretched palms.

"Phew, that was fun!" Schroeder's girlfriend says, sitting down. She looks at Schroeder. "You never want to dance."

"We were just dancing earlier!" he says, raising his voice a little like I do with Trent when I'm fucking with him.

"Well, you could have gone out with me just now, too," she complains.

He rolls his eyes and she grabs his arms, starts shaking them, pulls him up. Courtney reaches down, I take her hand, and Schroeder's girlfriend leads us to the middle of the dance floor. Ling-Ling points at Justin's feet, tells him to move more, not just his arms, and Schroeder slowly steps back with one foot, then another, jokingly moving away from his girlfriend. Thrilled they're dancing, she giggles and pulls him back, hugging him tightly. Courtney puts her hands on my hips, moves to her left, then right, pushes herself off me, spins back, and Justin grabs Ling Ling's hand, twirling her around a couple of times while she giggles.

Sweating again, I wish that Schroeder's girlfriend would've just stopped at the edge of the crowd, and I regret not bringing the napkins, but it doesn't matter too much, because this ends up being the last song. When it's done, Courtney and I look over at Justin, his hands in his jeans pockets, and Ling-Ling, both of their bodies swaying back and forth, nervously yet in rhythm, their heels slightly leaving the ground together at the same time, in a smooth cadence. They smile at each other, Justin says something, then both of them nervously glance at the ground, and when Courtney asks me if I think "that" will ever happen, I answer, "This year?" then turn to her. "Or when we're fifty?"

The bar clears out quickly, and after Schroeder tells us to "hold on," he goes back to the table, picks up two plastic cups and pours them into the one he already has in his hand. When we get outside, there's a mob of people on the sidewalk – groups talking, single guys and girls looking for last-minute fucks, people getting into cars that are lined up on the street. On the way to the alley, Ling-Ling notices a girl from one of her classes, someone she says "is leaving tomorrow," so she runs over, gives her a quick hug, then says a few words while we wait, hugs her again, and jogs back.

"Maybe you shouldn't smoke," Schroeder's girlfriend says to him as he stumbles in the alley, trying to light one of the blunts. "You're already drunk." He doesn't answer, and after he lights it, he gives it to Courtney, who's looking at her phone, then pulls another one from his pocket. "Schroeder!" his girlfriend yells.

Justin takes a hit, passes it to me, then taps Courtney on the arm. "So, who are you going home with tonight?"

"Yeah, who are you fucking tonight, Court?" Ling-Ling asks.

Without looking up from her phone, she says, "Chris, if he fucking answers."

Changing the subject, Justin tells her, "Well I hope that you have fun with the Grandma tomorrow and enjoy lunch."

A few seconds pass, and Schroeder, who's standing behind Justin, raises his cup. "The Grandma!" he shouts, stumbling forward.

All of us laugh at him, and after a few minutes, Courtney's phone beeps. "Yep, Chris," she says, looking up at us.

"Well, you better fucking walk me home first."

"Of course I am," Courtney tells Ling-Ling. She turns to us, and slaps her legs with both hands, implying that she's ready to go. "Okay, guys," she says.

"ZZZZZZZZZZ...Pop!" The bulb that was flickering when we walked out, the same light from earlier, explodes, shattering and scattering glass on the ground below.

"Fuck!" Courtney shouts, jumping back. Ling-Ling flinches, says the same thing. Schroeder's girlfriend yells, "Jesus!" and Schroeder lets out a delayed "shit". "What the fuck?!" Courtney says, looking down at the broken glass, none of it really close to us.

Ling-Ling takes a pull, blows the smoke at Courtney and says, "Life is pointless, and entropy is unavoidable, and the universe is filled with callous and casual destruction."

Courtney, swinging her arms through the cloud of smoke in her face, asks, "LL, what the fuck are you talking about?"

Ling-Ling gives it back, and Justin rips it out of Courtney's hand quickly, tells her, "A thermodynamic quantity representing the unavailability of a systems thermal energy for conversion into mechanical work, often interpreted as the degree of disorder or randomness in the system."

He takes a few hits, hands it back to her, then looks at Ling-Ling, who's already smiling at him. I don't know what the fuck they're talking about, and I can't imagine anyone else does, and Courtney just stands there, bewildered. Ling-Ling snatches the blunt out her hand, takes a puff, gives it back, then says, "Lack of predictability."

Still baffled, Courtney asks, "What the fuck does that have to do with anything?"

"In other words, shit happens," Justin says.

Courtney rolls her eyes. "Whatever, guys. You two could have just said that shit in the beginning." She takes a few hits, extends the blunt to Justin, then pulls it back when he reaches for it, doing it again three times before finally handing it over.

"Come on, LL. Let's go," Courtney says, grabbing Ling Ling's hand. "I want to get laid, so I can get back home and get some decent sleep before lunch tomorrow with grandma."

"The Grandma!" Schroeder shouts again, halfway raising his cup. His eyes are barely open, and when he drops his arm, the cup spills, covering the front of his shirt. His girlfriend tries to take it from him, but he pulls it closer, telling her, "I'm fine!"

After giving us the same quick wave she always does, Ling-Ling glances at Justin, shyly smiles, and Courtney flings her other arm in the air, yelling, "See you guys tomorrow!" After a few steps, Courtney stops, leans over a little, and without turning around, she starts shaking her ass and shouts, "Thanks for the moves, Clarence!"

Justin

We ask her several times, but Schroeder's girlfriend tells us, "They'll be fine," that "there's no need to walk us home". With her arm around him, helping him to stand, Schroeder's girlfriend tells us she had a great time, that she really loves dancing, and that she wishes the two of them did it more often. Just then, Schroeder pops his head up, mumbles something, we think "the Grandma," and when we get to the end of the sidewalk, they go left, and we go right.

Not far from home, Clarence starts making fun of Trent, mimicking him sweeping the kitchen floor, washing the dishes and wiping the counters. "I wish I could go back two hours," I think to myself. "I wish I would have been more confident or made a move or something. She smelled so nice, and she looked so cute."

"Now that would be cool," Clarence says, pointing at a bus stop. On a poster behind some glass, four guys are standing on a set of cliffs in Philippines, a sea, six shades of blue behind them. In the clouds above their heads, in bright yellow letters, it reads, "Imagine a world where you have an endless number of ways to feel alive and trillions of reasons to never be bored."

When we walk back into the apartment, Clarence says goodnight, and I pour a glass of water, head back to my room, get a text from Ling-Ling as I'm locking the door. "Made it home. Have a good night ☺," it says.

"Thanks ☺ You too ☺," I type. After pondering it for a moment, I delete one of the smiley faces, then push, "send".

I pull the cord on the nightstand lamp, flick the lights off, then grab some lotion and a towel from the bottom dresser. Once I find some Asian porn on my phone, I start jerking off, and pretty soon I'm thinking about Ling-Ling, how beautiful she was tonight, her laugh, her skin. My excitement starts to build, and I'm not far from cumming when my phone beeps. Excited, I glance over, but I'm quickly disappointed when I see it's a text from my grandmother. "Just saw this scripture and thought of you, Justin," it reads, along with an attachment. I roll my eyes, look down at my softening penis, and when I try to slide her text out of the way, I'm not really paying attention and somehow I accidentally push the "share" button. Confused by what just happened, and in a panic, I press "agree".

"Oh...my...God." My mouth just hangs there, for a moment, after saying this and I quickly sit up, banging my head on the wall behind me. "Ow, fuck!" I yell, quietly. Hoping that I'm mistaken, I look at my phone, fast. "Did I just?" I ask myself, rubbing the back of my head. Realizing that I'm smearing lotion into my hair, I pull my hand back, and just sit in shock for a few minutes, staring at nothing. My phone beeps and a message from my grandmother pops up, covering Rod Serling's face. Not bothering to read it, I turn my phone off, shove it under my pillow, then push the lotion and towel to the side, and turn off the lamp. "I cannot believe that just happened," I say to myself, taking a deep breath, closing my eyes.

"Ohhhh."

"Ahhhh." The noises are coming from Harry's room, and for some reason, I think about what he told me when we were in the tenth grade, and I was still afraid of the dark.

"Jus, it's no problem. Before you go to bed, just cut all the lights off and make the room completely dark. Then get naked and beat off, saying things like, 'Oh yeah, you like that, monster. Oh yeah.' No monster wants to see that shit. He'll be gone after that."

I haven't used a nightlight since.

When I wake up a couple of hours later, I can still hear noises coming from Harry's room, and I think about Ling-Ling, start getting excited, and want to jerk off. So, I do.

In the morning, I can hear Harry, Clarence, and Trent, talking loudly in either the living room or the kitchen, and knowing I'm not going to sleep any longer, I get up. Halfway down the hall, I think about Ling-Ling, realize I forgot my phone, and then it hits me while reaching under my pillow. I remember, for the first time this morning, my grandmother. "Fuck," I say to myself, stopping in the hallway, leaning against the wall, turning my phone on. A barrage of text messages starts popping up, all of them from my grandma.

Reluctantly, I read the first one: "What is this?" then the second one, "Justin, why do I have a picture of a naked, Asian woman on my phone?" Cringing, I don't bother with the rest, erase them, and message her that Trent had my phone, and it was a joke meant for someone else. "I know she'll believe me, because she's met Trent," I say to myself. Looking at the time, I figure out the hour in Hawaii, send her the message, then decide to text Ling-Ling. "Good morning ☺"

"Well, look who's finally up," Harry says. He waves the spatula in his hand at me, then flips over some eggs, and I smell them for the first time. Trent is sitting on the counter next to him, picking pieces of bacon off a plate, and Clarence is on the couch playing a video game. Not taking his eyes off the TV, he puts his hand up, and I slap it on my way to the kitchen.

"What's up, Sir Beats-A-Lot? You want some orange juice?" Trent asks, pouring me a glass before I can answer. Harry throws salt and pepper on the eggs, then sprinkles on some parmesan cheese, spreading it out evenly with his fingers, and Trent hands me the glass.

"So, did you get pissed on last night?" I ask.

"You know it!" Clarence shouts from the couch, his eyes still on his game.

Harry points the spatula at Trent and tells me, "Dude lied and told us he hooked up with someone else, but Clarence told him he saw him leaving with Melissa last night, and he finally admitted it."

"Well, you are fucking cleaning today!" I shout, turning to Trent, motioning to the massive pile of trash in the corner.

Harry, still pointing the spatula at him, starts shaking it, splattering grease on the counter, telling him, "And it better be spotless!"

"Yeah, yeah," Trent says, waving us off.

Clarence pauses his game, turns around, and resting his arm on the back of the couch, looks at Trent. "Funny thing is, I never even saw you leave last night."

Trent stops chewing and with a full mouth, says, "Are you fucking kidding me?"

"Nope," Clarence tells him. He looks at us, back at Trent, then grins, starts chuckling and turns around, unpauses his game. He has the volume down really low, and I can barely hear the sound of Sully starting the plane and taking off.

"Fucker!" Trent shouts, bits of bacon flying out of his mouth.

"You know it hurts us when you lie to us," Harry says, resting the spatula against his muscular chest. I put my glass of oj over my heart, tell him how disappointed I am in him, that I just don't know if I can ever trust him again. He flicks us off, drinks the last of his Sunny D, then fills his glass back up. Still sitting on the counter, Trent reaches for another piece of bacon, and Harry slaps his hand with the spatula. "Wait until all of us eat, bitch." Harry flips half of the eggs over the other half. "How are you feeling, man?" he asks, turning to me. "How was the rest of last night?"

"It was fun," I tell him. Glancing down to the floor, I say to myself, "I should have done something."

"And...?"

"And nothing, it was fun."

"Jesus, Justin. What the hell!?" he says, slightly raising his voice. I take a sip, and the elated feeling I had once I started thinking about her again, dissipates, turning into regret when I quickly recall last night and wishing that I could have gone back in time two hours. Sensing my change in demeanor, Harry alters his mood. "Ah, whatever, man. It'll happen." He flips the eggs. "No rush."

Bummed out, I walk around him, grab two pieces piece of bacon, and after I eat them and reach for a third, Trent complains to Harry, saying, "What the fuck? How come he can have some and I can't?"

"Because he hasn't already had ten pieces," Harry scoffs. After a few minutes pass, Trent motions to the couch, blurting out Clarence's name, and when Harry turns his head, Trent snatches a piece of bacon from the plate. Before he can get it to his mouth, Harry cracks his hand, sending the bacon flying across the kitchen. Harry spreads his legs, bends his knees and eyeing Trent, shouts, "Hiyahhhhh! Don't touch my bacon, fucker!"

Trent makes a few more failed efforts, Harry smacking him on his hand each time, always slowly pulling back into some sort of "karate" pose afterward, waiting for him to try again. Eventually Clarence throws his controller on the sofa, his game continuing to play, and he runs into the kitchen and bear hugs Harry, who quickly tosses the spatula to me. I slap Clarence in the face with it, not too hard, leaving some grease on his cheek, and Trent jumps off the counter, shadow punches me in the gut, twice, causing me to throw the spatula in the air. After Trent catches it, we battle in slow motion, passing it back and forth, smacking each other with it, all of us using our best ninja sounds and impressions while kicking and hitting each other, Harry and I, versus Clarence and Trent.

"Good morning."

Surprised, we immediately stop what we're doing; all four of us look to the hallway, and the blonde I saw Harry talking to last night, the one with the equally hot friend Trent was trying to hit on, is leaning against the wall. Still wearing the same, small dress from last night, she blushes a little and moves some hair that's fallen and covered part of her eye.

"Good morning, Lily," Harry says, looking up at her, his head stuck. After a brief lull, Clarence remembers he has Harry in a headlock, let's go, and Harry stands up, adjusting his boxers.

"Good morning," Clarence says, standing up straight, yanking at his grey t-shirt. I tell her the same thing and Trent just raises his glass, hops back up on the counter.

Harry asks her if she wants anything for breakfast, and she brushes her hair out of the way again, tells him, "No, we have to go." She smiles and bounces forward, abruptly, after the same friend I saw her with last night runs into the back of her.

"Oh, sorry!" the brunette says, sliding her dress down, covering her stomach and pink panties, revealing her face. "I couldn't see." Giggling, she runs a brush through her hair and the blonde glances over at us. Indifferent to noticing us for the first time, the brunette continues to brush her hair and cheerfully says, "Good morning!"

It's silent for a moment, the TV sounding louder than before, and Harry asks, "Ginger, would you like something to eat?"

"No, thank you," she tells him, holding out the brush for Lily, who puts her hand up, motions she doesn't want it.

"Are you two sure?" Harry asks them again, lifting up a plate of whole wheat toast. "I can make you both something, and you can take it with you."

Both of them smile, say, "No, thank you," again, and Lily adds, "You are so polite," while fastening her hair with a small blue, hair-tie. They kiss Harry on his cheeks at the same time and leave as quickly as they walked into the room, both of them yelling back at him on their way out the door, "Call us!"

"Motherfucker," Clarence says, still looking at the closed door. He puts his hand out to his side, palm up; Harry slaps it, and Trent hops off the counter, gets down on the floor and starts bowing. I don't say anything, I just smirk, nod my head up and down at Harry, who chuckles, and Clarence smacks Trent on the back of the head. "Aren't you supposed to clean some shit up?" He motions to the trashcan in the corner, then to the living room. "The least you could have done was vacuum before we ate."

Trent stops bowing to Harry, stands up and hunches his back, starts shaking a little. "Yessah, Massa. I be real, good, Massa. Wanna make sure I gets my breakfast." He hobbles over to the closet, humming "Long John" and Clarence folds his arms, brings them high up on his chest, starts shaking his head.

"Of all the best friends you could have had," I say, still watching Trent.

"And I ended up with this fool."

When Trent pushes the button, the vacuum won't start, so he unplugs it and puts it in the lower socket. After a few failed attempts, he kicks the side of the vacuum, and Clarence yells, "Hey man, if a vacuum doesn't work, does it suck?"

"Most of this is your shit anyway," Trent complains, pointing at the Doritos bits on the floor. He shoots Clarence a mean look, starts staring him down.

"Uh oh," Harry says to Trent, turning off the stove, getting Clarence's attention, pointing at the cabinet to the right of the fridge. "Looks like you've got that mean Eminem stare going on again."

Trent flicks him off and walks back into the kitchen, passing me before I set the orange juice and his Sunny D on the coffee table. I grab four of the coasters he took last night that are in a pile in the corner, spread them around the table, and Clarence puts down his bowl, opens the cabinet, pauses, then looks back at us. "Why does that dude always look like he told a joke and nobody heard it, and then someone said the same joke louder and everyone heard it and laughed."

"I believe that is the most accurate description of Eminem I have ever heard," Harry tells him, laughing.

My phone beeps, and knowing that it's too early in Hawaii, I excitedly reach into my pocket. "Good Morning back 😊😊." I really like that there are two smiley faces and Trent, still laughing at what Harry said, opens the cabinet, gets some forks, and Clarence grabs four plates, taking the one off the top, handing it to Harry, who throws some eggs on it, and I have that same elated feeling from before.

Ling-Ling

"I told her not to leave this shit in here," I say to myself, grabbing the cucumber and lube out of the shower, setting them on the bathroom counter next to my phone. When I close the curtain behind me, I let the warm water fall down my head, hit my face, and after a while I open my eyes, look over at all of the adorable kittens on our shower curtain. "So, cute," I say, looking at a black one, a white one, another black one and then my favorite, an orange kitten playing with a ball of yarn with one paw in the air, swiping at it. I turn the music down on my phone before drying off, drops of water falling and landing on the screen; and when I'm done, I hang the towel up neatly, next to Court's crumpled one. After putting on one of my matching t-shirt and shorts outfits I wear when I'm at home, I unscrew the showerhead, grab the cucumber and lube, and walk into the kitchen. Looking in the cabinet on the second shelf, through the condiments and spices we, meaning me (because Court doesn't know how to cook) rarely use, I grab the box with the little head of a chicken on it and pull out a few bouillon cubes. When I pick up the cucumber and lube, I wonder why I brought them, return to the bathroom, put the cubes in the showerhead, and screw it back on.

Sliding my phone in my pocket, Tchaikovsky still playing, muffled, I walk towards Court's room. I know she's home because I heard her come in last night after fucking Chris, or whatever his name is. When I'm a few feet from her door, I hear, "Owwww. Fuck, fuck, fuck, fuck, fuck." Knowing she has a rule about bringing home anyone other than Harry because she doesn't want anyone other than him hanging around here in the morning, anyone that either of us would have to talk to, I open the door. Court, partially covered by her sheets and comforter, is grabbing one of her legs, rocking back and forth on her bed. "Fuck, fuck!"

"Let me guess, you pulled another muscle masturbating?" I say, giving her a look.

She stops writhing in the bed and holding her leg up in the air, she turns to me with a pained look on her face, gritting her teeth. "Yes! Fuck off, LL!" she shouts, kicking her other leg, revealing a purple vibrator under her sheets. "Ow, fuck, fuck! It hurts!" she yells, laughing.

"That's the third time this week!"

She stops, looks at me and unconcerned, says, "So?"

"You got laid like five hours ago!"

"Yeah, so. It wasn't that good."

"Whatever. Stop leaving your produce and lube in the shower," I tell her, tossing the small tube on the bed. Trying to hit Court on purpose with the cucumber, I quickly fling it, and I'm surprised when it smacks her right in the head.

"Ow!" she yelps, falling back, her legs popping up in the air. "Fuck, LL!" Rubbing her head, she looks at me for sympathy.

"I've told you, like, 20,000 times!" I shout, ignoring her sad, puppy dog face.

Losing some of her covers, she sits up in the bed and grabs the lube and cucumber. "Thanks a lot, I could have used these five minutes ago!" she says, her breasts exposed. I tell her thanks for the show, and she tells me, "It's just started," then puts the cucumber under the covers, between her legs. "Oh, Justin, oh, oh, ohhhhhhh!"

"Court, stop fucking around and get up. I want to finish that last episode before we go meet the Grandma." I look around her messy room - clothes on the floor, drawers half-pulled out, glasses of various tinted liquids on her nightstand, and I notice a bag of colored pills on her desk, next to the picture of us in Mauritius. "What the fuck are these!?" I yell, storming over to her desk. Grabbing the baggie, I hold it up and start shaking it. "Did fucking Chris give you these?" Concerned, I wait for an answer.

Court stops her fake masturbation show, and with her legs still in the air, she looks at me. Several seconds pass, she giggles, starts laughing wildly and when she tries to say something, she looks at the baggie in my hand, back at me, and starts cackling with glee. I look at her oddly, and when she finally stops and is able to talk, she gets out of the bed, puts her shirt on and says, "Come on, dumbass. Follow me."

After closing the drain in the bathroom sink, Court turns the water on, and when it's almost full, she stops looking at her teeth in the mirror and says, "Throw them in."

"What?" I look at the bag, then at her.

"Throw all of them in. The red and blue ones are the best."

Not knowing why, I hold the baggie upside down, letting the red, blue, yellow and white pills, fall into the water. Court turns on the shower and spreads the curtain out. "Aw, so cute," she says, and I know she's looking at her favorite one, a black kitten with wide eyes, curled up, three kittens diagonally up and to the right of mine.

"I knowww," I say, briefly forgetting about the pills I found on her desk.

After hearing her talk about her drunken walk home last night, she starts to undress, and while taking her panties off, she points at the sink I haven't been paying attention to. "Look," she says.

The water is filled with colorful, spongy dinosaurs. A blue T-Rex, a red Brontosaurus, a yellow Pterodactyl, and a white Stegosaurus. "What are you, fucking five?" I ask, grabbing the T-rex, squeezing it.

"I just thought they were cool," she tells me, grabbing her towel, flinging it over the curtain rod, and I dip the T-rex back in the sink, throw it at her. Somehow I miss from three feet away, and she picks it up, yells "Bitch!" and hurls it at me, hitting me in the face. "Now we're even!" she shouts, stepping in the shower.

After five or ten seconds pass, Court screams, "What the, what the fuck is.........LL!" She shuts the water off and throws the curtain back, neither of our kittens visible. "What the fuck did you do?!" She starts smelling her skin and with a disgusted look on her face, she bolts out of the shower and puts her arms out, trying to hug me, chicken bouillon-flavored water, dripping everywhere.

"No, no, don't touch me!" I yell, laughing, backing up into the corner, putting my arms out, fighting as best I can. It doesn't do any good, because she's much stronger and taller than me, and she puts me down on the ground, starts shaking smelly water all over me.

She stops. "Say it." I shake my head, tell her no, and she moves her head wildly, splattering me with drops. "Say it!" I don't comply, and she puts her hair in my face and moves it all around.

"Okay! Okay! You're the queen, and I'm a peasant in your kingdom!" I shout.

"That's right," she says, letting me up. "As long as you know that." She slaps me on the butt, I smack her on the arm, then unscrew the showerhead, and she giggles when I show her what I did. I stay in the bathroom, talking to her while she takes her shower, and she does the same for me, and before we watch the show, she makes us both Bloody Marys. We finish them on the couch, not paying much attention to what's on the TV because we're talking the whole time, and I almost choke on mine when Court reminds me of our bitch roommates, and her putting jalapeno juice on all of their vibrators the day we moved out.

Walking the curb like a balance beam, Court slowly puts one foot directly in front of the other, the bottom of her white, floral dress blowing up delicately in the light wind, and I look down at my matching black dress she asked me to wear.

"Let's look like twins!!" she screamed, turning off the TV, snatching my hand, running us to her bedroom. She grabbed her phone and the dress she bought on our trip to Mauritius, and we went to my room, where both of us got ready while dancing and singing to "99 Luftballoons". Mine had the same pattern, and we'd bought them at a mall, thirty miles from our resort. Court drove a rental car there, and she wasn't used to driving on the left side, so it took us forever. On the way back, we stopped and saw the Chamarel Seven-Coloured Earth, ate off of leaves at an Indian restaurant, and after a guy took a picture of us with three, huge waterfalls in the background, he handed my phone back to me and asked, "Are you two from America?" When we told him yes, he said he could tell because of our shoes.

Balancing on my toes, I start walking the curb and when I catch up to Court, I hop around on one foot, stretch both my arms out and point past her. "Look," I say. She turns and laughs when she sees the painting on the wall of a naked guy eating trees and pooping houses, then tells me about how the Grandma has a clause in her will that protects all of her property from development for the next one hundred years. "Shame there's not more of that," she says.

The bus comes shortly, and it's almost full, but Court finds two empty seats, and she takes the one next to the window, because that's where she always wants to sit and I don't care. The dark-haired girl sitting in front of us has her hair pulled up in a bun, and the pen she's using to hold it together doesn't have a cap and there are blue marks all over the back of her neck. I start texting my mom, and Court asks, "Awwww, are you texting your man, Justin?" She'd been teasing me the entire time we'd been sitting on the couch, complaining about how Justin and I still hadn't kissed, telling me that all of them had been waiting for years and that something had to be done. "Just bang him out already," she said, bringing her drink to her lips, accidentally stabbing herself in the eye with her celery stick.

"I'm texting my mom, idiot. I just need her to ask my dad something."

"Why don't you just ask him?"

"You know he's barely talked to me since he caught me using that calculator for Math 55 when they last visited. You know how he is."

Laid out on the couch in our living room, legs crossed, I was trying to finish my homework before my parents arrived. My dad called an hour ago, because he doesn't text, and before I could complete the last problem, my parents walked in the door I had left unlocked for them.

"Hi, my Sugar-" My father paused when he saw the calculator and puzzled, asked, "Wait, what is this?" He grabbed my mother's hand. "I have no daughter!" he yelled, giving me a look of disappointment, before storming out of our apartment, slamming the door shut behind him.

"Yeah, well at least your mom's sweet," Court says. The bus stops and I can see half of a comic book store and half of a coffee shop through the window. A pregnant, pale-skinned lady in her 30s gets on the bus and reaching up to grab the yellow strap above her, she stands next to us. "I remember when I first met her. Awwww, so long ago," Court says, staring ahead, and I look back out the window at the stores flashing by, recalling the first time Court met my mom.

It was freshman year, and Court was sleeping over. Already in our pajamas, we were sitting on my floor, playing Truth or Dare. We'd been playing for the last twenty minutes, but I'd chosen "dare" every time, because I hadn't done anything interesting in my life, much less anything with a boy, and I didn't want to be embarrassed about having nothing exciting to divulge.

"Hi girls. Dinner will be ready soon," my mom said, opening the door to my bedroom, peeking her head inside. "What are you girls doing?" she asked.

"Playing Truth or Dare, Mom. Want to play?" We both pleaded for her to play and after she said yes, Court and I explained the rules to her.

"Okay, truth or dare?" I asked.

"Truth."

Court looked around my room for a moment, then asked my mom, who I'm named after, "Miss Ling-Ling-" Pausing, she glanced under the bed quickly for her dog she brought with her. "Have you seen my puppy, Max?"

"Dare!" My mom yelled, changing her selection.

"Weird how I never found that dog. It just ran away, I guess," Court says, staring blankly ahead. The bus hits a speedbump, creating a new, blue scribble on the back of the girl's neck.

When our stop comes and we get up, the pregnant lady lets out a "Hmph" as she lets go of the strap. "How fucking rude," she says, loud enough for everyone close to hear.

Court turns around. "Fuck you, lady. You stood for, like, thirty seconds. We knew we were getting up soon. Nobody told you to fuck the guy with no car." A look of absolute shock comes over the lady's face as her jaw drops, and two young girls, wearing red and white jerseys with the numbers 5 and 22 on them seated behind her, burst out in laughter and start clapping. An old woman, wearing a dark brown furry hat with a bird on it, cracks a smile as we pass by; and when we hop off the bus, onto the sidewalk, Court looks to her left, says, "I wonder if she's already here," and then to her right. "I bet she is."

Looking over the green hedges that separate the outside dining area of the restaurant from the street, Court glances towards the tables with white cloths draped on them that are lined up in rows of four on either side of the walkway. All of the tables have umbrellas on them, and some of them are open, but most are not, and even though it's difficult to see the people who have their umbrellas down, we can tell the Grandma's not in there. At a table close to the hedges, an older, pretty, heavyset woman in her 50s squeals with delight after pulling some earrings out of a box. The bald man across the table from her pushes his large frame out of the chair, walks over and hugs her.

"Oh, never mind. She's here," Court says, getting my attention, pointing at a black Bentley, parked behind two motorcycles at the end of the street.

"I thought she had a Panamera," I say.

"No, she- Jesus!" Court yells.

"What?"

"License plate!"

I look down at the plate on the back of the car. It reads, "L8 4ANAL."

"Oh my God!" I shout. "That is-" Before I can get out anything else, we hear the Grandma's voice, and both of us quickly turn our heads.

"Girls, girls!" she shouts, waving her arm in the air. In her late 60s, the Grandma is small and cute with short, white hair. Her long, gold earrings are shaking back and forth as she walks towards us, and I can tell by the design on her matching pink sweater and skirt that she's wearing Lily Pulitzer.

"Oh, sweet, another boytoy," Court whispers.

A dark-skinned man in his 30s, with shoulder-length black hair is holding the Grandma's purse. He's wearing black pants, a blue, button-down shirt, and I can tell he's in excellent shape.

Court puts both arms out, taking in the Grandma and they hug, each of them moving left and right slightly, over and over for a moment. The Grandma lets go and looks Court up and down. "You look so beautiful, sweetie." She turns to me, says, "Both of you girls do" and opens her arms. "Come here, Ling-Ling." I give her a hug, and she feels good. I gladly give in, until she stops rocking me back and forth and let's go.

"You two look like twins!" she tells us. "Aren't those the dresses you girls got in Mauritius?" She paid for both of us to go on the trip, and the night we bought the dresses, we wore them out to dinner, sending her several pics and videos of us dancing and walking around drunk, thanking her for the vacation.

I loved the Grandma. She raised Court on her own after Court's parents had died. Court had told me many stories of their electricity being cut off, about cold winters and eating mustard sandwiches for dinner on a nightly basis. They only survived because Court had an unusually high number of "uncles" who would come by and visit the Grandma, stay for an hour or so, leave money and then go. One of the uncles was really rich, and when Court was in the seventh grade, he died, leaving the Grandma multiple properties and one hundred million dollars.

The Grandma adjusts the Rolex that's loose on her arm, sliding it down to her wrist, so that it hangs over her hand, then introduces us. "Girls, this is Julio; Julio, the girls." We wave, and I notice he's really quite handsome when he brushes his hair out of the way.

"Hola," he says, firmly squeezing the Grandma's hip.

She says something to him I only understand twenty percent of, pats him on the butt lightly, and he kisses the Grandma on the cheek, hands her the pink purse, then smiles and nods at Court and me before walking past us. "Let's go, girls," the Grandma says, putting her arms around both our waists, and we walk under the ivy-covered entryway into the restaurant.

We sit down and when the young, good-looking waiter comes over, the Grandma politely asks him if he can put up our umbrella. She winks at him afterward, and when he's done putting it up, she gives him $20 and tells him, "Can you be a dear and get us three bottled waters, please."

Surprised by the early tip, he partially lowers his head, says, "Yes, ma'am," and hurriedly walks away.

When he leaves, the Grandma keeps watching him, and picking up the white napkin in front of the Grandma, Court tosses it on her pink skirt. "Grandma, don't hit on the waiter, please," she says.

"Settle down, sweetie," she tells Court, turning her attention back to us. "Now what have you girls been up to? Been busy?"

Court tells her about last night and Harry going home with someone else, and the Grandma says merely, "Boys will be boys," while picking up the napkin Court threw at her. She flicks it in the air, spreading it out, and lays it down on her lap evenly. Not enthused by the response, Court starts to complain, until the Grandma interrupts and asks, "And what did you end up doing at the end of last night?" Nothing but silence. "Mmhmm, I thought so," she says, leaning back in her chair.

Maybe to be funny or perhaps to see if she can get somewhat of a rise out of the Grandma, because of her response about Harry, Court starts telling her about our morning and how she pulled a muscle masturbating.

"Nothing wrong with that, Sweetie," the Grandma says, indifferent to the topic of conversation. "I've pulled a lot of muscles doing stuff like that. Just make sure you try and stretch every day, so that you stay limber and flexible, no matter what you do."

"Grandma!"

"And breathe while you stretch." She points her finger at Court, shakes it. "It's not good to hold your breath."

The waiter brings our waters quickly, gives us our menus and wiping his hands on his dark pants, asks us if we need anything else. The Grandma says no; he glances at us, we shake our heads, and he looks back at her, stands there for a moment before saying anything, maybe expecting another tip. "Um, okay. I'll give you ladies a moment." When he walks away, the Grandma checks him out again, her eyes glancing down, and she nods her head, mutters something to herself, then looks at the menu. At the table behind Court, is a Hispanic couple in their late 20s. Their umbrella is up, and they're facing each other, but both of them have been looking at their phones since we sat down, neither of them saying a word. Court and the Grandma are both checking out their menus, and before I look at mine, I decide I'm just going to have an appetizer and salad.

"So how were final exams, girls?" the Grandma asks, adjusting her watch. Once I'm done telling her that everything went well and that I'm pleased with my grades, Court starts to make up things, joke with her, something she loves to do.

Court says most of her finals were not difficult, but she thinks she performed terribly on her last exam, explaining how hard she studied and prepared, although she doesn't think it mattered, and the Grandma looking concerned, starts rubbing Court's hand. When Court tells her, "Yeah, grandma. I walked in there, and everyone was using a ruler, and I don't know why!" she does an excellent job of selling the story.

I know Court wants to keep it going, but I can't help it, and I start giggling, and the Grandma lightly slaps Court's arm, tells her what she always does when Court jokes with her about grades. "You shouldn't tease me like that about school."

"What are you getting, grandma?" Court asks, looking at her menu again, and when I see the back of hers, I flip mine around and take a look, even though I already know what I'm going to order.

"I don't know," the Grandma says, propping her menu up, holding it at the bottom, scanning it up and down. She turns it around, looks at the back, but only briefly, then ask us what we're going to have.

After telling her, I'm ordering calamari and a salad; the Grandma says calamari sounds excellent, and she'll get that too, and Court says, "I think I'm going to have a burger and fries.".

I stop reading the French translations of the entrees on the back and give Court an odd look. "You never get that."

"I know. I just feel like a burger," she says. "I don't know why. You know I only get one, like, twice a year. I guess this is one of those times." Holding her menu out flat, she drops it on the table.

"I think I might ask him about the specials," the Grandma tells us.

Frustrated, Court asks, "Grandma, why? You always ask, and you never get any of the specials."

Paying no mind to Court, the Grandma motions to our waiter, who's standing and talking with a group of other waiters, under the shade of the canopy at the bar. They all have their arms lowered in front of them, one hand over the other, and when he notices her, he jogs the first few steps, then quickly walks the rest. "What are your specials, dear?" she asks.

"Um." Hesitating for a moment, he looks up and to his left. He starts to describe a fish entrée, and I glance over at Court, who's looking at the older couple we saw earlier before we walked in. The man is now sitting next to the woman, and she is thrilled, modeling her new earrings for him. Court lightly kicks me, then takes her finger and starts moving it in and out of a small circle she's made with her other hand, while pushing her tongue to the side of her mouth. I kick her back, slightly harder than she kicked me, and she stops, makes a face at me, and the Grandma glances at Court, but doesn't say anything, then looks back at the waiter. He can only remember one of the specials, the fish one I just heard part of and apologizing to the Grandma, he reaches into his left pocket.

"That's okay, dear. Take your time," the Grandma tells him.

After fumbling in his left for a second, the waiter worriedly reaches into his right pocket. Relieved, he pulls out a yellow piece of subject paper and unfolds it. He reads the rest of the specials, enunciating certain ingredients and foods with more emphasis, using his hands, either because he thought this would be a good idea or because this is something management told him to do.

"I need a second," the Grandma tells him. "What do you girls want?" she asks, picking up her menu again, holding it close to her face, her gold Rolex sliding down her forearm.

He looks at Court first, and she asks him to describe the colors of medium and medium-rare in their hamburgers. Putting his finger up, he reaches into his back pocket and excitedly says, "We actually have a chart."

"I think I'll just get a salad," the Grandma says, after we order, pointing at what she wants on the menu, and leaning down, the waiter writes on his pad while nodding. Noticing that she showed him the third salad down, but not being able to read her menu, I find what she ordered on mine, then recall her saying something about wanting calamari.

"What about calamari?!" For some reason, I mention this loud and quickly, looking over at her, then up at the waiter, fast, as if I'm going to miss him and if I do there will be no chance to place an additional order.

Jumping a little in her seat, the Grandma exclaims, "Oh, that's right!" She looks up. "Calamari, please."

"Good thing you asked to hear the specials, grandma. I knew you weren't going to get anything," Court says after he leaves.

"I just wanted to see, sweetie." She pushes her watch down. "You never know." Court sticks out her two front teeth, crosses her eyes. "How old are you?" the Grandma asks.

"Five," I answer, and I proceed to tell her about the pills I found prior to coming here, and Court keeps the same face, occasionally tilting her head to the right and left while I talk.

"That sounds like my granddaughter," the Grandma says, and Court makes another silly face, then another, and the Grandma can't help but giggle, afterwards asking, "So how are the job interviews going, girls?"

I let her know that my applications for a hospital internship have been going pretty well, that I have a couple of interviews coming up, and Court tells her about the interviews she's been on, the numerous jobs she's applied for, the countless applications she's filled out, and the Grandma, attentive, nods and listens the whole time. "Grandma, you won't believe how many companies don't even bother to get back to me, and if they do, most of them address me, 'Dear applicant,' and then tell me how although I have great talent and experience, they've decided to go in another direction. If I can take the time to fill out an application and interview, they at least could take the time to-" Ranting and starting to talk faster, Court suddenly stops, slides her hand towards the Grandma. "LL actually told me about a great opportunity, but I can't seem to get in touch with anyone in the company." She lifts her hand up, slaps the table, slides it back, and puts it in her lap while resting back in her chair.

"Well that's odd," the Grandma says, looking at me, and I have no idea what Court's talking about, because I've never mentioned any job possibility to her.

After waiting a moment, Court says, "Yeah, it's with Redbox." She nods her head up and down. "I want to work in one of the machines, you know, handing out movies and video games." She pauses, takes a deep sigh. "But every time I go to one of the red boxes and knock, no one answers." Throwing her hands up, she finishes with, "I've tried several of them." She can barely get out the last sentence, because she starts laughing, and I throw my napkin at her and the Grandma just shakes her head.

"Where do you come up with this stuff?" the Grandma asks.

"I saw something like it on a meme," Court tells her. I glance past her at the couple again, who have been eating for the past few minutes, neither of them on their phones, both looking around the restaurant while they chew, not talking between bites.

"What's that?"

Court and I try to explain it to her, both of us giving various examples, going so far as to read the definition from Court's phone; but she still doesn't get it, so we scoot our chairs closer to hers, and Court opens up "@9gag" on Instagram. We show her a few, and the Grandma doesn't understand some, but she likes most of them, especially the ones with animals.

The waiter comes over to drop off some bread, the Grandma orders a double Johnny Walker Blue, neat, and Court pushes the basket to the edge of the table, opposite the Grandma, since none of us plan on eating any. He comes back soon and not wanting to bother us, he lays the drink on the table without saying anything, walking away just before we start laughing at a video of a cat freaking out because he's seen a snake. The Grandma takes quite a large sip of her Blue Label between that video and the next one, and Court mentions two interviews that she has this week, one of which the company is flying her out for. The Grandma asks if they're paying for meals and lodging and other things. Court says yes, and the Grandma tells her she needs to keep up with all her receipts, that it's best to pay for everything with her debit or credit card, not cash, because, "that will leave a trail, just in case".

Balancing some of the plates on his forearm, the waiter sets them on the table, close to each other, because Court and I haven't moved our chairs back. He clasps his hands, looks at the Grandma and asks, "Do you ladies require anything else?" For some reason, his use of the word "require" seems odd to me, but I quickly forget about it and focus on my food, lifting one of the little monsters with tiny arms off my plate, dipping it in the sweet chili sauce.

The Grandma throws back the rest of her drink and hands him the empty glass. "Yes, dear. Another double." After he leaves, she motions her fork towards Court's phone, says, "Show me some more, sweety," then towards her napkin. "And put that on your lap, please." Court rolls her eyes but obliges both requests, and after finding another video, she props her phone on the umbrella stand in the middle of the table.

Holding it with both hands, Court takes a bite out of her burger, the ketchup and some other sauce squeezing out from between the bun and meat, onto her fingers. "Mmmm, this is good," she says, with a full mouth. I look at the burger, wanting a bite, and she can tell that I do so she stands up and leans forward, holding it out, still using both hands.

"Mmmmm. That is good," I tell Court, sitting back down, glancing at my food. Still happy with my choices, despite how good her burger was, I grab one of my circles, saving the rest of the little monsters until the end.

Court asks the Grandma if she wants a bite. "No, thank you, sweety," she says, cutting her salad neatly. She takes small bites, with sips of scotch in-between, her calamari sitting untouched. "You know, I remember my first job," she says, setting her knife down on her plate gently, without making a sound. "I was young, not quite sure what grade it was, sometime in high school." She brings her drink to her lips again, glances at the couple that's barely said a word to each other during their short meal.

They're leaving, him pointing at the entryway, muttering something, and she nods her head, then rolls her eyes when he turns around. The Grandma explains how she came home one day from school, and her father found money in her backpack. "'Where did you get this from?' he asked, holding the crumpled up, money in his fist out in front of me," she tells us, holding her hand out, squeezing her fist. She takes a swallow. "So, I told him that Tommy, a boy in school, wanted to kiss me."

"'Yeah, go on,' he said."

"So, I described to him, how I told Tommy it would cost 25 cents." She sets her hand on the table. "Now girls, he started getting hotheaded at this point, clenching the money tighter, his eyes narrowing." She sets the glass down next to her calamari and picks up a ring, pops it in her mouth. Court and I continue eating, stealing fries and calamari off of each other's plates, waiting for the Grandma to finish the rest of her story. "And then I told him that more boys wanted to kiss me, so I charged them 25 cents, too." Both of us stop chewing, look at each other, then slowly turn our heads towards the Grandma.

With some lettuce hanging out of her mouth and a bit of ketchup on her lip, Court asks, "How much was in the backpack?"

"About fifty dollars."

"Grandma!" Court shouts, spitting out some of her burger, and I can't believe what I just heard, but it doesn't hinder my eating, because my calamari is really good and it's rare to get really good calamari. "What the fuck, grandma!" Court yells.

"Miss Courtney! Watch your language." The Grandma doesn't care for cussing, and Court knows this, so she apologizes, then finishes what's in her mouth. The Grandma looks at me, winks, then motioning to my almost finished plate asks, "Did you like it, sweetie?"

Nodding my head, I tell her, "Here, try this." For some reason, her sauce is different and when she tries mine, she loves it, so I set it in between us and we share.

Court grabs two crispy, skinny fries from her plate and dips them in her ketchup. She doesn't particularly like fat or soft fries, so she's put those in a pile, on the other side of her kosher dill pickle that I know she won't touch. "So, grandma." She picks up a fry, inspects it, eats it. "Where did you meet, Julio?"

Motioning her fork to Court, she says, "Firstly, cover your mouth, sweetie." Another waiter sits a couple down, two tables over from us. The young, red-haired lady, wheels a stroller next to her chair and sits down. She puts her finger to her lips, quieting her husband, who's talking loudly, and I turn back to the Grandma. "I met Julio on my spiritual trip to Asia, at a yoga colony we were both visiting." She takes a sip and then, per my suggestion, after dipping it in my sauce, eats one of her little monsters. Once she wipes the corner of her mouth, she tells us, "But he's not my first, Latino. I've slept with a Brazilian."

"How many, grandma?" Court asks jokingly. All three of us giggle, Court starts to choke and the Grandma reaches over, pats her on the back, tells her to drink some water.

The waiter must have noticed because he comes running over from the flock of other waiters, all of them still huddled in the shade, holding the same pose as before; and concerned, he asks, "Are you okay?" With tears running down her cheeks and her hand resting on her throat, Court waves him off.

The Grandma touches the waiter's hand. "Everything is okay, dear. Could you please bring us two more bottled waters and another one of these for me?" she asks, shaking her almost, empty glass.

"Another double?"

She moves her hand to his hip, pats it a couple of times. "Yes, dear."

The Grandma lightly taps Court's back again, unnecessarily, and Court says she's fine and leaning forward, takes another bite of her burger and looks up at us. "Mmmmmmm, so good."

None of us have been paying much attention to the videos playing on Court's phone, so the Grandma asks her to turn it off, and when the waiter comes back, she finishes what's left in her glass. Resting her hand in his for a few moments, then pulling him towards her, somewhat, she tells him, "Thank you, dear."

When we're almost done eating, three old ladies who know the Grandma stop at our table. They're all wearing one-piece dresses that look like they're made out of old couch material, with ugly colors like drab brown, rust, and light olive. Only one of them speaks, the taller of the three. She has a large, protruding nose, skinny face, and she's not really polite, nor friendly, and I wonder why they stopped at all. Birdy McBird face - I've named her this, because her facial structure and bad makeup remind me of the California Condor - asks the Grandma about her trip. While the Grandma talks, Birdy throws in a few comments that don't surprise me, based on what I've seen so far. "Oh, I would have chosen a more exotic location. I guess that trip is okay for your type," she says, finally ending with, "It must be nice to have had a sugar daddy leave you all that money." The fat one giggles, reaches behind Birdy McBird face, tapping the other one; and when she laughs too, the fat one reacts like she's having a gelastic seizure for a moment, her stomach jiggling in her too-tight dress, making her look like a ten-pound sausage in a five-pound wrapper. I've named her Marin.

Unfazed, the Grandma looks them over and unconcerned, she leans back in her chair, takes a sip. "Oh, honey, you're just so upset because the best you can do is an artificial sweetener daddy." Motioning her hand to dismiss them, she says, "Now be a dear, take your stooges with you, and move the fuck along, Ruthie."

Court makes a fist, bites it, and says, "Fuck" loud enough so that everyone can hear it.

Marin stops laughing, her stomach stops jiggling, and the other one looks down at her purse. In a state of shock, Birdy backs up a couple of steps, says, "I, I-..." Looking absolutely defeated, she turns, and all three of them shuffle to the exit.

Court pulls the Grandma in, hugs her tight, telling her, "Grandma, you fucking rock."

"I know," she says, smiling, lying back in her chair again, not bothering to watch the trio leave. "And watch your language, sweetie."

"But grandma, you just-"

"Sweetie, do as I say, not-"

"As you do. Yeah, yeah, I know," Court says. The Grandma pulls a small, orange bottle out of her pink purse, flips off the lid and turns it over, tapping it on the side. A huge, white pill that looks like it's meant for a horse spills out into her hand. "Jesus, grandma. Is that meant for a person?!" Court asks.

The Grandma puts the large pill in her mouth, takes a taste of her Johnny Walker, jerks her head back swiftly, then tells Court, "It's just for a little something I picked up in Asia."

"Spiritual journey, huh?" Courts says.

She takes another drink. "Mmhmm."

I finish my calamari but not my salad, and Court eats her entire burger and all of the fries that meet her requirements, along with more than half of the Grandma's calamari. "Ohhhh, I'm full," Court complains, laying back in her chair, sticking her stomach out, cradling it with both hands.

The waiter looks down when he comes over, surveying the table, most of the plates empty, and says, "You ladies must have been hungry." He looks like he regrets saying it this way, but he relaxes when the Grandma tells him we were, and Court makes him aware of just how much she enjoyed the burger.

"Fantastic," she tells him, slowly lifting one of her hands off her belly, giving him a 'thumbs up.'

"Can I get you ladies anything else?"

Looking at us, the Grandma asks, "Do you girls want anything?" I ask him what they have, and he reaches into the correct pocket this time, reading the desserts off of the same type of yellow subject paper. Court decides she's not that full, and we choose to split a piece of chocolate cake and some vanilla bean ice cream. "No dessert for me, thank you, but I'll take another one of these," the Grandma tells him, lifting her glass a little. "And a piece of paper and pen, please."

"Certainly," he says, nodding his head, stuffing the yellow piece of paper back into his pocket. Pulling out the same notepad he used to take our previous orders, he rips off a sheet, gives it and a red pen to the Grandma and tells us, "I'll be right back, ladies."

Court giggles a little, and after he turns and leaves, she says, "You're giving him your phone number, aren't you?"

The Grandma doesn't look up from writing, and I glance at the piece of paper, recognizing the number instantly. "Yep," she answers. Her handwriting is immaculate. All of the neatly written numbers and letters seem to match each other in size and width perfectly, like they were produced by a machine, the bottom, and top of each one even, as if someone had used a ruler to stop any unrequired follow through on the lettering. Anything she's ever written to Court or me has looked this way: birthday cards, notes, letters, everything. It's the most, pristine and dexterous handwriting I've ever seen. Court says it's from when the Grandma was in the hospital at a young age due to a type of pneumonia that developed into arthritis. She would sit in her hospital bed, practicing her writing for hours a day, in between physical therapy sessions and other mandatory appointments. Court had saved everything the Grandma had ever written her: mailed letters, short memos, even post-it notes, from when Court was a child, with instructions on them explaining how to cook a dinner that had been left in the fridge. She keeps them in large, sealable plastic bags in her lower, left dresser drawer, along with her extra blanket and slippers she wears during the winter time.

Court and I get excited when we see the waiter with two orders of dessert instead of one, and we both start clapping, impatiently waiting for him to set the plates down. He barely gets his hand away before Court takes a huge bite of her cake. "Thank you," she says, her words scarcely understandable, her teeth caked with chocolate.

He gives her an odd look, says, "No problem," and I thank him while grabbing my spoon. I lop off a piece of cake, dip it in my ice cream, and stuff both in my mouth.

The Grandma hands him the piece of paper, along with a folded $100 bill. "Thank you. We won't be ordering anything else. Can you please bring us the check?" She tilts her head a little to the side, squinting her eyes at the sunlight that's made its way around the umbrella.

"Absolutely," he responds, grinning widely, and I wonder if she's the biggest tipper he's ever had. "Certainly, for the amount of work he's done," I think to myself, engulfing another mix of cake and vanilla bean. "I'll bring it over to you as soon as you're done," he tells her.

The Grandma lightly grabs him by his wrist. "I would like the check now, please," she says, politely. Tilting towards him, she tightens her grip and he crouches down, leans in, and the Grandma explains to him that she likes to have everything taken care of so that when she's done and wants to go, she can just leave when "it is fine by her". This is a phrase she loves to use. Anytime that Court asks her for anything, or we tell the Grandma where we want to meet her, she always says, "That will be fine by me."

He puts his hand over hers. "I wouldn't make you wait on anything."

"We'll see," she says, glancing at his hand that's holding her phone number.

Leaning down closer, in an intimate, softer tone, he says, "Anything." Court and my eyes widen, we give each other a look, and I wonder if they're going to make out right here.

He comes back with the check in less than a minute, and the Grandma scans it, places a few hundred dollar bills in the black check holder, then hands it back to him. "Thank you again, dear."

"Change?" he asks.

She shakes her head, and after he says thank you, the Grandma takes a nip, tells him, "Thank me later." He blushes, grins, starts to slowly lean down.

"Grandma!" Court shouts. Stopping, he jumps back quickly and acknowledging us, nods his head.

"Thank you, ladies." He glances back at the Grandma, and his smile gets faintly bigger as he backs a couple of steps up. "Enjoy your day, ladies," he says, with a slight bow.

"Playa," I say, sticking my hand out, and the Grandma slaps it, takes a swig.

Joking, Court snaps at me. "Don't encourage her!"

While we wait for the Grandma to finish her drink, she nonchalantly asks us how our sex life is going. I don't say anything because I don't have any kind of sex life, never have, and after looking around the mostly empty restaurant, then back at the Grandma, Court says a little too loud, "I'm not talking to you about my sex life! You know that!" The couple with the baby, who were quietly talking to each other, glance at our table.

The Grandma takes her last gulp, wipes her hands, then folds the napkin and sets it next to the unused soup spoon the waiter forgot to take away. "You see those lovely women over there," she says, pointing over my shoulder. I turn around and notice two women, older than her, both wearing dark-colored sweaters and light jackets. Sipping on tea, with pens in their hands, they're working on puzzles in small, paperback books, and the Grandma says, "Even they've choked on a dick at some point in their lives."

"Jesus, grandma," Court says, swiping her finger through some chocolate on her plate, licking it.

The Grandma slides her chair back, gets up. "Sweetie, don't tell me you're one of those people that can't even buy a dildo in a store." She pats Court on the shoulder a couple of times while walking behind her. "Just ask them for a card, too, and tell them it's a gift."

Court stomps her foot on the ground, twice, but the Grandma doesn't see because she's busy waving hello to the older ladies, and Court shouts out, "I have plenty of dildos and vibrators, and I bought them all on my own!"

When we get to the sidewalk, I look down the street so I can see the Grandma's license plate again, just for a laugh, but it's not there and neither are the motorcycles that were parked in front of it. "Oh, there he is," the Grandma says, pointing in the other direction. Julio climbs out of the Bentley, starts walking towards us; but when she puts her hand up, he stops, smiles, then waves and leans against the hood, crossing his arms.

"Why don't you have a front license plate?" I ask, disappointed at not getting to see "L8 4ANAL" again, instantly realizing it must seem like a really odd question.

"I just don't like the way they look," she says. "Besides, you don't put a front license plate on a car like that."

"Do you ever get pulled over for it?"

"Yes, but I get out of it every time," she tells me.

"Of course you do," Court says, extending her arms, walking towards her. Hugging the Grandma, she closes her eyes, squeezes tightly, and lets out a groan. "I love you so much, grandma."

"Ugh, I love you too, sweetie," the Grandma says, rubbing Court's back for a bit, eventually tapping her a couple of times. "Not so tight, sweetie." Court lets go and pulls back, wiping her red, teary eyes. She sniffles a couple of times, rubs her nose, and concerned, the Grandma asks, "Oh sweetie, is anything wrong?"

"No, no-" Court pauses. "I...I just love you so much." She wipes her nose, her face, hard, and starts to cry a little while laughing at the same time, something she does every now and then whenever she says goodbye to the Grandma.

"Oh, I know you do, sweetie," the Grandma tells her, motioning for Court. "Come here, come here, I know you do." Court buries her head in the Grandma's chest, and somehow she looks smaller in comparison while the Grandma gently rocks her back and forth, rubbing and patting her back. I've never seen Court get emotional or cry about anything except the Grandma – not Harry, certainly not any other boy, no silliness back in high school, not grades, nothing, just the Grandma. When Court pulls back, she seems better. Smiling and giggling, she apologizes. "Don't you ever apologize to me for something like that. You are my whole world," the Grandma says, squeezing both of Court's arms.

The Grandma motions for me, and after I get my hug and kiss her on the cheek, I whisper into her ear, "You both are so lucky."

She smiles and gripping my hand tighter, mouths, "Thank you."

"Do you girls need any money?" she asks, flipping up the gold latch on her pink purse, pulling out a small wallet with cherry blossoms on in it. We both say no, but she waves us off, then thumbs through the wad of bills, handing me two hundred dollars and Court, four.

Court hugs her; I give her another one, too, and Court embraces her once more, fast, because she has to have the last one. I antagonize her by grabbing the Grandma again, like I always do, and for the next minute we go back and forth, and the Grandma plays along, like she always does, giggling and saying, "Now, now, girls," and we both end up holding onto her, not wanting to let go.

"You let go."

"No, you."

"Excuse me." We look over and not far from us, two guys with over-gelled, blonde hair, maybe in their late 20s, are standing in the street. The taller of the two, who's wearing a dark shirt with some sort of speckled design that looks like a small dragon, gives us a peculiar stare before looking at Court and asking, "Can you tell me how to get to 402 Horizon Drive?" He smiles, puts one of his square-toed boots up on the curb. Court says she doesn't know, and he raises his eyebrows, asks her for her name and phone number. His friend, who's wearing a grey shirt with a skull and tribal designs on it, hits him on the arm, looks at me and grins; but I keep my neutral expression, my head still resting on the Grandma's shoulder, and I wonder what type of grown men would wear fucking shirts like that.

Annoyed, Court tells him she's not interested. "Dude, look at your shirt."

He looks down, then over at his friend and snaps back at Court. "Yeah, well you look like the type of girl who would eat an entire roll of cookie dough in one sitting!" His friend hits him on the arm, just like before, making both of them look like even bigger assclowns, and the Grandma pats our backs, puts her arms in front of us, and steps forward.

"Hmph, that's funny, because I was just thinking that you look like the type of guy that would cum in his pants before any girl could take hers off." She flicks him off. "Now fuck off, son."

"What-" He pauses for a moment, looks at her outstretched, middle finger, then back at her. "What the fuck did you say, old lady?" he says, stepping onto the curb. "Wanna make something of it?"

After putting her hand down, the Grandma calmly says, "Oh, no, no, no, I never get physical. I just get upset. And when I get upset." She gives a short chuckle, slowly turns and motions down the street, to Julio. "He gets physical."

Julio is no longer resting against the car. Unbuttoning his sleeves as he walks towards us, he pushes them up his muscular arms, balls up his fists, tilts his head to the left, then right, and without running, picks up his pace. Worriedly glaring at Julio, the two guys start to back up, and the taller one that was threatening the Grandma, puts his hands out, telling her, "I'm sorry, ma'am."

"Fuck off, junior," she says, flicking him off again, and they sprint off, both of them almost running into the back of a white car they must have forgotten was behind them. We watch until they make a quick left at the corner and disappear. When Julio calmly approaches us, he's already buttoned his sleeves, and he grabs the Grandma's purse while taking her by the arm.

With her other arm, she hugs me first, telling me, "You know you have to let her go last."

Court sticks her tongue out at me, then gets her last hug from the Grandma. "What's it like having such a good-looking grandchild?" Court asks, letting go.

"Oh sweetie, I wouldn't know. You'd have to ask your great-great grandmother."

"Boom!" I shout.

Julio smiles and nods but doesn't say anything, and turning around, the Grandma says, "Now remember what I always say, girls."

At the same time, both of us say, "We know. Good sex sounds like running in flip flops."

The Grandma shakes her finger in the air, says, "That's right, that's right." They get in the car, Julio looks over his shoulder, backs up into a short driveway, and when they pull off we see the Grandma's head move down, towards his lap, through the rear window.

Instead of the bus, we decide to walk home, holding hands part of the way, sharing stories of the Grandma. Usually when we go through this area, one of us will see something in a store that catches our attention, or we will stop to "look around," but we just enjoy the beautiful day and each other, adding to one another's stories, "people watching" while we stroll.

We get to our building, and Court walks to the end of the rows of mailboxes, stopping next to the bulletin board with different colors and sizes of paper on it, advertising various things: items for sale, people needing rides, roommates. I pull out my phone to text Justin while she opens our box and thumbs through our mail. "Most people die at 25," she says.

I look up at her, smile, and finish one of the Grandma's favorite quotes. "And aren't buried until they're 75."

Harry

We've been watching a documentary for the last hour about a group of young, new, female pornstars who are living in a house together, outside of Los Angeles. We've seen it before, but it came on after we watched *Pineapple Express*, and since the controller is dead, and all of us are too lazy and too stoned to get up, it continues to play. One of the girls, a petite, skinny brunette, is getting ready to go to her first boy/girl shoot.

She's been talking non-stop for the last ten minutes about how nervous she is and she's not sure if she can go through with it and she might not do it; and Trent, irritated because he hasn't seen more action, says, "Why is it that a chick can talk for three straight hours, but two minutes into a blowjob and her jaw starts to hurt?"

None of us have changed our clothes or bothered to move the empty plates and glasses from the table. I'm wearing only my boxers, sitting on the floor, the dead controller in my lap; and Jus is laying on the couch, behind me, texting Ling-Ling, not paying attention to the girl on the TV who's now giving an awkward blowjob to a fat, old guy with spots on his balding head.

Trent had just finished trying to get out of cleaning the apartment twenty minutes ago, saying, "Technically you guys said I would get pissed on, but since I left early and just got laid, I won." He argued a little more, pleading his case, and we even ran a mock trial with Justin and Clarence as the attorneys, and me, the judge.

When I had Trent raise his right hand, and I said, "Anything you say can and will be held against you," his only response was, "Titties," and Clarence, nodding his head, said, "Damn, he's good."

Eventually Jus ended the trial, winning with his closing statement when he yelled, "No, no, no. The fact that he snuck out and lied to us shows he knew he was in the wrong!"

Before that, we smoked what Trent had left of the weed he scored from Schroeder, that he most likely didn't pay for, and all of us ended up talking about trying to jerk off with our left hand, probably because this documentary had started. Everyone admitted to attempting it and not being able to get used to it. "Felt like I had Parkinson's," Jus said.

We hadn't talked about Clarence's job, my departure tomorrow, or Jus' leaving for his internship. I think we'd all done it on purpose, not because we would get particularly sad talking about separating and our new lives - well, maybe Jus, but because we just wanted to enjoy today as if it were any regular Saturday, not thinking about our inevitable separation, nor "right now" being a memory we talked about in the future.

I turn my head, look back when I hear our doorbell ring, and all of us point at each other, none of us wanting to get up.

Typing, Jus digs himself into the couch. "I'm definitely not getting up," he says.

We hear a knock on the door, and the bell rings again. A voice from the other side yells, "Delivery."

"Who's it for?" I shout back, craning my neck.

"Uh." There's a pause. "Clarence."

"Sweet!" Clarence says, pushing Trent's feet off himself. Trent had set them on Clarence's lap after saying, "Titties" during our mock trial, while smugly lying back on the couch, pleased with his quick response.

Jus stops texting, puts his phone down to watch the action, and getting up off of the floor, I sit next to him on the couch. The guy in the yellow and white uniform is holding his hand to his mouth, laughing when Clarence opens the door. "So, uh, you're Clarence?" he asks.

"Yep, what you got for me?" Clarence takes the clipboard, signs it, and gives it back to the guy, who's still chuckling.

He looks into the room at all three of us, then back at Clarence. "Oh, I get it," he says, nodding his head up and down, glancing back at me with no shirt on. Reaching down to the floor, he picks up a package, then hands it to Clarence. Looking at the outside packaging, Clarence turns it around, all of three of us start laughing and the delivery guy finally gets what's going on. "Ahhhh!" he says, putting his finger up, but he disappears when Clarence shuts the door.

Still holding it up, he turns to us. "Motherfuckers." When he walks over, Jus takes a few pics of him holding his "Congratulations" package, and Trent and I jump in the last photo. We push the plates and drinks out of the way so Clarence can set it down, and the three of us sit on the couch, watching, waiting.

It's addressed to: Clarence "Lieutenant Fuzz," and in big, red letters in all-caps; on the top of the package, it reads, "CONGRATULATIONS!! YOUR GAY TIMES SUBSCRIPTION HAS ARRIVED!!!" Clarence holds the top of the package out so that Jus can get a pic, and then he twirls it around, showing the different pictures taped to the sides with men in leather bondage gear, a few chained up, gags in some of their mouths. "Show us the bottom," Jus says, getting his phone ready. "DELICATE GLASS DILDO PACKAGE" is on a yellow bumper sticker, stuck next to a naked dude wearing a pig mask. "I had that made from some old guy who has a shop near Bull Branch," Jus proudly claims, sticking his chest out.

Trent grabs his half-full glass of Sunny D, drinks the rest and says, "Hey, do you guys remember that guy who would come into Bull Branch, and the bartenders, Leah and Sam, would always yell out his name as soon as he walked in the door, but put 'slutty' in front of it, because he always went home with someone?" He says he can't remember the guy's name, and neither can any of us, even though all three of us know who he's talking about.

Mimicking Leah and Sam, I say, "Hey! Slutty-... slutty-... hey-..." trying to fill in the blank, to jog my memory, or theirs, but it doesn't happen and we forget about it.

Clarence tears apart the top and starts pulling items out: a pair of pink, velvet handcuffs, some cheap, pleather boots, a one-piece cop outfit meant for a woman, regular handcuffs, lotion, a rainbow-colored wig, a fake badge and gun, a donut, and other various cop-sex-themed items. He holds up the donut and takes a bite while Jus takes another pic. Snatching up the pink handcuffs, Trent says, "Gross, you don't know how old that thing is, man."

Jus tells him that he got it two days ago and reminds him, "You were with me, dumbass."

"Oh yeah, that's right," Trent says, twirling the handcuffs. He reaches up towards Clarence, accepts a small piece of the old-fashioned donut and eats it.

"Guys, thanks, this is fucking great!" Clarence tells us. He gives us all quick hugs; we start picking through things on the table, and Trent puts the pink, velvet handcuffs on his wrists, locking them. Clarence picks up the one-piece cop outfit, dwarfing it when he puts it against his chest and stomach. Holding it delicately, he spins around. "What do you guys think?"

Glancing at the black mini-skirt portion that looks like a small handkerchief against his blue sweatpants, I say, "I don't think that's going to work, man, but I'm sure-" I grab the baton dildo that's next to the wig and fling it at him, yelling, "You'll get some good use out of this!" Somehow he catches it, mid-spin, while tossing the outfit at Trent.

Clarence crouches down and starts swinging the baton around, stabbing at us with the dildo end, making sure to smack each of us in the face at least once before he finally stops. He grabs the rainbow-colored wig and plops down on the couch, next to Trent. After putting it on and adjusting it, he says, "Okay, name a good sex story. Best one gets first go on the gravity bong."

Trent points at him with both hands. "Looking good, Lieutenant Fuzz!" He yanks at the cuffs a few times, glances down at the table, then pulls on them again. Jus hits me on the leg and slightly opens his hand, revealing a small, gold key with a pink ribbon tied to it. "You boys know I got this one!" Trent yells, still trying to get them off, and he goes on to repeat the story of when he attempted to charizard a girl. It's the millionth time he's told it, but we let him – not only because it's fucking hilarious, but because we continue to be amazed by his audacity to ask the girl, and her actually letting him do it. The three of us are bent over from laughter by the time he's done, all of us yet to be bored by the climax of his story – him frantically waving his hands, trying to put out the quickly spreading fire on her pubes that his cum was unable to extinguish.

Once we all catch our breath, I remind him that there will be no repeats. "You have to tell a new story!" I shout.

"Well I was doing a standing sixty-nine with this chick once-"

"Did she piss on you?" Clarence asks, interrupting.

"No, fucker, but she farted in my face!"

Clarence asks what type of fart it was and how bad it smelt, but before Trent can answer, Jus puts his hand up, stopping him. "We don't need nor do we want to know about that shit," he says. All of us know that anything goes with us most of the time, but Jus has always been disgusted by any type of bathroom humor that's too "bathroom," as he calls it, so Trent just says, "It was bad. I ended up gagging."

"Who wouldn't?" I grab the baton dildo, start poking Jus with it.

"So, she farts in my face, and I gag and drop her. She hit the side of my chair so bad that her neck looked like it went ninety degrees when she hit it." Trent bends his neck to the side as far as he can.

"Ohhhhhh," Clarence says, wincing.

We all agree that's pretty bad and gross at the same time, and Jus asks, "Was she okay?"

"Don't know. Never talked to her again. She went to another high school," Trent tells him.

I run through some of the crazy shit I've experienced, in my head, trying to choose something I don't remember telling them about; and Clarence asks Trent why he hasn't heard of this before, so Trent offers him a few more details, but Clarence finally waves his hands and gives up. I start telling my story about a girl from high school that was into throatfucking, and how I either injured or bruised whatever the muscle is that connects the tongue, to your mouth, when Jus interrupts.

"Frenulum," he says, grabbing a small piece of bacon from someone's plate, popping it in his mouth.

"Yeah, frenulum." I look back at Clarence and Trent. "She ended up having to get stitches, and she couldn't talk for," I flash two fingers, "two weeks."

Clarence says he's got a good one and noticing how silly the wig looks on him, I think to myself, "That's the beauty of it. He doesn't give a fuck, none of us do." I quickly recall some of the events we've been to, the dumb outfits, hats, and wigs we've worn together, and the friends and people we knew that wouldn't join us because they didn't want to mess up their hair, or they thought they looked "uncool." He tells us it was in high school and when he describes the girl, Trent recognizes who he's talking about.

"Oh, yeah. She fucked that guy that lived down the street from us. The dude we built the ramps with for our bikes when we were kids." He thinks for a second, then shouts out, "Bryan!"

Clarence starts up again, but Trent interrupts once more, telling us he thinks Bryan owns a farm in California now. "Does he really!?" Clarence asks, shocked. Trent nods his head, and Clarence continues. "Yeah. So, she's a terrible lay. She just laid there doing nothing, saying nothing, like a dead fish." Trent crosses his eyes, sticks his tongue out, leans his head on Clarence's shoulder. "So, I ask her to give me a blowjob and talk dirty, and she… fucking… starts rapping!" We laugh, I ask if they were at least good rhymes, and Clarence responds with a definite no. "When I stopped her and told her what dirty talk was, she said, 'Oh, I can't do that.'"

I ask the all-important question. "So, did you cum?"

"Nigga, please," Clarence says, leaning back on the couch, brushing his rainbow hair. "She just sat there on her knees, stone-faced, while I did."

"This girl, same resting bitch face all the time," Trent says, looking at Jus and me. He makes a sullen face, pouts his lips, gives us all the evil eye. "You're getting fucked!" Trent shouts. He goes back to the face. "It's your birthday!" He scowls at us. "Bitch, you won the lottery!" Again. Shrugging his shoulders, he leans back on the couch. "But I would cum too," he says. Knowing I wouldn't have a problem with it, I nod my head, agree, and aware that Jus won't have a story, I suggest gravity bong hits so that Trent will forget about it and not tease him.

When it's Trent's turn, he has trouble getting the cap on, and he looks like a T-rex trying to get high, the pink cuffs impeding his movement. We belittle him, laughing at him while he holds the burning top close to his face and puts his lips to the Sunny D bottle floating in the cooler. Once he pushes it all the way down, Jus tosses the key at him, hitting him in the head, and it falls in the water. "Fuckers," Trent says, lifting his head, coughing.

All of us plop down on the couch, don't move for the next hour or so, and we sit there talking, not paying attention to the TV, rummaging through the assortment on the table, all of us trying on the rainbow-colored wig. We agree it looks best on Jus, so he keeps it on until he sluggishly stands up and announces he's going to get beer and liquor, and Trent tells Jus he'll go with him because he has to get money for Schroeder.

"Well, that's mighty productive of you," Clarence says, laying on his side, putting his feet up. "Because I'm not going anywhere. I might even take a nap."

"I can't do naps." I say, sliding to the edge of the couch, banging the glass table for some reason. "Too much of a gamble. I either wake up refreshed, or like I have no idea where the hell I am, or what the hell is going on." When I get up, the water is vibrating in the cooler, the half-cut jug bouncing on one end, and I tell them, "I'll be right back, let me get some cash." The walls are bare in my room, the empty closet open, dressers cleaned out, and the only thing I have left to take back with me is what I traveled with, and my sheets and pillows on the bed. I'd taken everything to my parent's house when I drove down for the conference and didn't bring much back, because I'd been forced to return by train when my truck's transmission started acting up. The sight of the room bums me out a little, so I grab the money quickly and shut the door after cutting off the light.

While telling Jus what I want, Trent runs to his room and Clarence stops me, puts his finger to his lips, says, "Shhh, listen." A few seconds later we hear a loud, screeching air horn, followed by Trent's girlish scream, and Clarence starts laughing. Trent runs around the corner, holding an air horn with duct tape wrapped around it. "I taped it to his door," Clarence tells us. Trent squeezes the horn two more times; all of us put our hands up, tell him to stop, and he throws it into the kitchen, aiming for the trashcan, but misses and hits the wall.

"Pick that up and take that garbage when we go," Jus says, pointing at the mountain of trash.

Trent stands very straight, salutes him, says, "Yes, Deputy Fuzz," then grabs a trash bag from under the sink, and starts filling it with the garbage that's on top of the pile. Jus comes back from his room wearing different clothes - jeans, and a dark t-shirt, and I finish telling him what I want since Clarence's joke interrupted me earlier. Jus grabs the two trash bags off the floor, and Trent slings his much smaller, lighter bag over his shoulder, then flicks us off. Before closing the door behind them, Trent walks back into the kitchen and reaches under the sink.

"What the fuck did you forget?" Clarence asks, plugging in the PS4 controller.

Trent ducks down, disappearing behind the counter and when he pops up, I can hear the sound of the air freshener canisters in his hand. Laughing, he throws them at Clarence and me, then flicks us off on his way out. The cans are spraying scented mist everywhere, and they're not stopping because he's tied the triggers down with zip ties.

"Jackass!" Clarence yells, grabbing one of the cans off of the floor. "Where are the scissors?!" he shouts, looking at the table for the scissors we used to cut up Trent's bud.

They're not on the table, and after frantically searching the room for a few moments, we hear, "Hey, bitches!" Dangling the scissors in his hand, Trent smirks then slams the door, but not before flicking us off for the third time and shouting, "Later, fuckers!"

Trent

We laugh all the way down the stairs, both of us mimicking them, acting out the way we imagined they were reacting. "Shit, shit," I say in a deeper voice, trying to sound like Clarence, stopping on the landing between the stairs, waving my hands frantically in the air. Playing the part of Harry, Justin almost trips while backing down the stairs, and I start laughing even harder. In the hallway, while passing the pictures of different landscapes and mountains on the wall, Justin lays out an itinerary of where we're going, and in what order, like he always does whenever we go anywhere. Not listening, I respond with "Okay, mom," while looking at my favorite photo, a portrait of a Scottish home with an old, mossy rock wall lining the property, waves crashing in the sea behind it, rolling green hills dotted with a few sheep.

After throwing away the trash and opening the door to the garage, Justin stands there for a moment, staring, and then shaking his head, he says, "Fucking fuckers."

Looking past him, I see his car, and it's completely covered in pink and yellow post-it notes. I immediately lose it, start howling more than I did back in the stairwell, and Justin can't help but chuckle. While walking to the car, I profess my innocence, putting my hands up and telling him, "Dude, it wasn't me. I don't know anything about this." I look at the car again, then back at him. "But it is funny as hell."

Giving me a look of uncertainty, he says, "Yeah, right, doubtful," but when we get to his car, at the center of the driver's side window, in the middle of a group of yellow post-it notes, a pink one reads, "❤ Harry".

"See, I told you!" I yell, pointing at the note. I pull out my phone, start taking a few pics.

He starts taking some of the notes off the hood, and I take too long to look at the photos and unnecessarily tie my shoe, so I won't have to pull off as much. I decide I'll start at the trunk first, then work my way around, taking care of the middle and higher ones so I won't have to lean down, hoping he'll bend over and take care of the low ones. Justin starts laughing, and when I let go of my laces and stand up, he's pointing to the inside of his car. After asking him what's so funny, he says, "Come check it out for yourself," and when I walk around, I see that he's actually pointing through a hole in the post-it notes at a blonde blow-up doll in the passenger's seat. Wearing a t-shirt from a Lady Gaga concert the six of us went to last summer - it has *"The Fame"* written on it - and when I open the door, she greets me with outstretched, plastic arms, her mouth wide open. A yellow sticky pad on her hot pink shirt reads, "❤ Harry."

Letting out a single, short laugh, I say, "Fucking priceless." We both take more pics, start pulling off the rest of the notes, and because I'm excited about the joke, I don't mind bending down and I rip them off quickly, regardless of where they are.

Justin puts her in the back, buckles her in, and while pulling the shirt down over her pink taco as best he can, he tells me, "I don't want some kid seeing that when we're parked."

I agree, then send some of the pics to Clarence and Harry, and while we're pulling out of the garage, I check my balance in my account. "Fuck, after I get out fifty for Schroeder, I'll only have $87.62 left," I tell him.

Wondering where the hell some of my money went, I recall for the first time how I might have bought some shots and drinks for Melissa and me last night, instead of drinking off of our free tab, to avoid bringing her back to the table and losing the bet. Harry texts Justin, and because he won't look at his phone while he's driving, I read it to him. "Just in case things don't work out with Ling-Ling."

"Psssh, whatever," he says, turning on the radio.

After reaching into the backseat to grab one of the small piles of pink and yellow notes, I ask, "Hey, man, do you have a pen?"

"In the center console," he tells me, not taking his eyes off the road, pointing between our seats. "Look in there." With his window down and the music loud, Justin starts tapping on the yellow pad with "♥ Harry" written on it that he's stuck to the middle of the steering wheel. Reaching up to the top right side of the wheel, he slides his hand across it repeatedly, timing it perfectly with the scratching in "Mo Money Mo Problems," and he doesn't say anything; he just mouths the words to himself, looking directly ahead. I start writing things like, "I know what you did" and "I want to break up" on the notes, most of which are pink, probably done on purpose by Harry. Justin pulls into Paradise Market and cuts off the car, but leaves the music playing, and when it ends, both of us, out of respect to an old friend who loved this song, say, "Kenny," then open our doors.

I put a note under the windshield wiper of the car next to us, ask Justin if he wants any, but he says no and pushes the lock button on his keychain. "Are you worried someone is going to steal your new girlfriend?" I joke, sticking another one on a maroon Volvo station wagon. After placing several more on my way in, I throw the rest of the notes in a trashcan to the right of the automatic doors, and a massive display of chips, pretzels, and baskets of fancy cheeses with names on them I don't recognize greet us as soon as we walk in. A flag with our colors and symbol hang above everything, and graduation caps are placed between baskets with rolled-up diplomas scattered throughout the display. I follow Justin towards the liquor aisles, both of us stopping at the cheese section to sample the free different types of cheeses laid out, spreading them across various crackers. The guy who usually works behind the deli counter waves and I take another toothpick, sample some salami. His hair is blue this week, and he hands me a box of crackers that are supposed to go with the type of cheese we're eating. I put the toothpick in the plastic cup, with all the other used ones, and recall the time I came in here drunk, mixed up the cups, and ate off of used toothpicks. It grosses me out, but not enough to stop me from devouring another slice of cheese. We pick up everything, fast, but have some trouble finding Clarence's beer, so we ask a tall, stout, bearded guy with a black, button-down shirt that says, "Paradise" on it to help us.

The guy apologizes, says he's busy, and then speaking into the headset he's wearing; he asks for Mike, then tells us, "Just wait here, and someone will be right with you." He walks down the aisle, past the rows of different beers, cases on the left, six-packs and individual beers on the right, and I grab one that has a malted, wax top and a red rose on the label. Wondering why anyone would pay $15.99 for a single beer, I put it back on the shelf, next to another expensive beer that's covered in dust.

Mike has wild hair and looks like a mad scientist. When we ask him about the beer, he strokes his goatee, then pushes up his glasses and says, "Ommegang? Sure, we have that. Follow me." On our way to the next aisle, I ask him if anyone really buys that expensive, $15.99 beer, and picking up Clarence's four-pack, he says, "Sure, a lot of people. It's good." He hands it to me. "Anything else I can help you guys with?"

When we say no and thank him, he leaves, talking into his headset, and Justin quietly says to me, "He reminds me of a mad scientist."

A girl that I used to date, Tiffany, is working the front counter. Smiling, she waves at Justin as we walk up. "Hi, Justin." He greets her back, and she loses her smile, gives me a not-so-nice glare, then grabs Harry's bottle of vodka and runs it over the scanner. It doesn't beep, so she swings it through again, but it still doesn't work; irritated, she ends up punching in the numbers. After ringing up everything else, she asks Justin, "So, what are you up to tonight?" She looks at me out of the corner of her eye while he answers, chomping on her gum harder and louder. Out of nowhere, she turns to me and interrupting him, yells, "You're a fucking asshole!"

"What?" I say, shrugging my shoulders, acting like I don't know what she's talking about.

She takes his money, and the cash drawer opens, making that familiar sound they all do. "You fucking cheated on me!" she shouts. We'd been dating for one month when she caught me fucking a girl in Clarence's and my shower last year. He'd left the front door unlocked, and she'd walked over to surprise me. It wasn't the first time I'd cheated on her after telling her we were going to be "exclusive," it was just the first time I'd been caught.

"Fucking bastard! You cheated on me and didn't think about me at all!" she screams. Changing her face, she smiles, turns to Justin, hands him his money, and calmly says, "I hope you have a great night, Justin. It was so good to see you."

I grab one of the bags, leaving two for Justin, and make my way around him so I can exit quickly. "That's not true," I tell her. "I thought about you the whole time so I wouldn't cum early."

"Asshole!" Tiffany quickly brushes her hair back and picks up one of the bottles of wine that's next to the register, for impulse purchases, and brings it back behind her head. She looks like she's going to throw it, but after glancing at the middle-aged couple behind us, she puts it down. The husband is laughing, and his wife lets go of his hand, hits him on the arm, and he tries to stop but it takes him a moment.

With her still glaring at him, he puts his hands out, says, "What? It was funny."

"That was harsh, man," Justin says, pulling his keys out of his pocket. "Jesus, look at this shit."

I've been glancing around the parking lot, checking to see how many of the cars I stuck notes on have left, and when I look over, I notice some asshole in a BMW has parked his car inches away from Justin's. He has to pull out so I can open my door, and before I get in, I search my pockets. After finding my last zip tie in the fifth one, I pull a shopping cart around the BMW and fasten it to the driver's side handle. "Okay, now we can go," I say, plopping down into the seat.

While riding out of the lot, I interrupt Justin's second announcement of our schedule minus Paradise. "Look," I say, ducking down and to my left a little more, pointing up through the windshield. We run over a speed bump, and both of us pop up in the air.

"What?" he asks, stopping the car, looking up, the glare of the sun bouncing off the apartment building across the street, hitting him right in the face. Holding his hand over his eyes, he looks for a few seconds, then says, "Isn't that-"

Interrupting him, I say, "Yep, and I got a hundred bucks that says that's not a cigar."

Glancing over at me, Justin says, "You have $87.62 that says that's not a cigar."

Goodkat

The wind has picked up some, so the second half of the blunt is burning faster than the first half did when I was out here thirty minutes ago. Wearing only the towel I picked up off of my bedroom floor on the way out here, I'm standing on my balcony, leaning against the black railing. I pull the metal chain on the infuser, let it sink back down into the Mason jar, seeping the decaffeinated black tea with the Jack Daniel's and water. Some of what I flick off falls into a corner near the glass door, onto a tiny pile of ash created from previous smokes, and I wonder how something so small and so light can be directed into a corner and remain, rather than be blown away and lost by a stronger force. My cock is semi-hard, bulging through my towel and I take another two puffs while picturing Sarah Silverman, my celebrity crush, in my mind to stay excited. I run through some of my favorite images of her I've jerked off too, focusing on the spread she did for Maxim magazine. Slightly smiling when I think of her in the gorilla costume, I quickly concentrate on her butt in those pink and white striped panties, then her in the convenience store, wearing small green shorts, a tank top, and rollerskates. I pull a few more from my Silverman spank bank - her in a red dress, then in jean shorts, boots, and a flannel shirt at some fucking event for turtles, lastly picturing one of my favorites - her in a black miniskirt and black knee-high stockings at a birthday party for Howard Stern. After a final pull, I toss what little is left of the blunt over the railing, watching it spin and fall down towards the street, until I can't see it anymore. I take a huge gulp and looking at the glass, I wish I'd grabbed the jar with a handle, and on my way to the kitchen, I check two t-shirts that are hanging and drying on a chair. Still too wet. I can see the green-tinted Mason jar with the handle through the small window, but when I open the cabinet door, I notice my set of Peanuts glasses I've had since I was a kid; and suddenly feeling nostalgic, I grab one of those instead. After pouring until it's full, I drink what's left in the Mason Jar, then head back to my room.

I set the glass next to the controller on the nightstand that looks like a die and make sure not to hit my laptop or touch anything with my vaselined hand when I jump on the bed and position myself on the pillows behind me. Once I slide on my over-the-ear headphones, I hear Joanna Angel, the same girl I was watching before I went outside. After sticking my hand in the Vaseline jar to my right, I scoot further back, sit up more, and check out the blonde in a plaid mini-skirt on my 55-inch TV hanging on the wall in front of my bed. With black stockings, she's lying back on a yellow couch, hands on her ankles, legs spread. Using my thumb and fingers, I slather the Vaseline around my hand, start to rub it around my still-hard dick, then grab the controller off of the huge, red die next to me and lie it down in front of the laptop to my left. I grab my phone, punching in the code while simultaneously looking at the video on my computer, and open up Snapchat to see if any of the girls I messaged when I started jerking off had responded while I was smoking outside. One of the four had - Cara, a cute, bubbly, young blonde with short hair. We'd hooked up last semester after she'd taken my final exam several hours earlier, making her no longer a student of mine. She was at a garage, getting one of her tires changed and she'd gone into the bathroom, lifted up her white tank top and sent me a few pics. I take a screenshot of two of the three, then look at my computer and watch Joanna get railed out, for a minute. After grabbing the controller, I flip through the other fifteen photos on the TV a few times, eventually stopping at number five.

I can see her red, high heels in this one. Playfully sticking her tongue out, she's halfway turned around, pushing her butt out from under her lifted skirt, her small, red thong showing. Grabbing the Peanuts glass next to me, I notice Charlie Brown. "Why is having fun so much work?" he says, as he struggles to paddle down a river, Snoopy's hook caught in his raft. After taking two large chugs of my Jack and black tea, I set the glass back in the same white, circular pip, then pick up my phone. I message Cara to drop her shorts, stick her tongue and butt out and take a pic in the mirror. Instead of looking for something else, I keep the same image on the TV, and move my cursor to Pornhub's "search," type in "Joanna Angel," then hit return. When the results come up, I notice some Vaseline or something, smudged on my cursor pad, so I wipe it off with my bedsheet, then scan the videos, letting the brief previews play, trying to decide on one to watch. Browsing through several pages before I find one I haven't seen, I start it, but three out of the six minutes are her being interviewed, so I go back to my choices and look at my phone. Nothing.

Still massaging my dick slowly, I search through several more pages of her videos while glancing at the TV and checking my phone, finally finding another one on page six. Wearing different colored stockings, yellow and red, she's getting dp'ed and facialed in the preview, and once I push play, Cara sends me a pic from the garage. She's sitting in the waiting room, sticking her tongue out at the camera, and her message reads, "Sorry, I was talking to the guy that fixed my car, and I just got this." Below her text is a gif of a dripping, glazed donut, along with several emojis – a bomb, an eggplant, a fist, rain, and a tongue. I tighten my grip a little, start to jerk faster. Pushing my hips up, I look at the TV quickly, then at my computer, the sounds of Joanna on her knees, slurping on three cocks, all I can hear. I take two long sips while looking at the screenshots again, wishing Cara had sent one with her tongue out, showing her tits, and I start thinking about Sonya and last night. I picture fucking her on my balcony, holding her legs open, her yellow panties pushed to the side, sliding in and out of her while we passed a blunt back and forth, both of us occasionally glancing at the people down below. They've been dp'ing Joanna for the last minute and a half, but the video is close-up, and when I preview the final two minutes, it's the same camera angle. Knowing the sight of two dudes' asses won't make me cum, I click on one of the videos below it - not necessarily because I'm interested, I've seen it before, but because I don't want to go back to page six and keep searching. I think about changing the pic on the TV, but after almost thirty minutes of jerking off and searching through photos, I decide it's the one that's aroused me the most, mainly because of the model playfully sticking out her tongue, so I don't. Knowing I won't use it anymore, I put the controller to the side, and a few minutes into the new video, Joanna balances herself on a couch over one of the three black dudes she's fucking and shoves his cock in her ass. The other guy, who's wearing a white t shirt, enters her pussy, and she squeals, "I want a dick in my mouth." The third guy obliges and I think about opening Skype, videoing a girl in England that masturbates with me on camera, but I decide I don't want to take the time, and I take another swig while glancing at the TV, then concentrate on my computer. They have her flipped around now, the same tattooed, muscular guy standing up, in her ass, the other guy in her pussy, her tits bouncing up and down, one arm reaching out to the back of the couch for balance, the other for the last dick. I decide I can cum to this, despite the fact that I've used it several times in the past, then my phone beeps and I get even more excited when I see it's another photo and message from Cara. Sitting in a van, she's lifting her shirt up, sticking her tongue out. Her message reads, "Haha. Sorry, I'm back in my parent's minivan. I had to use it to move back for the summer." The text includes the same emojis as before. When I look at the screenshot I took, I notice a cardboard, packing box over her right shoulder and over her left, resting against a fan, the brown teddy bear with weird, orange eyes I threw on the floor when I fucked her in her dorm room bed. I glance back at her face, her breasts, then her face again, my dick swelling in my hand, and I know I'm going to cum, so I turn my laptop around, stand in front of the dark blue towel, and start rubbing my balls against it and the corner of my bed. Looking over quickly at the blonde on the TV sticking her tongue out at me, I think of Sonya in her matching yellow lingerie and nutting all over her face on my balcony. Turned on and eager to nut, I widen my stance, concentrate on the video on my computer, and not long after Joanna starts asking for jizz, she takes her first load, then her second, and my body juts forward, and I bust hard, spraying cum all over the dark towel.

After a moment, I turn my attention to my phone, message back, "HOT, THANKS! ☺," throw it and my headphones on the crumpled comforter, shut off the PS4 and TV, then close my computer. Folding the blue towel over, I use the underside to wipe myself off, and toss it in the laundry basket next to my shoes in the closet. When I put the Vaseline back after washing my hands, I look in the mirror and turn, comparing my lower stomach with a side-view picture a friend took of me at the edge of some cliffs in Jamaica ten years ago. Pleased, I gargle some mouthwash while swiping my armpits with deodorant, then brush my teeth and head back to my bedroom. The Peanuts glass is practically empty when I pick it up and finish it and when I throw my red boxer briefs at the laundry basket, they catch, hanging on the edge. After sliding on my blue plaid bathing suit I was wearing earlier, I grab a black v-neck because the other ones are still too wet. Once I'm done washing and drying it, I place the Peanuts glass along with the others, and I'm relieved when I see a pair of black, below-ankle socks in my tennis shoes next to the door, because I don't have to go back to my bedroom and find a pair. I snatch my keys, then my cash that's folded over my driver's license and debit card from my desk and while slipping on my socks, I notice the left heel is showing a small hole, and the right one's not in much better shape.

Halfway down the stairs, while sliding my t-shirt on, I remember I'm parked in the lot across the street behind the building. For some reason, I'd left my truck there instead of the garage this morning at 4 a.m. when I came back from taking Sonya to her place. After walking out of Billie Chambers alley and while crossing the street, I notice the stout, Italian guy who owns the pizza place I love, Rocco's. Smoking a cigarette in his eating area, he's sitting on an orange metal stool, leaned over, his elbow on his black pants that are covered in flour. He nods his head, waves, scratches his goatee, and motioning with my hand, I say, "Hey man." He doesn't say anything, takes another puff of his cigarette, and leans back down on his knee. He might know my name from my debit card, but if he does, he never uses it; he just says "buddy" most of the time, and I don't know his. The lengthiest conversation we've ever had was after one July 4th party, where I drunkenly stated to him many times that his pizza was the greatest I'd ever had. He might have even been sitting in the same chair. Other than that, we'd never said much to each other, but he was always polite.

Two local college girls - both dark-haired, one a little taller than the other - are feeding the gray cat that hangs out in this parking lot. Squatting down, both of their heels are sticking up from their flip-flops, their butts poking out while they feed the cat his fiftieth snack for the day, and I notice a man in his early 20s, wearing a green hoodie and carrying a backpack. He takes the last bite of a candy bar he has, then drops the wrapper on the ground before walking into the convenience store. "Unbelievable," I say, under my breath, shaking my head.

When I check my rearview mirror to back up, I tap the blue and silver, bone-shaped dog tag that reads "Scrapdog" hanging from it. The only pet I've known, my mom used to tell me stories of her cleaning and vacuuming when I was a baby, and how Scrapdog, terrified and shaking, would bark and stand between me and the monster she thought might get me. Her dog collar has hung from the rearview mirror of every car I've owned since she died.

Two old biddies are crossing the road in front of me, so I have to stop. They're both wearing purple hats and moving slowly, one helping and guiding the other, who's using a walker, her white purse swaying from its handlebar. "41," I say to myself, and I start calculating multiple ages of when I could die, subtracting the former from the latter. At first, I give myself about 40 years, but unpleased that number is lower than 41, I raise it to 45, then 50, because it sounds better. The fact that I'm right at that halfway point doesn't bother me at all, and I recite a quote to myself from

Epicurus, a Greek philosopher I remember studying in college. "Why should I fear death? If I am, death is not, if death is, I am not. Why should I fear that which can only exist when I do not?"

It only takes about ten minutes to get to the gym from my apartment if traffic is light, and it is. The first two stop lights I pass through are green, and when I go under the second one, I notice Shannon, a black dude I know from the sidewalk outside of my apartment. He has some illness that confines him to a wheelchair, and I've seen him rolling around town, but only ever talked to him near my place. He's thin with a salt and pepper colored beard and has kind, brown eyes. Always wearing some sort of Colts paraphernalia, he thanks me every time I light his cigarette for him, once saying, "Most people won't talk to me, because they think I'm going to ask them for money." He's laid back in his chair, Colts hat on, chilling out in front of the assisted living home with some of his other friends - a black and white guy who are using motorized wheelchairs as well, all of them smoking cigarettes. He's never seen me in my car, so I don't think he'd recognize me, but I roll my window halfway down anyway, stick my arm out and beep as I drive by.

The assisted living home is a little more than halfway to the gym, so I light up the small blunt I rolled earlier for the ride with the trucks' cigarette lighter because after searching, I can't find a regular one anywhere else. I watch the red, hot coils spark the end, smoke quickly flowing out the window, and I open it all the way, take a few long hits, lean out, and look at myself in the side mirror. The last stop light I pull up to is red, but no cars are coming from the other way, so I drive on, ignoring the sign that says, "No turn on red," wondering why anyone would pay attention to it in this case.

Turning left into the gym entrance, I pass the silver metal sign attached to a rock column that says "Nnaight Athletics," take a couple more puffs, then throw the blunt away and reach for the small bottle of scented hand sanitizer when I turn the truck off, attempting to hide at least some of the smell because the sweet, old lady, who works here on Tuesday nights made a comment to me a few weeks ago. "I'll get you if I smell smoke on you again," she told me, shaking her finger. When I let her know it was bud, she immediately excused her previous comment and told me about how much she loved her pen.

Stevenson, a good looking, black guy in his 20s, greets me as I walk through the second set of doors, opened by him pressing a button underneath the desk he's behind. Welcoming me with his hand out, he's looking fly as usual, sporting a plum-colored shirt, with matching dark plaid pants, a bowtie, and black Buddy Holly-type glasses. "What's up, Goodkat? How's your weekend?" he asks.

"I'm cool, Stevenson. What's going on with you, man?" I say, slapping his hand.

When I first met him, he introduced himself as "Stevenson," but he told me, "You can call me, 'Steven,' if you like."

"Why would I?" I replied. "Not when you have a cool name, like that." He tells me his plans for the night, I say I have no clue what I'm doing, then I compliment his clothes, telling him, "Looking good as always, man."

A soccer match is on the big-screen TV in the sitting area to my right, and a young Asian kid in red sweatpants sitting on the blue leather couch kicks his feet against the side while playing some sort of game on his phone. Walking down the hallway, past the offices on the left, I move to my right to avoid a tall, skinny, wrinkled woman who's messing with her bag, not paying attention, and in the last office, the gym manager glances up from his computer, waves at me. Never having talked before, last week I stopped by his office to compliment Stevenson, and he gave me a logoed, black, Dopp kit, something I'd meant to buy for years.

As I'd expected for this time on a Saturday, the gym isn't crowded. Most of the elliptical machines to my right are empty, the treadmills too, and only eight or ten people are taking the class in front of me, behind the glass wall. I make my way to the vacant trainer's station and set my keys, cash, and cards under the computer, in a light brown and white marble compartment. I'd always placed my stuff on a small counter near where the yoga balls are kept, next to some hamstring and quad-stretching machines, until a couple of weeks ago when after working out, I went to pick all of it up and nothing was there. I came here and asked the cute, short blonde standing behind the same computer I just put my things under if anyone had turned anything in. "Here you go," she said, smiling, handing them to me. "I saw them over there, so I thought I would put them here for safekeeping."

"I still need to call her," I say to myself, heading to the elliptical machines.

I step on the grey footsteps, the small TV in front of me coming on after I turn on the machine, but I don't pay attention to the group of ladies talking. I'm too buzzed to really care enough to change the channel, so I just listen to some music, zone out, and get off after ten minutes. I search for a playlist, head towards the free weights, and while walking between the treadmills and stationary bikes, an older lady with fake tits and leopard yoga pants looks away when I make eye contact with her. The first song that plays, "Rock Show" by Peaches, I discovered from a cumshot compilation I jerked off to earlier this month. I take a few sips from the extremely long stream of water that shoots out of the fountain, walk past the rows of mirrors on my right without looking at myself, and lay the small, white towel on one of the maroon benches. After grabbing the 60 lbs. weights, I do fifteen reps of bench presses, holding each takedown for two seconds, the last one for five. When I'm done, I do one hundred high knees in the area I used to set my keys, then look for a black mat to do my stomachs. The place where they usually are is empty, so I walk into the classroom behind the glass wall and grab one from the rack, and some of the students turn around and watch me, possibly using me as an excuse to take a break from their exercise. Positioning the mat under my ass, I put my feet under the railing that holds the yoga balls and with my hands behind my head, I bring my elbows to the opposite knee, twenty times each, followed by twenty chin raises to the ceiling, making sure to press my tongue against the roof of my mouth during both exercises because it prevents neck pain. After holding a side plank for forty-five seconds and raising my left leg five times, I do the same on the other side and then a regular plank, hardening and tensing my stomach as if I'm about to get punched. I fling the mat back where I usually find them, get on the bike, set the difficulty level to twelve, pedal for seven minutes, get off and repeat the previous exercises. For the third and fourth round, I substitute butterfly for bench, using 45 lbs. weights, keeping every other exercise the same. On my fifth, I have to walk around a guy wearing calf-high white, Nike socks and a too-tight black long-sleeve spandex shirt. Leaning against the weight rack, he's stretched out across the entire walkway, working on his triceps, grunting too loud, staring at himself in the mirror, a gallon jug of water next to his feet. I've seen him here before doing the same sort of thing, and he doesn't say anything when I say, "Excuse me" and grab the 50 lbs. weights close to him. While I'm doing incline, a hot, young brunette sits down a few benches up from me. I can see her reflection in the mirror out of the corner of my eye - 5'7", 5'8" maybe, C cups under her black Lululemon top. She grabs some small weights before I return mine, and when I walk past her towards my one hundred high knees, "Sabotage" by the Beastie Boys starts up, the MTV Music Awards' version, and I throw my legs up high and fast, picturing them all wearing their tuxedos, tearing it "the fuck up" on stage. Two Asian ladies waiting for this class to end and the next one to begin are talking by the small walkway on the right that leads to where I do my stomachs, so I walk around the left side and do my exercises while a heavy-set guy in his 60s with wild, white hair uses the hamstring stretching machine. Looking on his phone, he doesn't have his right leg too far back, and when I come back to do another round, he has the same leg propped up, but at an even lower angle. Tina, the girl I still need to call, waves at me from behind the desk while she chats with a client. Continuing to talk, she points down towards where my stuff is and puts up her thumb. I finish up with two sets of fifteen reps of bent-over dumbbell reverse flys, using 20 lbs. weights, combining fifteen reps of triceps, using 40 lbs., mixing in my knees, stomachs and the bike. At the end of my workout, once I'm done with my last set of abs, instead of cooling down, I decide to do the stair climber at a difficult level because "Make 'Em Say Uhh" by Master P comes on, riling me up. I listen to it twice, forcing myself to get a certain number of steps before it ends, warning myself that if I don't, I won't make it out of here. This is something I do when I go running outside as well. I'll randomly pick a car, race it to a tree, sign, or curb, telling myself that if I don't get there first, I'll die. Feeling good, I look at the time when I'm done. One hour and fifty-two minutes.

I switch to Johnny Cash to cool down to and grab my debit card instead of cash because I don't feel like carrying sixty-seven cents around with me and back to my car. Tina isn't there anymore, and I take my time before I walk downstairs, meandering through the rows of equipment with my hands on my head, past the small, glass partition, towards the window that overlooks the pool.

After some small talk and telling me, "That will be $5.33, please," the cute, petite black girl working the café near the front of the gym takes my debit card and slides it through the side of the register. "I like your voice," she says.

She smiles and asks me to say something else and teasing her, I do, using her name. "I can do your voicemail, if you'd like, Hailey."

While walking back up the stairs, I wonder why I didn't talk to her longer, get her phone number, but I don't worry about it for too long and take a sip of my chocolate chip cookie protein drink, making a mental note to stop by once more on my way out the door. I walk around for a few more minutes, sipping on the bottle, shaking it, sipping on it again, and I look out one of the large windows towards the parking lot, then the woods past it, staring at nothing, thinking of nothing, for a few moments.

The old guy who was relaxing his hamstrings has left, and the two Asian ladies are inside the classroom, but there's no class. Instead both of them are wearing high-heeled shoes, one of them operating a small, grey boom box, the other twirling and swaying gracefully, moving to a dance I don't recognize. I stretch my quads, hamstrings, groin, upper back, shoulders, lower back, glutes, chest, and torso, in that order, for forty-five seconds each, then hang from the pull-up bar, letting my feet support about fifty percent of my body weight for an additional forty-five seconds. Because my bathing suit has holes in the pockets, the other reason I didn't want sixty-seven cents, I put my debit card back with everything else under the counter, rather than taking everything downstairs because I don't want to risk losing anything and leaving it here seems more convenient than dealing with the lock.

The locker room is empty except for two Indian guys talking to each other at the second group of lockers to my right. Wearing only towels, they nod to me, then say something to each other I can barely hear, definitely not understand. I walk to the next set of lockers because they're across from the mirrors above the sinks and I can get a nice, full-body view of myself after taking my shirt off. I look to the left, getting the same side view I did earlier in my bathroom. Even more satisfied, I turn forward, look at myself for a few seconds, then slide my bathing suit off and throw it on top of my t-shirt and phone in locker #222, not bothering to use the four-digit combination after closing it. After kicking my shoes that have my socks hanging out of them under the black marble bench, I fill up the plastic bottle I finished while stretching with more water, and grab two white towels on my way to the steam bath.

Noting the clock on the wall, I push the steam release button several times before opening the glass door and walking in. The room is empty, and I hear the sound that always radiates from behind the tiled wall before the steam shoots out of the grey pipe that's close to the floor. I wrap one of the towels around my waist and spread the other one on the second level of seating so I can spread out for the thirty minutes I'm in here. While lying face down, I turn my head to the right, left, and face forward for forty-five seconds each, taking long deep breaths, the eucalyptus spray in the air filling my nostrils. After what I think is twenty minutes, I get up and wipe the glass door, so I can see the clock. Five minutes longer than I thought. So that no dripping water from the ceiling will fall in one of my ears, I rest my forearms on my head, one over the other, covering them while I lay on my back. Not long after, two dark-skinned guys in their 30s walk in. Both of them are wearing small, tight shorts and they start talking loudly - Portuguese, I think - once they sit down. About ten feet from me and only a few inches away from each other, they shout as if they're talking across a large room, continuing to do so even after the steam stops, completely shattering any serenity that was left. I clear my throat, put one of my hands under my head and lift it up while I speak. "Hey, man, will y'all keep it down a little, please?"

"Why?" the larger one with a tattoo on his shoulder asks, annoyed. He turns back to his friend, continues to talk, but not as loud as before; and after a minute or two he spins around, and asks me, "Is it because we're talking Portuguese?" He pauses for a moment. "Because we're talking another language?"

"Come on, man," I answer, opening my eyes, sitting back up again. Irritated I have to deal with something that could have easily been avoided with simple manners, I say, "Do I look like the type of guy that would be like that? I've been polite to you. I just came in here to chill, man. It's a steam bath, not a hair salon. Y'all are right next to each other, just please keep it down some. I don't care what language y'all are speaking."

He changes his tone and starts apologizing, saying something like, "Some people are like that," and "You never know," and that he's here to get away from his wife, whom he had a fight with. The other one never says anything, and when they leave, the larger one says goodbye and "Have a good weekend," talking and gesturing to me like we're good friends. Another five minutes go by, maybe ten, and I don't bother to look at the clock on my way out. I throw the two towels in the bin with the other dirty ones, grab a clean one from one of the shelves above, and wrap it around my waist, forgoing my bathing suit because I know the pool and hot tub will be vacant or close to it, so it won't matter much - not that it would if it were busy, because I've gone au' natural under my towel then, too. The pools and hot tubs are entirely empty, except for a lifeguard who's lazily checking the chemicals in the hot tub, and I can hear the familiar water falling, and I look over to see it spilling out and over the top of a giant yellow mushroom into the kiddie pool it's standing in. I don't bother to push down my towel when it floats up, exposing my dick and the water's very cold in the lap pool, but I sink down further, acclimating to it, eventually dunking my head under and holding my breath for one minute and twenty-two seconds, according to the lap clock at the end of the pool. "Not bad, considering the amount of bud I consume," I think to myself. Sitting down on the stairs for ten minutes, I submerge myself every now and then, not trying to beat my previous time, just trying to cool down from the steam bath.

The air is colder in the locker room, and I throw the wet towel into the wooden circle, grab another one and walk quickly to the showers, enjoying the hot water only briefly. After my long, cold shower, I weigh myself before rubbing lotion all over my body. "175," the red digital numbers, read. Because I'm super mellow from the steam bath, I want to get my stuff quickly from upstairs and leave, without talking to anyone, so I put my earbuds in before filling the container with water once more and walk out.

I take the stairs, three at a time, lightly grabbing the railing on my right side, and remind myself about the young, hot girl that works at the café. Flicking my thumb up the screen of my phone without looking, I scroll through my song list, randomly stopping and tapping it, once I reach the second floor, selecting something. "I'll have to make an exception and see if she's still there when I leave," I think to myself, walking over to retrieve my things. The guitar begins slowly, softly, another one joins in playing louder, some light cymbals follow, then the drums start, and it all picks up from there, and without thinking about it, I softly say, "Hello, I've waited here for you."

She appears from behind a case displaying those watches that monitor your health and count your steps. Looking down at her phone and then around the gym, she glances towards me, then away. With shoulder-length, bright red hair and pale skin, she's easily the most beautiful girl I've ever seen. She looks like one of those models that you see in advertisements or commercials who you imagined had to be computer-generated of photoshopped. Someone who wouldn't, couldn't exist in the real world. She's so cute and beautiful and gentle and lovely, and the longer I gaze, the more amazing she becomes. She was terminally pretty. Enchanted by her loveliness, I didn't even notice her petite, tight body until I unconsciously started walking towards her a few moments later.

"Hi," I say, giving two, quick waves. "Fucking tool," I think to myself, putting my hand down. A size 0 or 2, she's wearing gray yoga pants with a yellow stripe on the side and a light grey t-shirt with a small cartoon of Pusheen attempting to make a pizza on it. I peek at the panels quickly, and it seems that by the end Pusheen has given up on making a pizza and ordered one, because "she is a cat".

She shyly says, "Hello," then glances to her left.

"Are you having a good workout?" I ask. She's wearing no makeup at all.

"It's okay," she says, slightly biting her lip.

"Just, just, wow." That's all that comes to my mind right now.

"Well, I just got started about fifteen minutes ago." She pauses, looks down, then back up at me. "How about you?" she asks, putting her hands together, locking a couple of her fingers.

Standing up a little straighter, I tell her I got here a couple of hours ago to work out. I make a light joke about the guy who was staring at himself in the mirror and people who do that in general, then let her know I ran up here just now to get my things after the pool and steam bath.

She laughs at my comment about the guy and the mirror, and when I'm done talking, she bites her lip again and I can't believe this girl exists, that this isn't a dream. Unlocking her fingers, she starts swinging her arms, a little and says, "Yeah, what's worse are some of the guys in here that are creepy as hell, staring at you while you stretch or walk by." She glances over at the group of treadmills, where a pale guy in his 50s with slicked-back hair, wearing a blue t-shirt that has its sleeves cut out, is walking slowly, pumping his arms up and down.

Noticing someone other than her for the first time since we started talking, I agree and say, "I can't imagine what some of you ladies have to put up with at gyms." I tug on my shorts for no reason, put my hands in my pockets, take two small steps back, one forward, then take my hands out of my pockets, my stuff still in my hand, because I don't want anything to fall through the holes. We talk a little more about the gym and she loosens up, but not much, still acting skeptical, maybe untrusting. I tell her the steam bath is the only reason I belong to this gym, that it's the nicest one I've been to in this area, adding, "It's the only one with eucalyptus spray."

She giggles a little, sways her hips briefly, then puts her hands back together. "That's a funny reason to belong to such an expensive gym," she says. "The only reason I can come here is that my parents pay for it while I'm in grad school."

"What are you studying?" I ask.

After telling me, she explains what she wants to do with her master's degree following graduation next year, and we talk about her possibilities and the jobs she's interested in, the places she'd like to live. "A city is good for work, but not to live," she says. "I lived in a city for three years after college when I worked in the financial sector, and I didn't care for it, at all." I mention warmer states, then islands, ask her if she'd like somewhere tropical. "To visit," she tells me. "I want somewhere that has four seasons."

I stop nodding my head, motion to her phone. "So, what were you listening to?"

She blushes, her upper body buckling slightly. When she covers her phone with both hands, probably not on purpose, I can discern she'd rather not tell, and I change the subject. "Your accent. If you don't mind my asking, where are you from?" I already have a pretty good idea. I've always been good with identifying people's nationalities by the way they look or talk, but I don't say anything for fear of being wrong and offending her.

After naming the town she's from, she continues, "It's capital of Republic of-" and I finish her sentence with her, naming the republic. Grinning, she hops twice, then reaches out and touches my arm. "Right, right! Very good!" she says. The guy with the slicked back hair from the treadmill, walks behind us, staring at her ass. She doesn't notice, even when he looks up at her once he passes. She's definitely more relaxed, and for some reason, I still feel a little like I did earlier, something I rarely experience: nervous. "I'm surprised that you know that. I mean, I don't mean to be rude, but-" She loses some of the excitement in her face, regretting her assumption I wouldn't know anything. I tell her to relax, that I understand, because most people who haven't been, view Russia as a country full of AK-47-toting, vodka-chugging, bear-wrestling babushkas and men known for making drunken videos while shouting the usual, "Blyat!" as they punch another guy or do something stupid. Relaxing, she giggles at my comment and brings her clenched hands to her chest. "I can't believe you've been!" she squeals, her excitement returning to her face.

"Yeah, twice. I've been to St. Petersburg and Moscow." I say.

Doe-eyed, she looks up at me, blinks once, then asks, "Where did you go?"

I begin with St. Petersburg because that was my favorite of the two, and I tell her about The Church of Spilt Blood, how amazing and detailed the artwork was inside. Next I mention the hotel where I stayed, the Corinthia, explaining how I was in the middle of everything in Nevsky Prospekt. When I bring up the Hermitage Museum, I let her know I had to regretfully rush through it on my last day, almost missing my flight.

Grinning, she listens, nodding her head every now and then, but she shows particular interest when I mention the Mariinsky Theatre. "What did you see?" she asks, interrupting me. She touches my arm. "Oh, I'm sorry!"

Smiling, I tell her, "I went to see The Nutcrac-" She lets out a squeal of excitement before I can get out the rest.

Calming down, but not too much, she starts pushing herself up and down moderately, her heels barely leaving the ground. "Did you like it?" she asks. "I love the Nutcracker!" She speaks loudly and quickly, and catching her overzealousness, she looks around to see if anyone heard her screeching. We both glance towards the treadmills at some black guy, wearing, short, yellow running shorts who's bending down, stretching and touching his toes. A little embarrassed, she speaks softly, even though no one's around. "Sorry, did you like it?"

Throwing my hands up to equal her excitement, I proclaim, "It was the greatest thing I've ever seen!" It was actually the truth. I'd never seen a performance, movie, or concert like it. The acoustics were amazing, the inside like stepping back in time, and the ballet itself was just excellent to witness.

"I've never been. I've only seen pictures or videos." She seems disappointed when she says this, so I try to lighten the mood by mentioning something funny that happened there. I proceed to tell her about renting a pair of old school, black-and-gold theater binoculars from a thin woman in her 60s with grey hair.

"She wasn't very polite," I say, with a short laugh. "When I rented them, I noticed a sign saying any binoculars not returned would be a 1200-ruble charge. So instead of taking them back, I decided to keep them because it converted to only, like, eighteen bucks." I chuckle again, recalling the old lady's boosted unpleasantness after I'd told her I'd misplaced them.

"Do you still have them?"

"Yep, on my desk at home." I imagine her walking around my apartment, wearing what she has on now, picking them up, putting them to her eyes and laughing while she looks at me through them.

"Sounds like you really liked St Petersburg a lot." She looks like she's going to say something else, but she doesn't, so I talk about the architecture of St Petersburg, how amazing it was. She agrees, mentioning Peter the Great's quest to make it more cosmopolitan than Moscow, telling me that he halted any construction of stone buildings outside of the city at that time. We end up talking about the university again, and I ask additional questions about her studies, what her interests are, and she tells me she loves movies. She mostly names foreign films, and I only recognize one, *The Lives of Others*, a movie about a police agent spying on a journalist and his lover set in the mid-1980s. When she describes the four-story home she was raised in and tells me about the large garden her grandmother, mother and her prepare meals from, I imagine what they look like, not bothering to ask her to describe them to me.

"Would they like me? Of course, they would!" I say to myself. I picture drinking the juice she mentioned they make from the berry trees standing in front of their house, all of us sitting around a table of food, leaning in together to pose for a photo taken by a fictitious uncle or neighbor I've conjured up in my mind. I'm surprised when she tells me they have a sauna in their house and right after she's done talking, which she's been doing for the last ten minutes straight, I ask if she has any plans for the night.

I immediately apologize for being so bold and not commenting much, even though she didn't give me much of an opportunity, assuring her that I was interested in what she had to say. "I was actually picturing your house and garden in my mind."

After giving me a skeptical look, she quickly smiles and says, "It's okay. I was probably talking a lot anyway. I can do that if I feel comfortable with someone."

Her last statement makes me feel fantastic. "No, not at all," I tell her. Someone wearing dark clothes, I think a woman, passes by my left side and I wonder if it's the first person that's walked by in a while, or if I just haven't noticed.

"And no," she says, shaking her head, adjusting herself a little. She pauses, then clears her throat. "I don't have any plans for the night."

"Would, uh, would you like to do something? Like, go get something to eat or some libations?" I scream at myself, "Libations?! Fucking libations?!" I tell myself to be cool. "I could give you my number, and you could call me after your workout."

"Okay." She smiles her prepossessing, sublime smile, and playfully drops her head for a second, then looks back up at me. Halfway through giving her my phone number, I realize I haven't even introduced myself, and she giggles when I do, because I make light of my rudeness and stand up straight and stiff, military-like, extending my hand, saying my name, and after she tells me hers, she doesn't bother with her phone. "You know-" She shows her teeth, bites her lower lip.

"Just wow," I think to myself.

"I'm free to do something now if you want," she says, slightly swinging her hips.

"Absolutely. If you're done with your workout," I say, actually having to stop myself from popping up on my toes.

"Just let me get my things," she tells me, motioning to the stairs, and we walk together.

Sitting on one of the leather sofas, waiting for her to come out, I realize that for the first time in as long as I can remember, I'm not thinking about only sex. I feel like we could hang out in the library tonight and I would have an extraordinary time. Just listening to her talk, getting to know her more, watching her laugh, sitting next to her sounds superb to me. My phone beeps, and it's Schroeder. Wondering why he'd be texting me since we just saw each other yesterday, I read the message.

"Hey, Dr. G. Just got the best bud I've ever seen. The stuff I was talking about. This shit is unreal. Saving you a q. Hit me up."

This news excites me a lot more than it usually would, and I respond quickly, smiling while I type. "Right on, man!... might be busy rest of the day! If so, I'll text you tomorrow! Have a cool night!" I immediately push "send", and not long after, she walks out of the locker room, looking more beautiful than before, even though I know she didn't change a thing.

When I ask for her bag, she seems surprised I offered, and while pulling the door open for her, I ask, "What would you like to do?"

It's much more beautiful than it was earlier - brighter, sunnier - and both of us take it in for a moment, before she turns around and giggling, says, "It doesn't matter."

I can't even begin to describe what she makes me feel, and I wonder when was the last time that I missed or cared about anything.

Schroeder

"Hmph, that's odd," I say, yanking my boxers off, wiping the fog from my screen with them.

"What, L-?" my girlfriend shouts, over the water and orchestra music playing from her phone.

"Nothing, S- P-" I tell her, both of us using the pet names she only allows us to call each other at home, or when no one else can hear, because she says it's just for "us." She goes back to humming along with the melody. "Looks like a text from my little sister," I say to myself, setting my phone on the counter, next to my girl-friend's six bottles of differently scented body lotion. I pick up the one labeled, Summer Breeze, take a sniff, and look into the foggy mirror, checking out what my girlfriend describes as "the perfect dad bod". After drawing a penis on the mirror, I add some ball hairs, and just when I finish putting the third hair on the right one to even it up with the left, my girlfriend turns off the water. I quickly put down the bottle, positioning it so that the label is out like the others, the way my girlfriend prefers it. After tossing my phone on the floor, I turn my back to the shower, bend over, tuck my dick and balls between my legs and stare at the door, waiting for the curtain to open.

"Jesus, Schroeder!"

"Sorry, just had to get this," I say, casually picking up my phone.

Shielding her eyes, she slaps me with the towel she's drying herself off with. "Just get me something to put on before you get in the shower." She glances over at the penis on the mirror, rolls her eyes, then looks back at me. "Now, please."

I walk back to our bedroom and grab the knee-high leather boots that are lying next to the leather dominatrix outfit, on the floor. Before we had sex this morning, she told me she would wear whatever I wanted because, apparently, last night in a drunken state, I kept yelling, "Get off of me! I have a girlfriend!" while she tried to unclothe me and put me in bed. She was so happy this morning that I woke up to an already made breakfast and her tell-ing me I could smoke as much as I wanted to this weekend as well as do whatever I'd like once we got back to the bedroom. Testing the waters, I asked a couple of questions while she made coffee for herself.

"Cum on your face?" I asked, going for the gold.

Giving me a disapproving look, she bluntly answered, "No."

"Anal?" I showed my teeth.

Narrowing her eyes and glaring at me for a moment, she responded with an even more definitive, "No."

Naked, with one leg propped up on the counter, applying one of her lotions to her smooth, dark, perfect skin, she looks over at me and the knee-high boots I'm carrying. "Schroeder, what the hell? Quit fucking around. Get me something to wear." Laughing, I jump in the shower, the water not taking long to get warm, and my girlfriend reminds me for the fourth time in the last twenty minutes to shave my balls and face. "I don't want to choke on your hairs again," she says, pausing for a moment. "Or no making out! You irritated my pussy this morning when you licked it!" I fondly recall being on my knees, tongue between her legs, her standing against our closet door, hitting me with a whip.

"S- P-, You don't have to remind me about something twenty-five times!"

"Well if I don't, you'll forget, like you always do!" I roll my eyes, and she raises her voice. "And don't yell at me!"

Sticking my head out of the black curtain, I tell her, "I'm not yelling at you, S- P-. I raised my voice because of the water and because you were yelling at me." She smiles, blows me a kiss, and I can't help but think about the comedic value of how whenever we get in any type of argument or any conversation where she raises her voice, it's fine, but if I do, she becomes "Miss Sensitive." I put my shampoo back, behind her seven bottles of various shampoos and conditioners and when I get out, I ask, "S- P-, why do I have one bottle for everything and you have seven in the shower." I motion towards her collection in the shower, then the one on the cabinet. "Look at all that stuff. I have one shampoo. It cost ninety-nine cents." Drying myself off, I mutter, "I use it for my entire body." Still mumbling, I fling my blue and red, striped towel over the rack, next to her neat towel. "Shit, I'll use it to wash my car, degrease something, wash dishes."

"Schroeder, I'm a woman, damn it!" she shouts, slapping her other leg that's now propped up on the counter. Glancing at my towel, she gives me a look, tells me to fold it, so I take it down, straighten it out, and bring the sides together, slowly and meticulously, to tease her, then put it next to hers on the rack.

"And fold it," I say, turning around. "And fold it, and fold it." I repeat this over and over, in an annoying voice, sticking my tongue out, squinting my face, dancing around her. Forcing herself to pay attention to her leg and not me, she smiles a little, even though she's trying not to, and I open one of the drawers, grab her hair dryer.

Irritated, she tilts her head to the side. "What're you doing now?" Without saying anything, I plug it in, push the red button marked "Lo", and start running it over my dick. Looking even more irked, she leans forward, rests both her hands on her leg and asks again, "Schroeder, what are you doing?".

"Nothing." I start humming to her music, wait a few seconds, then look up. "Just heating your dinner."

"Schroeder, get me some clothes to put on!" She puts her foot down, turns around, slaps me on the arms and chest a few times, and I dance around on one foot, trying to shield myself from her blows.

"Ow, ow, ow," I tease, something I always do when we joke around like this, and she stops hitting me. "Hold on," I tell her, putting my hand up, grabbing her towel off the rack, draping it over her shoulders. "Now you're super angry!"

She doesn't appreciate my joke, at all, and starts slapping me with the towel. "My shorts and t-shirt, please!" She stops striking me, tells me to put the towel back "where I got it from," and to fold it; and after putting her leg back up, she starts rubbing lotion on the top of her foot, reminding me for the fifth time, "And shave your face." I'd shaved my balls in the shower, not doing that great a job because I'm still kind of hungover, and I tell her I was planning on it, even though I'd forgotten. I tap a bit of my shaving cream on her nose, and she leaves it there, eventually asking me for a yellow bottle of lotion with a lemon on it, that I remember getting with her last week along with some other bottles. 4 for $26.

"How about a sweet 'stache?'" I ask, running the blade under one of my sideburns.

"How about no making out?"

"Well, that's harsh. You just can't handle how hot I look with one," I tell her, shaving under the other one. "All of the girls would want me."

"Uh, huh." She squirts some lotion into her hands, runs them over her chest and stomach.

I strike some sort of model pose, look into the mirror, narrow my eyes. "No 'stache, a seven out of ten." I put my finger over my lip. "With a 'stache, a fuckin' twenty out of ten!"

"Pssssh, more like a negative twenty out of ten." She gives me a nauseated look. "L-, please shave it. You look awful with one." Following my first swipe below my nose, she smiles and pleased, asks, "So are you bummed out tonight's your last night with all of them together for a while?" I don't respond, not wanting to talk with the blade running down my jugular. "I mean, I'm sure all of you will get together again, even after Justin leaves," she adds.

I hadn't really given it much thought. I mean, it was true that I'd rarely hung out with people I sold to, and they were solid guys I really liked; but people move on, live in new places, make new friends. You can't hinder that. I just answer with, "Eh, it is what it is, S- P-. That's life," and she doesn't say anything else.

We both finish what we're doing at the same time, and after she tells me to put away my razor that I'd set on the counter, I embrace her, then kiss her on the lips gently, smelling the lemon on her soft skin. "I love you, S- P-."

"I love you too, L-." She kisses me back, twice, and I remind her that she wanted me to go to the store. "Oh yeah, you forgot to remind me, like I told you," she says.

"What? Are you ser-"

"And you forgot to get my clothes." She puts her finger up. "Hold on, I'll make you a list."

I don't even bother to argue. I tell my girlfriend, "Just text it to me," then grab her again, pull her close and whisper, "You should have let me keep the 'stache.'"

"Cassava roots? Nopal? Watercress?" I say to myself, reading the list she just sent me. "We eat this shit?" Looking around the store, I find an employee unpacking bananas. "Can you show me where these are, please?" I ask, holding my phone out to the thin teen, who's wearing a yellow apron over a green polo shirt, his skinny arms barely filling the short sleeves.

After glancing at it, he says, "Sure, this way." Taking his time, he shows me where everything is, and one of the vegetables, the root, I recall seeing on our kitchen counter two weeks ago. I'm done with her list sooner than I thought I'd be, and I pick up two bags of gummy bears and mini-Heath bars, throwing them on top of the bagged vegetables I've already forgotten half the names of. Organic milk is what she prefers we drink, but when I read the labels, I can't remember which one of the five it is. One reads, "DHA OMEGA 3 SUPPORTS BRAIN HEALTH" and after considering my lifestyle for a moment, I set it in the basket.

When the automatic doors open, a blast of air hits me from above, again, as I walk through and when I get outside, another young teen in a green shirt almost hits me with a row of shopping carts he's pushing. He reaches a few handles forward, pulls them back, nods, doesn't say anything, and after making the quick walk back to our building, I set the three plastic bags down on the ground and lean against the brick wall. Without looking to see who's around, I light up the blunt I brought with me, take a few pulls. Across the street, a young kid, nine, maybe ten years old, wearing a black hat and jeans, is sitting on a bus bench, pushing his skateboard back and forth with his foot. "I wonder if he can actually skate," I say to myself. "Probably not." Before I'm finished, he stands up and performs a kickflip, jumping from the curb to the street effortlessly. Impressed, I nod my head, saying to myself, "I guess so." He rides off, leaning back a little, gracefully disappearing around the corner of a building, and I notice the wall in the alley across the street. Someone's written in yellow chalk, "history has stopped...nothing exists except an endless present in which the party is always right."

"Ain't that the truth," I say out loud.

My keys are in my other pocket, so I have to switch my groceries to my left hand once I get to our apartment and as soon as I turn the lock, I hear a scream from inside. Dropping the groceries and flinging the door open, I sprint to the kitchen. Screeching and pointing up at the ceiling in the opposite corner, my girlfriend is shaking in the space between the refrigerator and the wall. I follow her tearful eyes and trembling finger to the biggest spider I've ever seen in my life. "Holy shit!" I yell.

"Kill it, L-! Kill it!" she shouts, crouching down, bringing one of her legs up.

"But what if he just thinks he's our roommate? You know, he's been helping us out all along and we didn't even know it, killing flies and other insects and stuff."

She glares at me. "Schroeder!"

"Okay, okay, bad joke." I look around for something in the kitchen to hit it with, something long, but since I never really clean or sweep, I'm not sure where any mop or broom would be. Looking back at my petrified girlfriend, I ask, "You have hairspray, right?"

"Yyyyeah," she answers, stuttering, glancing at me quickly, looking back at the mammoth of a spider. "Under the bathroom sink." When I run out of the kitchen, she yells for me, pleading, "Schroeder, don't leave me!"

After rushing back, I grab the lighter from my pocket and inch my way forward. Feeling her hands on my shoulders and still holding both up, I glance back. "You know you're getting closer, right?" She lets out a small shriek, backs up into her corner. After repositioning the can and small flame, I start calculating when to strike, and I end up making a spontaneous decision that "now!" is the correct time, when I see the giant, black spider flinch.

My girlfriend howls as I let out a manly roar while lighting the kitchen up with a huge, yellow flame. The spider falls to the floor, crinkling into a black ball as I continue to burn it, its legs forming together, and I stomp up and down on its charred remains several times, my girlfriend chanting, "Die, die, die!" She runs over and gives me a hug, kisses me, tells me she loves me, then pulls back. "Did you smoke?" she asks, pulling on my shirt, sniffing it.

"Huh? Jesus, honey. No," I say, motioning to the ceiling, then to the spider corpse. "I just lit this place up with a flamethrower, S-P-!" Turning back to her, I put hands on my hips and add, "Well, also, those same guys were smoking outside near our door again." These are the same fabricated waiters from across the street I've mentioned a few times when she's caught some clue of me smoking. I remind her of last night's good deed. "And it doesn't matter anyway. You said I could smoke as much as I wanted to today."

"I hate when people do that. I hope you said something, L-," she says, believing me, walking over to the cutting board. While she chops tomatoes, I grab one of the pamphlets we get in the mail, advertising twenty percent off to a store we've never been to, and sweep the spider onto it with a paper towel, then throw it all in the trash.

"Here you go, S- P-," I say, setting the bags of groceries next to her feet. I take everything out and place them on the counter in front of her, so she can use what she needs, put away what she doesn't.

"Dinner will be ready in forty minutes," she says, without looking at me, leaning towards me, accepting a kiss on her left cheek.

Before forty minutes have passed, she yells at me from the kitchen, "It's ready!" and lacking any rationale, I shout back, "Okay, mom! I'll be there in a second!" Not realizing what I said, I continue to play, racing my kart into 2nd place when she walks in.

"I'm your girlfriend, you fucking idiot!" She throws the orange towel at me, and while walking back into the kitchen, she says, "Come and get our plates." I stuff the two empty wrappers that are under my leg into the grocery bag of sweets hidden behind the couch, then follow her.

Whatever she's cooked smells terrific, so I stop, and put my nose in the air. "Ahhhhh, that smells really good, my love." I pull out the plates, pass them to her and grab a glass from the drying rack. "What do you want to drink?" I ask, popping my head up from behind the refrigerator door."

"Pink lemonade," she answers, filling the plates. Glancing back at me, she motions to my hand. "No, not that one."

After pulling the cup she likes from the cabinet, I show it to her. She smiles, nods, and I fill it with pink lemonade, not bothering to take a glass for myself.

"S- P-, what do you want to watch?!" I yell from the bedroom, setting her glass on the table on her side of the bed, the carton of pink lemonade on mine.

"What?! I can't hear you!" She screams something else, but I can't make out what she's saying from the kitchen, and we yell back and forth a few times before I finally give up.

Something is heating in the microwave when I walk back in, so I step in front of it, grab the counter, read the timer, then start shaking my ass. "You only have seventeen seconds left of this," I tell my girlfriend, looking back over my shoulder.

She glances at me, rolls her eyes and goes back to cutting small slices of Havarti cheese for herself. "Yeah, guess I'll miss out," she says.

"Your loss!" I say, still gyrating my hips, even though she's not paying attention. I keep it going until the microwave beeps, and when I turn around she's smiling, holding our plates out, showing off what she's prepared.

"What do you think?" she asks.

"Mmmmmm," I say, pulling my nose from the plates. I smack my girlfriend's butt, something she would only allow at home, before grabbing her bowl of soup out of the microwave, and we go back to the bedroom.

"L-, make the bed better," she tells me, waiting on my side. I pull the sheets, adjust her pillows, and she sets down my plate, then scoots around the front of the bed, to the side I moved from when we started dating because it's "near the window," where she likes. We decide to finish a movie we were watching last week but had stopped because she was tired and wanted us to go to bed. Leaning back against our pillows, plates on our laps, the movie starts and it's not long before she asks, "Do you like your meal?"

"Are you kidding me?" I tell her, scooping up some of the mashed roots with my fork. "It's delicious."

Swirling her spoon around her bowl, she says, "You usually say something. You know, if you like it."

"Honey, it's great. Your meals always are." I put my hand on her lap. "Sorry I didn't say anything, S- P-. You just have to give me a minute. Why do you think I never want to go out to eat?" I tell her, thinking to myself at the same time, "I wish she'd used penne pasta." She smiles, stops playing with her spoon, then tells me she tried something different this time, added some new ingredients to see how it would taste.

Glued to her phone, my girlfriend hasn't taken a bite of her food or her soup in the thirty minutes we've been in here. Mostly watching cat videos, she's handed it over to me several times, saying things like, "Look, L-, how cute," taking my attention away from the movie. Every so often she looks up at the TV and asks like she always does, "Who's that?" or "What happened?" and I have to pause the movie, then explain what happened or who someone is.

"My food's cold," she complains, moving her fork around, pushing the pasta and vegetables on her plate.

"Do you want me to heat it up?" I ask.

Nodding her head, she smiles, hands me her food, then plays another video.

"You look so handsome shaved," she says when I walk back in the room and set down her plate. "Why don't we spice things up tonight?" she suggests between bites.

"Honey-" I, decide to seize my opportunity for a good joke. "You know I can't eat some of those hot spices you use." I turn back to the TV. Pointing a gun, one of the robbers starts to count, and with each number, Captain Spaulding proceeds to tell him various female family members he can go fuck.

"In the bedroom, my love," she says, swirling some pasta around her fork.

Putting my hands out, trying to act serious, I say, "Honey, you know I'm allergic. I can't eat it anywhere."

She tilts her head, gives me a look. "Sex, Schroeder. Sex."

"Calm down. I was just joking."

"Like I don't know," she says. After making a face, she opens her mouth wide and chomps down on her fork.

Before taking her dishes to the kitchen, I ask, "Do you want some dessert or anything?"

"Noooooooo," she moans, stretching out on the bed, pointing her toes, her arm almost knocking over the lamp on her nightstand.

"Are you sure? No ice cream?"

"Yesssssss." She closes her eyes, rolls over towards me, and extending her arms and legs, sticks out her torso.

When I get back from doing the dishes, she's on her stomach, lying diagonally on the bed. "L-, will you give me a massage. My neck and back hurt."

"My love, aren't you, like, six massages behind?"

She pouts her lips, gives me her "sad face" and shakes her head. "No."

Folding my arms, I say, "Yes," and lean against the doorway. "I've given you six massages since my last one."

"No, that's not true." She keeps shaking her head, then mentions the massage she gave me on Tuesday night.

"Honey," I say, walking towards her. "That massage was one of the worst massages I've ever received. You barely touched my feet for five minutes while we watched the movie." Sitting down next to her, I start stroking her hair and she closes her eyes, begins to moan.

Acting like she can hardly talk or move, she barely gets out, "It wasn't that bad," and after letting out another groan, she says, "Rub harder, and move towards my shoulders, please, L-."

"Honey," I say, slightly annoyed, but not really. "It was-"

"Are you telling me, I don't give good massages?"

"Jesus Christ, honey. Take your shirt off, so I can get your back and shoulders and lay down." I actually don't mind giving her massages, plus it will keep her quiet and I can finish the rest of the movie without pausing or rewinding. Smiling, she hops up quickly, takes her shirt and shorts off, tells me she loves me, then falls back down on the bed, wriggling her feet and shaking her butt in excitement. I grab the lotion out of the small nightstand on my side and throw it on the bed. "I love you too, S- P-. Hold on a sec, hon," I tell her.

Before straddling my girlfriend, I message Harry, Clarence, Trent, and Justin, "Be prepared for the dankest bud you've ever experienced tonight!"

Five or ten minutes in, she looks back at me and asks, "L-, why have you only been massaging my butt for the last few minutes?

Harry

"Oh yeah! A little something special for the last night!" I shout, tying off a red balloon Clarence just passed me. We've been at it for about thirty minutes, and Jus' room is almost full.

"And you know it has to be good if he's bragging about it," Clarence adds. The red one was the last one in the package, so Clarence grabs another, and rips open the bag. We picked them up at the same place we rented the air machine, and after shuffling his hand around in the see-through package, he says, "Man, there are a lot of yellows."

"Maybe it's that stuff he's always talking about," I say, tossing the balloon. "You know, that bud he says he can never get." We're done with the rest of the room in under twenty minutes, and I'm surprised when Clarence tells me we've only filled up 192.

We hold back as many balloons as we can, some of them drifting past our hands and arms, while Clarence shuts the door; and leaving the pump and extra plastic bags in the hallway, we walk back to Trent's room. Clarence had already started there when I walked in on him an hour ago and told him we should work together. "I think it'll be quicker," I said.

Clarence picks up where he left off, setting up red Solo cups alongside each other, next to Trent's bed. "Over there," he says, pointing at a case of cheap beer, next to Trent's brown dresser. I pick up the silver and blue box, along with a bag of cups, walk over and kneel down next to him. When I pop the top on the first one, it sprays all over me, and I quickly put my mouth over the small opening, taking several swallows of the warm, tasteless beer. Looking up, Clarence smiles but doesn't laugh, accepts it from my extended hand and takes a large drink. Starting in the corner between Trent's bed and the wall, he starts pouring small amounts in each cup, handing me the empty cans when he's done. I continue to lay out cups in front of him, handing him a full beer every now and then, each of us taking a swig. When I start to open the closet door, he puts his hand up, stopping me. "Don't worry about the closet. I already took care of that." He winks, then points to where I'm standing. "And don't worry about in front of the door either. I'll get that, too."

I give him an odd look, but he doesn't see because he's already started pouring again, and we talk while we work, mentioning the guy's reactions, tonight, the two girls from last night, tomorrow, our new jobs, and both of us eventually end up sitting on the floor across from each other, him leaning against Trent's bed, me against the wall. Almost done, we'd stopped working for the last few minutes, both of us talking seriously about our futures while sharing a beer.

"Man, I can't wait for tomorrow. I'm ready," Clarence says, passing me the can. I shake it back and forth, the minute amount left splashing around inside.

"Thanks a lot, man. I appreciate it." Finishing it anyway, I slide him a beer from the half-full box we opened fifteen minutes ago, and tell him, "We should do the rest of this before they get home."

While putting the air pump back in Clarence's closet, I hear Jus and Trent, get home. When I walk into the living room, the blowup doll I put in his car is on the sofa, and Jus is telling Clarence about a jogger they followed on their way home. "I was playing, 'Eye of the Tiger-'" He pauses for a second, gives me a nod, looks back at Clarence. "And Trent was hanging out the window, cheering him on."

"Dude even slapped my hand," Trent says, setting two pizza boxes on the counter. Immediately after he puts them down, Clarence walks over and opens the top one slightly, before closing it and sliding it to the side. He picks up a piece of sausage pizza from the bottom box and takes a bite.

Ignoring what Jus said about the jogger, I slap him on the arm, then motioning to the couch, say, "I see you brought your new girlfriend home to meet us."

"Of course, man," he says sarcastically, nodding his head. "You know I'm not going to get serious with anyone until I know you like her." He picks up my six-pack of Blue Moon Trent sat on the floor, and reaching into the cabinet, I grab Jus and my identical glasses from Jamaica on purpose, knowing he'll like it, then snatch an orange out of the fridge. After cutting it, they all hold out their glasses for me to drop their slice in, and Trent asks for a bottle opener.

Dipping his crust into the heated cup of marinara sauce, Clarence tells him, "You don't need a bottle opener, dumbass. It's Blue Moon."

"Oh, yeah," Trent says, twisting the top. Just then his phone beeps, and he takes two huge bites before looking at it.

I take a swallow, and the beer tastes perfect with our pepperoni and mushroom pizza, and I smirk a little, thinking about what's waiting for them in their rooms. "Thanks for the beers and food, Jus," I say, lifting my glass to him, and Clarence wipes his mouth, does the same.

Trent looks up from his phone, takes a bite and with a full mouth, says, "Uhhhh, u'r wlcumb."

"I highly doubt you paid for any of this, Sir Unemployable," Clarence says, turning to him.

The three of us laugh, and he stops typing. "No need for specifics. You required beer and pizza. I came back with beer and pizza," he says, motioning to the boxes. He picks up his bottle with the same hand he's holding his slice in and takes a swig. Jus, who's sitting on the counter, looks past Clarence and asks Trent what he thinks his next profession will be.

Before he can answer, Clarence turns around from leaning on the counter and puts his hands down. Standing between the two of them, he looks over at Jus, and tells him, "Man, I don't think there are many left that he hasn't been fired from."

Shrugging his shoulders, Jus casually says, "He could be a urine farmer for hunters."

"Those exist?" I ask.

"Uh huh," he answers, smirking.

"Or a professional cat catcher," Clarence adds.

I throw in "golf ball diver," telling Trent, "imagine how useful you could be at all of the local country clubs."

"How many jobs have you been fired from?" Jus asks.

"Including this latest one?" Trent says.

"Yep."

Trent glances over at Clarence, who immediately answers, "Twenty-nine."

"Twenty-nine," he says, looking back at Jus.

"Jesus!" I exclaim, hitting the counter, almost spitting up my mouthful of pizza. Clarence smirks, shakes his head, chuckles, and Jus simply says, "Unfathomable."

He flicks us off individually, goes back to messaging on his phone, and the three of us reminisce about our fond memories of Trent's multiple firings.

"Constantly setting off all of the alarms to go off at the same time after you left work at that department store," Jus says, turning from us to Trent who, recalling his prank, looks up, already grinning.

I remind them of the time he was fired from that Chinese restaurant for replacing his "l's" with "r's" while talking to everyone. "What did the manager say he was fired for?" I ask, looking at Clarence.

"For being an asshole," he says, chuckling. Coughing a little, he starts laughing harder and tries to talk. "And for having a, a-" Unable to stop, he keels over, not speaking again until he catches his breath. "For having a ching-chong speech level of a 1 out of...100!" Clarence can barely get the last part out, and Jus and I join him, all three of us howling hysterically at the burn the old dude delivered. "And that's an old Asian guy saying that shit!" Clarence yells, finally pulling himself together. "That's cold!"

"Don't you mean, 'rever 1 out of a 100," Trent says, chuckling.

"Aaaaaaand the time you were fired for having five dead grandmothers," I blurt out, sticking my hand up from behind the fridge door. I pull out another beer from the bottom shelf and halfway through closing the door, Clarence asks me to grab him one.

"And the granddaddy of them all." Clarence closes his eyes, shakes his head, starts smiling. "Your first firing." Opening his eyes, he looks over at Trent, who put his phone down. Grinning with pride, because he knows the story Clarence is going to tell, Trent puts his glass to his lips and holds it there. "The time you babysat our coach's eight-year-old son and gave the kid Nyquil to knock him out, so you could fuck his sister after the two of you drank the coach's liquor!" Clarence bows his head, then quickly jolts it back up, looks at Jus and me. Yelling even louder, he says, "And then panicked when the coach came home early, tossing the comatose kid into bed next to his naked, passed-out sister, forgetting a used condom on her bedroom floor on the way to pretending to be asleep on the living room couch!" Clarence brings his glass down, hitting the counter hard.

Shaking our heads, Jus and I mock Trent while he holds his glass above his head, blowing all three of us kisses, and then his phone rings.

"Hold on a sec," he says, putting his finger up, answering it. "What's up, motherfucker?!" When he walks into the living room,

Clarence says something about Trent being fifty and living in an apartment in his basement, and when Jus asks him if he would charge rent, Clarence tells him that if Trent had a job, he would.

"So, no then," I say, taking a swig.

We all laugh loudly again at our friend's expense, and Trent quickly looks over at us, making Jus cackle. He flicks us off, grabs the blowup doll, and walks back towards the kitchen, saying into the phone, "Okay, I love you too, mom. Bye."

On the TV, a news reporter is interviewing a guy in his mid-30s, who's much shorter than her. She holds the microphone down as he describes finding twenty thousand dollars in a bag on the street and turning it into the local police. Taking his hat off, revealing his balding head, he says, "I did it to set an example."

"Pfh. An example of what not to do!" Trent yells, at the TV. Shaking his head, he pats the blowup doll sitting next to him on the leg, and whispers in her ear, "I'll be back soon, baby." He finishes the last bite of his slice, takes a sip of his beer, then walks past me towards the hallway, saying back to us, "If that were me, that bag would be sitting in my bedroom now." Not five seconds later, we hear, "Woohoo!" and all of us head towards where it came from. When we get to Trent's door, I look over Jus' shoulder and down to the floor. Picking up cups with his left hand, Trent's pouring them into one in his right, then setting them on the floor, inside each other.

Clarence playfully pushes Jus' head down from behind. "Enjoy that warm beer," he says, resting himself on Jus' shoulders.

Surrounded by cups of beer, Trent seems pleasantly pleased with our prank, and I tell Clarence, who's pushing Jus down even more now, practically hanging on him, "Maybe we should have switched."

"Nah, man." He gets off Jus, stands up straight. "I got something else," he whispers, grabbing Jus' arms, shaking him.

Once his cup is almost full, Trent takes a large gulp, finishing half of it, then lets out a long burp. "Nice trick, toolbags." He looks past Jus, at Clarence, then me. "This is perfect for pre-gaming," he says, swinging his cup around, taking another swig. "Ahhhhhh, and free, too."

"Alright. Well, you might as well enjoy the good beers," Clarence tells him, motioning towards the closet. "We used a couple of Justin's for the cups in there because we ran out." I know he's lying because we still had a few cheap beers left in the case when we were done. They're behind the couch.

"Sweet!" Trent says, clearing a path to his closet.

"What the fuck, Clarence?!" Jus complains, turning around, glaring at Clarence, who tries to calm him down.

"Shhh, I didn't," Clarence whispers, shaking his head. He looks back to see if Trent's watching, but he isn't, and after Clarence gives me the same wink as before, he pulls out his phone and starts recording.

Immediately after Trent slides open the white door, he lets out an even worse girlish shriek than earlier and falls back onto the cups behind him, spilling cheap beer on the floor. Jus jumps a little but I don't, because I was expecting something, and Clarence, who's still recording, nods at the knocked over cups around Trent, and says, "That's why I told you, 'I'd get those.'"

In the closet, a baby is propped up on some sort of wooden stand that Clarence put together. Covered in blood, its head and upper body are sticking out of an old, grey, hooded sweatshirt, a menacing, creepy smile on its face; huge, disturbing, yellow eyeballs staring at us; its freaky, little arms, reaching out.

"Motherfucker!" Trent shouts. He looks at the evil creature for a moment, then turns to us and points at Clarence. Smirking, Clarence waves to him and stops recording. "Fucking good," Trent says, standing up, brushing beer off of himself. He looks back at the baby, kneels down again and panting a bit, says, "Really fucking good."

When we walk back into the living room, Jus announces he's going to make drinks. "I'll help," I tell him, following him into the kitchen. Clarence grabs their pizza, Trent picks up his plate and the blowup doll, and they both head to the couch. "Thanks for the help," I say.

"No problem!" they shout, raising their glasses simultaneously, the back of their heads facing me.

Jus grabs my vodka, then four glasses Trent stole from one of his jobs, asking me as he opens the cabinet, "Will you get me a beer and the cranberry juice?" I grab one that Clarence lied about using, pull out the carton, get an ice tray, and when we're done and walk over, Clarence is already playing the video he'd just taken. He pauses it as soon as Trent squeals, and laughing, he shows it again.

"What do you guys want to watch?" Trent asks, picking up a piece of sausage that's fallen onto the floor, popping it in his mouth.

Jus snatches the rainbow wig off the couch, flings it at Clarence, and sits down. "Doesn't matter to me."

"How about another documentary on hookers?" Trent suggests, nodding his head.

"How about no," Clarence tells him, grabbing the controller out of his hand. Disappointed, Trent tells him to at least pick something cool.

Clarence flips around for a few minutes, displaying the same selection of movies, TV shows, and documentaries we've been choosing from since the beginning of the month. We can't decide on anything to watch as a group, so per Jus' suggestion, we agree that the one who tells the best story about a joke he's pulled can determine what we watch.

When Trent starts his story about dressing a mannequin as a ninja and taking it around last Halloween to get free candy, Clarence gets up to walk back to his room. "You're going to miss my story!" Trent yells. Clarence waves him off, tells him he's heard it before, that we've all heard it before, and by the time he gets back Trent's telling us the location of where the good neighborhoods are for candy, and that he can't believe, "People still leave bowls out with instructions, actually expecting trick-or-treaters to only take one!"

Clarence sets a couple of nugs on the table in front of Trent, asks him to break them up, then walks into the kitchen. After leaning over the trash can for a minute, he comes back with two hollowed-out blunts. "Have you talked to Ling-Ling yet?" Clarence asks Jus, licking the wrapper.

"No, not since they went to lunch," he says, pulling out his phone.

Trent falls back into the couch and starts fucking with Jus. "Are you going to hit that tonight or what, man?! When the hell are you going to make a move!?" He grabs the blowup doll by the hips and starts popping her up and down on his lap. "This is what you need to be doing tonight!" He motions to Clarence and me. "All of us made bets two years ago on an over/under timeline, and we have to keep moving it back."

Jus turns to me, and I shake my head back and forth, mouthing "no," but then I stop, start nodding my head up and down, and mouth "yes". Not paying any attention to Trent, Jus reaches over the table, towards Clarence, and takes one of the blunts he's just lighted.

"Alright, man. Just let us all know when it finally happens, and we're all living in a retirement home," Trent says, extending his hand. Clarence lights theirs, takes a few pulls, then blows some smoke in Trent's face.

After a couple puffs, Jus passes me our blunt, starts texting, and Clarence reminds him to ask Ling-Ling about her friend. He says he will, and satisfied, Clarence takes one more hit, then passes it to Trent, who before smoking tells me it's my turn to go.

"You fuckers should drink for how good this was." I look over at Jus. "You should have known I would win this! We are definitely watching *Getting Doug with High!*" When he gives me a look like he did it on purpose, I chuckle, take a few drags, and behind a cloud of smoke, start to tell the story of the time I ordered a midget, transvestite stripper for Jus' birthday.

Ling-Ling

I look up from my book, smiling when I see it's Justin. Laying it down on my lap, pages open, I text him back, asking him what they're doing, and he replies, "Just telling stories, hanging out, and drinking. You? ☺☺."

"Reading. What are you drinking?"

"Vodka and beers. When are you two coming over? ☺"

"Hold on ☺," I message. Getting up from the couch, I head towards Court's room but not before returning quickly because I forgot to put my bookmark in.

"Comfortably Numb" is playing softly on the speaker next to her bed when I open the door. It's dark, the shades are drawn, and she's taking a nap, trying to catch up on what sleep she lost last night.

"Hey! Dumbass!" I yell, breaking the tranquil atmosphere.

She sits up suddenly, darts her head around the room. "Huh, what?" Looking at me with one eye open, her hair all over the place, she sleepily asks, "What time is it?" A wad of pink gum is entangled in her hair, just above her right eye.

"Chewing gum before you went to bed?" I ask, walking into her room.

Smacking her lips, she looks around her bed. "Yeah, LL, please, just thirty more minutes." She closes her one eye and lies back down slowly.

"Okay, but just so you know, you have gum stuck in your hair." I close the door, and before I even make it to the couch, I hear Court screaming.

Still shrieking, she runs into the living room, holding up a mirror, looking into it. "LL, what the fuck do I do!?" She starts poking at the clump of gum, pulling on it, yelping some more, stomping her feet. "LL," she pleads.

Despite knowing that she's looking for me to be just as over dramatic as her about the situation, I respond like I always do when she's ranting about something - which she hates - with sound logic and reasoning. "Well, poking won't help," I tell her. Casually stretching back out on the couch, I glance at my phone, set it on my lap, look back at her and calmly say, "Leave it alone until we figure out what to do." After thinking for a second, I suggest, "We should call the Grandma."

"Yeah, she'll know what to do! Move over." Court hits my legs, I bring them to my chest, then lay them out on her lap when she sits down. Putting her phone on speaker, she holds it up, and I can see the contact name that Trent changed a year ago when he borrowed her phone. It reads, "THE MOTHERFUCKIN GRANDMA!!!"

While it's ringing, I tell her we should try and leave by 9:15. She points at her hair, and giving me an irritated look, puts her hands up. The Grandma picks up after the third ring. "Hello, sweetie?"

"Grandma!" Court squeals into the phone. "I've got gum in my hair! How do I get it out?!"

"Ok, sweetie, relax." We can hear people in the background. "I've had cum in my hair so many times, I couldn't begin to count. Now calm down, and just go wash it out with shampoo. It'll come out."

"Gum, grandma, gum! What the fuck?! I've got gum in my hair! G – U – M."

"Oh, sweetie." More background noises and some music starts to play. "I can't hear well on this thing. Let's do that video thing, and you show me what it looks like.

The phone is too close when the Grandma answers, and we can only see her eyes and part of her nose. "Pull the phone back, grandma!" Court impatiently barks.

"Leave it alone," I tell Court, pulling her arm down, and both of us look at the screen.

The Grandma isn't wearing a shirt, and we can see the top of the straps on her bra. They're thick and made of leather, with shiny spikes on them, and behind her, over her left shoulder, through the large, square opening in her dining room wall, we can see two women kissing in the kitchen. They're wearing similar, leather bondage-type gear and a man who looks remarkably similar to our waiter, starts licking one of the woman's breasts. "Grandma! What are you doing! Turn the phone!" Court screams.

She casually looks behind her right shoulder, then her left. "Oh, sorry, sweetie," she says, turning around, indifferent. Waving her hands, she instructs whomever is holding the phone to move with her. "Here, here, okay, stop. That's good."

"Okay, girls," she says, looking back at us. The only thing in the background now is a painting hanging on the wall behind her that Court made in high school. Surprisingly really good, it's a portrait of a tulip field. A small stream runs through the middle of the rows of orange, red, yellow, and purple flowers that mix together nicely, creating new colors. At the far right of the painting, in a dark, brown tree, a petite, cute, older bird is perched on one of its branches, and next to her, in the nest they share alone, a baby bird is sleeping.

Showing her the gum, Court asks, "Grandma, what do I do?"

"Sweety, relax." Pretty calm for receiving a video call in the middle of an orgy, the Grandma goes on to explain what to do while we try not to laugh. Too much. "Do you girls have any olive oil?"

Not knowing the answer, Court looks at me, and while standing up, I say, "We do."

"In a bottle?" the Grandma asks.

"Yes," I say, leaning back down.

"Well, you better let her out!" The Grandma starts laughing at her own joke, and so does the person holding the phone, who I can now tell is a man.

Irritated, Court shouts, "Grandma, it's no time for jokes! What if I have to cut my hair!" The Grandma tells her again to calm down, and after I get back from the kitchen and show the bottle to the camera, she instructs me to completely cover the gum and surrounding hair in olive oil, using either my fingers or a toothbrush.

"Then just wait a few minutes, girls, and remove the gum."

"Thanks, grandma!" Court says, waving. "We have to go! I love you!"

"I love you too!" I shout, sticking my head close to the screen.

"I love you, girls!" the Grandma says, a hand appearing on her shoulder. It's Julio. Not wearing a shirt, he smiles, nods at us, then says something in Spanish to the Grandma, and she hands him a black leather mask with filtered eyes and a tube for a mouth.

"Grandma, what is that!?" Court asks, laughing.

"Oh, it's just Julio's anti-snoring device, sweetie. Don't pay any attention to that. I have to go, girls! I love you!" The camera breaks off to the right, panning to the ground, and before the video shuts off, we can hear the Grandma say, "Now be a good boy and get down on your knees, Julio," and then something in Spanish.

Still giggling, I look at Court. "Have I told you how much I love the Grandma?"

"Yeah, everybody does. Now get this shit out of my hair."

Jumping off the couch, I clap my hands together a few times. "Let's make drinks first!" I say, grabbing her hand. "Come on!"

After snatching the pineapple-flavored Cruzan rum from the freezer, along with a blue ice tray, I set them on the counter, then slap Court's arm. "Leave it alone," I tell her. We'd tried the rum on a trip to St Croix this past Spring Break. It was in the first drink served to us when we checked into the resort, and we both loved it so much that it was the only liquor we consumed for the rest of our trip, mixing it with orange juice, Coke, fruit punch, and coconut water. Within a month, we'd finished the three bottles we'd brought back with us from the duty-free in the airport, but luckily, on the way back from a last-second hiking trip suggested by Court last weekend, we found some in a small liquor store 5.4 miles off the interstate. We were only an hour away from home, but both of us were in the mood for a beer, so Court found two stores on her phone, and even though this one was further away, we chose it because we'd already passed the exit for the other one, and I didn't want to turn around.

"I can't believe it!" Court yelled from the next aisle over. She'd made a habit of looking for the Cruzan rum anytime we visited a new liquor store, always striking out. Kneeling down, with one bottle tucked under her arm and two in her hand, she waved me over, excitedly shouting, "Check it out!" We bought the eleven bottles they had at $9 a bottle.

"Make mine with orange juice," she says.

"Exactly what I was going to have!" I squeal, reaching into the fridge, grabbing both. After mixing our drinks, I motion to the sink, tell her to "lean over," and she puts her phone down. Our glasses make a "ping" sound when they meet, and we both take a sip. I coat the gum and surrounding hair with my fingers, tell her to wait a minute, then wipe my hands with a paper towel.

"Like, exactly a minute?" she asks, turning her head, looking up at me.

"Let's give it two, to make sure."

"Okay, well hurry up." Tilting her head, she takes a swallow, and some of the drink misses her mouth, pouring down her left cheek.

"Sure, Court. I'll just make time go faster."

"Okay, good," she says, closing her eyes, and I roll mine. When I bring the glass to my lips, the scent of the rum, processed by my olfactory bulb, travels to my amygdala and hippocampus, eliciting memories of our trip. I can easily picture the beach, mid-day, both of us laid out, the green and white striped hotel towels underneath us, the sound of the ocean breaking in front of us, the smell of lunch cooking at "The Pirate's Cove" fifty feet away.

Court calls for me, and my pleasant memory abruptly changes to us hiking over the small mountain that was filled with Caribbean Hermit Crabs, to some tide pools, her complaining the entire time, sweating profusely and taking breaks, asking "How much longer?" every five minutes.

"LL, Hello?" She'd already said my name twice.

Snapping out of my haze, I pull at the gum, and most of it comes out easily. Around twenty percent won't, so I tell Court to wait another minute; she tilts her head back down, and I start stroking and scratching her head. "Mmmm. Will you go around to the sides and do in front of my ears too?" she asks.

Moaning, Court moves her head around, non-verbally directing me where to rub, and I massage for longer than sixty seconds. When I tell her, "Time's up" and "Let's see if I can get it out," she asks if I'll continue for another minute. Unbothered, but out of habit, I roll my eyes again and looking out the window at the wooden lawn chair on the balcony, I recall three years ago when the Grandma rented us this apartment.

It was freshman year, and I'd been studying all night, and the yelling from the living room had woken me up from my two hours of sleep. It was early, 8:02 a.m. when I looked at my phone. I knew Court had a class, but it was at 8:00. "I wonder what's going on?" I thought to myself, walking across our room, pulling on my white robe with yellow, blue, and red stars on it.

Stopping once I heard my name, I peeked through our barely open door, not opening it any further, because it creaked. The roommates we'd been living with for the past month-and-a-half were complaining to Court, telling her that I just wasn't "cool" and they wanted me to move out, find other housing. "We want you to stay," Tabitha told her. *"You're fun to hang out with."* None of the four had given any type of effort to be friendly towards me since day one, all of them acting rude, arrogant, and disrespectful, despite any efforts or forgiveness on my part.

"Listen, Bitches." I don't know if it was from Court saying that, or her actions that created the loud bang I heard shortly beforehand, but all four of the girls let out a gasp, then backed up, and I could now see a little of someone's blue dress, and Jenny's gold purse, swaying back and forth, disappearing and reappearing in the entry-way from the hall to the living room. "Let me be fucking clear. LL is my best friend," she told them. "You cunts are nothing more than acquaintances - fucking douchebag tools we were roomed up with. You, you, you, and you, go fuck yourself!"

Three hours later, Court woke me up. Holding a brown, paper bag, she was sitting on the edge of my bed. "Come on, we're moving," she said, taking my hand.

We moved into this fantastic, two-bedroom apartment, a place that my parents nor I could ever afford half of. The Grandma, wearing a matching yellow sweater, jacket, and skirt greeted us at the door. Giggling, she was jingling our keys above her head. After touring our new place with them, I walked out on the balcony, sat in one of the wooden chairs and watched the people four stories below for a few moments. I opened the brown paper bag, took a bite of the pink frosted donut Court brought me, and it was the best donut I'd ever had.

Turning her head and opening her eyes, Court says, "Okay, want to see if it will come out?"

The gum comes out effortlessly, in one piece, when I pull. "All out," I tell Court, tossing it in the trash, slapping my hands together.

She grabs the brown towel next to the sink and asks, "What time did you want to leave?" While rubbing her head, she moves out of my way.

"9:15," I remind her, washing my hands, and she asks if I want another drink. Motioning to my half-full glass, I answer, "No, I still haven't finished that." She doesn't listen, grabs the icy bottle from the counter, and starts pouring until I yell "stop!" which doesn't take long. When she's done fixing hers, Court starts teasing me about Justin, telling me that I need to step up my game.

"And this is an actual conversation I overheard between you two!" she says, loudly. Turning to her left and right, she mimics Justin and me. "Well, no one asked me to the formal," she says, copying my voice.

"Yeah, me either. What are you going to do?"

She turns. "Stay home if no one asks."

Copying some of his movements, she says, "Me too, but it would be fun to go."

"I agree. It would be nice to go," Court says, talking slowly, acting dumb, mocking me, her head tilted to the side.

Done with her theatrical performance, she turns to me. "I agree? It would be nice to go!? It would be nice to go?!" she yells. "Seriously, LL?! That's the best you two can do?!" I look away, down and to the right, more embarrassed about actually hearing our terrible conversation out loud than Justin and my slow time table. She starts up again. "And this one I overheard from the hallway! You two were studying. What was it? Two weeks ago?" She looks at me for affirmation, and when I don't say anything, she turns to her left, and trying to sound like him, says, "So, this guy I know likes this girl I know, but she's been completely oblivious to all of his signals, so what does he have to do to tell her he likes her?"

Putting her head down and acting like she's writing, just like mine was, Court talks without looking up. "I don't know, just tell her he likes her."

She tilts her head up, turns. "Like, I like you. Just like that?"

"Yeah just like that."

"I like you."

"Yeah, just like that." Squeaky voice, head down.

"I like," small pause, "you."

Glancing up, she shakes her fake pen. "Yep, you've got it, anything else? We really need to study, Justin."

"Anything else?! Anything else?!" she shouts, hopping around the kitchen, her shirt flying up, exposing her belly button. "Are you fucking kidding me?!" She throws her hands in the air. "Anything else? Yeah, how about you lick my pussy, Justin, while I take these stupid, fucking notes!" Shaking her head, she looks at me. "The shame and disappointment I felt in that hallway. Shame, LL, shame!" Hardly taking a second to breathe, she belts all of this out, loud and fast.

"Are you finished?" I ask, leaning against the kitchen counter, standing up quickly, looking back at my clothes to see if I'd rested in any olive oil.

"No." She splits her middle and forefinger apart and starts sticking her tongue in and out of them. "Mmmmm, Mmmmm, Justin," she moans.

"Ew, gross, Court." I try to hit her hand, but she dodges me, and still darting her tongue in and out of her fingers, she starts jumping around the kitchen again.

"Oh, Justin. Oh, oh, ohhhhh!"

"Haha. You are so funny, Court." I take a drink, not paying much attention to the fragrance this time, and she finally stops after I try to defend my actions. "We were studying! It was a huge final!" I yell.

"Yeah, yeah, you can still get laid." She takes a large chug, looks at me, then screams, "We are getting drunk, so fucking drunk and high tonight, LL!" With her arms out, she attacks me, hugging me tightly, and I hug her back. After letting go, she tells me to text Justin. "Tell him we'll be there around 9:30," she says, and she starts dancing around the kitchen again, mocking my voice, repeating, "Anything else" and "It would be nice to go," while doing the tongue thing again. When I try to walk to the sofa to get my phone, she blocks my way and starts gyrating against me.

"Get out of the way, Court jester," I say, shoving her. While texting Justin, I take several sips, and defending myself some more, I remind Court of what only she knows. "I'm still a virgin. You know I'm not good at any of this stuff." I take a large gulp.

She stops whatever silly dance she's doing. "You know, you should-" After pausing for a moment, she looks at me mischievously, then starts nodding her head up and down. I glance at my glass, notice I've consumed quite a lot in the last couple of minutes, and when I look back at her, she finishes. "You should shave your pussy tonight just in case."

Clarence

"They'll be here at 9:30," Justin says. He picks up the thin, white rope and pulls on it, tightening it.

"What about their friend?" I ask, tying my rope off onto one of the four wooden stands I made, along with the mounting for the baby, earlier this week. He says he forgot, and after fastening his rope to the higher of the two small eyebolts on the stand close to him, he sends her a message.

"Here you go," Harry says to Justin and me, throwing the pillows from mine and Trent's bed at us. After ripping off some duct tape, I secure one of the pillows to the bottom of the stand, then another one above it, slightly overlapping the two.

Justin's phone beeps and I look over. He nods, tells me, "She said their friend is coming," then he starts pulling his rope to the other stand.

"Awwww yeah. Going to make some moves," Trent says. Sitting on the couch, he's breaking up some bud I gave him before Justin and Harry, and I started setting up. He has two piles of weed in front of him - one for blunts, one for the gravity bong.

"How about you make some moves and help, instead of sitting on your lazy ass," I say. Working on the stand close to Trent, I hit him with the pillow I'm about to bind to the wood. "It's taken you fifteen minutes to do that when it should have taken two."

"Dude, don't knock over the weed," he says, covering the piles that I didn't even come close to hitting. He turns and puts one of his hands on the blowup doll's leg and starts stroking her hair with the other. "And watch out for Claudette!" I roll my eyes, don't even ask him how he came up with the name, and using his school ID, Trent unnecessarily breaks apart and moves one of the piles around, telling the three of us we didn't need his help and, "What's it take, anyway. Thirty minutes?" None of us pay attention to him, nor his usual laziness that we're all used to, and Justin and I finish what we're doing, and Harry hangs the strobe lights.

After stepping off the chair, Harry brushes his hands back and forth, and tells us, "Time to make some 'getting ready' drinks, boys." On his way to the kitchen, once he's behind him, Harry slaps Trent on the back of the head and says, "Go get that desk." Justin suggested we use his small desk tonight for the gravity bong, because the kitchen counter is too tall for the girls, and unlike the coffee table, they won't bend over as much, so it'll be less likely that anyone's hair will fall into the water like Courtney's did last time.

"Whiskey or vodka?!" Harry, yells, his hands on both the freezer and cabinet handles. He lets go of the cabinet once we all shout, "Vodka!"

We take gravity bong hits, a cloud forming in our kitchen, then Harry makes everyone a second round because our drinks go down fast. Several balloons litter the floor, and we've been tapping four of them back and forth in the air between each other for the last several minutes, trying to keep them from hitting the ground. Justin had gone to his room after his gravity bong hit, and when the three of us ran back after hearing him shout, we found him lying on the floor, swinging his arms and legs, like he was making a snow angel, and for the next ten or fifteen minutes, we took turns jumping into the sea of balloons in his room, landing on his bed. Noticing the time, I pull the top rope up and slide underneath, while stepping over the lower one. "I'm going to get ready," I say.

I take a quick shower, saying, "Motherfuckering, Trent!" when I pick up my almost, empty shampoo and notice my new bottle of body wash, half-gone. Turning to the side while toweling off and looking in the mirror, I'm glad I'm not in the shape I was two years ago. "That outfit would not look as good," I say to myself, imagining myself in it, stomach sticking out, upper body not as formed. I actually owe a lot of my success to Trent. After filling the fridge and cabinets with my favorite high-caloric snacks on the first day of my diet as a joke, he threw all of it away and mapped out a nutrition plan for me to follow as well as a workout regimen to adhere to. He would check in and ride me on a daily basis. Once, he found a stash of donuts, my favorite dessert, hidden in the back of my closet and taking the filling out of each one, he replaced it with baked beans. "Ugh," I think to myself, cringing, still remembering the revolting taste. But it worked, never cheated again. I recall the amounts and types of food I used to eat, something I wouldn't and couldn't do today - late night meals, large sodas, copious amounts of fast food, candy, Chinese take-out from the place down the street - then I quickly remember my aunt Irma trying to embarrass me on my mom's birthday last year.

"Real classy eating an entire large pizza by yourself, Clarence," she said.

"Yeah, real classy not knowing who your kid's father is, Aunt Irma," I replied. *"Shouldn't you be checking your food stamp balance on your $700 phone?"* She left after that.

Chuckling about the beauty of this prank, I slide on and yank at the glittery red-and-white spandex. It's easily one of the best ones we've pulled. The leggings fit fine after a few tugs, the knee pads easy to slide on, and after fastening the white laces on the red-and-yellow boots, I throw on the cape. The red-and-white mask is a little small, but not too bad, and after adjusting it a bit, I can see fine. I start flexing, watching myself in the mirror, the yellow tassels on the back of the cape swinging back and forth, while I turn and twist my body. "Fucking perfect," I think to myself, getting more enthusiastic about the look on Schroeder's face.

"Grrrrr, who's first?!" I shout, jumping into the living room, my hands out, ready for battle.

Applause erupts, all of them cheering, raising their glasses, and Harry puts his hands up as if to say he's already giving up, not willing to fight. I strike more poses, Justin takes some pics, Trent reminds him to send them to him, Harry and I do the same, and looking away from his camera, over at Trent, Justin asks, "Safe to assume this is going on a t-shirt?"

"You better fucking believe it," Trent answers. Sitting on the kitchen counter with his feet hanging off the edge, he picks up the microphone next to him, says the same thing and it blares loudly through the speaker. "You better fucking believe it."

When I walk over to the kitchen, Harry starts rubbing his hand along the spandex. "Oh, so nice," he says winking at me.

Justin, ruffles my cape, swipes at the tassels and says, "This is fucking great!"

We pass around the vodka, followed by cranberry juice, each of us filling our glasses. The carton runs out after I'm finished, and when Justin pulls the other one out of the fridge, he almost drops it when there's a knock at the door. "They're here," Harry announces over the microphone.

Two more knocks follow, accompanied by several lighter ones trailing down the door, Schroeder's usual beat. "It's Schroeder!" Trent shouts.

"Yeah, thanks, detective," Justin says, turning his head. Looking back through the peephole, he tells us, "It's all of them - Schroeder, his girlfriend, Ling-Ling, Courtney and their friend."

Quickly looking at Trent, Harry motions to the radio and strobe lights. "Make yourself useful!"

I get nervous thinking about the last part that came out of Justin's mouth. What will she think of this first impression? Will she like me? Brushing it off quickly, I reassuringly tell myself, "How could she not? This is hilarious…and humor is a characteristic a girl loves in a guy."

After sliding the mask back on, I pull at it, trying to make it looser, then look around the room to test my visibility. Checking the sound on the speaker, Harry whispers into the microphone while Trent turns on the music, lowering the volume immediately when he realizes it's too loud from when we had it on earlier. Justin, with his hands on the door and light switch, whispers to me, "Go, go!"

With my back against the wall, I hear all of the girls saying hi, Courtney introducing their friend, and after a few moments, Justin turns off the lights, tells Schroeder he has to show him something. I can see Trent flip the switch from where I'm standing, and the different colors start flashing rapidly, a new one every five seconds.

"Whoa, nice, you guys really went out," Ling-Ling says.

Harry's voice booms from the speaker. "Thank you."

Schroeder's girlfriend lets out a yelp, then asks, "Are we doing karaoke?"

"We can," Harry answers. He's turned down the speaker volume.

"Yes!" Ling-Ling screams out, excited about Harry's answer.

"Nice blowup doll," Courtney says.

Trent corrects her, shouting, "Her name is Claudette!"

"What the hell are these ropes for?" Schroeder asks, getting closer, Justin talking to him, guiding him like we planned.

Courtney jokingly asks Harry if we have enough balloons, and Justin almost has Schroeder in position. Purposefully waiting several seconds before he answered, Justin says, "Oh, they're for- here, just slide through." It's about to begin. I crouch down, start bouncing, and Trent turns up the music.

"And in this corner, weighing in at 190 lbs., the challenger, Schroeder!" Harry turns the volume up midway through announcing, and he and Justin and Trent start booing loudly, hollering at Schroeder. The strobe lights switch from green to red, and I can barely hear Courtney talking because the music has gotten louder. She's asking Harry if she needs a drink for this, and Schroeder yells, "What the fuck is going on?!"

Harry continues. "And in this corner, at a new weight of 240 lbs., the world champion, the terrifying, the terrorizing, unstoppable luchador, Big to tha Mutha-Fuckin C!"

Trent, Harry, and Justin start cheering wildly, and I wait a few seconds, letting the suspense build before I jump out, staring wide-eyed at Schroeder through my mask. Going through the ropes, I walk around our living room, circling the area where our coffee table usually is, yelling, "Oh yeah, oh yeah!" I flex my biceps, hold my arms in the air, glare at Schroeder and shout, "Time to get down, Schroeder!" Courtney and Ling-Ling scream and start pumping their arms, encouraging their friend, who looks beautiful in her red dress, to do the same and she does.

"You fuckers are crazy," Schroeder says, shaking his head. Not quite knowing what to do, he cracks a nervous smile and just starts looking around the room.

"Ding." The sound of a starting bell, played through Harry's phone, rings several times through the speaker, and Trent raises the volume, and the lights change pattern, a rhythm of yellow, blue, red, orange, green, purple, one right after the other, in that order, repeated over and over again. Shrugging his shoulders, Schroeder gives me a "why not" look, puts his arms in the air and lunges at me.

Courtney pulls on the rope in front of her, starts yelling louder, and Justin, standing behind her, laughs while looking back and forth between the match and Ling-Ling, who's clapping her hands, jumping up and down next to Schroeder's girlfriend, the only one rooting for him.

Schroeder's girlfriend yells, "Boo!" when I quickly put him in a headlock and begin guiding him around our homemade ring.

"He's got him in a headlock!" Harry announces. I pick Schroeder up, his legs kicking and flailing wildly in the air, while I spin around, and the guys make more noise, encouraging me to slam him on the couch. "He's got him in the air!" Before I throw him down, I catch a glimpse of Schroeder's girlfriend out of my left eye. She looks genuinely worried, concerned he might get hurt, visibly distraught in a crowd of people that want to see something she doesn't. The sofa makes a loud cracking sound, despite my tossing him on it much softer than I'd planned, and when he hits it, Claudette flies up into the air, landing on her stomach, butt out, next to us. "And he's down!" Harry begins to count, "1, 2-"

"Schroeder, are you okay?!" his girlfriend shouts. I let him up, the couch bending slightly in the middle when he stands, and he kisses his girlfriend's hand, reassuring her he's more than fine.

"And he's up!"

Motioning to Schroeder with my finger, I say, "Come here, ginger." Both of them look at me. "I'm going to fuck you up!"

"That's not funny, Clarence. Don't say that," his girlfriend says, serious.

I put both my hands up. "I apologize."

Schroeder turns to his girlfriend, winks at her. "Don't worry, my love. I won't hurt him." He gives her a kiss, then attacks me. I let him put me in an arm lock, and she smiles, screams, "Go, Schroeder!" but her claps and cheers are soon drowned out by the guy's jeering and boos. It's not long before I turn my arm to the right and stand up, towering over him. Looking up, his face changes when he sees the trouble he's in. I grab his black sweatshirt with the picture of three wolves howling at a moon on it, and fling him over my shoulder.

Trent yells, "Tag-team!" and slaps Schroeder's hand while I'm whirling him around. Snatching Trent immediately, I chuck him on the couch, ripping his red t-shirt.

"Despite two opponents, our champion is in solid shape!" Harry declares into the mic.

After lightly putting Schroeder on top of Trent, I sit on both of them, not allowing either one of them to move. "That's not fair!" Trent shouts, his arms flapping underneath both of us. Courtney and Ling-Ling's friend is laughing, having a good time, all three of them sharing a drink that's in a large, plastic cup, made hastily by Harry after Courtney's comment, and since Claudette's close, I snatch her and start humping Trent's face with her ass.

"1, 2, 3!" Harry proclaims me the winner, and everyone starts clapping, except for Courtney and Schroeder's girlfriend, who are both booing. "And still the world champion!" I smack Trent on the side of the head before letting them up and make my victory laps.

"Fixed fight, fixed fight!" Courtney screams, shaking the rope.

"You want some, little girl?!" I yell, pointing at her.

"Hell yes, I do!" She steps through the ropes, screams, "Let's go!" Rushing at me, she jumps, trying to put her arms around my head. To oblige her, I bend down, and she grabs on, straddling me with her legs. "Yeah, you like that! You like that!" she shouts. When I stand up, her body goes with me, and a surprised "oh shit" look comes over her face. Swinging her, I grab her legs, hold them up high in the air, and her eyes get even more prominent as I twirl her around a few times, eventually lowering her head to the ground, gently. "I give up!" she says, laughing.

Over the speaker. "A forfeit!"

"That was so funny!" Ling-Ling says, hugging me, giving me a kiss. She leaves her hand on my lower back and introduces me to her friend, somewhat pushing me towards her.

When I shake her hand and halfway hug her, she smells like honey. "That was really funny," she says, giggling, scanning my face, and I realize I still have the mask on.

Smiling, I pull it off. "Thanks."

"Here you go, man," Harry says, reaching between her and Ling-Ling. He hands me a cup. "That was fucking terrific!"

I take a chug, and we chat about the prank, how she knows Courtney and Ling-Ling, where she's from and after ten or fifteen minutes, I announce to everyone that if they want to take pics, they should do it now. Turning back to her, I say, "If you don't mind, I'm going to change."

I've decided on another shower, but I don't want to take a lot of time, so I pick up my pace and take longer, quicker steps as soon as I reach the hallway, clutching my towel quickly from my bedroom. After turning the knob, impatiently jumping in the cold water, cursing Trent's name again when I grab one of my bottles, and drying off, I realize I haven't brought any clothes with me, only the costume I'm not putting back on. Retaking long strides, wearing only a towel, and hoping no one sees me, I dart to my room.

"Long Tall Sally" by Little Richard starts blaring from the speaker on my dresser, but I start it again after ten or fifteen seconds because I don't feel like I've appreciated it enough. Breaking it down hard at first, to give the song the respect it deserves, I dance wildly around my room, singing, but not too loud. When putting my jeans and socks on, I slow down a little bit, syncing my getting dressed with the music, because I want the song to end at the same time I'm done. Gyrating around my room some more, getting excited about tonight, tomorrow, I shake my hips, then point at myself in the mirror with finger pistols, shoot, slide my dark polo shirt over my head, and belt out the last line.

They've taken the ropes down, moved the coffee table back, put Claudette in a corner, and Harry quickly picks up the mic when he sees me. "The champion, ladies and gentlemen!" I raise my empty glass to applause and boos, Schroeder and Trent screaming they want a re-match. "Come here, man. Let me take care of that," Harry says, motioning me over. He puts the mic down, turns off the speaker, then says something to Trent, who's standing next to him.

Trent

After kicking the two ice cubes I just dropped on the floor under the fridge, I fill half of Clarence's glass with vodka and grab the Red Bull. Surprisingly, I'm already pretty buzzed. "Probably from all of those beers on my floor," I think to myself. There's not much Red Bull left after I'm done, so I drink the rest of it and put the empty can back on the counter.

"We gonna have some fun tonight!" Clarence shouts, taking his glass, slapping my hand. "So, what do you think of her?" He tastes his drink, then turns to the living room where everyone else is, and nods his head towards the couch, at Courtney and Ling-Ling's friend, Arkansas, or whatever her name is. Knowing that I wouldn't make any attempts to hook up with her because of Clarence, I hadn't really bothered to listen to her name when Ling-Ling introduced us.

We talk about her for several minutes, and Clarence starts asking more juvenile-like questions, and I finally say, "Damn, man. Are we back in middle school?"

He flicks me off, I hit him on the arm, and after taking a huge swallow of his drink and without looking at me, he says, "Here goes," and walks off.

Schroeder gets up and offers his seat once he notices Clarence leaning down and talking. His girlfriend starts to get up too, but he puts his hand on her arm and says something to her. Looking at her glass, she disappointingly nods her head, and Schroeder kisses her on the cheek, whispers in her ear. She giggles, and smiling, watches him until he slaps my hand, then she turns and listens to whatever Clarence is saying.

"What's up, man?!" Schroeder says, clasping my hand, nodding towards the vodka and Red Bull on the counter next to me. "Hook me up."

I pick up one of the cans, shake it, put it back down, grab the one next to it. "Get some ice if you want some," I say.

Motioning towards the couch, he says, "She's hot." He takes a gulp of his drink, cringes, then looks at it. "Damn, man. How much vodka did you put in this?" he asks, turning to me, taking a smaller sip. I agree with what he first said, look at his cup, call him a "pussy," and glancing back at the couch, I wonder how I would have done with her, had I met her somewhere else. "The natural curly red hair is what does it," he says. Used to the amount of alcohol and the taste, Schroeder takes a larger swig.

Courtney shakes her hand through Harry's hair, messing it up, then she grabs both of their glasses, and before she gets too close to us, Schroeder quietly says to me, "Don't worry about the fifty bucks, man."

Shocked, I glance over at him, then quickly back at Courtney, to see how close she is. Harry's gotten up and is following her. "Huh? Are you sure?" I ask, looking at him.

"Yeah, man." He takes a gulp. "Don't worry about it."

Relieved, because I have only $137.62 and no job, but still feeling a little guilty, I say, "Thanks, man," and tap his already-extended glass.

"Hey guys," she says. Harry walks around the three of us, grabs the vodka next to Schroeder and some bottle of rum Courtney's pointing to that Ling-Ling brought in her purse. Looking hot as always, she's wearing a pink skirt, with a white tank top and she's dancing in place while talking to us. I use that as an excuse to follow her legs down to her black shoes, then back up, and I do it fast so as not to be noticed. "So, who do you guys think will hook up first?" she asks. Trying to hide it from anyone else but us, she puts her hand against her stomach, moves her finger towards the couch, then to the other side of the living room.

Justin doesn't seem nervous or uncomfortable, but he's certainly not relaxed. Rarely talking, mostly just listening to Ling-Ling, he's standing next to the cabinet, only taking his hands out of his jeans' pockets to grab his cup from the shelf.

Clarence, on the other hand, is tilted forward, smiling, using his hands as he talks. They're facing each other on the couch, and she leans her head back, giggling after he says something. She starts talking, and he nods his head, listening intently.

After we watch for a few moments, Schroeder, who's leaning over the counter next to me, stretches one of his fingers from his glass. Not trying to hide it, he points to the couch. "I'll go with that one," he says.

I don't hesitate. "Me too."

Courtney glances at both couples a few times, and Harry hands her a drink that's in a red Solo cup. "I'm holding my vote til later," she says.

"Tonight my boy's coming through," Harry says, lifting his glass, motioning it towards Justin.

"Out of a thousand nights," Schroeder says. He stands up, turns, looks at Harry. "Tonight is the night?"

Without pausing, Harry confidently answers, "Yep," and all of us chuckle, unconvinced. "You'll see," he says. He takes a drink, looks around the room, then back at the three of us. "So, gravity bong?"

"Sounds good to-"

"Nah, don't worry about that right now," Schroeder says, interrupting Courtney. "I've got a special treat for you guys since it's the last night." He puts his finger up, says, "Hold on a sec," then walks over to his green backpack that's leaning against the wall, near the front door.

Schroeder

"Are you fucking kidding me?! You made those?!" Harry says, leaning over us, looking into the Pac-Man lunchbox I've had since the second grade.

"Aww, so cute," Courtney says.

Picking the figure up by its neck, I place it on my palm and show it off, telling them, "I call this, 'the bluntasaurus.'"

"Unbelievable," Trent says, putting his hands on his hips.

"Let me hold it," Courtney says, putting her hand out. I give it to her, then reach back in.

"A native of Africa, 'the eleblunt.'"

Harry starts chuckling, shakes his head. "Dude."

"Is there weed in that whole thing?" Trent asks.

"Nah, would be a waste." I explain how we're going to smoke out of the trunk, telling them, "I've spaced out the bud in all of these, so they'll smoke evenly."

Harry leans over Courtney again. "What else do you have?"

"Ahhh, I'm glad you asked," I say, putting my finger up, handing him the eleblunt. "Another creature who calls Africa its home, the 'hippopotablunt.'"

Taking the eleblunt's trunk out of his mouth, Harry passes it to Trent, then says, "Damn, Schroeder, how much time do you have on your hands?"

Courtney's mostly been paying attention to the one in her hand, looking up for only a second at the other two. "I still like mine better," she tells me. Guiding the bluntasaurus along the counter, she holds it by its sides, tilting it back and forth while she walks it. She "jumps" it over the sink and yells, "Super-bluntasaurus!"

"Alright, settle down over there, or playtime is over," Harry says, patting her on the back.

I don't give much of an introduction when I grab "the blunt-eater," only asking them if they can guess what animal it's supposed to represent.

"Anteater!" Courtney quickly shouts out.

Infantilizing her again, Harry says, "Good, now you can have a snack after naptime."

She flicks him off, and Trent asks me, "Are these filled with that weed you were talking about?"

"Hell, no," I tell him. "That would be a fucking waste. This is just my usual, solid bud." I nod my head, wink, lift my drink, and Trent and Harry raise theirs.

They both say, "Respect," and all three of us take a swig. Courtney gives a delayed "respect", but she's not sure why because she was too busy petting the bluntasaurus and talking to it.

My girlfriend, uncomfortable being without me for too long in a crowded room, regardless of the company, walks over later than I expected she would. She gives me a kiss on the cheek, whispers in my ear, "I love you, L-." We say "I love you" to each other a thousand times a day, something mostly initiated by her, but I don't mind. She can be beyond controlling and moody sometimes, but I know she loves me and cares for me deeply, and she's the best thing that's ever happened to me.

Glancing at her half-full drink, I ask, "Do you want more?" She shakes her head, puts her arm around me, pulls herself close.

"Let's take shots!" Courtney yells, looking at my girlfriend, who agrees, even though I know she probably doesn't want to; and as expected she barely drinks any of it, leaving it on the counter, telling me, "It doesn't taste good."

They ask my girlfriend about my blunt sculptures, and she rolls her eyes, informs them that I should smoke less, then looks at me. "Well, you should." She squeezes my hip. "I just care about your health," she tells me, sincerely.

Pretty soon, we end up talking about the other four, like I knew we would when Trent mentions Clarence. "My man is killing it with Arkansas."

"That's not her name, idiot," Courtney says, giving him a look. He doesn't ask her what it is, and she doesn't bother to tell him;

instead, she looks over at Ling-Ling, who's laughing at something Justin is saying. "I agree with Harry," Courtney tells us. Not trying to hide anything this time, she points at Justin and Ling-Ling. "I think it'll be those two."

"My money's still on Clarence," I say, turning to my girlfriend. I lightly pat her on the butt. "What do you think?"

She hits my hand, not hard, letting me know not to do that in front of everyone; and looking at Courtney, she says, "I'll take Justin, too." Smiling at each other, they touch hands quickly, squeeze and let go. I pick up my girlfriend's unfinished shot glass, throw it back. "I was going to drink that," she says, noticing me.

Surprised but not, I say, "Yeah right. You nev-" I don't bother, grab the bottle on the counter and pour a shot I know my girlfriend probably won't drink, much less finish.

Just as I'm about to suggest we smoke, Courtney starts a battle, so I wait it out, let it finish. After being punched by the eleblunt, the bluntasaurus roundhouse kicks it in the face, sending it flying in the air, backward. It bounces off the rum bottle, landing on the counter. Harry turns the microphone back on. "The eleblunt is down, it looks like it's all over for him! We might have a new champion!" The other four look over, and the bluntasaurus leaps on top of the eleblunt, repeatedly kicking it in the face until it's no longer moving, and when the bluntasaurus stands on top of the eleblunt, triumphant, its victory inevitable, Harry counts, "1, 2, 3!"

While walking into the living room, Harry yells out to Justin, motions for him and Ling-Ling to come over to smoke, and when they do, Harry and Justin go back to their bedrooms, coming back with chairs, Justin, one, and Harry two, setting a couple of them at the ends of their L-shaped couch, one next to Courtney on one side, the other next to Ling-Ling on the opposite end, and the third one in the middle.

Everyone who hasn't seen them checks out the animals, we're about to smoke, and Ling-Ling and her friend agree with my girlfriend and Courtney, saying the bluntasaurus is the best one.

Sounding like Courtney, Ling-Ling says, "Awww, so cute," and picks it up.

I explain to everyone, "If it feels like it's not pulling or you need me to light it again, just tell me. I don't want you to fuck it up and waste it."

"Schroeder!" my girlfriend says, lifting her hand off my leg, hitting me lightly.

"I apologize," I tell everyone. "I just don't want anyone to ruin them, to fuck up-" I close my eyes, open them. "To mess up what I spent a lot of time putting together."

The rest of the girls giggle at my response, all of them moving their eyes from me to my girlfriend, and Courtney hits her on the leg, leans towards her, and says, "Nice."

Trent, sitting in the chair between Harry and Justin, gives me a hard time. "Come on, man. I'm a pro."

"Yeah, yeah, just don't waste it," I tell him, brushing him off, and he doesn't say anything else like he usually would, probably out of respect for my wiping his debt clean.

The girls take a few pictures before we light the animals up, pass them around, and both Courtney and Ling-Ling hold onto the bluntasaurus too long, spiting each other, both of them hogging it while waiving the opportunity to smoke the other animals as they pass by. "Give it up!" Courtney yells, hitting Harry, so he hits Trent, so he hits Justin, so he'll hopefully be able to take it from Ling-Ling.

It takes a solid fifteen minutes before they're done, all four smoking evenly and well, none of them having to be re-lit, and Harry starts clapping; everyone else joins in, and Courtney and Ling-Ling start chanting my name, "Schroeder, Schroeder, Schroeder!"

"Thank you, thank you," I say, taking two bows.

"Not only quality craftsmanship, but as usual, quality bud!" Trent shouts, clapping louder.

"Just wait," I say, looking at everyone. "There's more to come." I throw my arm up, take another bow.

Clarence starts stroking his chin. "Ahhh, the mystery weed," he says. His new friend, who's really high, eyes completely blood-shot and half-closed, giggles more than she should at his comment. We refill our glasses and cups, take more shots, chat it up, and after an hour or so passes, Ling-Ling yells out to no one in particu-lar, "Where are we going?"

Nobody makes any suggestions; in fact, no one answers until Courtney, who stops talking to Harry, takes her hand off his leg and yells back, "I don't know!"

Since we're still high as balls and it's the last night, we decide to play a round of Justin's game. After giving Ling-Ling a minute to explain the game to her friend, Harry looks around the room and sounding as if he plans to start, regardless of what anyone an-swers, he asks, "Do y'all mind if I go first?"

"Go ahead!" Ling-Ling, shouts. She taps her friend on the leg, tells her, "This is fun!" then starts clapping.

Looking at each of the girl's individually while he talks, Harry says, "If women say that all men are the same, then why do you wait on the right one?" He puts his hands up, leans back and all the guys laugh while the girls jeer.

My girlfriend starts rubbing my leg harder, and Courtney says, "Psssh, who's waiting?" She yanks her hand off Harry's lap, makes a face at him, then takes a shot. "I'll go next!" she announces.

"You were next anyway," Harry tells her, chuckling. Filling his shot glass to keep up with her, he knocks it back, looks at her and grins.

She sticks her tongue out at him, makes another face, then turns to us. "Okay, I actually thought of this the other day," she says. Harry starts tickling her, and she swings at his arm, then goes on. "If a vampire bit a zombie, would the zombie become a vam-pire or the other way around?"

After a collective response of "oohs" and "aahs," Harry pours a shot, Courtney asks him for another one and so does Trent. We talk about it for a minute, most of us agreeing that it would depend on who did the biting, and Justin and Ling-Ling argue against us, saying zombies have no circulatory system; thus nothing would spread via blood. Justin starts saying something about the lack of a soul in zombies, due to the ancient's belief it lived in the blood when Trent interrupts. "No, the vampire is stronger," he says. "They have, like, superpowers."

Justin chuckles. Ling-Ling eyes Trent skeptically, says, "Well, that could be true," and Clarence suggests we move on.

"Let's not worry about order!" Harry yells. He takes his shot, points his glass. "New girl, you go!" Courtney and Trent knock theirs back, and excited, Ling-Ling looks to her right and pats her friend on the leg.

She sits up straight, clears her throat. "Uh, okay. I'm not sure if this, counts."

Teasing her, Courtney says, "Say it already!"

She speaks fast. "We use sex to sell anything possible, but those who buy and sell actual sex get arrested." Darting her eyes around the room, she asks, "How was that?"

There's a brief pause, then Courtney and Ling-Ling cheer loudly, everyone gives their approval, and Clarence leans forward, touches her arm, tells her, "Not bad for your first time!"

"I like her!" Harry yells, standing up. He leans over the table, puts his hand out. New girl slaps it. Looking back at Courtney, he asks, "Why didn't you bring her around earlier?"

"No kidding!" Trent shouts. "Why does it matter if someone does that!?" Serious about what he's saying, he goes on. "It's a mutual agreement between two adults!" He looks around the room, unaware all of the guys here know about the time he snuck off with the overweight hooker who kept hanging around the resort on their trip to Jamaica.

Harry points at Clarence, and Justin shouts, "This better be good!"

"Oh, everyone will get this," Clarence assures us. "Okay, tell me if this isn't true. If someone tells you they're cold, there's a ninety-nine percent chance they're going to put their hands on you to prove how cold they are."

"That is absolutely a fact!" Justin exclaims, and we all agree, especially the girls, who tell us the odds are probably a hundred percent with a woman.

"We'll go next," I tell them. Turning to my girlfriend, I rest my hand on hers. "Go ahead, my love."

On the way here, she'd bragged about having a good one for the night, telling me I'd have to wait when I tried to get it out of her. "How scary would it be for a blind person to read, 'DO NOT TOUCH' in braille," she says, giggling.

Letting out a short laugh, I tell her I'm glad she made me wait, and everyone finds her comment funny, and they start shouting out different scenarios involving running machinery, hot metal, electricity, wet paint. Trent somehow comes up with a situation involving a blind person wandering around a sperm donor lab, and when Clarence asks him why anyone would be roaming around a place like that, Trent says, "Duh, cause they're blind." Justin rolls his eyes, tells me to go ahead.

I'd always loved trivia, and when the guys first introduced this game to me years ago, I got obsessed with weird, interesting facts, going so far as to search for them online for my own enjoyment. With a ton to choose from, I decide on an odd one I can add a punchline to. "Did you know there is a male octopus that rips off his penis and throws it at the female, so she can inseminate herself?" I wait a moment, then say, "If that isn't the definition of, 'Go fuck yourself,' I don't know what is!"

Harry looks down at the table, starts to laugh, then picks up the leftover trunk from the eleblunt, tossing it onto Courtney's lap. "There you go!" he shouts. She flings it back at him, makes a comment about it being bigger than his dick, and leaning forward in his chair, Justin puts his elbows on his knees.

"Yeah, it's the Argonaut," he says. Moving his hands close together, Justin starts to explain. "The males only tend to grow to a few centimeters in length, roughly ten percent of the size of the females." He moves his hands further apart, demonstrating the difference in size. We wait for him to continue, but Ling-Ling picks up instead.

"Yeah, so you guys might ask, 'How is reproduction possible when the baby daddy is such a small percentage of your size, right?'" she says, looking around the room, nodding her head. "Right?"

"Of course!" Courtney shouts after no one responds. She hits Harry on his leg, suggesting he should have.

"Exactly what I was thinking!" he says, snapping to attention.

Oblivious that Harry and most of them don't appreciate such an in-depth, intellectual perspective, Ling-Ling responds, "I know! Right?!" She goes on, acts like she's tossing something. "So, the male throws a modified arm containing spermatozoa at the female." She imitates the doggy paddle, and Justin starts to snicker. "And it swims towards her mouth, finding its way inside, fertilizing her eggs. It's fascinating!" Very excited about this bit of trivia, she puts her hands in her lap, then nods her head quickly.

"Yeah, thanks, Dr. Ling-Ling," I say, sitting up. "Thanks for ruining my joke!"

We laugh, then Clarence motions to Trent. "Alright, man, you go."

Smirking, Trent sits up in his chair, pauses for a second, then shouts, "If you watch Cinderella backward, it's about a woman who learns her place!"

Pissed, Courtney stands up, Harry pulls her back down, and all of the guys laugh, especially Clarence, even though he's trying not to, since "someone in particular" is not. She jokingly hits him on the arm. Trying to be serious, he tells Trent, "That's cold, dog, cold." He's still chuckling when he says this, his shoulders moving up and down slightly, and grabbing the balled-up wad of paper towels she used to clean up the vodka she just spilled on the table,

Courtney flings it at him. Still looking at Trent, Clarence catches it, then slowly turns his head to Courtney, winks.

"Okay, Ling-Ling!" Harry shouts, grabbing another bottle of vodka from the freezer. Closing the door, he looks back at her. "Keep it on our level!"

She says, "I'll do my best," and looking back at everyone, she pauses, starts giggling, tries to talk but can't, unable to get out the first word. It takes a few seconds for her to calm down, and nodding her head, her face red, she stops and jabbers while she can without laughing. "Are Medusa's pubes also snakes? Bahahahaha!" She loses it, doubles over in her chair, and when she sits up, tears are streaming down her face.

"LL, what the hell?! Are you okay?" Courtney asks.

We laugh at Ling-Ling's reaction more than her comment, and Clarence starts waving his hands and arms back and forth, close to her, fanning her off. "Cool down, girl, cool down," he tells her.

With one hand on her chest, Ling-Ling waves the other at Courtney, telling her she's fine, and when she finally catches her breath, she takes a sip from her glass. "Sorry, you guys. I just thought that was so funny," she says. Sitting up straight, she slaps both knees with her hands, then wipes under her right eye one more time.

I start sliding my hand up my girlfriend's leg, seeing how far she'll let me go, teasing her, something I like to do when we're in public. Stopping me, she guides it back to where it was. "Not here, L-," she says, quietly.

I decide to mess with her some more, talking loudly. "But Sw-" She turns, glares at me, and I know to stop.

Taking his turn, Justin says, "Why can't I punch hard in my dreams?"

"Ah, no shit, man!" Trent shouts, quickly pointing his drink at Justin, spilling some of it, and most of us shake our heads in agreement, familiar with his revelation.

"I've never really thought about it, but you're right!" Courtney says.

After a couple more rounds of the game, Clarence glances over at Trent, who's looking at his phone, then flings the vodka-soaked wad of paper towels at him, hitting him in the face. Trent flicks him off, throws it back, and Clarence catches it, hurling it back quickly, slapping Trent in the face again. Making a face I wish I could have gotten on camera, Trent's head pops back and he yelps, "Motherfucker!" He picks it up off the floor, takes his arm back, but Clarence doesn't flinch, doesn't make a move, he just sits there. Trent decides he's had enough, drops it, and just then Harry launches another ball of wet towels, smacking Trent on the other side of the face. "Fucking bastards!" Trent yells, throwing his hands in the air, stomping his foot on the ground. After everyone takes another turn.

My girlfriend leans over, whispers so no one else can hear her. "What time are we going out, L-?"

"Hold on, let me check," I tell her, patting her leg. Without turning my head, I shout, "Guys, what time are we going out?!"

Everyone's too busy laughing at Trent to respond, and after a few moments, Harry stands up, taking control of the room. "Okay, y'all settle down!" He waits for the room to get quiet, then asks, "Shots or go out!?"

"Shots!" Courtney yells, banging on the glass table too hard, making a loud, annoying sound. She cringes, shows her teeth and quietly, repeats, "Shots, shots, shots," while lightly hitting the table with her closed fist.

"Damn, someone's down for some shots tonight," Harry says. She kisses the air in his direction, and Ling-Ling, joining her, starts tapping on the table, chanting with her, trying to motivate their friend and Justin to unite with them. They both do, and pretty soon Clarence, who wasn't paying much attention to anything that was being said, is encouraged to do the same. "Shots it is!" Harry announces, throwing both hands in the air, one of them holding the bottle of vodka.

"What should we drink to?" Ling-Ling asks, looking at Justin, then around the room.

Talking slowly, acting as if she has some type of mental illness, Courtney says, "Uh, I don't know, LL. Maybe that it's these guys last night together, and Harry and Clarence are starting their careers tomorrow." Justin loses his smile for a second, forces another one, and pushes up his glasses.

"Well, technically I don't start 'til Monday," Harry tells her.

Courtney hits him. "You know what I mean." She looks back at Ling-Ling, who's been flicking her off for the last few seconds, and Harry asks Ling-Ling if Courtney is her best friend because she lost a bet. The girls stop joking with each other, turn their attention to Harry, and make him "take it back".

Once all the shots are poured, Trent stands up and gets everyone's attention. "Hey, hey, everybody!" All of us stop whatever we're doing and look up at him. He scans the room, starting to his right with Justin, then to the couch, at Ling-Ling, her friend, Clarence, me in the middle of the "L," my girlfriend, Courtney, and Harry, to his left. He waits for a second, then clears his throat, lifts his shot glass higher. Realizing what we're supposed to do, we all stand up abruptly.

Justin

Trent starts his toast. "We've been together four years!" Harry, Clarence, and I holler, pumping our arms in the air. He continues. "And tomorrow, tomorrow, it ends, and these two start new careers." He motions to Clarence, Harry, then puts his head down, and we all do the same, and Harry, Courtney, and Clarence, make muffled, sad noises, joking. That same depressed feeling rushes over me again when I think about the four of us going to the train station tomorrow, and one of us not coming back. My best friend.

"Fuck it," I say to myself, remembering something Schroeder told me during a serious conversation we had here one night when Harry was out hooking up, and Clarence and Trent were in their rooms, passed out. "That's life," he said. "You can't stop someone's moving on, living their life." Grinning, I lift my head and sit up, accidentally brushing against Ling-Ling's arm. For some reason, without thinking, I rest my pinky finger on her leg. She looks down, then over at me, and smiles, but not her usual, shy smile; and I feel something different, something I haven't felt in a long time: hope.

Courtney lifts her shot glass up as high as she can, then starts jumping up and down, trying to reach the height of Harry's. Trent fixes himself, adjusts his ripped t-shirt and yells, "To Clarence and Harry! May all your dreams come true, bitches!"

"Yayyy!" We all shout, bringing our glasses to our lips.

Trent puts his hands out. "Whoa, whoa, hold on." We stop, and he turns at me. "And to this fucker, for being the one pre-med applicant out of five hundred, but only because I didn't apply!"

"Yayyy!" We all yell again, start to drink.

"Hold it!" Trent says, stopping us again, and we all put our arms down for a second time.

Trent turns to Harry. "Congratulations."

Tapping his glass, surprised at his sudden seriousness, Harry says, "Thanks, Trent."

Trent looks at me. "Congratulations, man."

"Thanks, Trent. I appreciate it," I tell him, extending my drink.

He turns to Clarence, pauses, takes a small breath. Clarence nods. "Congratulations," Trent says. They both reach out, Clarence not saying anything. "Clink."

Trent looks around, then screams, "Congratulations to everybody!"

"Yayyy!" all of us shout.

Courtney hugs Harry with one arm, kissing him on the cheek when he bends down, and Ling-Ling yells, "Congratulations, guys!"

Hesitating, we look at Trent. He waits a moment, grins, then yells, "Heyyyyyy!" and we all drink.

"Schroeder, don't drink too much," his girlfriend tells him, after he downs her shot she didn't finish. He tells her to relax, then quickly turns and asks everyone if we want to puff on the bud he was talking about. Grabbing his arm, she suggests he not smoke too much, saying, "We just smoked not long ago."

"Honey," he says, putting his arm around her. "That was almost two hours ago." He starts to massage her hip, and Clarence looks at me, chuckles, and I do the same. This is a show we've seen many times. Still rubbing, Schroeder quietly tells her that we're only smoking this much tonight because it's a special night. She rolls her eyes, grabs his hand, moves it to her neck, instructs him to massage it, and Harry, snickering and watching also, glances at me, then at Clarence, and Trent hits me on the leg, points at Schroeder.

"So, what is this stuff called?" I ask, as Schroeder's reaching into his Pac-Man lunch box. Ling-Ling leans over, tells me that she's already really high, but she wants to see what this is like.

"ODT," he says, pulling out three blunts.

"What?!" Courtney, asks, looking at him. Schroeder repeats it, but I don't think she hears, because she doesn't really acknowledge it, and she turns back to Harry, shakes his arm and says, "Were you even listening?"

Pushing her body up, Ling-Ling starts balancing on her hands. She puts her legs out and asks, "What does it stand for?"

"I don't know what the entire thing stands for," Schroeder says, flicking the lighter, failing to produce a flame. He flicks it again, tells us, "I just know the 't,' stands for 'thrill.'" He passes the smoking blunt to his left, to Clarence, then picks up another one.

"Outstanding Dynamite Thrill!" Ling-Ling shouts, letting her body drop. Giggling, she looks over at me and takes a sip of her drink.

Courtney chimes in, "Omazing Dynamite Thrill!"

"Or just Ochen Dank Thrill," Schroeder suggests, the blunt hanging from his lips. After he lights it, he passes it to his girl-friend, who gives it to Harry.

"Ochen?" Trent says, looking at me puzzled.

"Russian for 'very,'" I tell him.

I take a couple of puffs, exhale out my nose, take one more. "Damn, man, that's nice," I say, inspecting what's in my hand. I hit it again, then nod to Schroeder, who's smoking the third one, and he winks at me while he takes a long drag.

"It tastes amazing," Courtney says. She looks at Ling-Ling. "Right?"

Clarence tells Schroeder he appreciates the bud, and a shower of "thank you's" follow. Laying back on the couch, Schroeder tells us, "No problem, guys." His girlfriend only takes one hit when he passes it to her, and she gives it to Courtney, who after a few puffs, hands it to Harry.

"Not a bad problem to have!" Harry proclaims, holding two blunts up, the smoke from each of them, joining, intertwining, flowing together above his head.

"Let me take a picture!" Courtney squeals, reaching for her phone.

Clarence blows out a cloud of smoke, suggests she hurry up.

"You don't want to waste that bud," Schroeder says, shaking his finger. After Harry crosses his arms and the flash goes off, Trent suggests we put the strobe lights back on for another pic, and everyone agrees, so he gets out of his chair quickly and hits the switch on the wall. Harry takes two pulls off each one, the flashing, multi-colored light pattern making the smoke around his face look cooler, and Courtney takes another one.

The bud is unbelievably solid, and we're all completely stoned. Little has been said for the last fifteen minutes, we've mostly just been sipping on our drinks, and Schroeder, glancing around the room, says, "I told you guys."

Harry, with one eye slightly more open than the other, looks at Schroeder. "Dude." Schroeder nods, takes a drink, and puts his hand back on his girlfriend's lap.

"I have nothing to say," Clarence says, standing up from the couch. He pulls at his shirt, plops back down, shakes his head and takes a drink.

"Then why did you say anything?" Trent says, chuckling, his comment making all of us laugh. Clarence flicks him off, adjusts himself, and I miss my mouth when I try to take a drink, hitting the bottom of my glass on my nose.

"That stuff was excellent, Schroeder, thanks. What do you call it again?" Courtney asks. After Ling-Ling reminds her, Courtney thanks him a second time, adding, "I didn't think I could get much higher after my cute bluntasaurus."

Ling-Ling interjects. "My cute bluntasaurus."

"We love you, Schroeder!" Harry proclaims, standing up, raising his arms.

Courtney and Ling-Ling yell, "We love you!" and Trent opens his mouth, sticks his tongue out, flicks it around at Schroeder.

"Okay, settle down, settle down," Schroeder tells us. He points at Trent. "You especially."

Clarence starts waving his hand in front of the face of Ling-Ling's friend, who's silently been staring past Schroeder and his girlfriend, looking at nothing in the kitchen for the last couple of minutes. She snaps out of it. "I'm sorry," she says, smiling, brushing her hair over her ear. As he stands up, Clarence asks her if she wants anything, and after she glances at her half-empty glass, she says, "Yes, please." She giggles a little when she hands it to him, then nods her head, saying, "Yes, please" again when he asks her if she still wants orange juice.

She starts explaining to Ling-Ling and me that she doesn't smoke that much. "I didn't even try it until college," she tells us, brushing her hair over her other ear. "I mean, all of my friends did it, I just didn't." When I ask her about her first time, she tells us that she tried it last year, simply because a friend told her it would help her sleep. She looks up at Clarence, smiles, takes her drink. "Thank you." She goes on to explain that she now smokes "about once every two weeks". When she takes a small sip of her drink, her lips barely touching the glass, she looks like someone who's testing the temperature of a hot tea. "Thank you, this is so good," she says, and I wonder how she can tell.

"We should make breakfast here in the morning!" Courtney shouts, looking over at Harry, waiting for him to agree, her hand rubbing his inner thigh. She's started getting more touchy-feely with him, rubbing his leg and lower back, leaning in close to him anytime either of them says anything.

"Or go somewhere! Like I suggested last night!" Ling-Ling says, hitting me on the arm, nodding her head, looking for my approval. When I concur and Harry says, "That's fine," she shouts, "Yes!" then turns to Courtney. "It's settled then. We're going out-ttttt." Both of them dance in their seat, and when Ling-Ling stops, she reminds Harry that it will be better for his itinerary tomorrow.

Trent sticks his arm up quickly and yells, "If we get up in time!" He puts it back down, looks back at his phone.

"Oh, oh!" Courtney exclaims. "I thought of a game!" She looks at me, puts her hand out. "Not as good as the one you guys play." Looking back at everyone, she explains, "Each person has three seconds to give a nickname for their, you know-" She stops talking, points between her legs, puts her other hand to her mouth and whispers to us, "Pussy". "Or dicks!" she shouts, jumping in her seat, pointing at all of us guys. Standing up, she pulls at her skirt and adds, "And if you can't do it in three seconds, you drink." When she sits back down, she thinks of something else. "Oh! And if you guys want we can add that if you fail three times in a row, you have to take a shot."

"Oh, Court. I don't want to do a lot," Ling-Ling whines, rocking back and forth on the edge of the couch. Schroeder's girlfriend says the same thing, turns to Schroeder, tells him he shouldn't either, and after Clarence suggests that each individual can decide should the need arise, we all collectively agree and move on.

"I'll go fir-"

"No, I'll go first!" Ling-Ling shouts, interrupting Courtney. She puts her hands under her legs, sticks her tongue out, and Courtney does the same. They both pull them back in, then after a slight pause, at the same time, they make faces at each other.

"Okay, since you're going first, that means I choose who goes next," Courtney tells her. She glances around the room, tells us she'll just randomly point. "And don't forget to drink!" she reminds us, shaking her finger at Ling-Ling, their friend, then Schroeder's girlfriend, who puts her hand to her chest and mouths, "Who, me?"

"Wait! Hold on, pass me that!" Clarence shouts, motioning to Harry, who tosses him the vodka bottle. I lean forward a little, out of habit, when I notice the ring left on the table, but then casually sit back once I realize the silliness of it all, especially considering where I am right now. After pouring, Clarence holds the bottle up, offering it to anyone who might want it; and when Trent puts his hand out, he passes it over, and Ling-Ling starts.

"Love button."

Courtney points at me. "Knob."

Out of the blue, Ling-Ling, points at Courtney, yells, "Your turn!"

"Furburger!" She says, making a face.

"Furburger?! What the hell, Court?!" Ling-Ling shouts.

Next is Harry. Laughing, he says, "Vlad the Impaler."

Courtney calls out Schroeder's girlfriend. "Apple pie," she says, shyly smiling. Schroeder pats her on the knee and goes next.

"Woody Womb Pecker!" he shouts proudly, sticking his chest out, raising his chin.

Not everyone has laughed yet, but all of us do at this point, and Trent proclaims, "That's going to be the best one of the night!"

Teasing her, Courtney shouts, "New girl!"

Giggling already, she says, "Heaven."

Courtney and Ling-Ling react the same way at the same time, both leaning back, looking at each other while saying, "Ohhhhhhh!"

Clarence's eyes widen a little when he hears her, the corner of his mouth slightly turns up, and he says, "Knob goblin," after Courtney yells his name.

When Trent says, "Weapon of ass destruction," Schroeder's girlfriend spits up some of her drink and starts coughing. "Are you okay, my love?" Schroeder asks.

"Yeah," she answers, wiping her mouth. "That just really took me by surprise." Swiping at her tight black-and-white striped dress, she asks, Trent, "How the hell did you come up with that?"

Clarence answers for him. "It's the name of a porn movie."

Squinting his eyes, Trent makes a fist and shakes it. "The greatest porn title, ever!"

Ling-Ling turns to Clarence and asks, "And how do you know that?"

"Yeah, how do you know that?" her friend asks, folding her arms.

Taking his opportunity, Trent answers for him. "He had the DVDs in high school. '*Weapons of Ass Destruction 2, 5, & 6*'."

Clarence's eyes double in size, and he quickly looks over at Ling-Ling and her friend, shakes his head and tells them, "That is not true at all."

Lying, Trent takes it back. "Ah, I'm just kidding with you girls. They were mine." He leans towards them, says, "You two don't understand how nice it was for me to see the preview for the sixth movie on disc five, knowing I had it waiting for me, next to my bed, ready to go." Creeped out and looking at him oddly, they both rest back on the sofa.

Next come pink taco, king dong, upright wink, clam hammer, and yogurt slinging purple monster, among others. Schroeder's girlfriend is the first one who can't think of a name in three seconds, and we all chant, "Drink, drink, drink" until she does.

We go a few more rounds, everyone except for Harry and Clarence having to drink, and we decide that Schroeder's "woody womb pecker" was the best, and Courtney says Harry and Clarence should have some sort of final round to declare the winner. As if to set the stage, the strobe lights change color and pattern, start flashing faster, and the two battle it out in a speed round, shouting names back and forth at each other, quickly, neither of them failing to come up with something after ten turns apiece.

"The male genitalia nickname knowledge you two possess knows no bounds," Ling-Ling tells them, raising her drink towards Clarence, then Harry.

They both nod, say thank you, and Harry sarcastically adds, "It's nice to know that someone appreciates it."

Standing up, Courtney stretches her arms out, one finger pointed towards Harry, the other, Clarence. "Final round. Each of you comes up with one name." She pauses. "For the lady bits!" Laughing at her own comment, she glances around the room, telling us, "I should have used that one earlier!" After asking if they're ready, they both nod, and she says, "Okay, I'll give each one of you five seconds." She waits three. "Go!"

"Penis fly trap and cave of wonders!" are shouted at the same time by Harry and Clarence, respectively.

All of the girls vote for Clarence, the four of them agreeing it sounds sweet, lovely. "Even complimenting," Ling-Ling says. As a result, none of us guys vote, because this makes him the automatic winner, and Harry throws his hands in the air, puts his head down, and walks away.

"Boo! Boo! Sore loser!" Courtney and Ling-Ling chant. Making a loop in the kitchen, Harry slowly jogs back, puts his hand out for Clarence, attempting to pull it away when he slaps at it, but failing because Clarence notices his move and extends his hand, mid-stroke, hitting Harry's palm perfectly.

"You guys ready to go?" Trent asks. His right heel has been moving up and down, tapping the ground for the last five minutes, and I can tell he's definitely ready to go. He looks around the room, takes a quick glance at the four "couples", then checks his phone for the fifth time in the last minute, sends a text.

Ling-Ling has been ready to go. Already standing up, she's on her toes, twisting her hips, the bottom of her red-and-blue plaid dress swaying just above her knees, and Clarence looks at his phone. "Damn, 12:30 already? That was fast," he says, standing up.

Schroeder gets up too, saying, "Yeah, that's cool," and his girlfriend, excited, looks at him and reminds him that he said he would dance again tonight.

"Hey, Jus!" Harry shouts, getting my attention. He points to the other side of the room, and when Courtney looks, he flicks her ear then says, "One last time. Give us a good one!"

"Alright, I'll make it quick," I tell him. Still really high, I think for a moment, contemplating, wanting to- "If light does not experience time nor space, does it mean that all of time has happened in an instant from the perspective of a photon emitted during the Big Bang?"

"We can thank Schroeder's weed for that!" Harry shouts, raising his glass. Walking over, he hits me on the shoulder pretty hard, then says, "Ahhh, what I've learned under your expert tutelage."

I tap Clarence's outstretched glass with mine, and Trent takes a shot, out of impatience I think, then pours another. After knocking that one back, he yells, "Justin, your mama's so fat, every time your parents have sex, it is the Big Bang!"

"Ohhhh," Harry says, sitting back in his chair. He stomps his right foot, looks at me, and says, "Jus, are you going to let him get away with that?"

Trent leans forward, motioning for me to "come on," with both hands, and I start to say something, but Ling-Ling leans down and touches me on the arm, stopping me. "I got this," she says. Falling into the same spot she was in earlier, she casually sits back, propping her left arm up on the end of the couch. "Trent, your mama's so fat that her shadow is thinner than her because her mass is so large that it makes light curve around her, according to Einstein's General Relativity, thus making her shadow thinner than her."

Schroeder's girlfriend starts clapping wildly, and Courtney looks at Ling-Ling, yells, "Oh damn, I don't know what the fuck that means, LL!" Then she turns to Trent. "But damn, Trent, you got burned, motherfucker!"

Trent

I have no idea what I'm going to say, but I figure I'll just go with whatever comes to me. "Oh yeah, Ling-Ling, well-" Shit, I can't think of anything. "I don't know what the hell that evens means, but-"

Interrupting me, Justin talks like he's almost protecting her in a way. "It means the female who carried you in her womb for your gestation period and later expelled you from her vagina has such an excess of adipose tissue that one could reap cardiovascular benefit simply from taking a brisk walk around her person."

"My man!" Harry shouts, laughing, pointing at Justin. Ling-Ling sets her hand out, palm up, and her friend slaps it. Clarence reaches over, hits it too, then Justin's, and I feel a huge buzz come on all of a sudden. "That's harsh, man," I say, closing my eyes for a second and when I open them, everyone is still laughing.

I re-check my phone again quickly, nothing, then look around the room, noticing for the hundredth time tonight that I'm the ninth wheel, and after a couple of minutes of me encouraging them, everyone is finally standing, but no one is going anywhere or even looks like they're thinking about going anywhere, and I want to get laid so I mention the time again. All of them slowly make their way to the kitchen, and Harry suggests shots before we go. Everyone agrees, except for Schroeder's girlfriend, and Ling-Ling says to use their rum from St Croix. Clarence grabs the bottle, pours them, Courtney says something about a toast, but I throw mine back fast, bang it on the counter, and say, "Fuck that shit, let's go."

"Okay, well, I guess no toast then," she says, shrugging her shoulders.

Harry and Clarence gather beers out of the fridge while I wave everybody through the door. "That's right, move it along, keep it going, no stopping," I say. When we get out to the hallway, the eight of us bang our bottles together, each of us making sure to hit everyone else's, Schroeder's girlfriend pretending with her empty hand.

As we make our way down the sidewalk, Courtney and Ling-Ling, holding hands and skipping, get ahead of everyone, so I check out their asses, taking some extra time to appreciate what Courtney's pink skirt reveals. I continue to hold off on texting Melissa because I'm not too fucked up, and I want to see what the bar has to offer first. Harry tells Justin that he's setting his phone alarm now because he's already really buzzed and doesn't want to forget later if he's drunk. "Or if I'm too busy having sex," he says, hitting Justin on the arm, nodding in Courtney's direction.

All of the shops and restaurants are dark, the sidewalks empty, and none of us pay attention to the orange blinking hand at the crosswalk. Skipping and strolling we cross the road because there's not a car in sight. Ling-Ling, still hopping and holding Courtney's hand, turns her head and asks, "Where are we going? Their friend taps Clarence on the arm, then jogs to catch up with them.

Without looking, Harry stops talking to Justin, motions for her to keep going and yells, "Just go straight! I'll tell y'all when to turn!" Not seeming to care, she turns back around and starts bobbing her head up and down again as she skips.

"Schroeder, we still haven't had them," his girlfriend says, from behind us. Sauntering, both of their hands around each other, her head resting against his chest, both of them have fallen back, causing us to slow down, creating a gap between us and the other three. I look back, and she's pointing at the new bagel shop that opened up about a month ago. I assume she's talking about the donuts, because that's all anyone ever says about the place, and every morning there's always a line of people stretching around the corner, waiting for them. Clarence and I tried a dozen the first week they opened, not having to wait in line because both of us woke up after 11. My favorite ended up being the maple and graham cracker donut. His was the chocolate and marshmallow.

"Come on, man," I say, taking a swig of my beer, motioning to Schroeder to pick up the pace. He tightens his grip on his girlfriend's waist, and both of them walk faster. Remembering the favor he did for me earlier, I apologize. "Sorry, man. I just want to get there." I glance at my phone, look back at him.

Waving it off, he says, "No big deal, man. I got you." He glances down to his left, notices his girlfriend's not paying attention, the side of her face nuzzled against him with her eyes closed, so he grins, nods his head and says, "I totally understand."

"Take a right!" Harry shouts after several blocks. All three girls are holding hands now, and their arms stretch out, each one separating further from the other, as they swing right onto Vernon Street. "Just keep going straight! It's down there!" he tells them.

"Check that out," Justin says, pointing at some words written in pink chalk on the brick wall, below the black sign to a bike shop. Written in all lower-case letters, it reads, "the trouble is, you think you have time, you never think the last time is the last time…you think there will be more… you think you have forever."

I turn to Justin. "Yeah, I thought I had forever until I saw the time when I looked at my phone."

"I hope there are some hot girls here," I think to myself.

"Some art student did that," Alaska, or whatever her name is, says. She tells us that a senior art student went around town, using different types of mediums to convey messages. "It was her final," she says. "A friend of mine told me she did one of a guy eating trees and pooping houses."

"How long does it take to get there?" I ask, not caring at all about what any art student did.

"We saw that one!" Courtney tells us, taking a picture. Ling-Ling leans in front of her while saying they saw another one in an elevator, too, then makes a face, and Courtney snaps her last one.

Schroeder and his girlfriend walk over to the wall, and he puts his hand up, rubs some of the pink chalk with his finger. "Schroeder, don't do that! It's dirty!" she says, scolding him, hitting his arm. She reaches into her purse, then holds out a small bottle of hand sanitizer. He shakes his head, rolls his eyes, but takes it, and smirking, Clarence, Harry, Justin, and I look at each other.

Before I can ask again, after we've walked two more blocks, Harry says, "This is it." He motions to a small bar ahead that's on the left side of the almost vertical street we're walking down. Standing fifty feet from it, I hadn't spotted the place until he pointed it out. With two small, shady windows and an inconspicuous door, it was difficult to notice. The bouncer, old enough to be my grandfather, is sporting a huge, white beard and wearing a tie-dyed t-shirt with the name of a band I've never heard of, cargo shorts and sandals with white socks.

"This place looks great," I say. Disappointed, I look over at Harry. "What type of prize do I get if I win bingo?"

"Relax. It's going to rock." He points at my shorts, then at the bouncer. "Look, your grandfather's already here."

Patting me on the shoulder, while the guy takes forever to check my ID, Clarence adds to Harry's joke, saying, "Damn, man, family troubles?" He glances down at the guy's shorts, then mine.

"I figure you'd get in here easy, being family and all. Look at you two, not even talking."

Not bothering to check any of the girls, the guy smiles and opens the door for them, looking each one up and down as they walk past. Halfway through, Harry stops and loudly says, "Thank you, sir, thank you so much," and with the same facial expression of the girl in high school that tried to rap to get Clarence to cum, the old man says, "Yeah, yeah," while letting go of the flimsy metal door, and Harry has to stop it with his foot, so he doesn't get hit.

After a short, five-foot hallway, we walk through another door and into the bar. Framed black-and-white photos of guys wearing cowboy hats and holding guitars are scattered on the dark blue walls, two fancy chandeliers hang from above, and behind the short, wooden bar, red lights are dangling from used liquor bottles, on a shelf above a mirror. All of the stools are taken, and I look to my left, through the hallway that leads to the dancefloor, at the flashing lights, the people jumping up and down, waving their arms. Noticing a few hotties, I stand on my toes and lean forward, trying to see around the corner of the wall and it doesn't do much good, so I rest back on my heels and slap Clarence on the ass for no reason. He doesn't pay attention, and a hot blond wearing a tight black t-shirt and black leggings, passing by us, walks over to the server's side of the bar and starts talking to the dark-haired bartender. The bartender's white tank top is barely covering her huge tits, and she has a tattoo of a bird on her shoulder. "Not bad," I say to myself, nodding my head, looking back and forth between the two. "Either one would be fine." All of us are standing close together, and there's not much room between us, the bar, and the oddly placed black metal railing that Clarence is pushed against, so Schroeder, pointing to his right and down a few stairs, suggests we take one of the open tables below.

While Harry and Clarence push several tables together, the rest of us grab some chairs and clear off the leftover glasses, plates, silverware and used napkins off, placing them on an empty table, near the bathrooms. I grab a bowl of almonds from nearby, sit down, and I'm bummed out they're not salted after I eat a few. Regardless, I stuff small handfuls into my mouth, while Harry, Justin, and Schroeder are at the bar.

They bring drinks, and then all of them walk back, returning with shots, and I can't tell what it is, but it's clear, and I say to myself, "I hope it's not tequila." Harry starts to say something, but I'm not paying attention, because I'm trying to simultaneously look at the dancefloor and send a text. Still holding off on contacting Melissa, I've sent messages to six different girls and gotten no responses. While talking to Arizona, Clarence leans over me, trying to block my view. With no time for jokes, I push him back, scan the dancefloor, see nothing different, and Harry repeats something about the future and someone, I think Courtney, mentions the pink chalk outside. I take my shot without checking to see what it is. Glad that it's rum, I slam the glass on the table, look back at my phone, then past Ling-Ling and Justin to the bar. That feeling I had earlier hits me again and I regret drinking all of that cheap beer, then wonder if that shot was a wise decision. Opening up my contacts list, I find and text a girl I fucked last year. Within a minute, my phone beeps and I get a rush, glance down quickly. "Fuck off," it says. I lift my glass to my lips but don't drink anything. "Either I drank too much or smoked too much. Probably drank too much," I say to myself. Turning, Clarence hits me on the leg, says, "Right?" and I nod my head lamely, don't say anything, and he continues talking to Schroeder.

"Come on, LL," Courtney says, standing up to go to the bathroom. They look at their friend, who brushes her hair over both ears, then gets up. Schroeder's girlfriend doesn't acknowledge them, instead, with her arm around Schroeder, she sits listening to him talk to Clarence about whatever. Courtney hits her hands on the table, and tells us, "And we're dancing when we get back!"

"Good," I say to myself, looking past Justin. "We've been here almost thirty minutes, and I want to see what's out there." Suddenly I feel dizzy, queasy, and I know I need a drink of water or some fresh air, maybe both. Looking at my phone, I act as if I need to make a call and can't hear, then hit Clarence on the leg. "I'm going outside," I tell him.

"Uh-huh," he says, not turning around, still talking to Schroeder.

I trip, not too bad, on the second step, and when I open the cheap second door and step outside, it's drizzling. Small drops sporadically hit me, and the old dude is talking to some guy that looks like he's fifteen, telling him he can't get in.

His friend pleads his case for him. "Come on. It's a state ID," he says, pointing at the license in the bouncer's wrinkled hand.

Surprised by the rain, because Justin said it was supposed to be sunny for the next few days, I tilt my head back and let it hit me in the face. Just for fun, and so that I can get a taste of something other than alcohol, I open my mouth, eventually closing my eyes, but I feel dizzy after a few seconds and have to open them again, and I wonder If would've thrown up if I hadn't walked outside. Because I either read somewhere, or someone told me once that it was the most effective way to breathe, I inhale through my nose and exhale out my mouth, slowly, not even knowing if it helps someone who drank too much. The rain starts to fall faster, harder, and after a while I actually start to feel better. "Hmmmm, maybe it does," I say to myself. Lowering my head, I check my phone and the two guys leave, both of them looking back down at the bartender, mumbling to each other while they walk up the steep hill.

"Dumbasses," the bouncer mutters to himself, not acknowledging me as he walks by. He leans against the wall to the left of the door, lifts up his leg and pulls on one of his white socks. I don't say anything, neither does he, and for the first time ever I second guess my go-to shorts of choice.

Squeezing between a tall, bearded guy wearing a plaid shirt and a dark, skinny guy with earrings and purple hair, I order water from the bartender with big tits. When she comes back, I ask her what her tattoo means, but she doesn't answer. "Probably because I didn't order a drink and didn't tip," I say to myself. Swaying a little as I sip through the straw, I look past the guy with purple hair, at our table, to see if anyone had noticed me go outside or come back in. None of them are even looking in my direction, and after taking two huge pulls off the straw, I set the glass down, then jump down all of the stairs at once to prove to myself I'm not too wasted.

"Let's gooooo," Courtney whines, pulling on Harry's arm. He's in his chair, not moving, Schroeder, doing the same thing, both of them jokingly acting like they're talking to each other about something important, justifying why neither of them is getting up. Once both of the girls stop trying, Harry and Schroeder get up with ease, both of them calmly asking, "Ready to dance?"

"Fuck, this sucks," I complain to Clarence, after we pass through the hallway, into the much larger room. It's packed, but there are way more guys than girls and the majority of girls I do see are already with dudes. Sipping on my drink, I glance around the room some more, soon realizing that the only single, hot girls are the same two I saw through the hallway from the bar when we first walked in. "Kind of like watching a movie because of the preview," I say to myself, taking two large gulps without thinking about it, out of habit. "And finding out every good part of the movie was in the preview."

Ling-Ling walks in from behind us and stands next to me. "Look, a pool!" she exclaims. I turn my head to where she's pointing, noticing for the first time, a blue, circular, kiddie pool in the corner, with an inflatable palm tree and flamingo behind it, beach chairs on either side and a unicorn float with rainbow stripes bobbing up and down in the vibrating water.

"We should have brought swimsuits!" Courtney yells, Schroeder's girlfriend agreeing, and I look both of them up and down, say to myself, "Yes, you two most definitely should have."

All of us have been dancing for a few songs, and Justin and Ling-Ling are both bent over, talking, barely shuffling their feet, not moving their arms, so Courtney lets go of Harry's hand and squeezes in between the two. "Shut up and dance!" she yells, looking at them, grooving back to Harry. Moving with even less effort than Justin, I scan the room again, noticing an overweight, pale, chick, in jean shorts and a striped, flannel shirt. Looking doable, she's dancing near the pool with her friend, who's wearing a similar outfit. I think about walking over, but when she turns to the side, her belly shaking up and down over her too-tight shorts, I change my mind and question my judgment. Because I'm either getting drunk enough to not care about my partner or drunk enough to pass out, I finish my drink, and not worrying about either outcome, I start jumping up and down next to Clarence.

Justin and Ling-Ling stop talking, start to move more, and the music gets louder. We all get into it, gyrating our bodies to the sound coming out of the speakers, jumping, dancing, grabbing each other's arms, shouting things that none of us can hear, enjoying, "our time," together. I chuckle to myself, thinking about the words on the wall outside. "Sure, college went by fast, but we have so much time," I think to myself. "Plus, we'll see Harry and Justin all the time." With his arms around her, clutching her from behind, Schroeder and his girlfriend are moving together, slowly, despite the fast-paced beat. She tilts her head back, kisses him on the cheek, then gazes at him, and he smiles, and they look peaceful, content, happy, in a mob of screaming, unruly people, and they dance this way for the next several songs, both of their feet moving together, neither of them going anywhere.

After a while, the DJ turns down the music, announces last call, and I answer yes when Harry asks if I want anything. Looking down at the empty cup in my hand, wondering why I'm still holding it, I drop it on a pile of others in a nearby trash can and that same nauseous feeling creeps back, hard. Off-balance, I put my hand against the wall, and don't really respond or pay attention to anything happening around me for the next several minutes. When Clarence, Harry, and Justin appear from the hallway with our shots and last drinks, I notice the girl in the flannel shirt again. "Maybe just a blowjob," I say to myself, and Clarence shouts, "To all of us and our futures!" He hits me on the shoulder, I raise my glass, and we all take our last shots together.

Ten or fifteen minutes pass, and Schroeder abruptly tells all of us that they're leaving. "Noooo!" Courtney and Ling-Ling yell, reaching for Schroeder's girlfriend. They give her a hug once their friend does, and Schroeder clasps each of our hands, then tells us, "I'll see you boys in the morning." The two of them disappear into the hallway, Schroeder pulling her by the hand, his girlfriend looking back, her other arm extended to us, and Courtney and Ling-Ling reach for her again, shouting, "Noooo!"

"Fuck it," I say to myself. "Might as well." Swaying, I try to focus on the heavyset girl's striped shirt, so I can walk a straight line. I slowly stumble towards her, take the last gulp, then toss the empty cup towards the trash can, missing it by ten feet, and the pink flamingo in the corner catches my attention, and I can't help but think of our trip to Jamaica and how-

Justin

"Fucking shit! Look!" Clarence yells, pointing at the kiddie pool in the corner. Passed out, Trent is in the water, his arms and legs stretched over the sides of the pool, his body squashing the unicorn underneath him, the extra air causing its head to balloon out and sway frantically from side to side.

When we walk over, he's saying something about how a flamingo stopped him from trying to get a striped shirt. After a stranger takes several group pics of Ling-Ling and Courtney lounging in the chairs, Harry and me with our hands above our eyes, "looking out" from behind the palm tree, and Clarence sexually posing the flamingo with our drunk friend, Trent opens one eye and looks up at Clarence. "The water feels so nice. You should come in," he says, slurring his speech. "And one more thing!" he shouts, raising his hand quickly, dropping it just as fast.

"What?" Clarence asks, looking at us, laughing.

Speaking out of the side of his mouth, saliva dripping down his chin, Trent says, "You're my best friend. I lo-" His eye closes, and he drops his head.

"Okay, let's get you out of here," Clarence says, picking him up with ease.

"Woohoo!" Courtney screams, putting her head back, throwing her arms in the air.

Her and Ling-Ling start dancing in the street, letting the rain hit them, not caring, their friend declining their invite, staying under the cover of the front entrance, talking to Clarence. Ling-Ling closes her mouth, drops her head and looks at me. Giggling, she says, "I can't believe it went by so fast." Not a minute later, their friend says goodbye to everyone, hugs Courtney and Ling-Ling, and Clarence passes Trent, who's being woken up from the steady rain, over to Harry. The entire way down the street, she walks close to the wall because of the direction of the water, trying her best not to get wet, Clarence shielding her with his arms, and they vanish into the shadows between two tall buildings.

"Goodnight," Harry says, laughing, throwing his hand up, trying to turn around.

Crouching down lower, Courtney pushes him harder, towards his bedroom, and waving back at us, she shouts, "Goodnight!"

"Goodnight!" I say, too loud, putting my hand down quickly, wondering why I was waving it in the first place. We hear his door shut, and Ling-Ling stops shaking her hand, turns to me but doesn't say anything. With wet hair and a single drop of water falling down her cheek, she takes a step forward, blinks, widens her smile, and I tell myself, "This is it! Do it now!" Nervously leaning into her, I-

"Goodnight!" Trent screams from the couch, throwing one of his arms up. We glance over, and it drops, then his head falls to the side.

I turn back to her, the moment gone and since I can't think of anything else to say, I ask, "So, do you want something to drink?"

"Sure!" she squeals, jumping a little. She leans against the counter and watches me fix our drinks, while we talk about the night.

"So how do you feel?" I ask, handing her the red cup.

"Not too bad, actually," she answers. I tap her cup, and she takes a sip, sets it on the counter, then continues. "I didn't really have much when we went out. I gave most of my drinks to Court." Folding her arms, she asks, "How about you?" She unfolds them, picks up her cup.

I lie, tell her I'm not that buzzed, then bring my drink to my lips, but barely taste it. Grinning at each other, both of us still wet, we stand in silence for half a minute until I glance over to the living room. "So, want to smoke?" I ask, squeezing my cup.

Happy that I broke the silence, she responds, "Yep!" and we both look at each for a moment, neither of us saying anything, until she says, "So, the couch?"

I reach for what's left of the bluntasaurus, the only animal remaining, and grab the lighter off the table. Pausing, I look at Trent, who's still comatose on the other end of the sofa. "Hey man, do you want to smoke?" I loudly ask. No response.

"Maybe we should give him a minute," Ling-Ling suggests, giggling, touching my arm. She leaves her hand there, and a warm sensation runs through me.

Most likely because both of us are nervous and this show provides a comfortable activity that relieves both our tension, we watch him for a minute or two, each of us making small, funny comments. When I light the torso, take a puff, and pass it, I tell Ling-Ling, "Bummer since it was so cute." I say this because I know she'll agree and it's an easy, simple conversation starter.

She frowns, says, "I know," then inspects what's left of it. After taking a couple of pulls, she holds it out towards Trent. "Trent! It's waiting for you!" she says. He twitches, and she hands it back to me.

Standing up, I walk over to him, put the bluntasaurus' tail in his mouth, and without moving an inch, he inhales, blows the smoke out of his nose, repeats both, then mutters something. "Are you kidding me?" I say, quietly. Dumbfounded, I look at Ling-Ling, then back at him. "Trent! Trent!" I yell. He smacks his lips a couple of times, scratches his balls. Shaking my head, I set Claudette next to him, walk back, plop down on the couch next to Ling-Ling, and we both hear noises coming from Harry's room.

"Sounds like they're having fun," she says, adjusting herself.

I force a laugh, don't say anything, and one of the legs falls off when I pass what little is left to her. The smoldering appendage burns out on the table and feeling inadequate, I push up my glasses, then tell her, "I think it's done."

"We should draw on him."

"What?" I say, looking at her.

"We should draw on him," she says, scooting closer. "Court used to do it to me all the time when I passed out." She touches my leg. "Do you have any markers?"

Surprised by her suggestion, it takes me a moment to get out a "yes". "I'll go get them," I tell her. Jogging back into the living room, I hold them both up and ask, "Blue or red?"

"Red, definitely!" she says, hopping on the couch. She takes the marker, pops the top off, then leans over Claudette. "Do you want to do the glasses or the mustache?" she asks, balancing the tip over his right eye.

"Mustache, definitely!"

Her round, red glasses actually look good in comparison to Trent's facial structure, and when I comment on this, she giggles, tells me, "I know, that's why I chose them." Making it so that a few of the whiskers flare out at the tip, I finish my last stroke. "Nice handlebar mustache," she says, drawing a bridge across his nose.

She jumps off the couch, takes a few pics of him, me, and Claudette, then gives me her phone. "Here, hold these," I tell her, handing her the markers. She lifts them up and gives that same cute smile she does in every picture.

"Do you want to do his arms?" she asks, giggling, glancing back at Trent, and I snap one last pic. I quickly look, and it's my favorite one. Unaware I was taking it, she's turned to the side, her mouth half-open, a genuine look of joy and excitement on her face. "I want to use the blue one," she tells me, handing me the red marker. The top falls off and rolls under the sofa when I kneel down, but I don't even bother to find it, I just write. When I'm done, I glance over. With her head slightly tilted and her tongue clenched between her front teeth, she looks like she does when we're studying, and after making one last rapid poke near his wrist, she lifts her marker in the air, looks at me, and excitedly says, "Done!"

"What did you do?" I ask, standing up. When I notice what's on his left arm, I cannot believe it. I absolutely cannot fucking believe that out of all the things in the world she could have drawn on his arm, she chose the exact same thing I did - the most beautiful equation in the world.

"Euler's Identity," she says, giggling, looking at his right arm. I watch her look at what she wrote for a moment, and she pops her head up quickly, her mouth slightly open, and I know that we're going to kiss. I've never been so excited in all my life. My gut starts to tingle, a rush bursts through me, and both of us move towards each other, leaning over Trent and Claudette as our lips meet. We start to kiss passionately, slowly, our tongues just barely touching one another. "I can't believe this is happening," I say to myself, as I reach up and touch her arm, stroke it. Her hair feels so soft and gentle when I place my hand on the back of her neck.

We don't hear Clarence when he first walks in, neither of us noticing him until he tries to quietly shut the door. "Click." When he sees Ling-Ling and I quickly and embarrassingly pull away from each other on the couch, he cringes, puts his hands up, shows his teeth and slowly inhales. "My bad," he says. Walking fast towards his room, Clarence's eyes widen when he looks down and notices Trent and Claudette underneath us as he passes by. He stops, does a double-take.

Embarrassed, Ling-Ling give Clarence her short, quick wave, and for some reason, probably out of awkwardness, I feel compelled to say something rather than just nod. "Have fun with Alabama?" I ask.

He waves at Ling-Ling, glances at me and grins, then makes his way to his room.

Clarence

I'm already awake when the alarm goes off. Up for the last hour and a half, I've been digging my head into my pillow, trying to fall back asleep, knowing I won't. I look at today's schedule again, checking my name that's highlighted in yellow for the twentieth time this morning, and after dropping my phone next to me, I quickly remember that I wanted to play some music, so the picture of my mom and me comes up again, and I flip through my playlist. Once the music starts and the guitar starts ripping, I jump out of bed, dancing as soon as I hit the floor, my hips shaking wildly. Realizing that I'm way more excited than I was even ten seconds ago, I break it down even more, skipping and swaying around the room. Chuckling at myself in the mirror, I shoot my arms and legs out, moving less synchronized than I usually would, shuffle to my door, back to my mirror, continuing to watch myself gyrate like a fool while singing, "Kickstart My Heart."

Harry's coming back from the kitchen when I walk into the hallway. Looking barely awake, he's carrying a glass of water and rubbing his bloodshot, half-open eyes. Seeing me, he suddenly peps up, reaches his hand out and says, "What's up, man?!" I slap it. "You ready to rock?" he asks, sensing my mood.

"Fuck yes, I ammmmmmm," I tell him, leaning to the left, then the right. I start doing "The Running Man," the new school, more-compact version, and he joins me.

Harry

While quietly shutting the door behind me, I glance over at Courtney who's still asleep, her head buried under one of my pillows, then I check my phone for the time. "Really?!" I say to myself. I start filling my backpack with clothes, putting any dirty ones in a plastic bag before stuffing it in a side pocket, then throw in anything else I won't need until I get home. Looking around my room, I make one last check, reality hitting me hard, when I notice my vacant closet, empty dressers, bare wall, and I start to feel a little sad. I shake it off, lie down on my stomach, then look under the bed, turn to the dresser, and slide across the wood after I notice a lone sock. When I stand up and take my first step, I accidentally stub my left pinky toe on my dresser because I'm looking over at Courtney's breasts sticking out of my sheets. I start to yell "fuck!"

but control myself, and instead pull up my left foot, grabbing my toe. When I stop hopping around, she groans a bit then turns her body, slightly revealing her butt. Forgetting about the pain, I think about last night and ponder having another round. I look at my phone, realize there's no time, and she moans again, shifts to my side of the bed, revealing her pink thong. I lock the door, deciding I can make the time.

Laying down behind her, I put my hand on her hip, and reach around to her stomach. Groaning, she puts her hand over mine. "What are you doing?" she mumbles.

"Nothing."

Taking my hand out from under hers, I reach between her legs, slide my boxers down with my other hand, and start kissing her neck. After massaging her pussy and clit, once I'm inside her, she moans loudly, turns and sticks her tongue in my mouth. I go deeper, hold it, and start squeezing her breasts while sliding in and out, smoothly. When I go faster, further, she stops kissing, looks at me, then the ceiling, and opening her mouth, she moans in pleasure, "Ohhhhh, Ohhhhh, Ohhhhh."

"Shhhh," I say, laughing a little, lightly placing my hand over her mouth. She flings it off, grabs the back of my neck and yanks my head down, shoves her tongue in my mouth again, then pulls back on my hair and looks at me, tells me to fuck her harder, faster. When I say I'm going to cum, she hops on the floor, gets on her knees and looks me in the eyes until I spray all over her chest.

"Damn, Harry, that was more than last night," she says glancing down at her cum-covered breasts, then back up at me. She makes a face. "Now get me something." I wipe her off with two of the green washcloths that I'm going to throw away, then grab a few hand wipes from my "lady drawer," giving two to her to use, while I clean what's left on her right shoulder.

"Do you want something to drink?" I ask, putting on my shorts, catching my left leg, tripping, a few coins falling out of the pocket.

Laughing, she says, "Good to know your moves are better in bed, Sonic." She hands me the used wipes, and I throw them in the small trash can next to my empty, bare desk. "Can you get me an orange juice?" she asks, curling back onto the bed, covering herself with my sheets.

When I come out of the hallway, Trent's still asleep on the couch, his arm and leg draped over Claudette; Jus, who's not wearing his glasses, and Clarence, who's in his uniform, are in the kitchen. "What's up, fuckers?!" I yell, unconcerned if I wake up Trent. "Looking good, man," I say, pointing to Clarence.

"I know," he says, slapping my hand. He reaches into the fridge, pulls out some milk.

"What's up, bitch?!" Jus says, excitedly. I can already tell by the way he's acting and the look in his eyes that something good happened last night. He clasps my hand and yanks me towards him, hugging me. Pushing me back playfully, he tosses me an apple he just washed and Clarence pours some milk into a bowl.

"No glasses?" I ask, catching it.

"Nah, thought I would go with the contacts," Jus says, confidently. He turns to Clarence. "You're so fucked up."

"No doubt, man. Who the fuck eats cereal that way?" I take two large bites of my apple while watching Clarence shake the box, cereal pouring into his milk-filled bowl.

"Why don't you two leave me the fuck alone and let me eat my cereal how I like it," Clarence says, smirking. He shakes his ass a little, takes a bite out of his bowl.

Glancing at me, Jus whispers, "Fucked up."

"Fucked up," I whisper back.

"I bet when he gets dressed, he goes with sock, shoe, sock, shoe," Jus says. He hesitates before biting into his apple. "We could be living with a serial killer and not even know it."

Clarence starts shaking his hips, moving his ass around and he opens his mouth wide, shoves a spoonful in. "Mmmmmm," he moans. "So, good." Still dancing, he glares at us while crunching the cereal, loud and hard.

"Fucked up," we both say quietly, shaking our heads.

"Will you whores shut the fuck up! I'm trying to sleep over here!" We look over towards the living room, not seeing anything for a moment, and Trent's head pops up from the couch, then Claudette's. His hair is sticking out all over the place, and he's sporting a blue mustache and a pair of red glasses, courtesy of either Jus or Clarence, or both.

"Sweet 'stache," Clarence says. He leans down towards his bowl and takes two quick bites.

"When did you start wearing glasses?" I ask, grabbing one of the plastic cups so I won't have to wash anything.

Confused, he says, "What the fuck are you tools talking about?"

"Take a look in the mirror," Jus says, nodding to the wall.

It takes Trent a minute to get up from the sofa and stumble over to the mirror above the desk, where the unused gravity bong is still sitting from last night. He starts laughing. "Ahhhhh, looking good," he says, stroking his fake blue 'stache, turning his head. Strutting around the apartment, he acts as if he's adjusting his red glasses, and after making a circle around the living room, he walks over to us, "adjusts" them again, then bows his head and says, "Gentlemen." We laugh, and Trent rubs his head. "Man, I've got a fucking headache," he says.

Looking over at Jus, I ask, "So, how was last night?"

His eyes widen again. "Harry, it was-" he pauses, his smile growing. "Great."

I've never seen him this excited about anything, and I'm about to ask him to tell me all about it, but I remember Courtney's orange juice. Putting my hand up, I say, "I'll be right back, Jus. I want you to tell me all about it."

After leaving my room, I stop and lean against the wall before walking back into the kitchen, just to watch them for a moment - one last time.

Trent strokes his 'stache while picking and eating bits of cereal out of Clarence's bowl, the two of them listening to Jus talk about last night, and I'm glad it takes a bit of time before Jus sees me.

"We have to go in twenty minutes, bitches!" I yell and walking towards them, I tell Jus to start over.

Courtney

As soon as Harry closes the door, LL tightens her grip on my knee and swings her head back around quickly, her hair hitting her in the face. Grinning from ear to ear, she brushes it away and I take a large swallow of my oj. "So," she says, her grip tightening even more, her eyes growing more substantial, and I interrupt to aggravate her on purpose, since Harry already did and I know how excited she is to tell me about Justin.

"You can get a hair tie out of his drawer over there," I tell her, pointing to the bottom drawer on the right-hand side.

"Court! Don't inte-"

"Grab me one, too. And a brush," I say, talking over LL again.

"Let me talk!" She growls. She moves her hand down towards the top of my knee and squeezes hard, causing me to shriek and jump up quickly.

"Fuck!" I hit her, and she slaps me back.

"Now let me finish!" she says, getting up, walking towards the drawer. "So, we were both drawing on Trent's arms. I was on the couch and he was- Holy Shit! He actually has mini mouthwash bottles in here!" She picks one up, shows it to me, looks back in the drawer. "And disposable toothbrushes, facial cream, different types of hairbrushes. Jesus, you weren't kidding."

"I told you."

Still shocked, LL says, "I know, but I've just never seen it." Looking up at me, she says, "He's not fucking around."

"No, he's not," I say. "He also has organic moisturizer in there as well." I think about our sex just now, last night, and how happy I was when he asked me to come down next weekend to visit him and meet his parents, before kissing me and shutting off the light. I fall back into his pillows, catching his scent and watch the ceiling fan above me, trying to keep up with one of the blades while it rotates, but I can't and it starts to make me feel dizzy, so I stop. I can hear LL rummaging through the drawer, so I say, "Left side." When I sit up, she pulls out the green and white bottle of organic facial cream.

Letting out a single laugh, she says, "You weren't kidding!" She starts reading the label, and I can't help but wonder how much is left since the last time I used it two weeks ago.

"How full is it?" I ask. She twists the top off and tilts the barely used jar for me to see. Satisfied, I ask her to grab me one of the toothbrushes, telling her, "We'll just split one of the mouthwashes." Remembering what Harry said, I add, "Oh, and Harry said we can take whatever we want from there."

After scooping up some things, she hops back on the bed with her haul. "Can I finish now?" she asks. She loops a yellow hair tie around her thumb, pulls it back, shoots it at me. Continuing the story from last night, she tells it with such excitement and happiness, grabbing my leg, my hand, every so often squealing and clapping her hands when she reaches the end. "And then we kissed!"

"So, it was like a menage-a-trois?" I ask, giggling, running the brush through my hair. "Well, technically not, since Claudette was there, too." I put my finger to my lips, look up. "Hmmm. What do you call it with four people?"

"Court! No!" she answers, shaking her head, fast. "What are you talking about?" Putting her arms behind her, she rests back, looks up at the fan.

"You know I'm kidding," I say, lightly hitting her. "I'm so happy for you!"

"Yeah," she responds dreamily, staring at the fan, her head slightly moving.

"I never thought you two would hook up!" I hit her again and wonder if she's trying to keep up with one of the blades.

"I know!" she says, snapping out of her trance, grabbing my hand.

We hug and I hold LL tighter, longer than I normally would. While thinking about how truly happy I am for her, I realize how lucky I am to have her in my life, and suddenly letting go of me, she excitedly shouts, "We should get food on the way home from the train station and watch movies all day!"

"That sounds perfect!" I scream back, teasing her.

She makes a face and I jump briskly out of bed, not because I know we have to leave soon, but because I'm excited by the thought of the familiarity and feeling of being at home with my best friend.

Trent

"Whoa," I say, almost running into Courtney when she comes out of Harry's room. "Hey."

"Hey," she says, darting her eyes around my face. She brings her hands to her mouth, starts giggling, Ling-Ling joining her when she sees me over Courtney's shoulder. Remembering what's on my face, I stroke my 'stache, nod my head. "Ladies," I say, continuing to the bathroom, still stroking all the way.

They're still laughing when I shut the door, and I turn on the shower, wash my face as best I can, twice, then scrub my arms, trying to get whatever the hell this is that's written on them off. Attempting to recall last night, bits and pieces start coming back, and I barely remember the bar or how I got back here, mostly just the apartment beforehand and our walk there. The "fuck off " text comes back to me and I really focus on the word "fuck," then thinking about how I didn't get laid last night, my dick starts to get hard. Imagining my favorite pornstar, Riley Reid, I picture her gorgeous body, perfect tits and her giving that wild, hot smile. I run through some of my favorite images of her I've jerked off to - her posing in a yellow, flowered sundress and pink panties, cosplaying as Harley Quinn, sucking a dick through a gloryhole. Finally deciding to concentrate on a solo video of her I busted to earlier this week, I put one hand on the shower wall, balancing myself, and work one down quickly because I know we have to go, and also because Clarence's bodywash only works as a good lubricant for so long.

"Hurry up, fucker! We have to go!" Clarence yells, from either the kitchen or the living room, as I throw on a t-shirt after smelling it.

The five of them are in the kitchen, standing at the counter, Harry and Courtney on this side, Justin and Ling-Ling on the other, Clarence at the end. They're all laughing at something that Clarence is saying, and everyone turns and looks when Ling-Ling notices me.

"You're lucky to be alive!" Justin exclaims, looking up. He finishes filling one of the six shot glasses in front of him with orange juice.

Harry starts to sniffle, wipes his nose. "Yeah, if Clarence hadn't been there." Pausing, he dramatically hugs Clarence, then looks back at me. "You might not be here today." Courtney and Ling-Ling are giggling, hitting balloons in the air, not paying much attention, and my memory of walking over to the pool comes back to me; and then after a moment, I recall Clarence lifting me up, carrying me. Still sniffling, Harry walks over, his arms reaching out for a hug.

"Yeah, yeah," I say, brushing him off, walking past him to Clarence.

"That's the second time he's saved your life," Justin says, referring to a bullshit story Clarence made up about saving me from a small shark that frightened me when the two of us were snorkeling during our trip in Jamaica. He pours the last shot, and I ignore him like I did Harry.

"Lt Fuzz," I say, slapping Clarence's hand, grasping it. "I owe you my life."

"About fucking time. We have to go, fool," he says. "What were you doing, jerking off?" He tries to let go, but I hold on and start massaging his hand, rubbing one of my fingers against his palm, then I wink.

"Mmmmmm," I say, glaring at him, raising my eyebrows a few times.

"Fucker!" he shouts, yanking his hand away, walking quickly to the sink.

Harry puts his phone in his pocket, glances at Justin, then tells us, "Hey guys, we have to go."

"No Schroeder?" Ling-Ling asks, lifting her glass.

Laughing a little, Harry tells her, "That was as likely as us having a decent breakfast this morning."

Harry says, "To friends," and we shoot our oj fast because we're running late, and on the way out, Justin suggests we send Schroeder a group pic. They gather together in the hallway while Clarence pulls out his phone. "Hold on," I tell him, closing the door, looking back into the apartment, quickly noticing the framed fake police academy acceptance letter the three of us sent Clarence. We'd signed it using fake titles for ourselves, such as Commissioner Trent, Lieutenant Harry, and Commander Justin. I can't help but chuckle when I read the short, bodied letter: "Dear Clarence, You in Nigga!"

Schroeder

I put my arms around my girlfriend when I walk into the kitchen, give her a kiss on the cheek. "Did you brush your teeth?" she asks, looking back at me, still stirring whatever soup she's making. A carrot and a few potatoes pop up, then some noodles.

"Noooooo. I will," I tell her, holding out my phone.

"Awww, cute picture."

"Yep."

"So, what are we doing today after lunch?" she asks.

"Stay in bed all day, have sex, watch TV and smoke," I suggest. Just then, my phone beeps. "No objections?" I read Goodkat's message, then before she can respond, I quickly say, "Staying in bed and having sex all day while watching TV and getting high sounds perfect to you? What's that?! Even a massage, for me?! Fantastic!"

Goodkat

I put my phone in my pocket, open my door, sit down and look over. Her smile is even more beautiful today than it was yesterday, and while we're pulling out of the garage, I reach towards the radio, asking, "Do you want to listen to anything?" She shakes her head, and I pull my hand back. When my truck comes to a halt at the stop sign, just outside my apartment, I notice that only a few words from the new mural we saw yesterday evening are left, most of the pink chalk washed away from last night's rain. "You never think-"

She talks the entire way to her place - about her trip, how much time she has between the train arriving and her plane taking off, the connecting flight, what time her mother will pick her up. "4:20 p.m. their time," she says, smiling, staring out the front window, and I can't help but grin.

Her apartment, a tiny one-bedroom, is as neat and as accurate as I'd picture it would be. The kitchen to the left is small and simple, but everything is brand new; the appliances, cabinets, and counters, as well as the stainless steel oven and fridge, spotless. In front of me, under two large windows facing a brick wall, a white table top sits on top of two black sawhorses, serving as a desk. A closed black laptop and desk organizer are in the back, left-hand corner; a desk lamp and a framed picture of her, and who I assume are her mother and grandmother, in the right.

"Nice view," I say, joking.

"Yeah, it's not good," she says, laughing a little, glancing out the window. "But for the location, it's a great price." After mentioning the easy walk to campus and the train, she motions towards two suitcases on the floor near her bedroom door - one maroon, one pink. "I'm mostly packed," she tells me. "I just need to take a quick shower." I can't help but notice her large collection of stuffed animals on the dark wooden cabinet near her luggage. Various ones posed next to pictures, some hanging off plants, the top and bottom shelf filled with nothing but them, all of the animals positioned in such a way that none of them are cramped or hidden, all of their faces showing, not a one neglected. Noticing that I'm taking some time to look at her collection, she blushes a little and shyly says, "I like stuffed animals." I remind her of my stuffed woolly mammoth that I've had since the fifth grade, which I showed her last night, and she giggles, relaxes, then tells me, "Okay, so, I won't be too long." Halfway through shutting the door, she sticks her head back out and asks, "Do you want anything to drink?"

"I'm fine," I tell her. Take your time and get ready."

When I hear the shower, I sit down in the black chair in front of her desk and start pushing its wheels back and forth on the hardwood floor. Looking at the brick wall in front of me, my gaze shifts to a calendar, to the left of the window. It's showing the wrong month, February, along with a picture of a cute white kitten, surrounded by red heart-shaped pillows. I start to think about yesterday and last night.

When we walked out of the gym, she pulled out her phone, put it on airplane mode, asked for her bag, unzipped it and threw it in. We walked around for a couple of hours, both of us talking about nothing in particular: the weather, things that have happened on campus. I told her about a multiple-choice exam I gave, where all the answers were "C." We also talked about serious matters, what she wanted to do with her career, our relationships with our family members, good and bad. I told her about a book I was attempting to write, something I hadn't told anyone. Talking to her was so easy. I imagined us on a cross-country trip, rarely turning on the radio, laughing and talking like we'd known each other forever, enjoying the comfortable silences, while we both looked out the window, seeing new things, visiting new places together.

She ordered orange sherbet when we stopped for ice cream and for the first time in my life, I didn't think it was an odd, wasteful choice, like I had every time beforehand when I'd seen anyone order it. "Mmmmm," she said, when she dipped her spoon back into her bowl and asked me if I wanted to sit on a nearby bench. We watched a woman throw a tennis ball across the green lawn, her black lab chasing it down, bringing it back, the two of them doing it over and over again. She told me the current time back at home, and I wondered what both of us would be doing at this time tomorrow. When we finished our ice cream and got up to leave, the woman let a young boy throw the ball, and he got upset when the dog brought it back to her instead of him.

I asked additional questions about her family and friends when we walked through the park, and she told me more about her best friend, who was planning to have a baby, and the apartment her and her husband were hoping to buy downtown, where they worked. We both laughed at a guy wearing swim briefs, flexing his arms for a supplement ad on a bus stop, and I stopped and posed for her, tightening my muscles, while she clapped and gave me a rating of a "10".

Strolling around some more, we browsed through a consignment shop, played some games at a classic-pinball arcade, then stopped at a jewelry store because she saw something she liked in the window. She bought a necklace for her grandmother after I said, "I do," when the old, grey-haired salesman held it up, and she asked me if I liked it.

I couldn't believe the time when we got outside and I looked at the clock, above the bank entrance across the street. We agreed to get something to eat and found a small, quaint, Mediterranean restaurant, in between a ladies' hat shop and a vacuum cleaner store. She sat on the side of the table looking out to the restaurant like most women like to do, but when I pulled the chair out across from her to sit down, she asked me something no woman had ever asked me before. She asked me to come sit next to her in the booth. I liked it. Had anyone else asked, at any other time, I wouldn't have cared for it, but with her- . Thrilled, I sat down next to her, and both of us looked over the same menu while I held it. Our waitress bothered us too much, coming back so often to ask us if we were "okay" that I finally had to tell her to please give us at least thirty minutes alone. Periodically touching while we talked, she tried my food and I tried hers, while I told her about my college years in Virginia, my winters as a ski patroller in Colorado in my twenties, what I wrote my thesis on.

Just outside of the restaurant, we walked down a hill for another mile or so, to an area I had only been to once, maybe twice. It was another park, and this one had a little pond we walked around. When we got to the other side, we kicked our shoes off, laid down in the grass, and looked up at the stars. And the rest of the night went by quick. It drizzled on us for a while before getting harder and she eventually turned and sighed, telling me that she should get some sleep.

We drove back to my apartment, "Under one agreement," she told me. "That we will not be sleeping in the same rooms."

"No problem," I said, not minding at all. I couldn't believe it, but after pondering it for a second, I couldn't recall thinking much about sex with her since I'd left the gym. The exact opposite of my character.

After giving her a tour of my apartment, I fixed both of us a cup of hot tea, and we ended up in my bedroom. She showed me videos that she liked on YouTube - mostly SNL skits - and we kissed a couple of times, gently on the mouth, only our lips meeting. At some point, we both fell asleep. When we woke up this morning, next to each other, wearing what we had on last night, her arm and leg draped over me, one of mine under her, we just looked at each other. Smiling, neither of us said anything for a couple of minutes, until she cheerfully said, "Hi."

I hear the bathroom door open and turn my attention from the calendar I wasn't looking at, towards her. "I already knew what I was going to wear for the trip," she says, sticking her arms out to her side. "Do you like it?" She's wearing a white sweater and dark jeans that have floral and paisley patterns on them. Her hair's wet with no real form to it, and just like yesterday, she's wearing no makeup. She looks unbelievable, with absolutely no effort at all.

"Yes, I do," I answer. Smiling, I tell myself, "She could be wearing a potato sack and still look magnificent."

We pull into the lot at the train station, and I tell her to wait after we park. When I walk around and open her door, she leaps out of the car and hugs me quickly, letting go before I can squeeze her back. "Excited?" I ask.

"Very!"

When we get inside, it's busy, crowded, people moving all over the place, and I sit on one of the high-back wooden benches that are against the wall, her luggage beside me at my feet. She looks back at me twice while standing in line, smiling both times widely, waving once. Clutching her ticket against her chest, she walks back over and motioning to the coffee stand next to Terminal 5 & 6, I ask, "Do you want to get some coffee?"

"Yes!" she says, popping up in the air a little, and she stops me halfway there, looks back, and asks, "Do you think my luggage will be okay?" I chuckle, tell her it will be fine, that I can watch it from fifty feet away.

While waiting in line, with her arm wrapped around mine, she asks if I'm going to get anything. "No, I don't like it," I say, and I explain how I tried coffee for the first time when I was nine or ten, on a church youth retreat. I tell her that one of the counselors - whom I only remember was one of the kid's parents and that he was short and bald - had let a bunch of us kids try it one morning, during breakfast. "I just remember it tasting terrible," I tell her. "Leaving this awful taste in my mouth that I couldn't get rid of." Suddenly something comes back to me, something that I hadn't thought about or recalled in years, and I can't help but shout out, "Damn! I can't believe I didn't remember this until now!" An old, married couple in front of us turns around, and I motion to them, mouth, "Sorry," then grab both of her hands. Talking at a lower volume, but still excited, I say, "He always wore a pocket protector!" I laugh. "How could I not remember something like that?" For some reason, I start to imagine three pens in it, one of them blue, and now I think I'm just speculating.

Looking like she enjoyed my new discovery just as much as me, she giggles, then teases me, saying, "I'm glad you could recall such an important fact." She points out what she's going to get. "You can try some of mine. You'll like it."

The skinny teenager with pimples all over his face isn't paying attention when he hands me the coffee. Trying to pull his phone out of his pocket at the same time, he catches the bottom of the cup on the register, spilling a little of it on my hand and arm. The manager, a balding man in his late 30s, quickly runs over and apologizes, hands me some napkins, then tells me my coffee is free. He makes it himself, then apologizes again, even offering me a free donut, but I tell him, "Relax, man. It's not that big a deal."

Gripping it with both hands, she brings the cup to her nose, smells it, then takes a sip. "It's so good," she says, lifting it up to my mouth, offering me some. It has the same aftertaste as any coffee I've ever tried, and when she asks what I think, I don't lie. "Good, more for me," she says, smiling, taking another swallow.

"I'll be right back," I tell her. "I'm just going to find a bathroom and wash my hands."

She squeezes my arm, gives me a look like she doesn't want me to leave, but I assure her I won't be long as her hand slips from mine, our fingers letting go of each other. After noticing the bathrooms in front of me to the left, on the other side of the main entrance, not too far away, I turn around and walk a few steps backward, waving one last time before I go.

Trent

"What the fuck are you doing?" Clarence asks.

Bent over, I look up at him, then run my hand over a sticker that looks like an electrical outlet, fastening it to the wall. "Dude, it will be hilarious," I tell him. "Someone will think it's real and when they go to plug in their phone or computer or whatever - Nope! Sorry, just a sticker!"

"Dumbass," he says, shaking his head. He pulls up on his police belt, something he's done three times since we've been here.

"What? It's funny," I tell him, standing up.

"Yeah, it is," he says, chuckling. "Did you see, Goodkat?" Clarence points towards the bathrooms, and I notice an old man wearing a brown cardigan sitting on a bench that's next to the men's door. He's got a small suitcase and a set of golf clubs in front of him, and when he blows his nose into a handkerchief, then stuffs it in his pocket, I cringe a little and wonder why he wouldn't just use tissues instead of carrying that nasty thing around all day.

"No, was he-" A quick crackle comes over Clarence's radio, interrupting me, and then a female voice announces, "Robbery in progress at 507 Church Street. Send all units." A few moments pass and no one responds. "Ahem, robbery in progress at 507 Church Street. Send all units." Clarence shrugs his shoulders, and we wait for someone to answer. No one does, so she comes over the radio again, letting out a long sigh, before saying, "Young, black male-"

Immediately, we hear a police siren start up in the parking lot outside, even one on the radio, and several officers start replying.

"Units 6 & 2 responding."

"Unit 3 on the way."

"Terrible," I say, both of us looking at each other, shaking our heads.

The four of them walk back from the ticket counter, Justin talking about how we barely made it, Harry complaining about having to take the train instead of driving. He picks up his bag from next to Clarence's feet, then slings it over his shoulder. "All set," he says, holding up his ticket. "The train leaves in five minutes, so we should probably walk on over to terminal 7."

"Hold on, before you go," Clarence says, stopping him. He pulls several folded up, yellow sheets of posterboard from his satchel and starts handing them out. We had all quickly made the signs last night, each of us sneaking off individually to my room, using a pink marker Courtney had brought. When Clarence unfolds his, it reads, "FAREWELL, MY HARRY." Pink hearts are drawn all over it, some with arrows in them, and Justin, Courtney, Ling-Ling, and I start to unfold our large, yellow pieces of paper. He starts reading our signs, out loud, starting with Justin's, whose caption is surrounded by one, huge heart. "GOODBYE, MY PRINCE, HARRY." Courtney holds her sign up, high above her head, and just as he starts to read it, I hear something behind me that sounds like loud firecrackers.

Clarence

I recognize the sound as soon as I hear it. Scanning the room, I let go of my yellow sign, briefly seeing it fall to the floor out of the lower left corner of my eye as I reach for my gun. "Get the fuck down!" I yell to the five of them, pulling my weapon, glancing to see who I can get to. Trent and Ling-Ling are the only ones within reach, so I kick him to the ground, then quickly grab her, yanking her behind me. Several more shots are fired before I locate the gunman. About sixty-five feet from me, he's wearing a black sweatshirt and black jeans. His head is back, and he's gritting his teeth as he unloads an automatic assault rifle into a crowd of screaming and crying, women, children, and men. I notice he's not alone. Another gunman dressed the same is further away, near the ticket counter, shooting an identical rifle towards the waiting area and magazine stand. I look back at the first one, and he takes his gun off of a group of Asian tourists he's just mowed down, their bodies covered in blood, one slumped over the other. Screaming while he shoots, I still can't get a clear shot off because of the mob of people panicking and running in between us. Surprisingly calm, I repeat to myself what my instructor, Rob, told me, as I glance at the people past my target. "Be cool, just be cool, Clarence."

Ling-Ling, sobbing, and wailing, presses her body against mine and digs her nails deep into my skin. He aims his weapon at an old couple, dropping them instantly, and then he takes down a young kid wearing headphones. I stay focused, my finger forward, just under the slide, my firearm close to me, waiting on my chance, until I can't wait any longer.

Aiming the barrel of his gun at us, he starts to fire, killing a young couple and their crying children between us, and I tighten my grip on Ling-Ling with my left arm, guiding her and keeping her behind me as best I can while I step forward, moving my gun sharply to the right, to the left, down. A cloud of bullets flies past us, and to my right, I notice Harry trying to shield Justin and Courtney. Up, left. Now! Extending my weapon, I fire three quick shots, all of them hitting their mark. His head snaps back quickly with the first one, a spray of blood shooting into the air behind him, and both of his shoulders pop back, the right one, first, the left one, second, when my next two shots hit his chest. Falling to the floor, he lets off a few more rounds, sending bullets high into the wall behind us and the ceiling.

"No!" Ling-Ling cries madly from behind me, reaching out, trying to run to Courtney, who's on the floor, dead, her eyes open, staring back at us, a single tear falling down her cheek. "Clarence! No!" I keep Ling-Ling where she is, don't let go. Justin is dead, too, blood coming out of the side of his chest, stomach, and legs. Harry, his back riddled with bullets, is laying on top of both of them, his arms outstretched from trying to protect Justin and Courtney, his eyes closed forever. Trent is lying on the floor, curled up in a ball, shaking and crying, thankfully not dead, nor bleeding, as far as I can tell.

Looking back through the frenzied mob, I quickly find the other gunman. Unaware that his partner is dead, he's still firing, concentrating on the coffee stand, murdering a bald guy and teenage kid. Not far from us, a woman holding her dead husband is crying hysterically, and Ling-Ling keeps screaming for Courtney, beating at me to let her go.

Attempting to keep my gun on him and find a hole, I maintain control of her, and to my right, I see the bathroom door fling open.

Goodkat

When I open the door, it's absolute mayhem. With lifeless bodies scattered everywhere, people are wailing in pain, jerking on the ground, huddled together, bleeding and crying. I find her immediately where I left her. She's shaking, not moving, either from fear or shock, or both. Her white sweater is stained with coffee, the cup empty, rolling around on the floor at her feet. Terrified, she looks hopeless, tears streaming down her face, and then, seeing me, she turns in my direction, raises her arms, her hands trembling, and I notice the gunman in black start to turn towards her.

"No."

Grabbing the putter from the black golf bag to my right, I jump over the dead body of the nice, old man I'd greeted just a few moments ago, and watching only the gunman, I sprint as fast as I can, bringing the club behind me as I get close. With his back to me, I leap onto one of the flat, wooden benches, swinging at his head once I jump off. He turns around, mid-swing, and the putter connects with his left eye, the club splitting when it cracks through his eye socket. I feel a sharp, awful pain, and we both hit the ground. Taking the broken shaft, I jam it into his neck, as hard as I can, twisting it. With blood gurgling from the hole below his ear, I look into his open, lifeless eye, and I start to feel numb, weak, then I notice the pool of my own blood, underneath me.

She rushes over, falling to my side, and I try to reach for her, but I'm unable to put my arm or hand up. Sobbing, she screams, "No! Don't go! Don't go! Please!"

I can't feel her touching me, and it all flashes by, so fast.... seeing her for the first time, walking together, lying in the grass and gazing into the night at the stars, the rain hitting our faces, neither of us caring, waking up next to her not long ago.

I think of how amazingly enamored of her I was, the joy and sensations of life she'd brought me that I'd forgotten, that I didn't know I missed.

I wonder what it all would have been like with her if I had more time.

I am not afraid...but this is real...this is real.

Made in the USA
Columbia, SC
26 June 2020